STRONG AND STUBBORN

STRONG AND STUBBORN

 HUSBANDS FOR HIRE—BOOK 3

Kelly Eileen Hake

BARBOUR
PUBLISHING

Print ISBN 978-1-60260-762-0

eBook Editions:
Adobe Digital Edition (.epub) 978-1-62029-562-5
Kindle and MobiPocket Edition (.prc) 978-1-62029-561-8

For more information about Kelly Eileen Hake, please access the author's website at the following Internet address: www.kellyeileenhake.com

Cover design: Brand Navigation

Published by Barbour Publishing, Inc., P.O. Box 719, Uhrichsville, Ohio 44683, www.barbourbooks.com

Our mission is to publish and distribute inspirational products offering exceptional value and biblical encouragement to the masses.

 Member of the
Evangelical Christian
Publishers Association

Printed in the United States of America.

DEDICATION

*First and foremost, this is dedicated to the Lord.
Without His strength, no story would fill these pages.
It's a simple truth but sometimes not simple at all to
live with. When I alone try to wrestle the words
into submission, they fight back!*

*Second, this novel is dedicated to my amazing husband,
who encouraged me when I faltered, prayed with me when I
struggled, and celebrated each chapter. I am so incredibly blessed to
have found my partner in life, and I thank God for you every day.*

*Finally, this story is for the readers, without whom books
would not be published. Use your power wisely, well, and often!*

CHARACTER LIST

Hope Falls Heroines:

Naomi Higgins: Cousin to Lacey and Braden Lyman. Ex-fiancée of Harry Blinman.

Coraline "Cora" Thompson: Ex-fiancée of Braden Lyman. Sister of Evie Thompson. Best friend of Lacey Lyman.

Lacey Lyman: Cousin to Naomi Higgins. Fiancée of Chase Dunstan. Sister of Braden Lyman. Originator of Husbands for Hire advertisement and idea to turn the town into a sawmill.

Evelyn "Evie" Thompson: Fiancée of Jake Granger. Sister of Cora. Owner of Hope Falls Café.

Miscellaneous Ladies:

Charlotte Blinman: Estranged sister of Naomi Higgins. Wife of Harry Blinman.

Althea Bainbridge: Mother of Leticia Bainbridge. Mother-in-law of Mike Strode. Grandmother of Luke Strode.

Leticia Bainbridge-Strode: Deceased wife of Mike Strode. Mother of Luke Strode. Daughter of Althea Bainbridge.

Arla Nash: Widowed sister of Mr. Lawson, the sawmill engineer.

Dorothy Nash: Newborn daughter of Arla Nash.

Martha McCreedy: Wife of sawmill worker. Friend to Arla Nash. Helper in Evie's kitchen.

Hope Falls Heroes:

Michael Strode: Widower. Carpenter. Father of Luke Strode.

Luke Strode: Mike's son—though not biologically. Ten years old. Target of kidnap attempts by his maternal grandparents, the Bainbridges.

Braden Lyman: Brother of Lacey Lyman. Original owner of Hope Falls mine, caught and injured in the initial mine collapse. Ex-fiancé of Cora Thompson.

Chase Dunstan: Fiancé of Lacey Lyman. Hunter, tracker, wilderness guide. Originally helped Braden Lyman survey Hope Falls area. Came back to investigate suspicious mine collapse.

Decoy: Chase's silver-gray Irish wolfhound. Almost four feet tall and six feet long.

Jacob Granger: Fiancé to Evie Thompson. Family owns successful chain of sawmills. Originally came to Hope Falls under alias of Jake Creed to find his brother's murderer.

HOPE FALLS LOGGERS:

Volker "Clump" Klumpf: Good-natured German farmer turned logger, distinctive for heavy boots.

Rory "Bear" Riordan: Gentle giant of a Scots-Irish logger.

Gent: Oldest logger in Hope Falls with a penchant for top hats.

Bobsley: Youngest worker in Hope Falls.

Craig Williams: Arrogant logger who's tried to court every single woman.

Mr. Lawson: Mild-mannered engineer. Brother to Arla Nash and uncle to Dorothy.

HOPE FALLS MINE INVESTORS:

Mr. Draxley: Telegraph operator. Involved in mine sabotage, although not the mastermind. Attempted murderer of Lacey Lyman and Chase Dunstan.

Mr. Owens: Business partner of Braden Lyman and original owner of Hope Falls mine. Initially survived the collapse but died of injuries later. Discovered to have been part of mine sabotage.

Harold "Harry" Blinman: Ex-suitor of Naomi Higgins. Husband to her sister, Charlotte. Original investor in Hope Falls mine.

"Cautious" Clyde Corning: Original investor in Hope Falls mine. Interested in Cora.

PROLOGUE

Baltimore, Maryland, 1881

It should have been me.

Guilt crept around the edges of the thought, but Naomi Higgins brushed it away with the first of her tears—the first of an inevitable deluge. She'd held them at bay for far too long, and when the ever-present pinch behind her nose blossomed to a sharp tingling pain, Naomi sought solace in her favorite refuge. The books surrounding her showed more spine than she, who had abandoned her only sister's wedding reception.

It *should* have been Naomi, not Charlotte, who celebrated. It almost had been. After all, Harold Blinman became familiar with the Higgins household when he began courting *Naomi* a scant year before.

He'd wooed her just long enough to steal a place in Naomi's heart. Her advanced age of more than twenty-one years, though well beyond most ladies' first courtship, offered no protection against a handsome smile, a hand at the small of her back, and a whirlwind of dances.

Her advanced age did, however, offer Harry a reason to transfer his affections to her nineteen-year-old sister. The two looked astoundingly alike—so alike, in fact, that polite society recognized the switch slowly—fashionable hats and bonnets hiding their one clear difference. Charlotte dressed to impress and generally succeeded. She'd flounced home from her beloved French boarding school, only to flounce right back out the door with her sister's beau.

With their mother's blessing.

In fact, Charlotte's "success" led to endless edicts that Naomi abandon her love of books and take up her sister's ruthless study of fashion plates and scandal sheets. Delilah Higgins had long denounced her eldest daughter as "overly bookish," which somehow made her far too "adversarial and masculine" to attract a decent match. When Harry chose Charlotte, he as good as announced to the entire world that he felt the same way.

"Naomi Glorianna Higgins!" Her mother's hiss snaked through the room. "Whatever are you about, closeting yourself in here? Hasn't your reputation as a bluestocking cost you enough?"

Her tears halted as suddenly as if her mother stoppered their source. Showing emotion, Naomi learned long ago, issued an invitation for condescension, correction, or outright criticism. Speaking one's mind brought a more vehement version of the same.

For once, Naomi didn't care.

"If Harry spurned me for my intelligent conversation, my only loss is a miserable marriage." *Though that miserable marriage would have given me a honeymoon in Paris and moved me out of this household*, Naomi silently added. Saying anything more would prove disastrous—she'd never been a good liar.

Harry's defection still hurt. She'd believed he wanted her, been lured into wanting him, only to be told in no uncertain terms she wasn't woman enough to keep him. And while she didn't want a thing to do with the Harold Blinman who'd stood today in front of everyone and declared he would love her sister until death, a corner of Naomi's heart grieved for the Harry she'd thought cared for her.

"Harold." Her mother cracked the word like a whip, satisfaction in her smile. "Although he is now a bona fide member of the family, and thus you may claim the familiarity of his given name, you will never again use his pet name. Do I make myself clear?"

"As you please, Mother." Naomi shrugged, trying to dislodge her dismay at the way a single word betrayed her.

"Do not shrug. It's vulgar." Delilah Higgins made a moue of disapproval. "And you've ruined our hard work styling your hair!"

Glad for an excuse to turn from her mother, Naomi moved toward the massive mirror above the fireplace. She peered at the image of a tall woman, shown to advantage in an utterly inappropriate shade of crimson—her sister insisted that her maid of honor be clad in the Blinman colors in homage of her new husband—her hair loosely gathered into an intricate series of knots. The coiffure, meant to be sophisticated but not overwrought, was achieved by dint of dozens of hairpins *still* stabbing into her scalp.

But aside from a sadness lurking in her eyes, Naomi saw nothing amiss. In fact, the jewel tone suited her far better than the pastels typically deemed appropriate for any unmarried miss. *So I wear spinsterhood well.* The notion garnered a rueful grin.

"It seems secure and unfrizzled, Mother." Naomi kept her puzzlement out of her voice—uncertainty signaled vulnerability.

"Are you so secure in your resemblance to me that you presume others will discount your disfigurement? Your father wore his oddity well, but you're a woman. That coloring will mar your crowning glory until old age wipes clean any vanity."

"All and sundry know of it." Naomi couldn't fathom why her family persisted in fussing over her hair on today, of all days. The shock of white brightening black began just at her hairline and swept down to her waist. Eight hundred seventy-three strands of pure white amid the darkness—eight hundred seventy-three reminders of the first husband her mother hated too much to forget.

Naomi counted them at age nine as she plucked out each and every one in a desperate attempt to please her mother. Instead she'd been confined to the house for almost a year until the bald spot grew in sufficiently. No concoction brewed by the apothecary, beauty shops, or French maids could darken them beyond dull gray, and she'd long since given up trying to change herself.

"Yes, everyone has seen it, but out of sight, less in mind." Her mother pulled, twisted, and fluffed the hair to cover the telltale white then viciously stabbed more hairpins to keep the locks in place. "Now that Charlotte is wearing the Blinman ring, none shall mistake the two of you. It's to your advantage now to look your best, and all of Baltimore has turned out here tonight."

I know. Naomi closed her eyes against a sharp pain in her skull. Whether it sprang from her situation or her mother's hairdressing, she didn't ponder. *All the pitying glances and inane comments made me slip away in the first place.*

"There. Now you're presentable. Back to the party, young lady."

Naomi knew she should. Knew that walking out the door and joining the celebration with a smile on her face and a sparkle in her eye would help quell the gleeful gossips. But she hesitated. *Why run the gamut when I lost the race long before?*

Unexpectedly, her reluctance didn't wring a reprimand from her mother. Instead Delilah Higgins gave her eldest daughter a considering look, then crossed the room. Pulling on the axis of the massive standing globe, she revealed a set of cut crystal decanters and tumblers. Without a word, she poured a splash of dark amber liquid into a tumbler and handed the strong spirits to Naomi.

"I realize it's too much to ask that you be happy for your sister's marriage—try instead to be happy in spite of it. At the very least, paste a more convincing smile on your face. You look well enough tonight, otherwise." Her mother swept toward the doors. "Charlotte wouldn't fly against convention, but for once your stubbornness can serve you well. If you can forget yourself long enough to enjoy tonight, you'll out circle the buzzards yet."

Naomi gaped at the doors long after they shut. Only the sound of the fire collapsing into the grate startled her. She swirled the mysterious brew in her tumbler, wondering at its strength. Her mother—and society at large—never allowed her more than a glass of watered-down wine with dinner or a weak Madeira punch.

Forget yourself. . . . Her mother's advice was tempting. What would it be like to forget the troubles of Naomi Higgins, if only for an evening? What would it be like not to think about the mother who despised the living reminder of her first husband? Not to ruin a conversation by mentioning a fact or opinion about philosophy, history, or even politics? Forgetting that everyone knew the man she'd chosen had chosen her sister instead?

Yes, Naomi thought as she raised the glass to her lips and gulped its contents. She gasped for a few heartbeats, unable to breathe. The liquid seemed to burn a fiery path of determination straight through her. *It would be quite nice to forget.*

ONE

Boston, Massachusetts, June 21, 1887

H ow quickly you seem to forget, Michael." Althea Bainbridge raised one finely arched gray brow. "I, on the other hand, am blessed with a superior memory." Her tone indicated all too clearly that she believed herself blessed with superiority in every way.

"I remember." Mike saw no sense in wasting words on deaf ears. He could tell his mother-in-law just how exceptionally he remembered the deal they'd struck ten years ago. A single decade, after all, wasn't enough to fade the most important day of his life.

Or the worst.

"Then you know I'm right." Somehow the woman gave the impression of leaning back in satisfaction; something Mike knew couldn't be possible. Althea Bainbridge corseted the bend from her spine and the compromise from her conversation.

"No." As a matter of fact, the woman couldn't be more wrong.

"No?" Mr. Bainbridge, whose sole function as far as Mike could see was to fund Mrs. Bainbridge's ambitions, made a good parrot. But then again, the man had a lot of practice. Surely his only path to peace lay in agreeing with whatever his shrew of a wife demanded.

"Humbug." His mother-in-law looked as though she smelled something foul. "Despite the impression you give so readily, Michael, I know you are no fool. You've proven your good sense before. Dredge it back up from the mire you've made of things, and make the right decision."

Not for the first time, Mike wondered what the indomitable Althea Bainbridge would do if he upended her bone china teapot atop that ridiculous—and obviously ridiculously expensive—wig of hers. But he'd forgo outright fighting with the Bainbridges, for Luke's sake.

"I already have."

"Excellent." His mother-in-law looked at him expectantly. When he failed to react, her magnanimous mood vanished. "What are you waiting for? Go fetch the boy and bring him here at once! We've already outfitted the nursery and schoolroom. His new governess and tutors await, and I'll not allow my grandson's fine intellect to be wasted a moment longer. As it stands, it will take years to fix the damage you've undoubtedly done."

"I said I made the *right* decision. I won't leave my son."

"He ain't yours." Bainbridge looked pleased with that brilliant observation until his wife took him to task for letting his "unfortunate" background seep through the veneer of sophistication.

"Not, dear. Lucas *is not* Michael's son."

"'Xactly right, my dove." The man beamed, typically unperturbed by the fact they were discussing his only daughter's disgrace.

"Luke." It came out louder than he intended, but Mike didn't mind. "His name is Luke, not Lucas. I wrote it on the birth certificate myself." He'd had to literally yank the paper from his mother-in-law's grasping hands in order to name his son for his grandfather. Mike had been pulling Luke out of her clutches ever since, and today would be the last time. He'd made sure of that.

"I remember that." His mother-in-law lost her icy composure for long enough to glower at him. "But you will note that I am being gracious enough to overlook your audacity and rectify the error."

"*Gracious* is the last word I'd use for you." He allowed some of his rage to show. "Our agreement gave both your daughter and her unborn child the protection of my name. My name, *my son*."

"Give over, Michael. Lucas bears your name but not your

blood. Everyone here knows precisely why you married Leticia, and, more importantly, why our darling lowered herself enough to wed you. Your mother's familial connections combined with your father's unfortunate tendencies toward trade made you a beautifully unknown and marginally acceptable mate in the eyes of society. The marriage maintained Leticia's good reputation, but your usefulness to the family has reached its end."

She "lowered" herself to wed me because first she laid down for another man. Mike bit back the caustic words, knowing better than to let the past leach into the present. He'd known the situation when he married Leticia Bainbridge—though he hadn't anticipated the extent of his in-laws' constant interference in his household.

Leticia gained a new last name, quickly enough to squeak past too much gossip when her son emerged eight months after their nuptials. Michael gained money enough to buy whatever care could soften his mother's worsening case of consumption. Mama still passed on, but Michael's marriage bought her a measure of peace. She never knew the bitter truth behind his marriage, praise God.

"You're still wrong." Michael shook his head. "Leticia's life has ended, but Luke and I continue on. And we'll stay together."

"Sentimentality doesn't suit you. Think, man. Here Lucas will have every luxury, the best of educations, and more opportunities than you could possibly imagine. If you won't give us our grandson to ease our hearts or your burdens, bring him for his own good."

"He's already lost his mother." Though Leticia rarely saw the boy. "It's best for him to keep as much of the familiar as possible." Having spoken his piece, Mike headed for the door.

"We'll pay you!" Althea Bainbridge's reserve cracked, desperation making her voice shrill. "Whatever you like, however much. You'll take the money—I know you will. *You have to.*" She drew a loud, calming breath, oblivious to the fists now clenched at her son-in-law's sides. "You were bought once before after all."

"Yes, I was bought once." Mike didn't bother turning around. "But Luke never will be. My son is worth more than that."

"Of course. Lucas is worth anything." She spoke softly, consideringly. "There is no sacrifice too great for his sake."

Michael decided to ignore the vague threat and continued toward the door. A jarring crash against the far wall stopped him in his tracks. He stared at the shattered remains of Althea Bainbridge's fine Sevres teapot as a cup spiraled across the room to join it, sloshing tea across the Aubusson rug before it, too, smashed to pieces.

"Such a display of temper!" His mother-in-law calmly pitched the cream pot next. Then she surveyed the destruction and gave a smug smile. "I can't imagine what the servants will make of it. But perhaps over the next few days reports will arise as to your unstable and volatile nature, Michael." She tsked.

Her husband spoke up. "It's only a matter of time before someone in power sees to it that Lucas is removed from your care for his own safety. Our friend Judge Roderick will make sure of it."

"You've gone mad." But whether or not she'd lost a few of her marbles, Althea Bainbridge made her point. She had the connections—and the sick determination—to have Luke taken away from him.

"Well, I bore a fondness for that tea set." A hint of regret clouded her features before her lips thinned with heartless determination. "But, as I said, there's no sacrifice too great for my grandson."

"I will never allow him to be taken from me."

"We shall see. Since we both agree Lucas is worth more than your miserable life, you can't imagine what I'm willing to do for him." Something reptilian flickered in her gaze as she glanced at the shattered china. "Then again, perhaps you can. I was fond of my tea set. It served a purpose. But you? You're no more than a problem— and I have ways of making those disappear."

This brought things to a new level. Mike could push aside the prospect of a ruined reputation or vague threat—Althea Bainbridge just threatened to have him killed. The idea of being hunted didn't make him fear for himself, but the danger to Luke sent a chill up his spine.

No matter how much I have to give up, how far I have to go, the Bainbridges will never take my son. I won't let him out of my sight.

San Juan Mountains of the Colorado Territory, July 3, 1887

"Have you seen Lacey?" Naomi couldn't suppress her nervousness over the way her cousin kept flitting away from their company in favor of trailing behind Hope Falls's new hunter. The girl didn't understand that a good reputation was as fragile as spun sugar—and as easily shattered.

"The mercantile with Arla." Evie Thompson's mention of the sawmill engineer's widowed sister made Naomi relax. "She's drawing up lists of things to order. I don't know who's more anxious for the baby to be born—Lacey or its mother. Lacey keeps saying she needs to know whether it will be a boy or a girl."

"You know how Lacey loves to shop. Hope Falls may have reduced her options to catalogues, but she'll find what she needs." And a half-dozen fripperies besides, if Naomi knew the young woman she'd helped raise for the past five years. "Is Cora with them? She and Arla seem to have struck up a friendship."

"Not that I know of." A frown crinkled Evie's brow at the mention of her sister. "It seems unlikely she'd go pay Braden a visit, considering the way he's been acting, but I'm guessing you already checked the house."

"No sign of her there. Would you like to go check the doctor's?" At her friend's nod, Naomi hovered by the door as Evie draped the stained apron over a stool, plopped a lid atop a simmering pot, and banked the fire in her prized cookstove. The two women fell into step as they journeyed toward the doctor's quarters.

"Between you and me,"—Evie's words dropped heavily, as though weighted with regret and resignation—"I think Cora's had enough."

Naomi sighed. "Between you and me, it's a testament to how

well you raised your sister that she's stayed by Braden's side this long. Her devotion and commitment are stronger than he deserves."

"Heaven knows I didn't encourage her to withstand Braden's foul moods." A note of regret crawled beneath Evie's strong words—true words. "I didn't want her subjected to that kind of heartache. But I underestimated how deeply she loves him, and now I know I should have encouraged her loyalty and bolstered her spirits."

Naomi instantly understood Evie's change of heart. Now that Jake Granger came along and earned her love, Evie held a new appreciation for the bond between a woman and her chosen mate. Naomi could only pray that appreciation never became pain or bitterness.

"Your own loyalty made you protective," Naomi soothed. "In fact, I think knowing you would support her decision if she left Braden helped Cora to keep fighting for him." They came to a stop.

"Naomi,"—her friend shook her head—"you have a way of making something preposterous sound wise. I feel like if I turn it around enough times in my mind, I'll find the sense in what you say."

"Think about it, Evie." Naomi moved toward the benches lining the front of the mercantile and sat down. Despite niggling worries over Cora, she felt the other two of their foursome were safe enough together. Right now Evie needed some assurance.

Out of them all, Evie Thompson worked the hardest from sunup to sundown. She gave the most to make their fledgling town run and asked the least in return. Between cooking for two dozen lumbermen, falling in love with a man whose secret nearly destroyed them all, and trying to care for her sister, Evie handled more than her fair share of troubles. By all rights, she deserved a rest!

"Better yet, let me walk you through my reasoning so you can see the way I do." Naomi paused a moment to collect her thoughts. The extraordinary events since the mine collapse left a lot of ground to cover. How best to address the treacherous without losing sight of the triumphs? She silently prayed for the words.

"You financially supported Cora when your father died." Naomi began with the facts. "You emotionally supported her when she fell in love with Braden—or, rather, the man Braden used to be."

Here she paused as they both remembered that man. Braden, the handsome cousin Naomi never met until her family cast her out. Braden, whose immediate pretense that Naomi *honored* the Lyman family by becoming his sister's companion almost convinced Naomi herself that she hadn't been exiled in disgrace. How she missed *that* Braden!

"Yes." Evie broke into Naomi's recollections. "I stood by her side when she accepted Braden's proposal—but when I learned of his plans to start a mining interest, I should have told her to wait."

"Ah, but the Hope Falls mine seemed a perfect investment. All the geographical surveys, the rich geological samples, the location near the railroad. . . Braden gathered plenty of investors who saw the value of this place." Naomi looked around the now-empty town. "When he put up his inheritance and accepted your and Lacey's investments for a diner and mercantile, Braden had every reason to expect Hope Falls would be a success—and the perfect place to raise a family."

Evie gave a mirthless laugh. "Yes, it seemed perfect. We should have known nothing is. We should have realized—"

"That the mine would collapse?" Naomi's voice sharpened as she interrupted. "None of us could have imagined such a thing! You knew Braden would bring Cora here, so you bought in. I knew Lacey would follow her brother—and any opportunity for adventure—so I made the same commitment. Where love leads, each of us chose to follow."

"Of course you're right." Evie jumped off the bench to pace before it. "At least the first time. Investing in Hope Falls, the mine made sense. But surely we should have learned from that first disaster? After hearing Braden died in the collapse, we vowed to have nothing more to do with this place. Instead we jumped back in and compounded our mistakes! How could we be so *foolish*, Naomi?"

Talking this out wasn't helping much. Naomi wondered what on earth she could say to reassure Evie now. Because the truth was...

"I have no idea." Her own admission caught her by surprise. But she couldn't escape the fact that their mad scheme to save Hope Falls was foolish in the extreme. Except... "Except that when we learned Braden actually survived the mine collapse, nothing could have stopped Lacey and Cora from coming here. And neither of us could let them gallivant across the country without us. It wasn't safe."

"No, it wasn't safe for the two of them. But joining them didn't give much protection from the real danger here," Evie cried. "I followed Cora to her fiancé, only to watch my sister's heart break."

"You're wrong." Hearing voices inside the mercantile, Naomi realized that Lacey and Arla had left the supply room and might be within earshot. She rose to her feet. *The worst of it is that we brought most of the danger upon ourselves with that ludicrous ad!* But now wasn't the time to say so. There never would be a time to say so, now that the ad brought Jake Granger into Evie's life. And, unless Naomi was much mistaken, the same ad brought Lacey's match to Hope Falls. The sparks flying between her cousin and the town's new hunter had less to do with disagreements than a powerful attraction.

"How?" Evie's desperation held a hint of hope. "How am I wrong?"

"Let's head back to the café." Naomi tilted her head toward the store, where Cora's voice joined Arla's and Lacey's. She saw recognition flutter across Evie's face as they moved away.

When they'd reached the halfway point, Evie resumed the conversation. "I sheltered Cora too much, but I hated to see her hurting. Braden's enmity—so soon after her grief at news of his death—is too harsh a blow for my sister's tender heart."

"Cora's heart isn't broken. It may be badly bruised, but it's not broken." Naomi stepped off the raised wooden platform surrounding the store. "If your sister's heart had broken, she wouldn't persist in visiting Braden and weathering his storms."

Evie walked a few steps more before giving a grudging nod. "I still think I should have encouraged my sister not to give up. No matter how terrible Braden's become, he's still the man she loves."

"And I still think the opposite. Consider this," Naomi propositioned. "If Cora dragged you out of Charleston, uprooting both your lives and dragging you to the wilderness, how do you think she felt when Braden took away the reason you both traveled here?"

"Furious with his wretched, ungrateful hide. What else?"

"No, that's how *we* felt, Evie. Not how Cora sees things. Turn it around. What if it were *your* fiancé, and *you'd* asked Cora to give up everything so *you* could be with a man who no longer wanted you?"

"Guilty." Evie's eyes widened with equal parts of understanding and horror. "Oh, Naomi! Cora shouldn't feel as though she's to blame for the challenges we've faced. Hope Falls was—and still is—beyond what any of us imagined. She couldn't have changed any of it."

"To an extent, I think both she and Lacey do blame themselves." It had been Lacey, after all, who convinced them to write that accursed ad. But now wasn't the time to dwell on *that* mistake.

"How awful. What can we do to show them otherwise?"

"You already have." Naomi reached out to pat Evie's shoulder as they returned to her kitchen door. "That Hope Falls brought you a fiancé of your own goes a long way toward alleviating Cora's worry, I'm sure. But I think the fact that you never make your sister feel as though she had to stay with Braden helped. Cora knew she wasn't trapped by your expectations because she knew you cared more about her happiness than you cared whether you'd left Charleston for nothing."

Evie gave her a long look as though weighing the words. Finally her dimple surfaced. "I knew you'd turn out to be right."

"Of course!" Naomi opened the doctor's door. "Sometimes the best way to support someone is to let them make their own choices."

TWO

It's the right choice, Mike reminded himself with every mile he put between Luke and his grasping grandparents. There was no contest between losing a house and losing his son.

"Come back here." Mike wrapped a hand around his son's wrist and tugged it away from the open window and safely back inside the train car. This made the first of a days-long journey, and he knew from experience that he had to lay down the law at the start if he had any hope of keeping his ten-year-old's high spirits in check.

"I like the wind." Color rode high on the boy's cheeks as he beamed with excitement. "It makes it feel like we're going fast!"

"Fast is good." *The faster the better.* Mike wouldn't rest easy until thousands of miles separated his son from his in-laws' grasp.

His hand crept to his coat pocket, where a slip of paper linked this madcap flight to the possibility of a future free of the Bainbridges' threats. Softened from much handling, the telegram's short message offered opportunity, if not promises.

HOPE FALLS, COLORADO. *Stop.*
BETWEEN DURANGO AND SILVERTON. *Stop.*
NEW SAWMILL GOING UP. *Stop.*
MIGHT HAVE USE FOR CARPENTER. *Stop.*
ASK FOR ENGINEER LAWSON. *Stop.*
GIVE MY NAME AS REFERENCE. *Stop.*
SOUNDS LIKE A STRANGE PLACE. *Stop.*
GOOD LUCK AND GODSPEED. *End.*

Mike didn't bother to take it out of his pocket, just fingered the edges to make sure it remained in place. These days a man's word—especially a stranger's word—wasn't trusted. He needed the telegram itself as a makeshift letter of introduction and proof of reference.

For that matter, he needed the telegram for his own peace of mind. The way Mike saw it, even if this Lawson fellow didn't need a carpenter or joiner—or simply didn't need one yet, as engineers often lavished time upon blueprints and schematics before getting down to the real business of construction—he might find other work.

True, he'd only ever swung an ax to break up or square off logs already cut down. But from what Mike heard, a strong back and a way with wood were traits that served a lumberman well. So long as he could make arrangements for Luke to remain out of the way, Mike was more than willing to try his hand felling trees.

"It doesn't feel like we're going so fast now." Luke flattened both palms against the lower half of the window, which didn't open, squinting as though trying to make things blur by more quickly.

"We're going just as fast as we were with your hand out the window," Mike told him. "But this way a tree branch won't hit you."

Luke frowned in concentration. "If we're going as fast as the wind outside, then why does it feel so different?"

"How does it feel different, aside from being warmer?" Mike stretched his legs out, glad no one occupied the seats ahead.

"I don't know, 'xactly." Small fingers tapped on the armrest. "But the wind feels like adventure, and the train feels like. . ."

Mike suppressed a smile as his son reached for an explanation.

"Sitting!" Frustration seeped into the proclamation. "Like we aren't really doing anything much different than taking tea at home. If it wasn't for the noise, I'd hardly know we'd left!"

"Except the chairs at home are more comfortable," Mike teased. "And even if your hand isn't out the window, you can still see things whisk past. Before the trip is over, you'll see a lot of places and people you never would have if we were still home."

And hopefully none of the people we left behind, Mike prayed as

Luke settled into watching the world go by, his nose now pressed against the glass. And when he wasn't sleeping, Luke's nose pressed against the windowpanes of several other trains as the days and miles rolled past. By the time they reached Dallas, Mike fancied that the tip of his son's nose looked flatter than before the trip.

"Why do I have to stay behind?" A note of fear quivered beneath the question. "I thought we were leaving so Grandma couldn't take me away. I thought you said we were staying together and going on an adventure!"

"We are." Mike squatted back on his heels to be at eye level, searching for the words to explain his reasons for leaving. "But every adventure has different stages. For just a little while, until the next part of our lives begins, you need to stay with your aunt."

"But our adventure is supposed to be for both of us." Luke rubbed his eyes, though Mike couldn't tell whether he wanted to keep from crying or to work out grit from the train ride. "Together!"

He reached out to hold one of his son's achingly small hands. To tell the truth, those hands—and the rest of Luke—had grown by leaps and bounds lately. All too soon his son would leave childhood behind. But for now there was enough of the little boy about him to need his daddy—and Mike was glad of it.

"Yep. That's why we left Baltimore. This is all about making sure our adventures are always together. You know that." He gave Luke's hand a comforting squeeze, pleased when Luke squeezed back a little harder. Mike topped that, and they engaged in a short battle before Luke couldn't summon any extra strength and conceded defeat by trying to pull away. So Mike held on tighter and didn't let him.

His son tried to scowl, but his smile crept in around the edges. Luke didn't say anything about it, but Mike knew that their playful tussle assured the boy more than any words he could string together. Come what may, Luke knew that his dad was strong enough to get the job done and not let go of him in the meantime.

"As soon as I have everything settled and made sure I've found the right place, I'll come back and fetch you." He stood up, knees tingling. "If all goes well, I'll be back before you miss me."

Any possible response would sound childish, so Luke settled on a snort. It both dismissed the notion that he'd miss his father and dismissed the idea that he wouldn't. Then he spoke up.

"I don't much like waiting." Luke jammed his hat down and muttered, "So make sure the first place is the right place, all right?"

"I'll do my best." Mike couldn't get his son's parting request out of his mind for the rest of his journey.

No matter how he tried to tell himself that Hope Falls would be the answer to those prayers, doubts lashed him at every turn. *What if the Bainbridges were already having him followed?* He shook away the grim idea. Mike had purchased three different sets of train tickets in case someone tried to track them. He'd even boarded the first train, only to step off the back end and track around to their real ride. He'd closely watched everyone who boarded or left the train but saw nothing suspicious so far—which meant they'd gotten out of Baltimore free and clear.

But can we stay that way? That was an entirely different question. Someone might be waiting to snatch Luke away at the next train station. Or some dodgy back-alley tracker might sniff them out after they reached Hope Falls. He had no way to know for sure.

Of course, Mike had done his best to find a location few people ever heard of so no one could deduce where they'd go. From what he'd gathered, Hope Falls had been a mine of some sort before being turned into a sawmill. No one with a smattering of logic would think that Michael Strode—carpenter, joiner, and cabinetmaker— would take off for a silver mine. Particularly not one so far away.

Yes, the location seemed perfect. So why did that one line in his telegram keep streaming through his thoughts? What on earth could his old friend mean by *"Sounds like a strange place. Good luck."*?

Because, despite Mike's determination to build a new life and a safe home for Luke, he couldn't stop wondering. . .shouldn't all the bad luck have run out for a town that suffered a mine collapse? And, perhaps more importantly, just how strange could Hope Falls be?

Hope Falls, July 5, 1887

Strange how much effort it takes to accomplish so little. Braden Lyman gritted his teeth and leaned back to ease the strain on his knee. During the past week, the doctor had determined his kneecap well enough healed to be taken from traction. Then had begun the agonizing—and agonizingly slow—process of "training" his leg to bend again. Thus far, through a makeshift system of pulleys, bandages, and bars, the doctor had managed to manipulate his damaged leg to a far-from-impressive one-hundred-forty-degree angle. No more.

Yes, it meant a forty-degree improvement from lying flat, as he had for more than two months—but it remained a solid fifty degrees away from him being able to bend his knee as though sitting properly in a chair.

Which meant fifty degrees away from him getting out of this blasted bed and into the wheeled chair ready and waiting for him.

If he'd made enough improvement, Braden would be in that wheelchair *right now*. He would've rolled himself straight out the door, across the meadow, and up to the opening of the mine he'd hewn into the mountain. The very mine that collapsed on him three months ago, killing several of his men and leaving Braden badly concussed with a dislocated shoulder and shattered kneecap.

The mine, where his little sister was determined to uncover evidence that the collapse had been a cleverly engineered catastrophe—not a result of poor planning or careless construction, as he'd believed. Braden's fists clamped around twisted bedsheets, the twin bullets of hope and helplessness piercing him anew.

Braden sucked in a deep breath and tried—as he had been for the past hour or so—not to stare at his fiancée while she quietly sat beside him and read. If he allowed himself more than a glance, he wouldn't be able to tear his gaze from the red shimmers in her ginger hair, the pale perfection of creamy skin touched with saucy freckles. If he looked once, she'd catch him staring at her, greedy for the comforting presence of the woman he no longer deserved.

She shouldn't be here. Fury, sharp and vicious as barbed wire, squeezed his chest. *I can't provide for her from this sickroom. I can't protect her. I can't even make her go back home, where it's safe.* His rage coiled more tightly, crushing any last hopes.

"Why are you still here?" He lashed out against the woman whose presence reminded him of the man he'd been—and what he'd lost.

"Because, for the first time since I arrived in Hope Falls, you haven't ordered me out of your room." Cora didn't look up, merely ran a delicate finger along the seam of pages. "I suppose I took it as an encouraging sign." She paused. The page turned.

Her calm disinterest needled him. "Didn't I order you out of my room this very morning? Have I not said from the very beginning that you females should never have come to Hope Falls with your far-fetched schemes? At every turn I've said I don't want you, don't need you to do anything but leave here and behave like the ladies you've shown you aren't. Don't accuse me of inconsistency, woman!" The moment he spoke the words, Braden wished he'd choked on them.

Of course Cora could accuse him of inconsistency—he'd once pledged to love and protect her until his dying day. But Braden could no longer protect her. He could only love her enough to give her up. But the contrary woman made even that impossible. His glorious Cora wouldn't see reason, defied him at every turn, and obstinately refused to return to the safety and security of home.

"If I were to bother accusing you, Braden, inconsistency would hardly be the worst of the charges." She raised her head, pinning him with the mismatched gaze Braden swore saw straight through him. One hazel eye, one blue. . .both shimmering with unshed tears.

His throat closed. For every time he'd sworn he didn't love her anymore, didn't want her, would order her from his sight and his town, Cora had looked steadily at him and refused. For the first time, she allowed him to glimpse the grief in her remarkable gaze.

I'm sorry. He swallowed another of the thousand apologies he owed her and crossed his arms so he wouldn't reach out to hold her close and assure her how incredible a woman she was. *You deserve better. If the only way I can make you see that is to hurt you, I know it will still be best in the long run. You'll thank me someday.* And when that day came, he'd still be cursing himself.

THREE

Cora Thompson blinked back tears, knowing they wouldn't vanish. Tears lurked all too close to the surface these days, and every time she pushed away the sorrow, it returned more quickly than before.

At this rate she'd be watery-eyed in another ten seconds.

Braden knows it, too. Cora swallowed her hurt, refusing to cede her fiancé the victory. Instead she gave him the full force of her fury. "But since 'inconsistent' is the sin you want to address first, how about we discuss it. How dare you berate us—daily—for two solid months over putting ourselves in danger and then put up only a token protest when Lacey tromps off to the mines?"

"None of you listen to me anyway," he pointed out. "What you call a 'token protest' was a reiteration of what I've been saying—as you admit—for the past two months. None of you women should be here at all. At this point, does anything make much difference?"

"It should. Your vague, insulting objections to our presence hold no water when your only reason is our gender. When it comes to a mine that already caved in on top of you, I would have thought you could offer better guidance. Lacey's life is at stake!"

"The mine construction stayed sound, and they shored it up farther to pull me out. It's safe enough if Dunstan keeps to the main way and doesn't stay long. But you don't have to believe me. If it makes things easier, believe that I don't care about my sister, too. Accuse me of whatever you like." A sneer distorted his once-handsome face. "In the end, your words mean nothing to me."

Cora drew a shuddering breath, refusing to let him see how deeply that struck her. When hope waned and even her love itself began to falter, she'd found pride to be her saving grace. Ironic, when one considered how pride numbered among the seven deadly sins.

But, if she was honest with herself—and Cora always tried to be honest with herself, even if the thoughts were too outrageous to share with anyone else—she'd imagined that she'd lovingly support Braden and see him through his time of pain and suffering. Cora had thought of helping mend broken bones or closing wounds.

Instead, every moment she spent with the man she loved fractured her own heart a tiny bit more, prying open the scars she'd thought healed over with the miraculous news of Braden's survival. As his body began to heal, their relationship wasted away.

"Who are you trying to convince of that, Braden?" She concentrated so hard on keeping her voice steady, she almost missed the flicker of emotion in his eyes. It caught her off guard, since she'd begun to believe his pretense that he no longer felt anything.

"I don't have to convince anyone of anything." Again something shadowed his gaze. On him it looked like misery, but to Cora it looked as though hope wasn't completely lost after all!

"Yes you do because I don't believe this farce you've become. And until you can convince me, I won't release you from this engagement." She crossed her arms over her chest. "So now what do you have to say?"

Maybe we've finally come to the point where Braden can no longer cocoon himself in his own misery and anger. It's smothered him for long enough—he has to begin breaking free of the past.

Slowly expectation leaked from the air, leaving it brittle with unanswered anticipation. Silence crept in, softly at first, gaining ground, growing heavier with each passing moment.

Cora found herself holding her breath in spite of herself—but as a crumbling defense against the renewed onslaught of unshed tears. *Sometimes,* she realized as Braden turned his head to the wall, *the worst possible answer is no answer at all.*

I've lost him.

"So Lacey's disappeared again," Naomi murmured when she and Evie walked into Braden's sickroom a few days after their talk. Even stranger, the room held about enough tension to crack the walls.

Obviously Braden had said or done something upsetting. But right now she didn't have the patience for the troubles of Cora's engagement. Instead Naomi's worry had clicked up another notch.

"Where's Lacey?" It sounded more like a demand than a question, but Naomi knew her sharpness would be forgiven. After all, the young cousin she'd watched over for the past five years had a vexing habit of disregarding danger and disappearing into the forest surrounding Hope Falls. In the past month alone, the stubborn girl had been abducted at gunpoint *and* attacked by a cougar.

The mere fact that a cougar attack ranked as a *lesser* concern meant Lacey shouldn't be allowed in the forest alone. Ever. Naomi's stomach churned at the newfound proof that Lacey had wandered again.

"My peahen of a sister went off with Dunstan." Braden roused himself to glower at them as though it were all their faults.

Maybe it is my fault, Naomi conceded. After all, she'd been the one to help raise Lacey when the girl needed a mother. Worse, she'd gone along with the harebrained plan to save Hope Falls. *If I'd tried harder, maybe I could've talked sense into the others and saved us all.* Even as she wondered, Naomi knew better.

Lacey was a force of nature, going where she wanted and getting there in whatever manner she pleased. One could either go along with her or be swept to the side, and Naomi would always choose to stay with her cousin. *For all the good it seemed to do either of us.*

"Oh good." Evie sounded relieved. "She's not alone then."

"We have bigger concerns than that." Cora glowered at Braden.

Naomi believed she understood the larger issue. "She's without a chaperone." The attraction between Lacey and the hunter rapidly grew too obvious for things to continue this way. "This isn't the first time she's gallivanted off alone with Dunstan. I know we asked him to keep an eye on her, but it shouldn't be so blatant!"

Evie looked troubled. "Perhaps we need to ask our new hunter to stop taking Lacey on his expeditions. Our reputation as ladies is one of our safeguards out here. If the men begin thinking we're less than paragons of virtue, we'll have a situation on our hands."

Guilt fisted at the back of her throat, cutting off Naomi's ability to agree. *Paragons of virtue.* A laughable thought.

Braden snorted. "As though they believe that anyway, after the stunts you four pulled. The lumbermen are playing along in hopes of striking it rich, but deep down all of them see the four of you as the strange hussies who set out to hire their own husbands."

"Three," Naomi hissed at her cousin, a part of her longing to brain him with the bedpan. "Three of us set out to hire our husbands. One of us gave up everything to be at her fiancé's side."

"And who asked *any* of you to come here, hauling enough luggage to sink an ocean liner and attracting enough trouble to keep a dozen writers' pens scratching? There can be no peace with you here."

"Peace is what you had before, Braden?" Cora's tone went silky. "I would call it shame and the waste of a town."

Naomi gaped for a moment, struck by Cora's uncharacteristic attack. Evie, she couldn't help but notice, failed to hide a grin. Perhaps it was time for Cora to stop standing by Braden's ill humors and begin challenging them instead. Braden himself looked flabbergasted by the change—and well he should be. For the past seven weeks since their arrival in Hope Falls, his fiancée crossed him only in her refusal to dissolve their engagement.

Grin out in full force, Evie apparently decided to leave the estranged lovebirds to sort things out.

"Well, since Lacey's accounted for, I believe I'll go back to making supper. I wouldn't want to disappoint the men. And who knows? Maybe Jake will come back this afternoon." With that, Evie slipped from the room. They heard her footsteps speed to a near run as she made her way down the hall and through the doctor's front door.

"But Lacey needs—" Cora spoke too late to reach her sister.

"Granger won't be back yet," Braden predicted then muttered, "I wish he was. Then he could go help Dunstan in the mines and send Lacey back to keep company with the rest of you women. You're less in the way when the four of you stay huddled together somewhere."

As used to as she'd become to ignoring Braden's mutters, it took Naomi a moment to sift through his sulk and pinpoint what made her so uneasy. Surely no one was wandering around the collapsed mines?

"Dunstan isn't out hunting?" A lump blocked her throat.

"Oh, he's hunting all right." Grim satisfaction showed in Braden's first smile in months. "But this time, it's for proof."

"Where?" Naomi was desperate for answers. "Proof of *what*?"

From the way Cora eyed the pitcher beside Braden's bed, she was barely managing to restrain herself from dumping its contents atop her self-involved fiancé. "They went to the mines."

Naomi knew a vague pride that her knees didn't buckle. All of a sudden she understood Cora's newfound hostility. She felt a large dose of it herself and felt only marginally better as Cora ceded to temptation and upended the pitcher atop Braden's head.

"You let Lacey go into the mines?" Naomi seethed. "Your sister, who can't so much as go for a brief stroll without some disaster?"

"Yes." Braden raked a hand through his sopping hair, flinging drops of water around the room. "My sister, who *you* couldn't stop from selling our family home and planting herself in the middle of the wilderness without protection and no plan of how to handle things."

"We had a plan," she snapped back, stung by the bald accusation that she'd failed in her responsibility to watch over Lacey. Besides, Lacey *had* thought up a way to join her gravely injured brother and reenergize the town that almost stole his life. And although the idea proved incredibly foolish, quite probably dangerous, and definitely impractical, there had been a plan.

Which didn't make Naomi feel one whit better about having gone along with it. Nor did it alleviate her worries about Lacey now. Nothing would make her breathe easy until she saw her cousin safe and sound—and far away from collapsed mine tunnels.

"Which entrance did they take?" She began rolling up her sleeves—as though that might save the soft gray serge of her day dress from the dirt of the mines. "Eastern or southern facing?"

"How should I know?" He made an abrupt gesture drawing notice to his leg. "I'm stuck in here while they go search for proof that Dunstan's hunch is right. If I could be with him, Lacey wouldn't."

Naomi paused in the act of tightening the new Common Sense bootlaces she'd ordered from Montgomery Ward. Now that she'd had a moment to catch her breath and think about it, she couldn't deny how strange it was for Lacey to go into the bowels of a mountain.

Yes, her cousin dearly loved adventure. Yes, Lacey seemed to find particular delight in discomfiting Chase Dunstan, the new Hope Falls hunter. But at Lacey's core was a creature born of sunlight and sparkle who vigorously guarded the beautiful things with which she surrounded herself. Lacey wouldn't sacrifice one of her gorgeous gowns to dankness and dust without good reason.

"What hunch?" Naomi finished with her laces and leveled her stare at her still-soaked cousin. "Why would either of them go?"

"I hired Dunstan as our territory guide when I first came to set up the mine. After the collapse, he thought I was dead. Since my partner sold his shares so swiftly, the sudden news that I lived after all roused his suspicions." Braden shifted, betraying an uncharacteristic eagerness. "When he caught wind of my sister's featherbrained ad, he assumed it was either code or a scam and decided to look into the real reason behind the mine's collapse."

Naomi blinked, sorting through Braden's answer and finding more surprises than she liked. Questions sprang up where before there had been blind acceptance—the sort of blind acceptance she thought she'd left behind on the day of her sister's wedding. Her head pounded.

"It seems Jake Granger wasn't the only man to come to Hope Falls hiding his identity." Cora brought up one of the more troubling points. The women had forgiven Granger's deception—though just barely—because the man had been hunting a murderer. Though even that good reason might not have been enough, had Evie not fallen in love with the rugged lumberman and supported him after.

"Nah." Obviously seeing that the women were taking exception to these circumstances, Braden rushed to defend Dunstan. "Chase Dunstan really is his name. He's one of the most capable men I've ever met, and possibly the only one I think could hold his own against my sister. Since he's the best guide and hunter in these mountains, he's the best choice to keep an eye on Lacey—even if you couldn't have known that when you hired him. Just because you didn't look into the man's background doesn't mean he hid who he is."

"He hid his connection to Hope Falls," Cora contested. "Dunstan deliberately left out his reason for coming back then went out of his way to avoid you because you knew his connection to the mines."

"You deliberately chose to keep me in the dark—don't blame Dunstan for your duplicity. What were you thinking, hiring on another man—particularly one as potentially dangerous as a hunter/tracker—behind my back? You're lucky it was Dunstan!"

"Granger vouched for him." Naomi decided to cut off the brewing argument. They could snipe at each other after she fetched Lacey from the mines and wrested her cousin's promise never to go back. "You can quibble all you like—it doesn't change the fact he misled us. And while he's proven his ability to look after himself and Lacey in the forest, a mine that's already collapsed once is drastically different! Its construction is compromised."

"No! The problem wasn't in the construction." Braden punched the mattress with his fist. "If the mine was sabotaged, the design and supports of the tunnels were just as safe as I intended."

"Originally." Cora rubbed her temples. "But you know that your original design was ruined—even though they cleared debris and shored up the main tunnels to get you out, it left the entire network weakened, strewn with shifting rubble. Who knows what Lacey might disturb, bringing the whole thing down again?"

"You're right." From a man who'd spent the past two months telling them they were wrong about anything and everything, the admission offered little comfort. "We'll need to shore up the supports and send in a team for safety's sake. I shouldn't have let them go. Lacey was being stubborn and Dunstan goes his own way, but I encouraged them." He looked as though he was about to be sick.

Cora looked as though she might want to reassure her newly humbled fiancé, but Naomi yanked her friend out the door. When Cora would have run straight back to Evie's kitchen, Naomi veered them toward Lacey's mercantile. In a matter of minutes, she and Cora looped lengths of oiled rope over their shoulders and around their waists and grabbed rucksacks and shovels. If they had to brave the tunnels to fetch Lacey, they'd go in prepared. They headed for the door, only to freeze in place as the earth let loose a booming roar.

FOUR

T he train had already begun slowing for the upcoming stop, so for a moment Michael thought something had gone horribly wrong with the engine. A muted boom sounded before the train car shuddered, nearly tilting off the tracks as it came to a whining, skidding halt.

As it stood, Michael had a hard time distinguishing when the train itself stopped moving—because the earth itself hadn't stopped. The ground beneath the tracks shook; a mountain in the distance roiled enough to look like a mythical dragon sprung to life, stone suddenly struggling to draw breath. Rumbling, roaring, the quake sent dust swirling into the air and obscuring parts of the horizon.

Before the sound and motion ceased, one of the few passengers in the train car bolted to his feet, sprang through the door, and burst from the vehicle in an impressive leap. The man hit the ground running and kept going, headed for the nearest building.

Slinging his rucksack over one shoulder and grabbing his tool case, Michael disembarked. His first real glance of Hope Falls showed a bewildering contradiction. Chaos reigned supreme—the mountain he'd glimpsed before seemed to be sagging in on itself. The dust started settling but still caked several buildings with a tangible coating of catastrophe. But where were all the people? For such a sizeable outpost, there was hardly a soul to be seen.

Michael absorbed the details, sifting through possibilities and explanations. *I thought the mine already collapsed?* Which would account for the almost-abandoned air of Hope Falls. *Maybe the tunnels remained unstable, and the same mines caved in farther?*

That seemed the only way to explain the booming rumble that shook the mountainside. As far as where he could find the townsfolk, Mike could only pray that they hadn't been so foolish as to be poking around the old mine site and set off the earlier ruckus.

For now he headed in the direction mapped out by the other fellow. If he found no one and nothing else, at least he wouldn't be the sole inhabitant of the town. And for a town supposedly raising a sawmill, there definitely weren't enough people to get the job done. *Perhaps Hope Falls abandoned the sawmill idea?*

Acid clawed at the back of his throat at the very thought. Surely the Lord wouldn't have brought him all this way for nothing? Mike shook his head and kept walking, now hearing excited voices.

"It's all going to be fine." Deep tones rumbled reassurance.

"Lacey and Dunstan went to explore the mines!" came a sob in return.

"We're going after them." The beguiling, husky tone sent a shiver down Mike's spine.

He paused, now understanding the true nature of the crisis. The mine had, indeed, suffered another cave-in. Worse, it sounded as though this woman's friends might well have been caught in it.

"I'll send Lawson to get word to the men to come help." The unknown man, still trying to assure the women, began making plans. "The sooner we get through, the sooner we'll find them."

Lawson? Mike didn't have to check the well-worn copy of his friend's telegram to know that this was the name of the engineer. In spite of the tragedy he'd walked into, Mike acknowledged a surge of relief. *If the engineer is here, and there are 'men' to fetch, it looks as though the Hope Falls sawmill does exist after all.*

He set down his carpenter's chest and rounded the corner of the building, determined to give whatever assistance he could. In that moment he got his first glance at the occupants of Hope Falls.

Three women clustered around a doorway—and the man from

the train. Little wonder the fellow leaped from the car as though fearing for his life. By the way the plump, pretty gal in his arms stared up at him, the man had an awful lot to lose. Beside them hovered a wisp of a girl whose face bore some resemblance to the other. But the third woman caught Mike's attention and held it.

Her sensible gray dress used no ploys to play up feminine curves, but to Mike's eyes that enhanced the woman even more. Her skin was as pale and fine as smooth-sanded birch and all the more striking given her hair. That single streak of white racing through the dark tresses showed her singularity. Mike instantly knew she belonged to the incredible voice he'd heard before.

And in the same instant he knew a fierce joy that she wasn't the one cradled so protectively in the other man's arms. At some point, after he'd helped find her friends, he'd ask around to see whether the striking beauty was spoken for. But for now he needed to offer assistance and not a distraction from the task at hand.

"Came in on the train." He gave a nod of acknowledgment to the other man and received one in return. "What can I do to help?"

"My cousin looks to be trapped in the cave-in." The beauty studied him, seeming to measure his strength. "If you're willing, we'd be grateful for your help—though it may prove dangerous."

"I'm willing." Mike knew he'd be willing to do more for this woman than to dig out a collapsed mine tunnel but knew better than to say so. A few times in his life he'd summed up people within moments of their meeting. Without fail, he'd found his initial judgment eerily accurate. At least this time it was favorable.

"In that case,"—the slender girl took a loop of rope from her waist and handed him a rucksack—"I'll go fetch Mr. Lawson. You and Granger will make more headway than I could manage in his place." With that she trotted off, leaving Mike to follow "Granger" as he led them out of town and toward the ominously sagging mountainside.

Under normal circumstances, Naomi would be hesitant to accept a handsome stranger into their midst without thorough questioning.

Of course, she thought, suppressing a mild twinge of panic, it had been so long since she'd found herself in "normal" circumstances that catastrophes seemed more the usual way of things.

So here she stood, blatantly eyeing a strange man—who happened to be more than average in the looks department—and deciding that he looked fit enough to heft large boulders. *Splendidly fit.*

Naomi squashed the thought, accepted the stranger's offer of help, and set about agreeing with Cora. As much as she loved her friends, Evie or Cora should go fetch Lawson. Granger and the stranger—she fought back an absurd giggle at the phrase, knowing hysteria could manifest in inappropriate levity—were the only two here whose physical strength could start moving the mountainside.

There was no question of Naomi fetching Mr. Lawson herself. She hadn't already headed for the mines because she stood precious little chance of accomplishing anything alone. Her running ahead would only pull attention away from the task at hand, and everyone needed to focus on finding Lacey.

Alive, Naomi prayed. *Please, Lord, let Lacey still be alive.*

"Are you the kind of folks who'd want to pray before we head out?" Quiet words, spoken low but clear. The stranger knew how to command attention without distracting from the current crisis.

Of course, the others just stared at the man without answering. Naomi couldn't tell whether they were surprised and touched by the offer or abashed no one had suggested praying before now. It didn't much matter. At this point Naomi could only be grateful.

"Yes, Mr. . . ." She trailed off at the sudden realization none of them knew his name. A forgivable oversight, given the circumstances . . .but awkward nevertheless. "Thank you for offering."

"Strode." The stranger shifted his weight from one booted foot to the other. "Michael Strode, and I'd be honored to pray with you."

Naomi registered the newcomer's surprise as she reached out and twined hands with Cora. Cora linked with Evie, who held on to Jake Granger, who shrugged and held out his hand to Mr. Strode at the same moment Naomi reached out to close the circle. The stranger hesitated a heartbeat before joining them. His hand surrounded hers, as warm and strong and comforting as the words he began to speak.

His prayer washed over them all, a plea for the lives of those in the mines, an offering of thanks for the Lord's provision, a request for the strength to face what was to come. But most of all, the low words became a reminder that they weren't alone.

If asked, Naomi wouldn't be able to repeat a single sentence of it. She didn't need to. It was enough to take part in the asking and offering of comfort and protection. Somehow, prayer blunted the thin edge of panic and steadied the flickering flame of Naomi's hope.

"Thank you, Mr. Strode." She remembered herself just in time and restrained from the impulse to give his hand a grateful squeeze.

"You're welcome, miss." A brief smile graced his black-stubbled jaw before he turned his attention to Granger. "I see shovels already, but do you have any lamp helmets? Pickaxes?"

"This way." Naomi headed off and didn't look back to see whether or not they followed her to the mercantile. If they didn't, she'd just grab what they needed and hoof it up the hill behind them. So long as she hurried, they wouldn't lose any more time, and she wouldn't feel the gnawing sense that time was running out.

The tinkle of Lacey's customer bell when Naomi opened the mercantile door sounded more like an abbreviated lament than a cheerful welcome. Even so, she couldn't help but be grateful Lacey had recently come into the shop and set everything to rights.

When she considered the condition in which they'd found this store—boxes and crates stacked higgledy-piggledy, coated with a thick layer of grit and no clue as to their contents—Naomi breathed a prayer of thanks. If Lacey hadn't whirled into the shop and set everything to rights, they wouldn't have a prayer of finding things.

As things stood, Naomi veered left as soon as she entered the door, heading for the wall of tools. She reached for a pickax, only to have a strong arm reach farther, faster, and snatch it from her grasp. An unfamiliar prickle of awareness told her it was the stranger, but Naomi didn't tilt her head back to make sure.

STRONG and STUBBORN

With the men grabbing the pickaxes, she ducked away and made a beeline for the back counter. Behind the rear counter, she slid through the door to the storeroom. Tucked in here, she knew, Lacey stashed anything and everything originally intended to help outfit the Hope Falls mines. With the mines closed and the town now slated to become a lumber mill, the mercantile wouldn't see much business for the strange paraphernalia used solely by miners.

When she didn't immediately spot what she needed, Naomi began eyeing the crates and boxes stacked in the farthest corner. Knowing Lacey's penchant for order, she would have placed heavy items at the bottom to support the lighter or more fragile goods. In a matter of seconds, Naomi had pried open two boxes.

One held what looked to be small machine parts, and she set it aside. The second held small bottles of Sunshine Lamp Oil, which she kept close at hand. The next crate, with SUNSHINE LAMPS thoughtfully stamped along the wooden slats, defeated her. She set it aside as requiring a crowbar and reached for the next box. The sound of the crate being moved farther away made her jump.

A startled glance showed the stranger, Michael Something-or-other, scooting the crate for another few inches of clearance. Without a word, the man hunkered down and began working at the tacks with the tines of a hammer. Naomi watched for a moment before realizing that, at this pace, he'd not only have the lamps out of the crate by the time she unearthed the helmets, he'd have them filled with the Sunshine Oil she'd found mere moments ago.

With renewed vigor, she shoved open the box before her, relieved to see what looked like overgrown brown raisins. Once picked up and shaken out, the wrinkled leather took the form of stiff, close-fitting skull caps with a narrow pocket sewn to double thickness along the front seam. Naomi's triumph at finding the helmets darkened to dismay. Yes, this was what she was looking for—she remembered from almost a year ago, when Braden demonstrated how the lamp's long metal prongs tucked into the narrow openings.

But while these caps would hold the teapot-shaped lamps

43

emerging from the now-opened crate, they would only provide light. With such flimsy head-coverings, was it any wonder so many of Braden's miners had perished in the first collapse? The contraptions offered absolutely no protection from falling rocks.

And Lacey doesn't even have one of these. A small round stain darkened the leather between her fingertips, and Naomi realized she was crying. She gulped in a shuddering breath and rose to her feet.

Feelings interfere with getting things done, and emotions cloud judgment, she reminded herself. Today she could afford neither.

FIVE

Mike heard the other man—Granger—and woman rummaging about in the front of the store. When he'd seen the husky-voiced beauty slip around the back counter and through a door, his feet followed before he made the decision to go after her. Propriety, he knew, would have stopped him before he went through the door.

Mike smiled at the thought and kept right on walking. After all, he'd left propriety—along with the other inconveniences in his life—a few thousand miles behind him. *Why not enjoy the freedom?*

Besides, it seemed to Mike that while the other man bore the trademark signs of a leader, the quietly determined woman looked like she knew where she was going. Mike decided he liked her initiative—and her productivity. In the mere moments it took for him to catch up with her in the storeroom, she'd already begun sorting through a heap of boxes and crates in the far corner. As he watched, she shook her head and nudged a box to the side—out of her way—and kept on.

Mike grabbed a hammer from a nearby shelf and squatted down to lend a hand with the crate she'd just abandoned. Its tacked-down top would have taken too much time away from finishing her hunt. He pulled the thing closer, making the move louder than necessary in case she didn't already know he'd come into the room behind her.

She hadn't. A small jump tattled that he'd startled her, even before her wide-eyed glance confirmed it. *Green.* Mike hadn't realized until then that he'd wanted to know the color of her eyes. Such an unimportant detail in the midst of a mission, but in that moment it hit him hard. He'd never thought about it before, but it seemed he must've thought of green as a cool color. How else to explain his surprise at the warmth of this woman's gaze?

She'd turned back around and resumed working while he sat there like a fool, pondering the color of her eyes. So Mike made up for it by working his fastest. He didn't look up at her again until he'd opened the crate and unwrapped all of the teapot-shaped Sunshine Oil Lamps, which were to be fitted into leather mining caps.

A quick peek showed her still facing forward. Doubt speared him—what if they were unable to find the caps after all? They would have wasted all this time fumbling in a storeroom when they could have been helping scout out the mines or unblock passages!

If they were on a wild goose chase, he'd need to redirect their efforts to where they could do the most good. Mike craned his neck, trying to look over her shoulder without attracting her notice. The stack of goods seemed to have diminished somewhat, and he noticed the first box he'd seen at her side happened to be the oil for the lamps he'd finished unearthing. . .two parts of a three-piece puzzle.

And there, almost blocked by her bent form, stood the missing item. Creased and pressed into a box for who knows how long, the leather looked more like bark than hoods. Even so, their very necessity made them beautiful. Mike reached for one, only to pull back when he saw she already held a cap. *Then why had she stopped?*

As he watched, a drop of darkness wet the leather in her hands. Understanding dawned. Her sudden stillness meant she was crying. Or, he realized when her shoulders stiffened with resolve and she returned the cap to the box, she was trying not to.

Something clenched behind his rib cage, powerful enough to make him pause. *She shouldn't have to cry*, his instincts clamored. *And she shouldn't have to stop or hide her tears if she wants to cry*. Mike cupped his hand beneath her elbow and raised her to her feet.

"Let's go tear that mountain apart." Without waiting for her response, he dumped the oil lamps back in the crate, slammed the now-loosened lid back on it, and plunked the box of oil on top. Mike reached for the box of leather hoods, only to come up empty.

The woman—it began bothering him that he had no name for her, but right now it felt too awkward to ask—finished slipping the last cap into a large canvas bag, which she then slung over her shoulder. With coils of rope looped over her other shoulder and around her waist, she looked like a prim adventuress.

And if such a thing hadn't existed before now, in Mike's humble opinion, it was a terrible oversight. Since it wasn't his place to say so—*yet*, a small, determined part of his mind insisted—he snagged the pickax he'd grabbed earlier, hefted the stack of lamps and oil, and followed her surprisingly swift march out the door.

Outside, they found not only Granger and the lady Michael already thought of as Granger's woman, but also the girl who must be related to her. As they drew closer, the girl spoke.

"Mr. Lawson is off to the areas where the men are working today." She sounded winded. "They'll meet up with us at the mines."

"You're not going to check on Braden?" Granger's girl looked surprised, and Mike found himself wondering who Braden was.

"No. He shouldn't have let Lacey go into the mines." The girl held up her hands as though to stave off any disagreements. "I know he couldn't actually stop her, but he didn't even argue with her the way he's been arguing with us about anything and everything else."

"All right." The beauty at Mike's side handed the girl a shovel and turned away, squinting toward the sunken-in mountain.

"Do we know which entrance they took?" Granger looked the same way. "To my recollection, there are two, but I don't even know which one was the most cleared out from the first rescue."

"Southern," chorused the three women in response, and Mike wondered why the women would know that when the man didn't.

"Do you hear something?" The dark-haired beauty inclined her head to the side, as though listening for a faraway sound.

Everyone waited, almost holding their breath, as though whatever she heard might make the difference between finding their friends alive or facing failure. After a moment she shook her head.

"I must have imagined it, but for a moment I thought I heard Decoy."

"Decoy?" This time Mike couldn't reign in his curiosity. He powered on with the rest of them as they headed toward the mines, but his own mind raced far ahead—or behind. Everyone here knew far more than he did, and he didn't like bringing up the rear.

"Mr. Dunstan's dog," the young one answered. "And since Mr. Dunstan is the one who took our friend Lacey to the mines, it was probably just wishful thinking on Naomi's part. Because if Decoy's nearby, then they probably are, too. . . ." Her explanation faded away at the sound of frantic barking, coming from not too far ahead.

When a massive creature came tearing around the bend, Mike was glad he'd asked; if he hadn't been told that Decoy was nothing more than someone's pet dog, he might well have reached for his pistol. The beast was, quite simply, the largest animal he'd seen off a farm or outside of the circus. And it wasn't in a good mood.

The thing had to stand about four feet tall—at least that was Mike's best guess, since what he now identified as a brindled Irish wolfhound came to a stop several yards ahead. Agitated, the dog bounced about, prancing almost in place and shaking its huge head from side to side. The dog's message couldn't be clearer: *Hurry up!*

"He's alone." One of the women gave voice to the chilling truth no one really wanted to acknowledge. If their friends weren't with the dog, then their fears proved correct: the mines had taken them.

"We haven't lost them yet." Naomi urged everyone on, frustrated beyond reason by the way they'd all stopped to stare at Decoy. "The dog isn't the specter of death. If anything, he's telling us that Dunstan and Lacey are still alive. He's not crouched down, slinking around and whimpering. He's telling us to get a move on!"

At that, the others perked up visibly. They surged forward, filled with a renewed hope Naomi prayed wasn't false. As they drew closer to Decoy, the dog let loose an anxious howl and turned tail. He bounded up the mountainside a short ways then stopped and resumed what Naomi would call pacing if the beast were human.

As though reading her thoughts, Decoy raced back toward them, gave a sort of urgent growl, and darted back up the mountain. Again, he stopped to perform what Naomi decided to call the "I'm waiting for you to catch up, you slowpokes" dance. Somehow the dog's confident insistence that they follow him seemed comforting.

The troupe of them dutifully carried on their part in this dance, following the dog's lead up toward the mines. When Decoy began doing his impatient prance near the eastern entrance, Granger gave a grunt of. . .of what, Naomi couldn't be sure. In truth, she didn't decipher grunts very well, but it sounded like a good one.

Then again, maybe she was grasping at straws—anything to keep hold of the idea that they could still save Lacey when things looked increasingly bad. The closer they drew to the mountain, the more damage they could see. Boulders from much higher up had toppled from their lofty perches, knocking loose chunks of earth and smaller stones as they tumbled down the hillside. They left furrows in the dirt behind where they skidded to a halt. Dust hung heavy in the air, and Naomi reached for one of the bandanas she'd stuck in her apron pocket. Tying it around the lower half of her face made her feel oddly like a bandit, but maybe that was only fair. After all, she was trying to take something precious from this mountain.

She heard another grunt, this one conveying irritation. When she looked back at the newly sealed entrance to the mines, Naomi realized why Granger sounded so dissatisfied. Decoy had sidled to the left and back, almost out of sight. The dog was leading them to the other mine entrance—which was that much farther to go and that much more time they lost. Naomi stifled her own annoyed grunt, reminding herself to be thankful that the dog was pointing the way.

"Better to go the long way to the right place than start digging in the wrong one." She said it to raise her spirits as much as everyone else's. She fell, as she so often did, into prayer.

Thank You, Lord, she praised, *that Dunstan trained him so well.* Her silent conversation with her creator continued, falling into the rhythm of her steps. The prayer might not be formal, but it was heartfelt. *If he were a typical dog, we wouldn't trust Decoy's guidance today. You use all things to further Your plans, and I only ask that You find as much use for me today as You have for that dog.*

She drew as deep a breath as she could manage through the thick covering of her folded bandana and stepped aside when she couldn't fight the need to cough. The new man hesitated until she stepped back toward the main path, but Naomi was pleased to see the others pushing forward as swiftly as possible. She hurried to catch up, skirting around a giant boulder and almost tripping in the process.

After finding her balance, Naomi looked down to see what had caught her. It hadn't seemed as solid as stone, but nothing grew roots this far up the rocky terrain. Maybe it was a rucksack or Lacey's cloak and they shouldn't be following Decoy to the other entrance after all. A thick layer of dust coated everything, but a closer look erased any doubts. Naomi swallowed a scream and backed away, bile clawing at the back of her throat and stealing her voice and leaving her alone with her gruesome discovery.

Pinned beneath the biggest boulder she'd ever seen, obscured by the debris of a mountain's convulsions, protruded a pair of legs.

SIX

Mike noticed the way Naomi—as the youngest girl had called her—withdrew into herself as they walked along. Before she'd been determined, anxious, and practical by turns. Now *preoccupied* seemed the best word to describe her trek. With her face half hidden beneath the bandana she used as a mask, Mike couldn't tell whether Naomi strengthened her resolve or sank deeper into her worries.

When a short fit of coughing stopped her progress, she'd still thought to move aside. Obviously she wasn't about to slow things down. After he passed her, Mike hesitated, waiting for her to come back on the path. When she moved, he continued on around a turn. He wanted to wait for her but didn't want to make her uncomfortable. A few steps later Mike realized she still hadn't followed.

So he went back for her. Awkward or not, he needed to make sure she was all right. Mike went back around the bend, gaining speed when he spotted her. Half bent over beside a large boulder, with her breath coming in short, uneven gasps, she was in trouble.

Mike's first thought, looking into her wide, frightened eyes, was that she was choking. It sounded like she was still drawing air, so something must've stuck in her throat. . . . There was only one thing to do. He slapped his hand against her upper back, hard enough to dislodge whatever was blocking her airway. The thump of the blow made him wince—nothing but this could have made him strike a woman.

Mike peered at her. The woman remained doubled over, but the strange little gasps stopped. Fear gripped him—had he shifted the obstacle and made the situation *worse*? She wasn't speaking. . . .

He grabbed her shoulder and pulled her upright, yanking the bandana down. She gave a strangled-sounding hiss and jerked away, eyes narrowed. Yep, the lady looked angry, but since she was breathing again, Mike didn't care. He wanted to hug the woman.

"What are you *doing*?" Her indignation effectively doused his triumph. "Do you usually swing first and ask questions later?"

"You weren't choking." Now he sounded as foolish as he felt.

"No." The outrage vanished in a blink, replaced by tears as she looked back toward the massive boulder. "I just couldn't. . ." She swallowed visibly, struggling to explain and finally giving up. She gestured toward the base of the huge rock. "Over there."

Fighting back a terrible suspicion over what would so upset this woman, Mike moved over to look. What he saw made his own lungs stop working for a minute. Beneath the stone stretched the bottom half of a man's torso and his legs. A closer look revealed a hand covered in dirt, outstretched in a silent plea for help.

No blood caked the ground, but Mike knew the man's head had been crushed instantly. Without knowing what else to do, Mike gathered a grief-stricken Naomi in his arms, shielding her from the horrific sight. She buried her face in his shoulder and sobbed, unable to keep a brave face in the sight of a man's destruction.

Mike sent up wordless prayers, half-formed hopes for the man's soul and supplication that the other missing person—the woman—hadn't met the same fate. He'd gotten the impression that it was the missing girl whom Naomi held close to her heart. But a look around the area revealed nothing to suggest a woman had died there.

Reluctantly Mike eased Naomi from his arms. They needed to fetch the others and form a new plan. He cleared his throat to say as much but found it unnecessary when the others came storming into view. From their fast pace and the looks on their faces, concern for Naomi had won out over irritation at the delay—but barely. And as they saw her standing there, evidently unharmed, they slowed.

"He's dead." Naomi's announcement brought them to a stop.

Granger's woman started shaking her head. "We don't know that, Naomi. Now's not the time to become hysterical and lose faith—we might still find both of them safe and sound and waiting for us."

"She said *he*, not *they*." Mike gestured toward the crushing boulder and defended Naomi as best he could. "She's far from hysterical—though she has every right after what she found."

By the time he finished his sentence, Granger reached the boulder—and its victim. Other than an audible swallow, he kept calm and collected. "Ladies, hold off. There's no sign of Lacey, and no one should see this unless there's a darn good reason."

It looked like the young one wouldn't follow his instruction, but Granger's woman caught her arm and held her back. After some furious whispering, the young one decided to hold her piece. But Mike was inclined to attribute her change of heart to Naomi, who'd started up the trail to wait with the women. When she reached the others, they engulfed her in embraces and reassurances, all the while casting fearful looks toward the boulder below.

Now that Naomi was in good hands and out of harm's way, Mike returned his attention to Granger. The other man bent down for a closer look at the corpse. A puzzled frown creased his face, letting Mike know something was wrong beyond the obvious. But what?

"Let's hear it." Mike hunkered down and waited. Whatever Granger was thinking, it looked like he'd need a sounding board.

"Dunstan—the man who went to explore the mines—is a hunter. A mountain guide." Granger gestured toward the corpse's boots. Even coated in dirt and rocks, they had a stacked heel and rigid stiffness. "I've never known him to wear anything but leather boots worn so soft even a deer couldn't hear him move through the forest."

Mike swiftly realized what Granger was trying to say. "You're thinking this isn't our guy." He waited for a curt nod of agreement before taking it to the next logical step. "Do you know him?"

"Hard to say." A moment later Granger quit musing. He narrowed his eyes and considered a small lump in the dirt around the vicinity where the man's head should be. "What's that?"

It turned out to be part of a pair of spectacles, broken at the nose and the lens shattered within a thin gold rim. Granger palmed the piece, gave those boots a considering glance, and shook his head. Whatever he was puzzling over, it must not add up.

"You know him." Mike didn't press, but spectacles weren't a common item in a mining camp. Or a sawmill for that matter.

Granger nodded. "Only two men in town wear glasses, and Cora just sent one of them off to fetch the axmen." He used the spectacles to gesture toward the corpse. "That leaves the telegraph operator, Draxley. But for the life of me, I can't figure out why a man scared of his own shadow would be strolling around up here."

Mike saw that the wolfhound had tracked them and was now circling around the women, whining loudly and butting his head against their skirts in an attempt to herd them back to the mines. For all that the others trusted the dog, and it seemed well trained and admirably determined to rescue its owner, Mike didn't like the situation. He straightened up and started toward the women.

"Maybe Dunstan and the missing girl have the answer."

When the men finally joined them, none of the women could find words to ask about the body below. Naomi knew because she tried and failed to form a question. Part of her didn't want to know any details beyond the horrible sight already emblazoned on her mind. But the larger part needed to know something—anything—about what was going on. Maybe there was some clue to help find Lacey.

"Well?" For the first time, Naomi understood the appeal of one-word sentences. They moved fast and left no room for anxieties.

"It's Draxley." Granger didn't mince words, just pulled out the broken spectacles as evidence. "Or a stranger new to town."

Naomi sagged in relief—if she hadn't been holding on to Cora and Evie, she might have humiliated herself by sliding straight down to the ground. But shame swiftly chased away any relief. *A man is dead*, Naomi chastised herself, noticing that the other women looked as guilty as she felt. They, too, must have welcomed the news that the crushed corpse wasn't Dunstan, who should be protecting Lacey.

"Lawson's fine, so I think it must be Draxley." Cora came to her senses first. "No one new's come to town since Dunstan." She slid a glance toward Mr. Strode, the newcomer, and faltered. "Until today. But no other glasses."

Decoy butted his head against Naomi's skirts and issued a pleading whine. The gesture inspired Naomi's gratitude. Once they'd established it was (most likely) Draxley beneath the boulder, her thoughts turned right back to Dunstan and Lacey. But she couldn't see any graceful way to pull attention away from a dead man.

So when the dog prodded them back toward the caves, Naomi tugged her bandana back over her nose and mouth and made haste up the mountainside. Peripherally, she was aware when Cora spoke briefly with Evie and turned back toward town, but she didn't catch the reasoning behind it. Nor could she work up any curiosity.

As the entrance to the mine came into sight—or rather, what had been an entrance less than half an hour ago—fear spiked higher than ever. Dust hung heavy in the air, but even if it were clear as a mountain stream, Naomi would have had difficulty drawing breath. Where there used to be a tunnel, a heap of stone and earth cascaded from higher up the mountain all the way to the ground. The debris mounded high enough Naomi couldn't tell whether it had merely sealed off the mine or if the mine utterly caved in upon itself.

The sides of his chest heaving like bellows, Decoy leaped atop a medium-sized boulder and began frantically clawing into the gravel and dirt sealing it in place. Naomi rushed up beside him, scuffing her leather gloves as she grabbed smaller stones and heaved them out of the way. She heard Evie come alongside, helping with a too-heavy stone, while the men set to work on the other side of Decoy.

"Lacey!" Her shriek bounced around mountain rock, shrill echoes obliterating any chance of hearing a response from within. Naomi bit her lip and dug in with even more fury than before. Where were the men? If anyone should be coming to help rescue Lacey, it was all the lumberjacks she'd brought here by writing that blasted ad.

It felt as though hours passed before a dull thudding preceded the woodsmen. Using chisels and ax handles, pickaxes and shovels, they attacked the shifting mass of rubble with a vengeance. More than once Naomi fought silly little battles with men trying to dislodge her from her post. Her sharp elbows rewarded a few who reached for her arms. One unfortunate soul who misguidedly tried to grab her waist discovered just how sturdy her boots were. And, as occupied as she was, Naomi found herself slightly disgruntled that no one tried to move Evie or even Decoy from their stations.

Although, she conceded, *every man here knows they'll lose whatever hand they put on Jake Granger's fiancée, so Evie won't be bothered. As for Decoy. . .* Naomi wouldn't try her hand at ousting the wolfhound from his digging site. The dog dug like a. . .well, a beast.

In some distant, practical portion of her mind, Naomi knew the burly lumberjacks only wanted to help Lacey and Dunstan. Even worse, she acknowledged that their methodical use of strength and leverage would move things along faster than her frantic scurries.

But ceding her spot would feel like giving up on Lacey, and Naomi knew she'd cling to these stones like a barnacle until they found her cousin. Besides, the rhythm of scraping and digging, pushing and pulling, shoving and dislodging small pieces of the mountainside was the only thing drowning out her frantic worries.

Time scraped by, measured in fistfuls and shovels of dirt and a steadily growing pile of stones and boulders pushed away from the entrance of the mine. Eventually the thick grit of dirt and stone dust became a natural part of breathing. Naomi kept scrabbling at the stone separating her from her cousin, eyeing the progress they made. At what point should she shout again? Had they made enough headway for Lacey and Dunstan to hear voices through the blockage?

How could she keep on if she called and Lacey didn't answer?

"Lacey!" Apparently having waged the same battle with herself,

Evie called out before Naomi could bring herself to try again. At the sound of her voice, everything ground to a halt, waiting for a response as she called again. "Dunstan! Are you in there?"

SEVEN

"Somebody tell me what the hell is happening!" Braden's yells welcomed Cora to Hope Falls long before she reached the buildings.

"Stop swearing, you miserable, self-centered fool!" Cora knew she shouted at Braden to siphon away some of her frustration and worry, but the man deserved it. "You've been a wretch for weeks on end, and I won't listen for another minute. Right now we need to help Lacey and Dunstan, so your tantrums will have to wait!"

"Where's my sister?" he roared back, face shockingly pale beneath his dark hair. Braden leaned forward as though trying to escape the bed, and Cora noticed that his knee was bent farther than he'd managed even with the doctor that morning. "Where's Lacey?"

Oh, so now you care about your sister? Where was this concern when you let her go to the mines? Cora bit her tongue hard to hold it back. Blaming Braden for not being able to stop Lacey was like blaming a farmer for not stopping a tornado as it ripped through his cornfields—ineffective at best and downright dangerous at worst.

"We don't know." The words tasted every bit as bitter as those she'd just swallowed. Her best friend was either dead or trapped in a collapsed mine—just like Braden had been a few months before.

"Don't tell me what you don't know." Oddly enough, his snarling comforted Cora. So long as Braden kept on snapping and shouting at her, things seemed almost normal. "Tell me what you *do* know!"

"I know you need to stop cursing, shouting, sulking, and demanding, Braden Lyman." Cora matched his glower. "If you're going to help Lacey, I need you calm enough to think properly."

"Is she in the mines?" Fear made his pupils so large his eyes looked black. His hand groped for hers for the first time in months. "Tell me my sister isn't in the mines, Cora. Tell me she's okay."

"I—" Cora gave a hard swallow, but the tears won this time. She gulped out the words anyway. "I can't tell you that. No one's seen Lacey or Dunstan since they left for the mines, and we all know that means she's in some kind of trouble." Otherwise Lacey would be rushing like a whirlwind trying to make sure everyone was all right.

Braden closed his eyes, so still it looked as though he wasn't even breathing. When he opened them, Cora could see he'd banked his fear with determination. "Do we know which entrance they used?"

"Eastern." Cora pushed pencil and paper into his hands, giving him not only a purpose but something tangible to hold on to while he faced his own memories of the mine collapse. "I assume they thought they might find more evidence on the side not facing town."

"That's the side where I—" His throat worked for a moment before he changed the wording and finished, "—they pulled me out of."

"I know." Cora tapped the paper to keep his attention away from whatever horrors lurked in his memory. "Can you draw the tunnels? Do you remember at all which ones were cleared after the collapse and which were left alone? Once we get past the blockage at the entrance, we'll probably need to go farther inside to find them."

"God help me." Braden's eyes shut, and Cora knew he wasn't swearing this time but genuinely asking for help. "I don't know which branches they would have cleared out before they reached me. I know what they absolutely would have needed to clear to get there, but the rest. . . I just don't know." His knuckles went white. "If I could be there—I could tell you. I'd know just by looking."

"Your memory can go where you can't," Cora urged. "Braden, you can still be our guide. Think. When they emptied the tunnels needed to reach you, they shored up the supports, didn't they? So the strongest places are the only ones Lacey and Dunstan found access to—and the only places we should look. You can help us find them!"

Cora held her breath as Braden's pencil crawled across the page, first hesitantly then with more confidence. A web of lines spidered away from a single entry point. When Braden's hand stopped moving, Cora leaned close to peer at his makeshift map.

Her heart sank at the number of tunnels winding away from the entrance, deep into the mountain. *It's more of a maze than a mine.*

"Impossible." Braden's mutter echoed her fears, making Cora raise her eyes to meet his. But he wasn't looking at her. He tapped the pencil against the page before crossing through lines with dark Xs. "Lacey and Dunstan couldn't have gone this way."

He only meant one tunnel. Relief had Cora sagging into a chair beside the bed as Braden considered his sketch. *It's not impossible!*

"We started to close off this tunnel a week before the collapse. Found a footwall, decided it was safer to make a transverse passage to the highwall and pull it out from above. Less falling debris that way." He muttered obscure technicalities to himself, crossing out various branches. "Down here, groundwater kept rising. We made it a sump, to funnel drips from other areas." He cocked his head to the side and marked out another passage. "We had to abandon this adit when we hit a deep fissure—highly unstable. After the collapse, I wondered if we should have stopped sooner."

The admission caught Cora's attention, but Braden fell silent. Cora watched him studying the drawing but wondered what else he was sorting through in his mind. *How terrible for him, to shoulder responsibility for the tragedy. And now, when he begins to hope it wasn't his fault, he'll feel responsible for Lacey's fate.*

"Here." He thrust the paper toward her. "It's all I can do."

"Thank you. We won't be going in blindly—and with as much as you've crossed out, we won't waste time." Cora gave him an encouraging smile, not daring to reach for his hand a second time.

"Go on then." His irritable dismissal had her speeding to the door so fast she almost didn't hear the rest. "But come back."

She clutched the paper to her chest, refusing to turn around and invite the tears again. "You already know I will. I always do."

"Lacey!" Granger's woman called a stop to everyone's hard work.

Michael halted his pickax and held his breath, praying they would hear someone answer her. He knew it wasn't likely—every single man, woman, and even dog working against this wall of stone knew they fought fate. There were simply too many unknowns.

Were the people they sought—Lacey and Dunstan—even alive?

If they lived, were they awake and in condition to respond?

And if they were so fortunate, how far back were they?

Even given the perfect combination of circumstances, there was every chance the pair was much deeper in the twists and turns of the mines. There was no telling how many mounds of collapsed mountain they may have to get through before nearing the couple. Worse, there was no telling whether they had enough time to save them. Air might run out. A critical support might buckle.

Despite Mike's fervent prayers otherwise, the expedition was practically drowning in doubts. He imagined he could smell the sour scent of despair mixed amid the dust. They needed a reason to keep hoping—they needed a sign that God was working alongside them.

"Lacey!" The two women yelled in tandem, forcing their voices through the cracks. But nothing came back. Not so much as a moan.

"Oh God." Naomi sagged against the boulder, where she'd been working alongside the hunter's dog. She tugged the bandana—now encrusted with dirt—away from her face, and Mike could see her lips moving in soundless prayer. Dust caked her face, save where tears cut clear paths down her cheeks. Her eyes closed in supplication.

"Dunstan!" Granger's woman kept on screeching. "Are you there?" When she stopped, it seemed as though the mountain swallowed all sound. Despite the impossible odds, everyone still hoped to hear—

"Esh!" came a muffled female cry. "Eve wherin ear!"

"Yes!" Naomi clutched at the other woman. "Evie, they're in there!" The two wrapped each other in a dancing, circling hug.

"Donut drag he live on." The man's deeper tones came in echoes, difficult to decipher. "Sum of ewe want him down if you ax to."

Granger frowned, repeating the sounds in a furious whisper before his brow eased. "Don't let Draxley leave town." The rest of it seemed a greater challenge. "Hunt him down if we have to?"

Mike gave a quick nod. Once sounded out, without the distance and the interference, the words made perfect sense. Except for the fact they had no idea why Dunstan would want to hunt Draxley down.

"He won't go anywhere." Granger took care to speak slow and loud—apparently not caring that everyone could hear. "Draxley's just outside the mines, head crushed by a boulder from up the ridge."

Shaken from their hushed expectation, the men began murmuring to one another. Mike picked up on their shock—but he noticed no one seemed broken up over the loss of the town telegraph operator. Added to Dunstan's directive that they hunt him down if necessary, Mike pieced together an unflattering portrait of the man—as well as a few suspicions. A telegraph operator had no business lurking around the mines—on the very day Dunstan and Lacey decided to investigate. So what were the chances that this second cave-in was a coincidence?

Mike shook his head and kept his musings to himself. Who wanted to hear half-fledged theories from someone new in town? Nobody. If he turned out to be wrong, he looked insolent and self-aggrandizing. And if he turned out to be right. . .well, in that case, Hope Falls had enough to worry about without adding in a know-it-all.

The strike of a shovel against a nearby rock demanded his attention. Everyone else was looking at Granger, waiting to be sure the conversation with their trapped townsmen had ended. Everyone, that is, except Naomi. It seemed as though Granger's pronouncement shook loose her fears. The people trapped inside the mountain could still be crushed. She gripped the shovel handle with gloves torn enough to show the blood beneath, working feverishly to break through the wall still separating her from her unfortunate friends.

Mike knew he should do the same, should attack the rocky barrier with equal enthusiasm and twice her strength. His hands tightened around the pickax he'd been using to dislodge larger rocks and lever them away. Beneath his leather work gloves, he felt the ridges of the handle where the new tool had yet to be worn smooth by hours of friction. Calloused as his own hands were, the rougher surface hadn't registered until he spotted Naomi's gloves.

And now that he'd seen, Mike couldn't convince himself to turn away and get back to work. There was no way of knowing whether Naomi herself realized the damage—the woman was obviously caught up in the rescue and not giving a thought to taking care of herself. Before they heard the answering call, how long had it been since she'd paused for a breath? When was the last time she drank from her canteen? Mike didn't know, but he knew it had been too long.

Why hasn't anyone else noticed? Someone needs to look after the woman. Common sense warred with a surge of protectiveness, cautioning that it wasn't Mike's place to step forward. *She only turned to you earlier out of shock and grief.* To take care of her now would signal an undue interest and arouse suspicion.

He couldn't afford to start off on the wrong foot with the residents of Hope Falls. It would jeopardize his chances of bringing Luke to the isolated safety of the town. And as much as it went against the grain to leave a woman hurting, Mike couldn't risk it.

Lord, You've answered many prayers from these parts today, and I'm going to add one more to them. If You can give me an opportunity, any window to stop Naomi from shredding her hands without sacrificing my son's future, I'll gladly make use of it.

As he had many times before, Mike lamented that prayers weren't often answered immediately. He'd never manage to figure out the whys and whens of God's work, but he knew God heard him. Sometimes that had to be enough while a body waited for a clearer response.

With a sigh, Mike turned his attention back to the challenge he could handle. Women, with all of their complications, were beyond Mike, but some of his frustration eased with the work at hand. He wedged his pickax beneath the next stone and prized it loose. Too large to roll aside without endangering another worker, the rock had to be hefted over to the makeshift pile of larger rubble.

Setting his load down, Mike glimpsed a figure making its way toward the work crew. He squinted and realized it was the third woman he'd met—the one related to Granger's woman. He'd noted when she left, but now Mike had a moment to wonder where she'd gone. The girl clipped along at a rushed pace, clutching something in her hands. Whatever she carried, she obviously thought it important.

Too bad I'm not settled enough to be more involved. A powerful curious streak coursed through him, and Mike knew he wouldn't be able to satisfy many of his questions that day. The girl's message would be for a select few. Most likely Granger and the women.

Ah! That wasn't just a girl rushing up the hill—it was the opportunity he needed to get the shovel out of Naomi's hands!

Mike moved quickly, heading over to let Granger know of the girl's impending arrival. When the other man and his woman stepped away from their work and went to meet the newcomer, Mike sped over to where Naomi chipped away at the packed earth wedging several rocks in place. So intently did she work, she didn't hear him clear his throat. She didn't so much as slow down her furious pace.

"Miss?" Mike raised his voice but didn't yell at her—the last thing he wanted to do was try to grab her by the arm or waist. He'd watched from the corner of his eye when the lumberjacks joined in. The small skirmishes as Naomi protected her place made him smile at the time. But now he knew she wasn't going to take it kindly when he interrupted her work. So he called a couple more times.

The woman wasn't going to make it easy on him; she kept right on working. When it was clear she couldn't hear him, Mike knew he'd run out of options. He was going to have to take away her shovel.

EIGHT

She's alive! Lacey's alive! Naomi rammed the metal lip of her spade into the densely packed dirt cementing a slew of rocks in place. *It didn't even sound like she's hurt!* Again and again she thrust the shovel against the barrier, grinning as the debris began to loosen.

Of course, they'd barely managed to decipher Lacey and Dunstan's words at all, much less pick up on any tones of distress. If Naomi stopped to think about it, the fact Lacey didn't attempt to carry on a longer conversation could be seen as troubling. The Lacey Lyman that Naomi knew and that helped Mother would be shouting through the barrier, demanding details about Draxley's death. But for right now, Naomi refused to stop working long enough to think about it.

She took up the rhythm of striking and pulling back, chipping away at the chaos before her. The incredible noise enveloping the mountainside didn't distract her. Every sound of tool against earth or stone sang the praises alive in her heart. *Thank You, Lord.* Her shovel thunked against packed dirt. *They're alive.* A scraping clang as she hit stone. *Thank You, Jesus!* A dull thud then skittering pebbles as she pulled back. *They're right on the other side.*

On that happy thought, something ruined her rhythm. Or rather, *someone.* Naomi glowered at the huge hand that snagged on the handle of her spade. Unwilling to waste time arguing, she tightened her grip and tried to dislodge the disturbance by shoving.

The spade didn't budge. Naomi found herself having to take

a huge step forward to keep her balance, stubbing her toes in the process. Gritting her teeth against the sudden streaking pain, she readjusted her hold, keeping one hand above the interloper's and putting the other below it. Then she tried again. She pushed. She tugged. She even tried to wiggle the thing loose, but no luck.

"Let go," she ordered. Didn't the man know he was *in her way?* Finally acknowledging that the man couldn't be sidestepped, Naomi decided to look trouble in the eye. She needed to tilt her head back to manage it. *When did trouble get so good-looking?* The inane thought made her scowl fiercely as she tried to intimidate the new man in town. And repress a sudden memory of crying on his shoulder.

"Sorry." He loosened his grip but tightened it again when she would have snatched her shovel away. "I tried calling, but you didn't hear me. I thought you'd want to know your friend came back." A strong jaw tilted over to where Cora joined Evie and Granger.

"Oh!" Naomi would have dropped her spade if the man hadn't continued holding it. "I wouldn't have noticed. Thank you!" She reached down to grab her skirts, raising them enough so the fabric wouldn't hamper her steps while she raced over to her friends.

"Wait." His other hand shot out and circled her wrist, startling Naomi with the sudden warmth and familiarity of the motion. His daring left her breathless, unable to do more than stare at the sight of his broad, dusty fingers clamped around her small wrist. As she watched, he gently turned her palm upward, placing a clean bandana in her grasp before releasing her completely.

Only then did Naomi realize she'd worn her leather riding gloves—the thickest pair she owned—clean through. The tatters rubbed against his bandana while tiny pinpricks of red appeared on the green field of fabric, slowly blossoming into a field of crimson.

As the stain seeped into the fabric, its meaning sank in. Suddenly she identified the pulsing in her palms as the throb of pain. It sharpened when she clenched her fingers over the bandana, trying to hide the damage she'd done without even noticing it.

"Here." He produced a black bandana from his back pocket,

unfolded a knife, and sliced it neatly into two bandages.

Naomi watched, thunderstruck, as he draped the pieces atop the crook of her elbow and pointed her toward the women to have her hands bandaged. She stammered her thanks and left before she could waste more time making an even bigger fool of herself.

By the time she reached the Thompsons, Granger left to get back to work. Naomi drew a deep breath to clear her head and pasted a smile on her face when the other women noticed her. She didn't want them to worry, but Naomi couldn't very well bandage her own hands.

Cora's smile far outshone Naomi's weak attempt, clearly rejoicing in the news that Lacey and Dunstan were alive and in reach. Her friend's delight rekindled Naomi's own thankfulness. Compared to the miracle of today, what did it matter she'd waged an absurd war, wiggling her shovel at the new man in town? What did it matter that she'd ruined her gloves and blistered her palms? Gloves could be replaced, blisters healed, and embarrassments faded.

So Naomi hugged Cora and Evie and listened as Cora waved a hastily sketched map and explained what she'd been doing. Apparently, Braden dug deep in his memory and rendered the layout of the mine, indicating which passages Lacey and Dunstan might access.

"If they weren't right on the other side of the landslide, this would have been our best hope of finding them." Cora carefully folded the paper and slid it into an apron pocket. "I'm glad we don't need it, but I'm just as glad Braden made this."

Naomi nodded. "It couldn't have been easy for him to face his memories. Not just of his own time trapped in the mine but all the dreams and hard work he put into planning and building this place."

They all stood in silence for a moment, considering how selfless Braden had been. Naomi was sure she wasn't the only one hoping this was a sign that the curmudgeon who'd taken over her cousin would be departing soon. She'd missed the old Braden.

"Granger said it will be a couple more hours before the men get through," Evie ventured. "We're torn between staying up here and helping or going back to town. The men will be ravenous after this kind of work, and the least they deserve is to have supper."

"I want to stay," Naomi blurted out without even thinking. "When Lacey comes out of that dark, forsaken place, she'll need us. I can't go back and wait in the café for everyone to come down for dinner!" Frankly she couldn't believe Evie suggested it at all.

"No, no, no." Evie shook her head. "I left stew on the stove, and we already have bread and rolls. I was thinking of slicing up some ham for sandwiches then bundling it all up and carrying it back. It won't take very long, and we'll get everything taken care of."

"I think we'll be more in the way than helping if we try to go near the rocks," Cora confessed. "I don't want to slow them down because I'm too stubborn to admit that I'm not equipped for this."

Her friend's wisdom speared Naomi, making her feel her heartbeat in her injured hands. *I would be slowing the men down, trying to work like this. And if Lacey needs help once she comes out, I won't be of any use if I keep abusing my hands.*

That thought clinched things. Naomi nodded and held up her hands. "It's not as though I'll be of much use here anyway. I need to get these taken care of so I can help with other things."

Her friends' clucks of dismay vied with the clamor of men tearing apart the mountainside, both ringing in Naomi's ears as they made their way back to town. She enjoyed a brief interlude of quiet while the doctor inspected and cleaned her hands, the other women watching and waiting for his pronouncement. Naomi bore no illusions—she knew her friends expected her to make light of any ailment. They'd known each other too long and too well to pretend otherwise, though at one time none of them would have stayed alone with a male doctor—back when they'd thought more of guarding their reputations than rebuilding a ghost town or saving a friend in need.

At this point none of the Hope Falls women would meet the standards of polite society. Their unconventional choices, along with their story-spawning residence alongside two dozen lonely bachelors, managed to tarnish their once-sterling reputations.

Lacey, in particular, had shown a disturbing talent and enthusiasm for ruining herself. If word ever reached Charleston that her cousin had gone on long escapades in the woods with a hunter and finally been trapped alone in a dark mine for hours on end with that same hunter, Lacey Lyman's name wouldn't be worth a plug nickel.

Which isn't fair! Lacey deserves to be treated as the lady she is. No matter that she thought up the ad, Lacey's innocent. Naomi flinched as the doctor dug his tweezers into her flesh, picking out bits of stone. *If any of us should be ostracized*—she flinched again as shards of buried memories pierced through her—*it should be me.*

Not Lacey! Braden clenched his teeth against the urge to start shouting. If he started railing against God, he didn't know whether he'd be able to stop. *Not my sister! You already did this to me*, he raged in silence, as though even whispering the accusation might bring down whatever remained of the mountainside he'd once claimed.

His eyes burned from staring down the small wooden cross nailed on the opposite wall. Braden blinked, but his eyes still felt dry, swollen, and sore. He knew it was because he didn't close them often or long enough, but to do so meant succumbing to darkness.

Groaning, he closed his lids, pressing his palms against them as though to blot away his accursed memories. It didn't work. The nightmare that used to plague him only when the doctor forced morphine down his gullet had grown stronger over time. His breaths came short and shallow as the darkness pressed in on him, around him, surely seeping into his very soul through every breath. If he stayed this way much longer, he'd start to see them again.

He waited anyway. His eyes needed the rest, but Braden deserved what came with it. It began slowly...it always started slowly. Braden knew the collapse happened in a deafening, blinding rush of sound and suffocation so fast he barely knew what happened. But memories spooled more slowly, giving the destruction its due.

His partner Owens's angry words were drowned out by an incredible roar as the mountainside tore apart. Wooden supports buckled, stones tumbled, dirt rained until it gave way to clouds of dust coating Braden's face, mouth, throat—and his very soul.

Cave-in.

While it lasted, he prayed for it to end, but in the silence he heard the screams, shouts, and cries of injured men the next tunnel over. Oh Lord— what have I led them to? *It wasn't until he heard a moan but couldn't move toward the sound that Braden realized his legs were pinned beneath something—his hands told him it was a wooden support burdened by rock and earth.*

I can't feel my legs. *It didn't seem to matter. He lay, time measured by ragged breaths and unrelenting thirst. His men grew quiet. Braden strained to hear them, but silence steadily won until he prayed for even the screams and sobs from before.*

He opened his eyes to the harsh sound of his own breath, safe and sound in the doctor's home. The sunlight streaming through the window did nothing to reassure Braden that the nightmare had ended. How could it, when the same tragedy had just played out all over again?

Not Lacey, Lord. His chest hitched in a dry sob. *Don't let her suffer in the darkness.* He knew he was a beggar with precious little to barter, but Braden shed his pride. *Please, God. Don't take my sister for my mistakes. Take anything else. . .stop the healing so I never walk again, but let Lacey live a long and happy life.*

"Braden?" Cora's soft question jolted him from his pathetic attempt to strike a bargain with God. Concern creased her brow, making Braden notice the fine lines he knew were his fault.

"Where's Lacey?" He peered past Cora, hoping against hope.

"We haven't broken through the barricade at the mine's entrance yet." Cora crossed the room to fold his hand in hers. "But we're close— and we spoke with Lacey and Dunstan. They're right on the other side, so we won't have to go searching once we break through!"

Her touch, her words, offered a warm comfort Braden wished he could sink into and soak in forever. *Lacey's been found, and soon she'll be freed.* He could have cried out with the relief of it. But there was still so much he didn't know. Were Lacey and Dunstan going to be all right once pulled out of the mine? Were they hurt? There would be no way of knowing their condition until then.

"We didn't stop working long enough to talk much, but I'm told they sounded in good spirits." Cora squeezed his hand, making Braden realize how pathetic he looked if she thought he needed assurance.

"What took you so long?" he snapped, swallowing his fear and guilt. They weren't for her to see. His pain wasn't hers to pity. Braden could keep that burden at least from her slim shoulders.

"Naomi wore through her gloves and blistered her hands bloody from trying to dig through the landslide." She didn't say anything more, but the unspoken accusation stung him. *Because Naomi is doing your work—we all are and have been since we came to salvage Hope Falls from the mess you made of the town—and our lives.*

"Fool." He snorted back a bellow of rage that he couldn't be out there, tearing his own hands to bring down the mountain. What was a woman doing up there, taking on a man's work? That was the problem with all four of them—they didn't know their place, so the women found themselves in a heap of trouble Braden couldn't prevent. "After today you girls should learn to stop sticking your noses into men's business and just stay where you're wanted."

Cora didn't speak for a moment, instead staring at their joined hands. Slowly, as though handling a snake that might lash out at any sudden movement, she withdrew from the contact. She drew a deep, shuddering breath, squared her shoulders, and headed for the door.

"I have more questions," Braden shouted. "Where are you going?"

She paused but didn't turn back to him. "Where I'm wanted."

"Wait!" Braden called out and reached for the woman he'd always loved, but it was too late. She was too far gone, and so was he.

NINE

There wasn't a man on the mountainside who didn't sense the women's return long before they rounded the bend. Never mind the distance. Never mind the noise. Never mind the dirt and debris weighing the air.

Stew. Mike's stomach rumbled after the aroma winding its way up the mountain. The few cold biscuits he'd eaten early in the morning didn't even make a decent memory now. The men around him paused in appreciation of the heavenly scent then attacked the earthen barrier with more vigor than they'd displayed in the past hour.

Mike followed suit, loathe to appear idle when the women appeared. The work distracted his grumbling stomach—or, at the very least, disguised it. Once he smelled supper, nothing could actually stop his stomach from sulking. Loudly. Not even the last of the warm water sloshing in the bottom of his canteen muffled it.

He put his back into the work and tried to keep his mind off his stomach by keeping one eye on the road. The rhythm of his pickax became a series of countdowns awaiting the women. *Three. . . Two. . . One. . .* Nothing. *Three. . . Two. . . One. . .* Still no sign of them, but Mike's nose stubbornly insisted that supper stayed nearby.

Suddenly his gut clenched—and it had nothing to do with an empty stomach. Images of a faceless man crushed by a massive boulder flashed across his mind. If their excavation caused more damage, the men wouldn't have heard the rumble of rocks cascading down the side of the mountain. Given enough speed, it wouldn't take a large one to hurt somebody standing below. *What if the women were hurt?*

Mike almost dropped his pickax at the thought but caught himself and the tool before anyone noticed. Leaving the implement leaning against one of the multitude of rocks lying around, Mike scrambled down from his perch. He noticed some of the men watching him, saw the scowls darkening their faces, and knew the axmen assumed he was trying to get a jump on the supper line. Earning the enmity of the men he hoped to work alongside wouldn't serve his son well. Mike glanced around for an acceptable reason to leave.

A pile of canteens caught his eye. Earlier the women had filled the extras and left them for the men. By now Mike suspected the men had drunk every drop. Digging was dry, dusty work. He snagged one, forcing himself to look disappointed when he discovered the thing was bone dry. Shrugging, he looped a dozen of the things over his shoulder. Fetching water—especially enough so that other men could partake—made an excellent pretext for heading down the mountain. He rounded the bend in record time, only to pull up short.

There was no sign of the women, save that same tantalizing aroma. For a moment Mike wondered whether hunger muddled his mind, that he smelled supper when there was in fact no supper to be found. To his right stood the outcropping where Naomi found the body. Mike had heard Granger instruct a team of men on how to retrieve the body and had seen the men return, so it was safe to surmise the stones no longer hid the corpse. Nor did it seem as though any dangerous pieces had shifted. In fact, now that he could take time to think it through, Mike figured that any trouble would've raised the type of caterwauling and carrying-on sure to bring the men running.

Then again, Mike had thought it safe to assume that the death site would be the last place any woman would think to set up supper.

So with no sign of trouble and no sight of the women up ahead, Mike stopped in the middle of the road, stymied. The copse of trees to his left should preclude that area—who would want to dodge trees and underbrush while carrying cookery? But as he stood staring, he glimpsed a flash of blue skirts swishing between the trees.

Relief had him heading toward the trees without a minute's thought. Sure enough, he spotted all three women almost right away. The trees didn't signal the start of forestland, as Mike assumed. Instead they shaded a wide clearing. *The women probably chose it because they knew the sight of food might make the men stampede.*

It sure smelled good enough to stampede for. Now that Mike knew the womenfolk were fine, he should head back. The canteens wouldn't fill themselves, and his fellow workers might note his long absence. But Mike found himself loitering near the trees, mouth watering as he watched the women set up no fewer than three stewpots atop makeshift fires. A large stump held baskets of some kind of bread with stacks of tins waiting to be filled and served to the men.

At that thought, Mike managed to pull himself away from the welcoming sight and hurry off to what he'd nicknamed Canteen Stream. Water flowed clear and strong into the empty containers. Mike filled his own canteen and emptied it in long gulps until the cool water washed away the layer of dust coating his lips and throat. Mike would take the honest freshness of sawdust over mountain dirt any day of the week; at least sawdust smelled good.

Though the water helped, persistent thoughts of dinner got him to thinking about how bad he must look if his face matched his hands. The idea of Naomi handing him a plate made Mike plunge his hands back in the water for a good scrub. For good measure, he splashed his face free of dust and the grime made where sweat met dirt. Mike remembered too late that he'd given away his clean bandanas, leaving him less grubby but sopping wet instead.

Oh well. At least he wouldn't show up filthy to his first dinner in Hope Falls. Besides, he might have time to bake dry before being called in for supper. *Unless. . .* Mike frowned. Any work dust he gathered in the meantime would probably make him a muddy mess.

"Here." A soft, feminine voice made him spin around. There stood Miss Higgins, holding out a fresh bandana in a now properly bandaged hand. "With my thanks for your thoughtful loan earlier."

Unsure how to thank someone who was thanking him, Mike nodded and accepted the gift, swiftly mopping up before shoving the bandana into his back pocket. His search for something to say ended when he spotted the buckets. One rested on the ground beside her, where she'd obviously laid it down so she could dig out the bandana. A second swung from the cradle of her other freshly bandaged palm.

He shrugged his canteens so they clanked against his back and grabbed the bucket at her side. When she made no motion to give him the second, he reached out and offered, "Let me help with that."

"Oh no." She gave a shy smile. "You're already toting all those canteens. Besides, I came down here to get water for you—well, all of the men—to wash up for supper. It's little enough to thank you for the hard work you're putting in to save my cousin."

"Believe me, miss,"—Mike grinned—"if the rest of the men are anything like me, they'll be glad enough to see dinner that they might miss the washtub altogether in their rush to appreciate *your* work."

"*My* work?" Naomi discovered that once she started smiling, it was hard to stop. Maybe it was relief over knowing how close they were to saving Lacey. After so much worry, she might have gone a little giddy to know her cousin would be home soon. But honesty forced her to admit—if only to herself—that the day would have held far fewer smiles without the man standing in front of her. *Mr. Strode.*

There was something endearing about him. Despite his size, strength, and calm capability, Naomi found his good-natured awkwardness most appealing. The way he'd smacked her back, mistaking panic for choking. The mulish glint in his gaze when he grabbed her shovel. The sheepish look on his face when she caught him shaking like a dog because he'd forgotten he had no clean bandanas left. For a man named Strode, he managed to stay a little out of step.

Naomi understood. No matter how hard she tried to keep ahead of Lacey, she usually got caught in the wake of her cousin's search for adventure. Today's disaster proved more the exception than the rule.

"Your cooking." Mr. Strode patted his stomach as though in anticipation. "There's no thank-you like a home-cooked meal."

"If I didn't already know that you're newly arrived, that comment would give you away." She felt the bucket slip along the soft surface of her bandages and tightened her grip. "Everyone in Hope Falls knows that Evie deserves the credit for our cooking."

"True. The mountainside hadn't finished shaking when my train pulled in." Something akin to concern flashed across his face too fast for Naomi to gauge it better. "In all the commotion, I clear forgot about my hopes for lunch—so you can probably see why I'm happy to give credit to anyone who stepped foot inside a kitchen."

Hopes for lunch. . . Naomi frowned at the implication behind that phrase. *Had he planned to get back on the train after he ate but stayed and helped out of nothing more than Christian kindness?*

"If needed, we'll replace your train ticket." She couldn't dredge up a smile at the thought of him going. For a town with more males than females, Hope Falls was short on hardworking gentlemen. It would be a shame to see such a helpful one ride off so soon.

"Ah. That won't be necessary since I planned to stop in Hope Falls." His shirtfront gave a faint crinkle when he patted the pocket. "This is a letter of recommendation to give to Mr. Lawson."

"Lawson?" Naomi hid her grin at his response by sidling closer to the stream. "Are you another sawmill engineer looking for work?"

"Not quite." Mr. Strode stepped forward alongside her, his big boots making it more of a shuffle. Before she could dip the bucket into the water, the warmth of his large hand brushed against hers, slipping the handle away from Naomi's suddenly nerveless fingers.

Blaming her clumsiness on her bandages, she waited until he filled both buckets with water before reaching to reclaim one.

"I've got them." He hefted both of the large buckets easily.

"But you shouldn't," she protested. "I'm supposed to be—"

"Resting your hands so they heal?" He raised his eyebrows. "Because I'm fair certain the doctor didn't list hauling heavy water buckets around the mountainside as a recommended activity."

"He didn't give a list of recommended activities," she shot back. "Only to change the bandages daily and keep them dry." Naomi knew she'd lost as soon as she said it. If Mr. Strode's brows were high before, by now they rose practically up to his hairline.

"My mistake." To her astonishment, he set the first bucket down. "Here I thought the weight and friction might aggravate your wound, but I should have been concerned with the water itself."

"I'm not likely to spill upward." She moved for the bucket, only to pull up short when his arm slid behind her back. Distracted by his proximity, at first she didn't notice that he'd removed his collection of canteens and looped them over her shoulder instead.

"Just in case." His voice went low as a whisper, catching her as surely as his brown gaze. The moment passed as quickly as it came. Mr. Strode retrieved the bucket and gestured for her to lead on.

Naomi shifted the canteens—which were heavier than they looked—to shake off her bemusement. It had been ages since a man looked at her with admiration and far longer since one left her so unsettled.

As she led the way back to their makeshift supper station, Naomi had plenty of time to think about how foolish she'd made herself. Yes, it had been an emotional day, and it wasn't surprising that the newcomer who'd been so much a part of it would unsettle her. But that was all. Lacey would come out of the mines, and life would return to some semblance of normality again. *Besides*, she reminded herself, *I'm much too old for a handsome man to turn my head.*

All the same, she caught herself looking back more than once.

TEN

N aomi ignored the speculative glances Evie and Cora cast her direction when she returned with Mr. Strode at her heels. What she couldn't ignore quite so easily were their loud remonstrances.

"I couldn't believe it when I saw you'd slipped away with those water buckets!" Evie shook a wooden spoon to illustrate her ire, making Naomi swallow what would have been an inappropriate chuckle.

From the corner of her eye, she saw Mr. Strode marshal his features into a mask of polite concern. *He's having just as much trouble as I am, trying to keep from laughing at the spoon of wrath.*

"You know I would've seen to it." Cora's softer chastisement didn't strike Naomi as so humorous. "Think of how upset Lacey will be when she sees the way you've injured yourself trying to help her. Take better care of yourself for her sake, if not your own healing!"

"You're right," she conceded more humbly. "I don't know where my good sense has gone today. Without Mr. Strode's help"—she gestured for him to move forward, thinking that "help" seemed like a weak description for his determined assistance throughout the day—"I wouldn't have noticed that I'd hurt myself in the first place."

"Mr. Strode, is it?" Cora gave an unladylike grunt as she hauled the heavy metal washbasin farther away from the foodstuffs. "It's rare that a man becomes a blessing to an entire town, but you've managed it in a matter of hours. We owe you our thanks."

The man made a noncommittal sound as he emptied the buckets into the washbasin. "Kind words, but the blessing will be when we work through the barrier and get your people home safe and sound. Then we ought to be giving all our thanks to God for His mercy."

"You're right." Naomi felt like she could snuggle under the weight of his words, burrowing into their comfort like a blanket. "We have much to be thankful for." *And I've been busy worrying about all of it for the past three months instead of enjoying it!*

"This is a mighty big basin and could use more filling." Mr. Strode kept hold of the now-empty buckets. "I'll be right back." With that, he left the three of them to finish setting up dinner.

And, apparently, to gossip. The minute he passed through the trees on the edge of the field, Cora and Evie began interrogating.

"Did he follow you to the stream?" True to form, Evie sounded like a concerned mother hen looking after a wayward chick.

"No, I stumbled into him while he was filling canteens."

"Still,"—Cora managed to look both solemn and pleased at once—"it seems the new arrival has taken special notice of you, Naomi."

She huffed away the idea at once, seeing where her friends were heading. "The poor man's been thrown alongside me since the moment he stepped off the train. He's done more for Lacey than anyone else, but no one would speculate he's taken some sort of interest in her."

"That's ridiculous. He hasn't even *seen* Lacey," Evie countered.

"But if he had even glimpsed her, we'd all be thinking he was working so hard because he's sweet on Lacey." The truth of that statement tasted sour to Naomi, but she knew better than anyone how a young girl could turn a man's head—especially a beauty like Lacey.

"She does have a way of catching attention," Cora agreed.

Even when she's not present. Naomi smiled at the realization. Her younger cousin's zeal for life transformed those around her, and Naomi knew God had made the exile to Lyman Place her saving grace. Newly grieving her father, a younger Lacey needed love, guidance, and stability just as much as Naomi needed a reason to rejoin the world. They found it in each other, and neither one would have changed it.

Though, if possible, I would've changed a lot of things since.

Naomi shook the maudlin thoughts away. Regrets didn't change the past—but they had a sneaky way of staining the future if they weren't caught and corralled early on. The trick was to focus on what was possible today and how today could make tomorrow better.

So she put all her energy into making supper run smoothly, knowing that well-fed men could break down the wall more quickly to get Lacey back. Besides, work helped her keep her mind from worrying. It distracted her from the way the shadows stretched on the ground as the sun slowly sank behind the mountains.

Indeed, the light had grown thin and pale by the time Mr. Lawson came running through the trees, arms flailing like a rag doll's. "We broke through!" He gasped for air. "They're saved!"

Time itself seemed to speed up at his words—Naomi certainly did. She hiked up her skirts and raced across the clearing, through the trees, and up the mountain path almost before she blinked.

Panting, she skidded to a halt just in time to see Lacey wriggling through an opening in the stone wall, her hands clasped in Granger's as he steadied her progress. No one made a sound, afraid to distract them. Maybe afraid that one of the now precariously stacked stones might shift if they dared breathe too heavily. Then Lacey was out of the mine, and Naomi was running once more.

As soon as the lady—for the life of him, Mike couldn't remember her identity beyond the fact she was Naomi's cousin—emerged from the mines, pandemonium broke loose all around her. If he was honest, Mike would ascribe some of the chaos to the woman's garb.

On the one hand, a man could admire her practicality in wearing britches. On the other hand, a man couldn't help but admire the fine figure she presented in those same britches. From the furious whispers flying around, the workmen focused on the latter.

Mike stepped back, farther away from the hub of activity, trying to give everyone as much space as possible. Even so, he caught an elbow to the gut for his trouble. From what he could make out, the perpetrator was a terrified lumberman trying to scramble away from the wolfhound. Once Mike got his wind back, he forgave the fellow. After all, it was taking the efforts of a behemoth to hold Decoy back while they maneuvered his master up out of the mine.

Amid the high-pitched cries of the women, the loud cheering of the workmen, and the hoarse barks of the wolfhound, Granger called out. No one seemed to hear him—even Mike, who'd seen the man's mouth move from his detached viewpoint, couldn't make out the words. The man beside Granger tried waving and adding his own shouts, but the chaos around the rescue site swallowed the sound.

The lady who'd already been pulled out tried to get everyone to calm down and listen but was ignored in the clamor. When she tried to scramble back up to help the rescuers, the other women pulled her away. Their efforts added more deafening noise but not much else.

Mike pushed through the crowd—which managed to be very dense for fewer than two dozen people—and climbed up to where Granger had the man from the mine half in and half out of the opening. The thick layer of dirt caking the man's skin and clothes couldn't hide his grimace of pain or the way he gritted his teeth against it.

"What do you need?" Mike surveyed the situation, noted the way the man was lying on his side, obviously keeping weight off his left arm and rib cage, and deduced that the poor fellow had broken something. His shoulder. . .a rib. . .maybe even his collarbone.

"Shoulder's dislocated, and he has at least one cracked rib." Granger's detail of the man's injuries explained why they weren't simply pulling him free by his arms or even bracing beneath his underarms. "We'll need to construct a rigging to pull him out."

"Right—are you wearing a belt?" Mike directed the question to the injured man, trying but failing to remember his name.

"Yep." He drew a deep breath. "Can't stand suspenders."

"They would've come in handy." The shorter man beside Granger, who happened to be wearing suspenders, spoke with a German accent.

Mike decided to forgo pointing out that a pair of button suspenders wouldn't hold a sturdy man's weight without the buttons popping loose. Instead he focused on finding a workable solution.

"Here." Mike slid his own sturdy leather belt from its loops, and he saw Granger do the same. "If we loop them around his belt, one on either side, we should be able to pull him through with the least amount of strain on his injuries." He paused, unwilling to be less than honest. "It's still going to hurt like the devil."

"It'll hurt worse once Dunstan's out and I pop his shoulder back," came Granger's grim prediction. "I wish we could do it without the ladies present, but there's no prying them away now."

"Bite on this." Mike slid his knife off his belt, stuck the blade in his boot, and offered the thick leather sheath to Dunstan. In a matter of moments, they'd rigged their belts and began pulling.

Dunstan grunted and bit down on the leather sheath but otherwise issued no sound of protest. Sweat beaded on his brow, but he held firm until they'd pulled him completely free of the mine. Then he spat out the sheath and lay there, panting until his breaths grew more normal. When he finally nodded, they helped him to his feet and removed their makeshift rigging from around his waist.

The stocky fellow picked up Mike's knife sheath and tried to return it to him, but Mike pushed it back to Dunstan. Resignation was written in every dust-creased line of his face as he turned his back to the crowd below and accepted the sheath once again. To his credit, he didn't give more than a low groan as Granger jerked his shoulder back into place. He didn't manage to bite through the leather but left such deep impressions Mike wouldn't use it again.

Nor did he care. They'd managed to get both victims free of the mine without causing more damage or further upsetting the women.

"Draxley." Dunstan ground out the dead man's name as he cautiously picked his way down the slow grade of the rocky incline.

"Dead." Granger spoke with finality, sending the other man a look that cautioned against going into further detail. But this response seemed to satisfy the other man, who gave a short nod.

Leaving Mike to wonder again just how Draxley—supposedly the town telegraph operator—came to be by the mines during the collapse. And, more importantly, why the man they'd just pulled from that mine seemed reassured by that fact. The mystery awoke Mike's curiosity.

Once they reached the ground, Mike hung back. It wasn't his place to come between the townspeople and thrust himself in the midst of their joyful reunion. For all that had happened since the train pulled to a stop, he remained an outsider to Hope Falls. But being an outsider was a good reason to observe very carefully.

He watched as the rescued woman barely restrained from flinging herself into Dunstan's arms, not bothering to hide tears of relief that they'd both made it out safely. Mike saw the way Dunstan moved as close to her as possible, angling his body to keep the rest of the men distanced from her while he wrapped her in the warmth—and, it had to be said, concealment—of a cloak. Anyone with eyes could see that those two were as much a couple as Granger and his woman.

More interesting was the way Dunstan's dog, Decoy, reared up on his hind legs as though to give his master a canine hug but immediately dropped back to all fours when Dunstan snapped his fingers. The wolfhound, impressively trained, pressed against the man's uninjured side and stayed there during the walk to town.

Unsurprisingly, Mike found the most interesting member of the scene to be the woman who'd caught his eye from the very beginning. Naomi—Miss Higgins, he tried to remind himself—kept to her cousin's side. Eyes shining with love and gratitude, she positively beamed.

And Mike wasn't the only one to notice. All the way back to town, the lumbermen all stared at the trio. Understandably, their gazes went to the couple they'd worked so hard to free. But just as often the men stared at Naomi. Their expressions ranged from considering to downright greedy, and while Mike couldn't blame them—he caught himself staring the same way—he didn't like it one bit.

He wanted to shield her from prying eyes, and he wanted to know what she and her friends were doing in a town full of rough axmen. No other women showed up to help with supper, and it was clear as could be that no man laid claim to Naomi or the younger girl with mismatched eyes. But even without any obvious protector lurking nearby, the men deferred to them with more respect than could be explained by their gender or even the fine food they served.

Now that the immediate danger had passed and the crisis averted, questions crowded Mike's thoughts. And underscoring every query was that unexplained line from his telegram about Hope Falls. *"Sounds like a strange place,"* his friend warned. *"Good luck."*

As Mike stepped back into the small town, unsure where he should go or whether he could even count on being allowed to stay, Hope Falls seemed far stranger than he could have imagined.

Cora slowed her steps when they reached town and the doctor's house moved into view. Since she'd left Braden earlier, she'd managed to submerge her thoughts of him beneath all of the evening's activity. But now they'd gotten through the rushed shifts of feeding the men and finishing the rescue. Now the sun, which stayed in the sky so late during these long summer days, had finally set. And now, as the day's excitement faded, darkness crept across her thoughts.

I left him. I left Braden. Cora drew in a deep breath and held it, trying to stop what was promising to become an unending mantra. It didn't work. The refrain stuck stubbornly in her mind and heart. Even as every step drew her closer to returning, her thoughts wouldn't budge from the prospect of leaving. After all, she'd already done it once. *How much harder would it be to keep it up?*

She didn't know whether her obsessive ruminations were meant to encourage her decision or scold her against it. Did her feet drag because she dreaded the idea of apologizing or because she didn't want to have to walk away again? Did it even matter which one?

Ultimately, it came down to the same issue. Spending time with her fiancé had become a pain rather than a pleasure, and time wasn't making any improvements. Neither was patience, nor, it seemed, prayer. Yet sometimes no response was, in and of itself, an answer.

It was time to let Braden go. The doctor seemed pleased with his physical progress, confiding his belief that Braden would be rolling about in a wheeled chair before the week ended. Then the fresh air and stimulation of movement should encourage recovery. Such freedom meant that Braden wouldn't need to rely on her help.

She'd done her duty, stayed by his side for as long as he truly needed her. Now that he wouldn't, Cora owed it to the independent man her fiancé had been—and was trying to become again—to step back. *But I never thought that stepping back would mean walking away.*

Lost in her musings, Cora didn't realize everyone else had stopped until she practically ran right into her sister. Evie merely reached out a steadying hand and gave an encouraging smile. Her sister probably thought Cora worried about Braden's reaction to seeing Lacey. She didn't know Cora had effectively ended things.

Or that Cora had only barely accepted that she'd ended them.

But now wasn't the time to think about these things. No matter she was seeing Braden for the first time since she'd done what he'd been demanding for three months and left him alone. Right now the denizens of Hope Falls had more pressing matters to resolve.

Cora normally would have gone in ahead of everyone to absorb the worst of Braden's anxieties and give him a chance to collect himself before facing everyone. Tonight she stayed to the back.

She watched while Granger directed Riordan and Clump—his almost comically mismatched pair of right-hand men—to take the men back to the bunkhouse and settle everything in for the night. Cora waited when Naomi steadied Lacey's elbow and drew her toward the doorsteps, distracting her while Granger moved to support Dunstan's climb up the stairs.

Dunstan took shallow breaths for the majority of the walk, and it hadn't escaped Cora's notice that the men used far more time and careful effort to pull him free than they'd used for Lacey. Dunstan tried to mask his pain, but stairs would most likely jar whatever injuries he'd sustained. *That's why Naomi guided Lacey ahead.*

They all tried so hard not to upset each other, and the funny part was that they were going in to see the one man who would try to upset everybody in the room! Cora shook her head at the irony of it.

That's when she noticed the new man. He was hanging back, too, shifting in the uneasy way of a man who doesn't know what to do. With a start, Cora realized that he probably didn't know what to do. In all the hullabaloo of the day, the new arrival hadn't been officially interviewed, accepted into town, or given any welcome.

Mr. Strode saw a town in trouble and pitched in without complaint. Normally Granger—or if Granger happened to be out of town, Dunstan—would have gotten to know the new arrival and found a place for him. But with Dunstan out of commission and Granger overseeing the fallout, their new guest was left out in the cold.

"Come on in." Cora gestured toward the door, eliciting a pair of surprised glances from first Mr. Strode and then Granger.

Understanding dawned on Granger's face then warred with an obvious reluctance to invite a stranger to what would certainly be a very specific and private discussion about Hope Falls business. His hesitation reminded Cora that Granger only returned to town that same afternoon and doubtless would have had a lot to talk over with Braden and Dunstan even if the mine hadn't gone and collapsed.

Which also meant that Granger didn't know Dunstan came to town to investigate the first cave-in or that both he and Braden now believed the mine was sabotaged. And wasn't it strange the way the second cave-in happened on the same day they went to investigate?

Oh yes. Tonight's conversation should be very interesting. *And won't it bunch Braden's britches to have a stranger stroll into the middle of everything?* That alone was worth inviting Mr. Strode!

"Er—yes." Granger had reached the forgone conclusion that they couldn't very well ignore the man after all he'd done today. He even showed the grace to look somewhat abashed at the oversight.

For her part, Cora tried to ignore her sister's questioning glance. Evie could wonder why she'd invited Mr. Strode, but in the end she probably wouldn't ask. Somebody had to see to the man. Besides, there were far more interesting questions to ask tonight.

ELEVEN

W here's Dunstan?" Braden craned his neck, trying to peer around the people who'd crowded into his room. He saw his sister, looking a complete mess but otherwise safe and sound, edging toward the door. "Lacey! Come and let me see you. Where are you sneaking off to?"

"To check on Dunstan," his sister called back. "I know he'll be fine, but he's not the sort to take kindly to doctoring."

"What does Dunstan need doctoring for? What happened to him?" Braden locked eyes with Granger, who he hadn't even been told had returned to town. How long had he been back in Hope Falls?

"A mine caved in on him." Cora gave the obvious answer with no further explanation. Obviously she was still upset with him.

"I know that!" He waited for Granger to fill him in, chafing anew at the fact he hadn't been at the scene in person, helping.

Granger seemed to sympathize with his frustration. "Doc's binding his ribs. Dunstan got pinned under a beam in the collapse."

Braden swallowed against a sudden onslaught of memories. He'd been struck by a falling beam in the first cave-in, and the mere mention of the same thing befalling another man made him taste bile.

But cracked ribs would heal. It could have been so much worse.

"You look all right, sis." He desperately tried to be positive.

"Out of all the opportunities to give me a compliment, only you would choose the night when I'm covered in grime." Lacey quirked a small smile at him. The smile grew when he opened his arms in invitation, and she bustled across the room for a long overdue hug.

Thank God, you're all right. He gave her a last squeeze. Now that he had her back, he realized how much he would have missed Lacey if he lost her and how disappointed he would have been if she'd obeyed him and left Hope Falls as soon as she'd arrived.

He suddenly realized he couldn't remember the last time he'd seen his sister's smile. *How much of that can be laid at my door?* Guilt snagged away his satisfaction in knowing she and Dunstan would be all right. *They shouldn't have been endangered to begin with.*

Thankfully, Dunstan's entrance pushed away Braden's gloomy musings. The hunter shouldered his way toward the bed—an impressive feat for a man with a couple cracked ribs and a dislocated shoulder.

"Do you want the good news to start, or do you want to get the bad news out of the way first?" Dunstan's attempt to lighten the mood failed when Braden saw the way Lacey sidled up to him and put her hand on his arm. Even worse, Dunstan folded his hand over hers!

"Depends." He fought to keep his voice level. "Is the bad news that you've fallen for my little sister? Because I have to warn you, Dunstan, that might be the biggest catastrophe of the day."

Lacey's blue eyes widened then narrowed. "Don't make any assumptions," she hissed. "It's not yet midnight, and who knows what might befall a beloved brother with a mouth two sizes too big!"

"That's my sister, always ready with a retort." Braden tried to return her scowl but felt the edges of his mouth quirk upward. He was gratified to see her fighting the same losing battle until they stood there, grinning at each other. "Some things never change."

"And others do." Dunstan looked at Lacey when he said it, but Braden felt the impact of those words in the pit of his stomach.

"What did you find?" Now that there'd been a second cave-in, Braden didn't know what to think. His hopes from the morning seemed no more than a faint memory, the shining idea that one of Braden's own mistakes hadn't taken the lives of several men. The hope, odd as it may seem, that an unknown party deliberately sabotaged his mine.

But even if Dunstan managed to find evidence of tampering amid the original destruction, it would be long gone by now. Worse, if their suspicions were confirmed, it would bring today's cave-in under question. Secondary landslides, smaller collapses caused by the destabilization of an original cave-in, were common enough to be expected. But what were the chances that the second incident would take place only when Dunstan began investigating?

Coincidences like that, in Braden's experience, were no coincidences at all. So, did the saboteur remain in Hope Falls? Everything rested on the answer Dunstan wasn't giving him. The longer the hunter remained silent, the more frustrated Braden became. He looked around the room, searching for an explanation among the friends gathered around him. He found a surprise.

"Who's he?" Braden pointed at a stranger leaning against the wall, almost hidden in the corner farthest from the bed.

"Mr. Strode." Naomi gave the man's elbow a light touch, nudging him forward. No one else seemed to find it strange that she'd shown such familiarity, but it didn't sit well with Braden. Naomi was the oldest and, if such a thing could exist amid a group of women, the voice of reason and sensibility. If Naomi slowly abandoned the edicts of propriety, what would happen to the rest of the girls?

The thin threads binding them all to polite society frayed the instant the ladies placed that benighted ad in the paper. Their arrival in Hope Falls and subsequent antics further unraveled the order of things. Wasn't it evident in Lacey's headstrong adventures? Even more so in Cora's sudden denouncement of him?

Braden eyed the newcomer with suspicion, wary of both the man's calm confidence and his sudden appearance on a day already filled with chaos. His timing was enough to make Braden wonder. *Why did he come today? Can this be the saboteur they were looking for?*

Cora paid to that notion immediately. "I know what you're thinking, Braden, but he arrived on the same train as Granger."

Why is Cora supporting the stranger? Robbed of a reason for his mounting animosity, Braden still couldn't welcome the man. For one thing, the man had an unpleasant effect on the town's women. Braden supposed the fellow was attractive enough, but that didn't help matters. A sudden thought grabbed hold with a vengeance. *Is Strode the reason Cora walked away? She thinks she found a better option?*

"What are you doing here?" Braden didn't try to sound friendly. He wasn't inclined to waste time making nice to some Lothario.

"The young miss asked me in." The fellow gestured toward Cora, and Braden immediately lost track of anything he said afterward.

"Why?" He gritted the question at the man but kept his gaze on his errant fiancée. What was she thinking, inviting a stranger to take part in an important meeting? Braden might not like having a town council made up mostly of women, but he accepted that they'd all earned their places. The stranger had no place among them.

Mike hadn't felt so conspicuously out of place since his wedding. He hoped this town suited him better than the arrangement with his late wife. Just like then, the commitment would change his life. And, just like then, he had someone counting on him to see it through.

Why am I here? Against all odds, Mike found humor in the question. He didn't know many people who hadn't asked that question, along with a plethora of others related to it. *Why am I here? What is God's purpose for my life? Am I doing the right thing?*

Too bad the answers were harder to come by—especially when an entire room filled with people was waiting for his response! But Mike knew one thing for sure: he didn't intend to begin his stay in Hope Falls as a target for anyone's bad temper. A man started the way he wanted to finish, and Luke needed him to start strong.

"If you're asking why she invited me,"—Mike kept any hint of emotion from the words—"I couldn't tell you. Every time I try to figure out a woman's reasoning or speak for her, I get it wrong."

Granger let loose a guffaw, Dunstan gave a chuckle, and even the grump in the bed seemed to soften. The women seemed surprised, pleased, and amused by turns. It couldn't have turned out better.

Encouraged by the response, Mike ventured further. "Now, I haven't caught everyone's names, but I don't think I'd be far off the mark in thinking you're the ones running Hope Falls?"

He addressed the room at large, not wanting to alienate the women. Mike sensed they held more power than women usually managed, but he'd steer clear of making assumptions until he knew more. As things stood, his lack of knowledge about Hope Falls put him at a severe disadvantage. He hadn't had the time to research the town before taking off and had relied on talking with Mr. Lawson first.

"You're correct." The rescued lady kindly took it upon herself to make introductions. "I'm Lacey Lyman. This is my brother, Braden." She indicated the invalid. "Together we own the bulk of Hope Falls, including the town, the mine, and the surrounding forestland."

"Granger's asked to purchase shares in our sawmill venture, and we're allowing that because his expertise is invaluable." Braden Lyman took over. "Otherwise, the women own the remaining shares."

"I'm Evelyn Thompson, and I run the café. For now we can call it the diner." Granger's arm around the amber-eyed woman provided the rest of her identification. "This is my sister, Cora Thompson,"— she indicated the girl Mike already pegged as a relation—"and on your other side is Naomi Higgins, Lacey and Braden's cousin."

"Chase Dunstan"—Granger looked like he wanted to clap the man on the shoulder, but thought better of it at the last moment— "hired on as our hunter. He knows these mountains better than anyone."

"And you are?" Not surprisingly, the pointed query came from Braden. The man looked like he was itching to get rid of Mike.

"Michael Strode. I was referred to Mr. Lawson in hopes your new sawmill could use a woodworker for carpentry, joinery, and so on." Mike ignored the sea of names, faces, and details pushing for places in his memory, instead concentrating on the task at hand. "If Hope Falls isn't at that stage yet, I can swing an ax and work a saw."

"We aren't at that stage yet," Braden Lyman said flatly. "And as far as I know, we aren't looking to hire any woodsmen."

The words slammed into Mike with the force of a sledgehammer, knocking the air from his lungs in a sudden rush. He'd been so focused on getting to Hope Falls, he'd not let himself consider where he'd take Luke if things didn't pan out like he hoped.

"Aren't we? We lost a hefty percentage of our workers when we kicked out the brawlers." The younger Miss Thompson looked toward Lacey Lyman, who stayed snuggled up against the hunter. "And Granger's and Dunstan's increased involvement changes things."

Mike knew he'd missed something, but for the life of him he couldn't figure out what the girl was talking about. If he hadn't seen the way everyone responded to Granger's command throughout the day, he would assume that the workmen didn't like Granger and Dunstan. But that wasn't so, which left Mike wondering why everyone looked like somebody snuck up behind and goosed them. Miss Higgins, in particular, looked pale and delicate as fresh-hewn birch.

Whatever hid beneath Miss Thompson's speech, it gave him one last chance to make his home in Hope Falls. Why, then, did it make Miss Higgins look like she was being frog-marched toward a noose?

TWELVE

N aomi made a strangled sound. Then she had to cover it by clearing her throat. Hopefully everyone would chalk it up to the amount of dust she'd swallowed during the course of a long, trying day.

But they knew better. Cora's comment forced them to examine the implications of Lacey's newfound fondness for Dunstan, and there was only one conclusion for everyone to reach. The same conclusion that made Naomi's mouth turn dry and her fiercely stinging hands go numb.

Wanted: 3 men. Thinking about the words they'd once written so boldly now made Naomi feel violently ill. *Object: Marriage.*

It didn't matter that Cora's commitment to Braden was weakening—Naomi knew she wasn't the only one to notice that Evie introduced her only as her sister and not Braden's fiancée. With Evie promised to Granger and Lacey now all but announcing her engagement to Dunstan, two of the three women were already brides-to-be. Now for them to make good on their promise to the workmen of Hope Falls, Naomi had to shed her spinster status and select a husband. Her time was up, and all at once everyone in the room realized it.

Everyone, with the exception of Mr. Strode, who was trying and failing to hide his puzzlement. Apparently the newest addition to Hope Falls would be the only man who hadn't been lured by their ad. A strange mix of gratitude and disappointment swirled together at the realization that Mr. Strode hadn't come seeking a bride.

Naomi wouldn't allow herself to wonder what he'd think once he learned about the advertisement. *It shouldn't matter one whit what he thinks*, she told herself. But somehow it did anyway. Just like it mattered whether or not he was able to stay in Hope Falls.

She cleared her throat again, this time because she had some difficulty getting her words out. "Yes, things are changing in Hope Falls. I like to think they're changing for the better. The men we lost are men we'd escort from the grounds if they ever returned."

Vehement nods met this proclamation as the women gave their full support. Granger did the same, his opinion chiming in to the tune of ominously cracked knuckles. Obviously Evie's fiancé hadn't forgotten the time he stopped four men determined to break into the women's house in the dead of night. Naomi hadn't forgotten either.

"I can't speak to what progress has been made in my absence," Granger admitted. "But I can say that hiring more men will be very difficult. Warm weather makes the sap run too freely—most loggers stop working altogether in the summer, wary of the difficulties."

If Mr. Strode found the prospect intimidating, he didn't show it. To the contrary, there seemed to be a glimmer in his eye, as though he welcomed the challenge. Or perhaps he merely welcomed the opportunity, since Braden so quickly tried to turn him away.

"They've mapped the route for the main leg of the flume and managed to clear most of it." Dunstan's assessment surprised Naomi, mostly because she hadn't thought the hunter was keeping track of matters related directly to logging and establishing the sawmill.

Keeping Hope Falls in fresh meat and keeping Lacey out of trouble was more than enough work to keep him busy, but Dunstan continued. "They've also cleared and leveled the sawmill site. Soon we'll be ready to order ready-cut lumber and begin construction."

"I hadn't realized we'd come so far." Braden sounded surprised but not entirely pleased, and Naomi guessed at its cause. How frustrating he must find it, not being able to oversee his town.

"Evie's cooking makes the men able and willing to work hard." Granger's boast wasn't far off the mark. If it weren't for Evie's cooking, they would have lost the remainder of the men in a blink.

"Miss Higgins mentioned that credit for the cooking goes to you," Mr. Strode addressed Evie. "Now, I know hunger seasons any dish, but your stew can settle a man's stomach and soothe his soul."

"She's spoken for." Granger good-naturedly tightened his hold on a blushing Evie. "But for as long as you stay on, you'll be able to fill up on her cooking for breakfast, dinner, and supper."

"Wait a minute," Braden protested. "Who says he's staying?"

"I do." Naomi surprised herself by speaking up first. "Mr. Strode barely stepped off the train before he started hauling equipment up the mountain and breaking down the barricade. We didn't have the chance to welcome him, but his actions surely make him a member of Hope Falls."

"I agree." Lacey slapped her britches to emphasize her point, raising a visible cloud of dust. "Any man who helped haul Dunstan out of that mine is welcome to stay on. That's all there is to it."

"I couldn't argue with that even if I wanted to." Dunstan gave an uncharacteristic grin. "But, for the record, I vote he stays."

"Especially since he and Naomi found poor Mr. Draxley." Cora's contribution shaded things a little, but Naomi forgave her.

"Poor Mr. Draxley, my eye!" Lacey looked mad enough to spit, mad enough that she didn't notice Dunstan and even Braden trying to get her to hold her tongue. "The weasel just about killed us!"

"What?" Mike's confused question got swallowed whole in the pandemonium following Miss Lyman's denouncement.

Her brother sat bolt upright in bed, demanding details in a voice better suited to commanding new troops. Dunstan, whom Mike had seen try to hush his woman, sighed at his failure. The ladies shrieked and gasped, save Miss Lyman, who seemed pleased by the uproar. Granger got over his surprise fastest of all and seemed to be mulling over the startling revelation.

Which made the carpenter in Mike start fitting pieces together for himself. He hadn't bothered to ask why Dunstan and Lacey went into the mine in the first place—it wasn't his place. Furthermore, by the looks of them, he hadn't been able to discount the possibility that the couple had sneaked off for a private interlude. Once he'd understood that this wasn't the first collapse, he'd entertained the idea that the couple had somehow brought on the second cave-in by being too loud or knocking into a precarious support. What he hadn't questioned was whether it was an accident.

This missing clue shifted the entire picture. From Miss Lyman's statement, Mike understood that the destruction was intentional—and possibly intended to kill the people trapped inside the mine. This created new questions about what the couple had been searching for, but Mike put that aside to examine later. For now he was fiddling with bits of information about the late and unlamented Mr. Draxley. Now he knew why the telegraph operator left his post to poke around the mines. Now he understood that the type of man capable of such deception wouldn't be the sort to inspire goodwill in everyday life—hence the lack of grief at the news of Draxley's death.

"So did Draxley cause the first cave-in, too?" Mike realized he'd spoken aloud when every head in the room whipped toward him.

Silence reigned for several heartbeats as the denizens of Hope Falls regarded him. Surprise, suspicion, even admiration played across their features as they considered his question. And, if Mike didn't miss his guess, considered his sudden involvement. It didn't take much brainpower to know that Dunstan and Lyman hadn't planned on making this part of the conversation public. But it was too late.

Even Miss Lyman held her tongue, now aware of her mistake.

Dunstan, in particular, stared at him with unnerving intensity, grappling with the problem he posed. All the same, it was the hunter who spoke first. "You don't miss much, do you, Mr. Strode?"

"Not if I can help it." Mike walked a fine line. "Woodworking takes attention to detail and an eye for piecing parts together. I take note when something doesn't fit or goes against the grain."

"In Hope Falls,"—Miss Higgins sounded a warning—"people

and projects are never predictable."

"Yep." Dunstan raised his brows. "You'll fit in just fine."

With that acceptance, Mike relaxed. Everyone understood without saying the acceptance was conditional upon his performance. So Mike didn't mention Luke. First he'd prove himself. Then when they valued him and his work, he'd be able to bring his son home. Thankfully, the people seemed smart enough. It shouldn't take them long to notice how hard he worked and the quality of his results.

"I want to know how you got the idea Draxley caused the first cave-in." Respect mingled with suspicion in Lyman's request.

"Others mentioned this was the second cave-in and that it was strange to find Draxley so far from his telegraph station." Mike paused then decided to speak plainly. "Judging by the reactions, he won't be much mourned. Miss Lyman indicated that Draxley intentionally caused the cave-in today."

He waited for Dunstan and the lady to confirm this. After they nodded, he continued. "So either Draxley set out to kill the two of you, or he had another purpose. The only reason I could devise for creating a second cave-in was to destroy evidence that might remain from the initial collapse."

"I didn't connect it so quickly, and I've been involved for months." The cook blinked at him.

"No matter how damning it seems, any proof that the original cave-in was caused by sabotage has been thoroughly eradicated by now." Lyman leaned back again. "It's all conjecture at this point."

"Not quite." His sister edged over and perched along her brother's bedside. "Although it isn't proof you can hold in your hands and show to the world, Braden, we know for certain. Draxley confessed that he'd brought down the mine back in the spring."

"How did you coax that from him?" Lyman looked desperate to believe her but didn't dare.

The depth of the man's emotion confirmed Mike's suspicions. Braden Lyman lay in this bed because he'd been trapped in the first cave-in. No one said so—even if it weren't common knowledge, it wasn't the sort of thing loved ones gossiped about—but it made sense. It made even more sense when Mike considered that Braden Lyman owned most of Hope Falls. The mines predated the sawmill venture by at least a year—it stood to reason that Braden Lyman began them. And the man who oversaw the mines would, by default, shoulder any responsibility for unstable design implementation.

It explained why a man would be so eager to hear that his property had been sabotaged. Why else would Braden Lyman seem filled with hope instead of rage that another man ruined his life?

It's easier than thinking he ruined his own life. Mike breathed deep. He and Braden Lyman shared more in common than he'd thought.

THIRTEEN

No, you're wrong." The muffled moan emerged from beneath a heap of bedclothes, followed by the glare of a bleary-eyed Lacey Lyman. Hair mussed and pout in place, she looked much the way she had five years before when Naomi first met her cousin. "It's not morning already!"

"For all the hundreds of times you've attempted to argue the sun away, I've yet to see you succeed." Naomi tapped her small pendant watch before dropping the chain back inside her bodice. "It's already half past four, Lacey. Bread doesn't bake itself."

"To hear you tell it, anyone would think the sun was shining and I'm a slugabed." Lacey pushed herself up and stretched. "But how can I argue the sun away when it hasn't even shown itself?"

"Piffle." Naomi loved the whimsical word but rarely employed it. When something was overused, it became underappreciated, after all. "After all the trouble the men went through to dig you from the mines, you need to dish out a few smiles with their breakfasts."

"Don't you think my smiles would be more genuine if I could sleep in for another half hour or so?" Lacey never could resist getting the last word, even though she'd already gotten out of bed.

"You're difficult to drag from bed, but that doesn't mean you need to sleep in. Besides, you're the woman of the hour. Enjoy it."

"Ah. . ." Lacey looked over her shoulder as Naomi tackled the tangled ties of her cousin's corset. "But *I'm* not the woman of the hour, am I? Everyone will have guessed how things stand between

100

me and Dunstan, even before we make an official announcement."

Suddenly Naomi wanted to crawl beneath the covers and not come out. "That doesn't make me anything more than I was yesterday."

"The only single woman amid a dozen or so bachelors?" Lacey tackled the wayward wisps of her blond hair, utterly oblivious. The girl was prophesying doom but viewed it as a dream come true.

"Now, Lacey, don't go putting it like that." Naomi sat down on the bed hard enough to make the ropes creak. "You know as well as I do that a good portion of those men didn't list me as one of their choices. It's not as though I'll be surrounded by the entire dozen!"

In the early days, when bachelors descended on Hope Falls en masse, they'd asked each man to list which two of the three ladies they'd like to court. Unfortunately, they'd never worked out what to do with the men left over after the first two women made their choices. That left Naomi with a handful of men who'd listed her name—and an even larger handful who'd wooed but not won their women.

"That's true." Evie and Cora trooped into the room with Naomi's favorite part of the morning—hot chocolate and sweet buns.

"What are we going to do with the men who chose me and Lacey?" Evie settled herself beside Naomi on the bed, concern creasing her temple. "Now that they've lost their chance at winning a bride, we can't expect them to stay on for nothing more than room and board."

"Even if we scraped up the wherewithal to pay the. . .erm, if I call them losers, you'll all know that I don't mean it negatively. If we pay them fair wages, we couldn't expect Naomi's suitors to go on as before." Lacey cautiously lowered herself to perch atop a rounded trunk.

"I say, Lacey." Cora sounded somewhat awed. "However did you manage to bend so much without losing your balance? That's amazing."

For a brief moment, Naomi remembered the two times Cora had fallen from her chair. The first time she'd been informed of Braden's death. The second, she'd been told he was still alive. Both times, after she came around again, Cora's corset made her employ some vaguely turtlish movements to get up off the ground.

"It's that new Pivot Corset I ordered!" Lacey practically jumped to her feet then resumed her seat with impressive ease. "It expands to let one bend. I can't tell you how grateful I was to be wearing it yesterday. A traditional corset would have made breathing impossible, and I hate to think about the cost if I'd fainted."

Everyone took a restorative sip of chocolate at the thought. Naomi engaged in a silent argument with herself, trying to decide whether to draw out Lacey for a more detailed account of her experiences or if her cousin and friends needed a moment of levity. She looked around, seeing that ultimate social signal that someone needed to steer the conversation: the sweet buns sat untouched.

"Marvel though the Pivot Corset may be,"—Naomi allowed a wry note to enter her tone—"it wasn't the new garment that caught everyone's attention when you reappeared. You ordered something else from the Montgomery Ward catalog without telling us, didn't you?"

Lacey stuffed an overlarge bite of bun into her mouth, chewing slowly to delay her answer. Evie and Cora began nibbling during the wait. Naomi smiled and enjoyed a bite of her own pastry. She'd made the right choice. The conversation now offered both amusement and instruction, holding Lacey accountable for those appalling trousers.

"Well." Even if her cousin typically arose in an amiable mood, her tone would have been overly bright. "I could've sworn I'd pointed them out to everyone since the name is so clever. And yes, I wore my new Waulkenphast half boots yesterday. Although they are plain, I can't complain about comfort. They're entirely practical." She shifted her skirts and flexed her foot, displaying the boots.

"While an admirable attempt to *sidestep* the issue. . ." The rest of Cora's comment was lost amid a round of good-natured groans.

"I hadn't realized it, but it's been a long while since any of us punned." Evie grinned at the revival of their old game. "Lacey took last honors. After Granger caught him, she told Twyler that my chances of hitting him brought new meaning to the term *long shot*."

"That wasn't so long ago—just over a month." Naomi briefly relived that awful day. Granger revealed that he'd come to Hope Falls tracking his brother's killer. Spooked by Granger's pursuit, the murderer panicked, kidnapped Lacey, and forced a showdown. Justice had been served, but Naomi couldn't help but worry. "Please tell me you won't make a monthly habit of terrifying us, Lacey!"

"I don't plan to." Lacey sniffed. "Listening to you, anyone would think I asked Twyler to abduct me or begged Draxley to light that fuse. It's not as though I routinely endanger my own life!"

"Of course." Evie took a dainty sip of cocoa. "It must have been another woman who donned britches and raced off to investigate a sabotaged mine. What were we thinking to make such a mistake?"

"Touché." Lacey shook her head. "Though exploring the mines was more of a calculated risk. They'd been stable for months and in all likelihood would have remained so if it weren't for Draxley."

"For a moment, we'll ignore the myriad of perils presented by any mine, much less a system of tunnels already compromised by a cave-in." Naomi paused, allowing everyone to imagine those unnamed perils. "Tight trousers are no calculated risk, Lacey. Our comportment as ladies is one of our few protections against lascivious advances.

"It was bad enough when you insisted on accompanying Dunstan on his hunting trips, but at least the workmen didn't notice your absence. Now it escaped no one's attention that you slipped off, indecently clothed, to spend time with Dunstan in a secluded space."

"I'm sorry it seems so unsavory." Lacey sounded duly contrite. "But I couldn't let Dunstan go alone, and if there was any chance to bring back proof, I couldn't let Braden down. Showing him that the cave-in wasn't his fault is the only way to bring my brother back, and in spite of all that happened, I can't say I regret going."

Naomi knew she'd already given one lecture but couldn't stop herself. "Frankly, Lacey, it's fortunate that you and Mr. Dunstan stopped fighting long enough to acknowledge your attraction to each other. If he hadn't offered the protection of an engagement, you would have opened yourself to dishonorable advances. At the very least, you would have ruined your chance of marrying a good man."

She stopped there, unable to speak past the lump in her throat. Dimly, she heard Lacey apologize for endangering them all, but Naomi didn't believe her cousin truly understood her precarious position. Lacey's life wasn't in danger any longer, but her way of life was. A fallen woman had no hope of happiness. And the worst part of it was, Naomi couldn't tell her cousin the true reason behind her concerns.

I don't want you to go through the same heartbreak I did. Part of Naomi longed to give Lacey the truth. *That kind of sorrow, the constant shame and uncertainty, is no way to wake up every morning.*

Mike woke up groggy and disoriented, the noise of the bunkhouse reassuringly unfamiliar. The splash of the washbasin and irregular thunk of men shoving boots on their feet almost varnished over a few last stubborn, spluttering snores. It was about as far away as a man could get from waking alone in an overly elaborate Baltimore bedroom.

Galvanized by the realization he was one of the last to rise, Mike lurched from his bed and just about clocked himself on the upper bunk. In truth, the loggers' bunks were little more than two wooden shelves, built wide and well supported at frequent intervals, running along three of the four walls. The pallets were rendered comfortable by exhaustion rather than padding, but Mike didn't mind.

He'd worked hard enough yesterday to fall asleep on the bare ground, and he fully intended to work that hard all day, for six days a week, until he'd secured a home for himself and Luke. With only two exceptions, his bunkhouse mates stood tall and broad as the trees they felled, testimony to a logger's strength and endurance.

Their swift exit from the bunkhouse gave another testimony— that Mike needed to hurry if he wanted to enjoy some breakfast! Mouth watering at the thought, Mike made short of his morning wash. He threw on his clothes, strapped on his teeth-marked knife sheath, and wondered whether he could make it through the day without shaving.

Stubble pricked the palm of his hand when he felt his jaw, making Mike grab his straight razor and soap. He'd seen a cloudy mirror hanging above the washbasin, but another man was using it. Oblivious to the dark streaks running from his obviously blackened hair, the man methodically finished shaving and rinsed his razor.

"All finished." When he turned around, Mike could see that the man was a good bit older than the others he'd seen. The man eyed Mike's bar of soap before producing a small brush. "Would you like to borrow this? I always need one to make a good enough lather."

"Thanks." Mike accepted the offer and quickly filled his face with thick suds. After rinsing and drying the brush, he returned it.

"Anything to welcome the new man in town." He returned the brush to his shaving kit. "You can call me Gent, by the way."

"Mike Strode." Making quick, short strokes of the razor, Mike couldn't shake the man's hand. "Any reason why they call you Gent?"

"Old-fashioned wisdom." His new friend donned a top hat, carefully tilting it at a jaunty angle that hid his bald spot. "A fondness for good manners, and of course, my sense of style."

What did a man say to a logger sporting a top hat? Nonplussed, Mike splashed away the soap residue while he thought it over.

"I can see I surprised you." Gent spared him having to answer. "Good of you not to look concerned, since I'm entirely sane. Besides, you'll soon see that an acceptance of the unusual is a valuable trait for someone choosing to set up in Hope Falls."

"You're comfortable in your skin, that's all." Despite his oddity—or perhaps because of it—Mike warmed to the man. He offered a grin. "Seems to me we ought to worry about the people who aren't."

FOURTEEN

Try as he might, Braden couldn't make himself comfortable. He couldn't ignore the persistent throbbing of his injured knee, which he'd pushed hard this morning. At least he could bend it farther than yesterday. He kept imagining that if he just tried hard enough, he could push past some crucial point of pain and he'd be beyond it.

So far Braden hadn't passed that point. *Maybe tomorrow.* Or the next day. He was determined to be able to bend his knee ninety degrees before the week's end. At that point the doctor promised Braden would be permitted to use a wheeled chair. For now, the doctor refused to bring the contraption into the room. The man claimed it was unhealthy to fixate beyond the current goal, but Braden harbored his own suspicions. Most likely the good doctor kept the chair out of his reach because he knew Braden would seize the thing, muscle his way into the seat, and wheel himself away if given the slightest chance. Or, at the very least, he'd try.

"Leave it to you to enlist the services of a retired army surgeon," Dunstan griped by way of greeting. "The man is small, but I'd wager Doc gets his way more often than you or I manage."

"If I kept a tally, I'm afraid he'd have a hundred to one ratio against me." Braden tried to keep the bitterness from his tone. Doc, after all, was the one who'd signed over the management of Lyman Estates to Lacey. Even after Braden recovered from his concussion, Doc refused to rescind the orders. Apparently he'd seen too many men make uncharacteristically poor decisions after suffering trauma.

"That's why it's best not to keep score." Dunstan moved more slowly than usual, cautiously lowering himself into the chair. Although his friend didn't complain, Braden recognized the signs of suffering. "Besides, we have more important matters to discuss."

"Draxley." It was a name, a question, and a curse in one.

"Last night I didn't go into detail. It didn't seem prudent."

"I wish Lacey shared some of your prudence." Braden sighed. But what was said couldn't be undone, and the newest addition to Hope Falls knew more than he should. And what the man didn't know, he showed an uncanny ability to deduce. "What else did you discover?"

"As we suspected, the original cave-in was caused by carefully placed explosives, rigged together and detonated in one fell swoop." Dunstan shifted in his chair and wordlessly accepted the pillow Braden passed his way. Once he'd wedged the brace against the chair back, Dunstan seemed more at ease. "Much the same way Draxley set his charges yesterday. Lacey discovered the fuse while we poked around, but it was too late. Draxley engineered things so that we'd be trapped in the bowels of the mountain long after he ran out."

Braden's rage at Dunstan's revelation squeezed his chest and cut off his breath. He couldn't begin to calm himself until black spots swam across his vision. He'd known last night of Draxley's duplicity, had surmised that the greedy telegraph operator intentionally made the mines collapse atop Lacey and Dunstan. But something about the way the hunter spoke about being trapped in the bowels of the mine triggered memories of other men who'd suffered the same fate—but weren't fortunate enough to tell their story.

"But before he left us like rats to scramble through his own maze, Draxley grew chatty. His partner disappointed him on the day of the cave-in by racing back into the mines." Dunstan paused as though unsure whether to divulge more. "Trying to save you, Braden."

The tight, squeezing sensation abruptly ended, leaving his skin and skull feeling oddly swollen. Refusing to become light-headed, Braden grappled with the implications of Draxley's confession. Very few men knew of the massive gold vein they'd unearthed in the midst of the Hope Falls silver mine—and only one of them came rushing in, gasping with panic, moments before the world turned upside down.

"Why are you here?" Owens had shouted. *"You shouldn't be here!"*

"My partner." Braden sagged against the headboard, staggered at the depth of the betrayal. "I don't want to believe it of Owens, but it makes a horrible sort of sense. He'd known me for years. Knew me well enough to guess that I wouldn't be able to reopen the mines if I thought I'd made a fatal mistake and gotten all of our workers killed. I would've given him my share to try and make amends."

"Honor isn't something to regret, Lyman." Dunstan's words did little to comfort Braden as he added, "Integrity itself isn't a flaw, but the predictability of an honorable man can be exploited."

"If you're trying to cheer me up, you'd do better to call Doc back in here." Braden gave a slight stretch and ended the experiment with a hiss. "Telling a man he's easy to exploit is bad for morale."

"If you want to look at it that way, it's disheartening."

"How else am I to look at it?" Braden seethed. Even when he'd been whole, he'd been unable to protect those who depended on him.

"I read some redemption in the loyalty you inspire. It's convoluted, but Owens forfeited his own life trying to save yours."

"The death of a trusted friend—however unworthy—is cold comfort." Braden choked on an impossible mix of grief and loathing. Owens survived the collapse and Doc sent him home to recuperate—but he never made it. A damaged blood vessel burst in his brain before they took him off the train.

"Maybe you should be looking to strengthen your resolve." Dunstan's brows lowered. "Because Draxley and your partner weren't the only ones responsible for the collapse. They answered to someone else, someone powerful enough to put the plan in motion."

"Who?" Fists clenched, Braden had to remind himself that he couldn't leap from bed, find the fellow, and throttle the dastard.

"Beyond implying that the man was a Hope Falls investor, it's the one thing Draxley wouldn't tell us." Far from looking defeated,

Dunstan grinned. "So how about you and I exploit that reputation of yours one last time and lure the mastermind back to Hope Falls?"

"If you've got a plan," Braden promised, "I'm listening."

"This can't go on much longer." Lacey flounced in with a frown.

Naomi's heart sank. She'd reached the same conclusion even before breakfast, but hadn't come to terms with it. Unfortunately, she didn't have time to dither. Perhaps if Lacey and Dunstan's courtship had been more measured and conventional, she would have found a solution before they announced their engagement. Then again, Naomi should have known better. Lacey bucked convention at every turn, and Dunstan could hardly be termed traditional.

"We're going to have to do something." Lacey plopped down on one of the kitchen stools. "This has to be settled today!"

"Jake took care of it yesterday." Evie's calm pronouncement shook Naomi. "So we wouldn't be obligated to make arrangements."

"How did he take care of it?" Naomi thought back over breakfast but couldn't remember anything out of the ordinary. Shouldn't there have been some sort of upset? Even if Granger managed to make most of the men happy, there would still be a few grumblers. And what if they needed to overturn Granger's high-handed arrangements because they didn't have adequate funds? "He didn't get our approval or even discuss how much we should pay!"

Lacey looked equally unsettled. "I know he's your fiancé and he has more experience than all of us put together, but Granger is not the owner of Hope Falls. He can't take over our accounts."

"What on earth are the two of you going on about?" Cora didn't seem to share their sense of outrage. "I, for one, am grateful to Granger!"

"Changing our arrangement with the men," Naomi burst out. "I know now that Evie and Lacey are taken, we'll need to address the issue, but I'm not ready to abide by whatever Granger set in place."

Heart pounding, Naomi nevertheless noticed that no one blinked.

Wide-eyed, they stared as though she'd sprouted a second head.

"Hold up," Evie raised her hands. "We're talking at cross purposes here. Jake hasn't changed our agreement with the men!"

"Is that what you thought, Lacey?" Cora looked confused.

"I was talking about the larder," Lacey ventured. "The last two supply orders haven't arrived, and we're running out of foodstuffs. But Granger isn't in the position to authorize the use of funds."

"He didn't do that either." Evie settled herself on a stool. Now that she no longer needed to defend her man, she looked at ease. "Though Lacey's right about how badly the pantry needs restocking."

"Then what did Granger take care of?" Naomi felt like a fool.

"He had the men move Draxley and cover him with stones. He called it a cairn." Cora grimaced. "To keep scavengers away."

"I knew that, and I am grateful to Granger." Naomi stifled a shudder. "Draxley deserved his fate, but we couldn't leave him."

"Let's not think about it any longer. Naomi looks ill." Lacey took her arm. "We'll go try our hand at sending telegrams."

"Wait." Naomi pulled her arm free. "Foolish as I sounded earlier, we still have a problem looming. We can't expect the men to continue working without pay—and we need to decide their wages."

"I say that any man who wants to court Naomi should stay on as agreed," Lacey sniffed. "Because she's worth as much as Evie or I."

"But we can't very well expect to ask my. . .um. . ."—Naomi needed to swallow before she could say the next word—"suitors to work without wages alongside men who are paid for the same day's efforts."

"Agreed." Evie looked thoughtful. "The trouble lies with those men who elected myself and Lacey. We can't expect their free labor when they've no chance at winning one of the Hope Falls brides."

"What if they still had a chance?" Cora lifted her chin. "I mean to say, what if Naomi wasn't the last Hope Falls bride?"

Evie slapped the countertop loud enough to make them wince. "Absolutely not. Cora, whether you leave Braden or not is your own decision, but we all agreed you aren't ready to wed someone else."

"Naomi isn't ready to marry one of these loggers, but we all expect her to choose one of them in the near future." Cora's lower lip began to tremble. "Why should the burden rest on her alone?"

"It doesn't!" Naomi hurried to assure her friends that she was willing to do the last thing she wanted. "Evie and Lacey are holding up their part of the bargain—they chose men who came to Hope Falls and helped set up the sawmill. It's only fair that I do the same."

Except it isn't fair, is it? Naomi's conscience sounded as dejected as she felt. *Whatever man you marry won't know he's taking on damaged goods, not a virtuous woman. How can that be fair?*

"No it's not." Cora frowned. "I know you, Naomi. You'll rush your decision to end the tension among the men and because you don't want to make Evie and Lacey wait to marry the men they chose."

"Yes." Naomi seized on the opportunity. "It would make things less rushed if Evie and Lacey went ahead with their weddings."

Silence blossomed as the prospective brides thought it over. Anyone could see that they didn't relish the idea of waiting, but it didn't take long before both of them were shaking their heads.

"No. We've already found out the hard way that it's not safe. Even with four of us living together, we had to bring in Mr. Lawson." Evie's logic couldn't be assailed. If it weren't for Granger's fists, the men would have broken in under cover of darkness to "claim their brides" and take away their choices.

The reminder sent a chill up Naomi's spine. Afterward, Mr. Lawson and his widowed sister moved in with the women. The engineer made his bed in the downstairs study. Even then, his presence wouldn't be acceptable if Arla weren't so heavily pregnant.

"Besides, we all planned to marry on the same day," came Lacey's more sentimental logic. "I want us all to stand together as united as when we came to Hope Falls. The joy of the day can't be complete unless we've all found the husbands of our hearts."

"Then I might as well go up alongside Naomi." Cora's quiet resolve ruined the romance. "Because unless he can convince me otherwise, and I don't think he can, I won't be marrying Braden."

FIFTEEN

Can't say that I blame you." Granger's voice made Cora jump. "Sorry, I didn't mean to startle you. Just popped in to ask if anyone needed to add their telegrams to the ones Braden gave me."

"As a matter of fact, we haven't received the last two supply shipments we ordered." Lacey expertly smoothed things over, sparing Cora from having to reply to Granger's comment about Braden.

The thing of it was, Cora wanted to reply. "You don't?"

"Nope." Granger didn't miss a beat. "In fact, I'm glad to hear it. Braden's a friend, but he needs to break through that crusty cocoon he's built up around himself and come out a better man."

"You think that's possible?" Cora caught her breath. She might not be willing to marry Braden as things stood, but she couldn't help but hope that would change. And even if he couldn't change her mind, her feminine heart still wanted him to want her enough to try!

"All things are possible through Christ." Granger angled over to Evie. "It's a matter of whether or not Braden's going to lean on God's strength or his own as he recovers and gains independence."

Lacey frowned. "We Lymans have always had trouble with that. Braden's gone sour *because* he's lost his independence."

"Helplessness is a harsh torment for any man," Granger agreed.

"There's more to it than that." Cora didn't want to defend Braden, but there was more to his transformation than thwarted independence. "Pain doesn't improve anyone's disposition." *And the festering pain of his guilt makes things ten times worse!*

She bore no illusions. Braden probably wouldn't be improving at all if it weren't for the absolution of Dunstan's discovery. Her love certainly hadn't been enough to pull him from his despair. If anything, Cora wondered whether her steadfast support hadn't enabled Braden to wallow in his own misery. She could only keep praying.

"It doesn't mean you have to marry him," Evie argued fiercely. "And it certainly doesn't mean you have to marry anyone else!"

"What?" Granger, normally so stoic, looked shocked. "Who?"

"I don't know." Cora flapped her hands as if she could shoo away the question. "Naomi shouldn't be the last Hope Falls bride when there's another one of us who isn't engaged to be married."

That set off another round of vehement protests from the women. Interestingly enough, Granger didn't look nearly as appalled as he had when Evie first mentioned the possibility. He looked as though he were considering the option and finding it had merit.

"Why not?" He broke through the arguments being volleyed about the kitchen. Granger even ignored Evie, who looked as though she'd dearly love to apply a cast-iron skillet to her fiancés thick skull.

Cora knew that look as well as she knew her sister, and it couldn't help but make her smile to see it directed at someone else. Of course, it didn't hurt that Granger was taking up Cora's cause.

"She doesn't have to marry anyone," he clarified. "But why not let Cora decide whether or not to allow a man to try and win her heart? The men will all know she's fresh from a broken engagement, and we can make sure they won't expect any speedy decisions."

"I don't think distracting her from Braden is the answer." Now that the tides had turned, Naomi looked deeply concerned. "A hurt heart seeks comfort, and affection can be mistaken for love."

"I'll be careful, Naomi." Cora couldn't help but give her friend a warm hug. "My friends will always be my greatest comfort and trusted advisors. Remember, we set up safeguards. At least two of you have to support my choice before I can marry anyone."

"Including Braden?" Evie had a shrewd look, and Cora realized that her sister didn't trust her not to fall back in love with him.

"Are you joking?" Lacey was fervent. "*Especially* Braden!"

"It's a wise woman who knows when to walk away," Granger encouraged. "And a wiser one still who knows she's worth the chase."

What if Braden doesn't come for me? Cora ruthlessly squashed her first thought. She deserved a man who valued her—a man who looked at her the way Granger looked at her sister. And besides. . .

"Braden's spent a lot of time trying to chase me away." Cora gave a tiny grin. "Now we'll see if he's man enough to catch me."

"A man's only a man when he works hard for those he loves." Dad's advice cut through Mike's growing fatigue as steadily as his saw bit through felled trees. Back and forth, give and take, progress made and measured in mere inches. But every inch brought Mike closer to the time he and Luke could call Hope Falls home. Together.

As an admitted "sapling"—the logging equivalent of a greenhorn—he'd been paired with Gent as a "bucker." Bucking consisted of stripping the branches from felled trees then using a two-man whipsaw to cut the massive pines down to more manageable sizes. It made for less dangerous work than wielding an ax and less skilled labor than making precise undercuts and swift, even back-cuts to determine which directions the trees would fall. But what bucking lacked in those areas, it more than made up for in the monotonous, muscle-straining push and pull pattern of the crosscut saw.

As Gent put it, "One of the best things about working as bucker is that it means keeping well clear of the fallers so you don't get hit by mistake. The team foreman, and for us it's Bear, doesn't tend to bother so much with buckers either. We're pretty much left on our own, so long as we get the job finished in good time."

Come noon, Mike noticed a drawback to the bucker's isolated position. By the time he and Gent heard their team's echoing calls to come 'n' grub, the other men were already cracking open the lunch pails. Thankfully, their team leader held out their fair share.

"Here now." The massive redhead passed them a pail kept cool beneath shady underbrush. In spite of Gent's observation that buckers were left to their own devices, Bear Riordan didn't stint when it came to checking on the "sapling" throughout the morning. The giant gave Mike a nod of approval and added, "You've earned it."

"Feels like your arms are going to fall off, don't it?" The youngest member of their crew looked like a stiff breeze could blow him over, so Mike figured that he was commiserating, not teasing.

All the same, Mike wasn't about to complain. No one liked a whiner. "What kind of workman would I be if my own arms detached?"

"That would, I believe, depend on if you can reattach them." It was easy to recognize the short, stocky German with a fondness for suspenders. His ready grin rendered him instantly likeable.

"I wouldn't want to find out." Mike brushed away the idea that he might have to. From the ache across his back, he'd be stiff as untreated oak when he tried to roll out of bed tomorrow morning.

"*Ja*, neither would I." Even without the accent, the amiable man would have been recognizable. The unexpectedly thick soles of his boots made for an unforgettable clomping sound when the man walked, reminding everyone of his nickname with every step he took.

Easy to see how Volker Klumpf earned the nickname Clump. Just as it took no time at all to realize why the impressively burly Rory Riordan went by Bear. With Gent rounding out the crew, Mike began to suspect that loggers hid a fondness for creative nicknames.

"Ah!" Bear sounded absolutely delighted as he pulled something from one of the pails. "Slap me if they didn't make Scotch eggs!"

"This is from an egg?" Clump squinted at one of the large brown balls. "Looks more like fried chicken. What kind of egg is this?"

Trying not to be conspicuous about it, Mike surveyed one of the round objects presented as lunch. It didn't look like anything he'd ever eaten before, and he wondered whether that was a good thing. Mike downed half his canteen, waiting for Bear Riordan's summation.

"Mam used to make these," the large man rhapsodized, emptying the contents of his pail onto a clean bandana. He then upended the pail and transferred the bandana atop it as a sort of makeshift table. He flicked out a blade and set to slicing one of his Scotch eggs. "First, she'd boil and peel the eggs. Then she'd wet her hands and mold seasoned ground pork sausage all 'round each one."

He split the thing neatly in two, revealing the boiled egg in the center. "From there, she dipped the sausage-covered egg in beaten egg, rolled it in bread crumbs, and fried it in hot oil."

By then, Mike caught up with the foreman. He'd laid open one of his own eggs and had it halfway to his mouth before realizing he hadn't prayed. It took a fair bit of will to set down his lunch and give thanks, but at least he was sincere. From the inroads made in the food, it looked like Scotch eggs tasted as good as they sounded.

And better than they look. Mike made short work of the first and reached for a second. Crispy fried sausage with a spicy kick, cooled down by the chewy egg, lent the portable meal an array of texture and taste. The butter-baked biscuits made a welcome addition. They gave the food it's due, making their way through the first two-thirds before slowing enough to allow for some conversation.

"I don't know much about logging," Mike hedged, "but it was my understanding that the teams were much larger—say twenty-five men?"

"That's the way of it." Bear sounded grave. "But Hope Falls doesn't have so many men at the moment. Besides, men disperse even when working in a team. It's not safe to set two teams of fallers working close, nor should the buckers stay nearby. The work's dangerous enough without trying to clump men together. If the foreman can see his whole crew, then one tree can crush them."

"For now," Clump joined in, "it doesn't matter whether the units are small. We're mostly clearing a path for the flume. Once that's up and running, work will really begin. Granger can gauge the labor and determine whether to keep smaller teams or change over."

Mike rolled his neck and stretched, his muscles protesting the idea that this wasn't the "real" work. "Thanks for letting me know."

"I say it depends on the donkeys." Bobsley, the youngster, grew animated. "The more donkeys, the farther apart you can set up."

"The farther apart you *have* to set up," Bear corrected. "I doona trust the newfangled machinery. Steam engines are fine for ships and trains, but for hauling logs? Bah. One cable snaps, it cuts down two trees and three men before coming to a halt."

"Sounds like a different sort of donkey than gets hitched to a wagon." Despite Bear's obvious dislike of the machines, Mike couldn't help but be curious. "If Granger's bringing in steam engines to move the logs, why are we bothering to build a flume?"

"That's the trick of it. The Colorado River runs through these mountains—Lawson's building the mill atop a strong-running off-shoot to power the wheel—but it winds. Donkeys could haul sectioned logs straight to the river, but they'd float right past the offshoot." Bobsley filled in the gaps. "If the donkeys haul the logs to the right place upstream, a good flume can rush them straight to the mill."

"Provided we have the manpower to set things up." Gent made his first contribution to the conversation. "Given recent events, the ladies will have to make some changes to keep things progressing."

"That's not for us to speculate on." Bear quickly cut things short, leaving Mike completely in the dark. "Until things change or you decide to pack up and leave, we've an agreement to keep."

As Mike followed Gent back to the Douglas fir they'd been breaking into thirty-two-foot segments, he tried to make sense of the cryptic conversation. *What did Gent mean, the ladies would have to make some changes? Why would any of the men suddenly pack up and leave?* And, perhaps most mysterious, *What kind of agreement?*

SIXTEEN

W e're going to have to offer wages to all the men." Naomi broached the topic again once she, Lacey, and Granger were en route to the telegraph office. "Especially now that Cora's set on joining me."

"You know how much I hate to say you're right." Lacey sighed. "So I'm not going to say it. We're just going to have to figure out what makes a fair wage and how meals and lodging factor in."

"I can help you there." Granger reached the telegraph office first and held the door open for them. "Though it varies by outfit."

"Any guidance would be helpful—" Naomi walked into Lacey, who came to an abrupt stop at the threshold. When she recovered, she saw why.

"What on earth happened here?" Lacey edged over to allow Naomi and Granger entrance. "This could be an entirely different office."

Naomi knew what she meant. The haphazard stacks of paper, crumpled missives, and skewed stacks bore no resemblance to the office she'd seen as recently as last week. Draxley had kept the place so obsessively tidy she'd wanted to mess it up a little.

"He must have panicked after the picnic." Lacey shook her head.

"What picnic?" Granger obviously couldn't make the connection. He'd been all the way in Baltimore, taking Twyler to trial.

"We had a picnic a little while back in the same clearing where we served supper last night," Naomi explained. "Draxley became very agitated when someone suggested we take a stroll around the mines."

"Something triggered this." Granger bent down and began retrieving fallen missives, plunking them atop the desk. "I remember every time I came to his office, he'd neaten his papers into perfect piles, made everything parallel. I'd put the pencil down sideways, just to see how long it took him to straighten it."

"Not long." It sounded as though Lacey spoke from experience. For a while, there was nothing but the sound of papers sliding and shuffling together as they made a collective sweep around the room.

"Little wonder our supplies never arrived." Naomi smoothed out a badly crushed order spilled from the overturned wastebasket. "It looks as though he threw them away as soon as you left the room."

"When's the last time you received an incoming telegram?" Flipping through a stack of paper filled with barely decipherable scratches, Granger looked troubled. He tapped a page. "There are several messages here in the hastily penciled translations of incoming telegrams. I'm not seeing any of the official ink copies."

"The lazy, scheming reprobate!" Lacey huffed. "You'd think he could have at least done his job properly before trying to kill us!"

Naomi giggled before she could even think to stop the sound. And once she started, she couldn't stop. By the time she caught her breath, the other two were chuckling. "Only you, Lacey," she gasped, "could work up such indignation over a murderer's filing skills."

"*Lack* of filing skills," Lacey justified. "In all fairness, I would have granted him much more leeway about the state of his office if he hadn't done all of those other nasty, terrible things."

"I think we can all agree that Draxley exceeded his allotment of terrible deeds." Naomi managed to keep a straight face this time.

They got back to work, creating various piles of paperwork. As the sorting continued, it quickly became evident that Draxley had been negligent long before the picnic. He'd just hidden it better.

While the stack of penciled translations grew high, there were precious few official ink telegrams. Several outgoing messages were found balled up beside the wastebasket, making it doubtful that Draxley ever sent them. Even worse was the expanding pile—it became too large for a simple stack—of undistributed post office mail.

"He abandoned his post long before that picnic." By the time they'd gotten everything sorted, Granger was downright irate. "I'll start resending the messages and orders we found in the trash."

"You know Morse code?" Lacey's brows rose, and Naomi shared her surprise.

"Yep. I've set up several logging outfits. Finding a telegraph operator isn't as easy as you'd think, so if I needed to get messages out I had to learn. It was easier than learning how to wait on someone else." He grinned at their chuckles.

"Why don't you give me the pencil copies?" Naomi offered. "I can probably make out the messages. It can't be any worse than trying to decipher Braden's letters." She smiled at the memory.

"I'll organize the post then." Lacey lowered herself to the ground with an ease that reminded Naomi to order a Pivot Corset.

For the next hour the tapping and mechanical clicks of the telegraph were the only sounds in the room. Finally, Granger pushed away from the desk and stretched. "That's the last of them."

"I'm just about finished here, too." Naomi blinked and rubbed her eyes.

"I hope you didn't tire your eyes already." Lacey wore a satisfied grin as she pushed a large pile—by far the majority of the post—across the floor. "By the looks of them, these belong to you."

For a moment, Naomi couldn't imagine who might have sent her so many letters. It wasn't until she plucked one from the pile that she realized what had happened. Across the envelope, the smudged lines were addressed, appallingly enough, *"To My Future Bride(s)."*

"Oh!" She dropped it as though its author might emerge from the envelope then used her foot to push the pile back toward her cousin. "Stop looking so pleased, Lacey. Those do not belong to me."

"I doubt Dunstan wrote this." Lacey plucked the offending letter from the pile and waved it in the air. "So it's not mine."

By then Granger had ambled over to see what was going on.

With a shrug, he plunged his hand into the heap and brought up another letter. "This one's to 'The Three Fair Maidens of Hope Falls.'"

Naomi couldn't even blame him for snickering when he reached the "Fair Maidens" bit. The whole thing was absolutely ridiculous.

"The sad thing is this was the kind of response we'd hoped for—oh, don't look so quizzical, Granger. I don't mean the overblown forms of address. I mean that we'd anticipated going through letters and selecting a few men to come visit Hope Falls in person."

"Our welcome committee disabused us of that notion." Lacey was obviously remembering the day they'd arrived in Hope Falls, believing that the men gathered around the train were recent hires. "I don't know why we never thought to check the post—we should have realized there might be some men who replied as requested."

"I know why." Naomi set aside several other obvious ad responses. "We haven't had time to think beyond the basics." *And even then we haven't managed to handle things very well.*

Naomi flipped through a few more. "We should burn them."

"No!" Lacey grabbed them back and cradled the replies to her chest, looking for all the world like a mother protecting her child. "How could you even suggest letting all of these go to waste?"

"Yeah." Granger flipped another find toward Naomi. "Think of all the fun you'll have opening these. Hours of entertainment."

A snort escaped her as Naomi glimpsed the writing on the letter Granger selected. "'To the Lovelorn Logging Ladies.'" She snickered.

"We're also known as the 'Sawmill Sweethearts.'" Lacey set this gem to the side but wrinkled her nose at the next one she picked up. "'Wilderness Women'? Why does that make it sound as though we parade about in grubby buckskins, brandishing firearms at hapless men?"

"I'm sure they didn't mean it like that," Granger soothed. "Though this one probably did." He tore up the envelope but not before Naomi was able to decipher the words *Shameless Hussies.*

The indictment wandered through Naomi's memory, a painful echo.

"You're going to Charleston, where my brother needs a woman to guide his daughter. You're not fit for the position, but it's your last chance to make something of yourself. If you can't find some fool to marry you and cannot control yourself in any other way, simply stick your nose back in a book. It's better to be known as the bluestocking you were than the shameless hussy you've become."

"Naomi?" Lacey's call, accompanied by a nudge against her boot, recalled her to the present. "Whatever is going through your mind?"

"Oh. . ." She searched for an acceptable answer. "Only how unlikely it is that I can find a good husband by reading these." *Or at all.*

"Pish." Lacey brushed away her protest. "That's no reason to look so glum. You can't read a man by looking at his envelope."

"There's some wisdom to brighten your day." Granger stood up, holding out a letter Naomi didn't have the heart to take. "This one's different. Looks like a lady wrote it, and it has your name."

Naomi fought to keep her hand from trembling as she accepted the envelope. In return for the scores of letters she'd sent to her family during the past five years, she'd received one response. A terse telegram from her sister advised that their mother's funeral had been the day before and Naomi should cease writing home.

She peered at the envelope as though it could somehow prepare her for its contents. Who would bother writing to her from across the country? And more importantly. . . *What can they possibly want?*

"Supper's ready and waiting," Miss Lyman assured a hungry crowd.

"Then what's it waitin' on?" someone grumbled, loud enough to be heard but not so loud Miss Lyman couldn't graciously ignore it.

"An announcement." Dunstan's growl warned away more grumbling. When the men stopped shifting on the benches, he relaxed. "I'm pleased to tell you that Miss Lyman has agreed to be my wife."

For a moment the men all looked at each other. It wasn't as though they hadn't seen the writing on the wall, but they still seemed at a loss how to handle the proclamation. From where Mike sat, the problem had nothing to do with whether the men respected or even liked Dunstan. This wasn't even about the supper holdup.

The problem stood beside Dunstan. Covered in dust and sporting britches, Miss Lyman turned heads. Dressed up in pink frills, she shimmered like an oasis. And now Dunstan had made her unreachable. Little wonder the room full of lonely lumbermen wasn't cheering.

From the growing displeasure on the ladies' faces, supper might never come out of the kitchen. So Mike did what any exhausted man with an empty stomach and a waiting bunk would do. He started clapping. Not loudly, just prompting the other fellows to join him. Granger helped ease the tension by offering hearty congratulations.

"Course *he*'d be happy for them," muttered one of Mike's tablemates. "Granger already got himself the cook, didn't he?"

"Now Dunstan's gone and nabbed the dazzler," another lamented. "That means I'm out. First frost, I'm heading for another outfit."

"Leave sooner," Bobsley urged. "Less competition for me!"

"Didn't you hear me?" The man who'd spoken of leaving peered sadly into his empty coffee mug. "I'm out. No more chances. Only reason I'm sticking around at all is for the food. That's worth staying for, so long as there aren't paying jobs someplace else."

Mike blinked at that last bit. "You aren't getting paid?"

There had been too much going on last night to broach the subject of wages—considering the mine contretemps, Mike figured he was lucky to have gotten a bunk to sleep in and an offer of employment at all. He hadn't pushed about further details because it would've done him more harm than good—and he hadn't cared. Mike didn't lack funds. The Bainbridges gave him and Leticia a house as a wedding present, and he'd recognized a good profit even on a quick sale.

All the same, this lack of logging wages was a revelation. Maybe the employees of Hope Falls expected to receive a lump sum once the mill was up and running? That might explain Gent's earlier comment about changing the agreement.

This could be the advantage Mike needed. *I'll gladly work without wages until the mill's set up—if they let me bring Luke.* Mind galloping along, he almost missed what came next.

"In light of these changing circumstances,"—Miss Lyman could be awfully loud for such a delicate-looking thing—"we understand that some changes are in order. Tonight we modify our arrangement."

The resulting swell of sound swallowed anything more the women might have said. Mike recognized that the women had foreseen this problem. In a bit of brilliant strategizing, the elder Miss Thompson used the one weapon guaranteed to inspire fear, reverence, and awe.

She rang the dinner bell.

SEVENTEEN

Conversation ceased so abruptly it might have been cleavered. Speakers stopped midsentence. Every man perked his ears and sniffed the air as though he hadn't already noticed the aromas wafting from the kitchen. It went so still, Mike fancied he could hear the rumbling of a dozen stomachs. *Or maybe mine is just that loud.*

"Now that we have your attention,"—Miss Thompson lowered her dinner bell to continue—"we'll explain the terms of our new offer."

Mike couldn't help wondering about the terms of the old offer—particularly since so many men had taken them up on it, and now he wouldn't get the chance to find out if he would have done the same.

"As you know, Mr. Granger is an authority on the lumber business, having left Granger Mills to join us in Hope Falls."

Mike puzzled over the ladies' pointed mention of Granger's pedigree. Perhaps they wanted a subtle reminder that they knew the business and wouldn't be taken advantage of. More likely, the mention of Granger's connections was a warning not to cause trouble.

Granger himself took over at this point. "Beyond industry standards, Hope Falls has high expectations and plans to pay well for its workers to meet them. We're offering each man a working wage of thirty dollars a month, less fifteen dollars room and board."

Aside from a few hushed whispers, men just nodded. New as he was to this side of the industry, even Mike understood this to be an excellent offer—practically engineers' wages. He'd known factory men paying fifteen dollars a month for a bunk and mediocre meals. For Miss Thompson's fare, they would have gladly shelled out more.

"Sleep on it. I'll be asking for your decision come morning." Granger most likely didn't want to hold up supper any longer.

"Is the girl still up for grabs?" one logger wanted to know. "Or is she hands-off for anyone who signs on and works for pay?"

Mike felt a surge of sympathy for the young Miss Thompson. Obviously the girl in question, she betrayed her discomfort by beginning to fidget. The fellow who asked if she was "up for grabs" needed a knock upside the head and a lesson in how to treat a lady.

"None of us was ever 'up for grabs.'" The girl's sister came to her rescue. "And to answer your question, nothing has changed save the addition of your wages. If you wish to woo a woman, you may still try, provided you remember to keep your hands to yourself."

"Y'all got no entertainment hereabouts." Someone's holler set off a fresh round of speculation. "When you gonna put up a saloon?"

Mike craned his neck for a clearer view of the idiot. Men like that needed watching. Sometimes they just needed to be steered in the right direction. Meanwhile, they needed to be steered clear of the women. Mike would start with the latter and pray for the former.

"Never." Naom—*Miss Higgins*, Mike caught himself—bristled like a stepped-on porcupine, every inch rigid with warning. She looked as though she knew precisely what "entertainment" was. Or, at the very least, she was thinking of the sort of saloon that served more than whiskey and cards. In short, exactly the sort of saloon most loggers wanted.

"Your wages are your own." She softened her approach slightly. "But no part of Hope Falls will become a venue for hard drinking, gambling, or anything else you wouldn't want to tell your mamas."

"While the ladies head back in the kitchen to bring out supper,"—Dunstan waited while the women dutifully filed out, staring down the audience and bearing a striking resemblance to the snarling cougar someone had suspended on the wall behind him—

"I'll remind you that Hope Falls is a decent town, run by ladies. You will address them as such, or you'll be escorted aboard the next train."

"Ladies," snorted the man who said he'd stay for the food.

"*Ladies*," Mike growled back, ready to stick him on a train.

"What would you know about it?" his companion jeered. "You're what, a day old? Fresh off the train and thinking you know anybody?"

"I know you're not staying long." Mike pushed back his mug in case he needed to move quickly. "And I know a lady when I see one."

"What tipped you off to how proper they are? The britches?" He gave a knowing smirk. "Not that any of us are complaining about that privileged sight. No, it's the starched-up, skunk-haired one—"

Mike choked off the flow of bile by grabbing the man's grubby shirtfront and twisting. It tightened around the neck and gave Mike a good enough grip to haul the arrogant cuss off the bench. He got halfway through the diner before the other men realized what was going on. He almost made it to the door before they hit their feet.

A shadow slipped past him just before the room grew too small for Mike to move any farther. Surrounded by a dozen suddenly silent loggers, Mike didn't know if they were interfering on behalf of the wriggling idiot in his grasp or if they wanted to watch a fight.

The door creaked open, making heads swivel. There stood Granger, ushering them outside. In a whisper obviously not meant to carry back to the kitchen, he ordered: "Not in Evie's diner."

With that, the seas parted to let Mike haul his opponent into the evening light. Until he felt the cool breeze on his face, Mike didn't realize how hot his blood boiled. The men, now less quiet, filed out behind him and formed a much larger circle. An arena.

Mike abruptly realized he hadn't thought beyond evicting the foulmouthed fool from the diner, where the aspersions he cast on the ladies wouldn't do any further damage. He didn't plan on a fistfight and wouldn't engage in one to satisfy a blood-thirsty mob—unless of course the aforementioned fool forced him into it.

"What do you do with men who belong on the next train?" He addressed Granger, wondering whether the obvious leader of the

Hope Falls loggers had already needed to deal with this type of thing. Mike also noticed Dunstan picked up on the fracas and joined them.

"Depends." Granger planted his feet in the dirt, a little wider than his shoulders, and issued his first order. "Let him down now."

Mike's sudden release made the man stumble, even though he'd only been high enough to keep from bracing his heels. As soon as the man steadied himself, he swung a clumsy punch at Mike's midriff. Mike sidestepped him, wrapped his arm around the man's wrist, and flipped him on the ground. A wave of quickly hushed cheers followed.

"Never can trust a man who leads with a blind punch." With that, Bear Riordan established himself as Mike's supporter and ally.

"What about a man who grabs another by the collar at the supper table?" The whine came after Mike's opponent regained his feet.

"Depends," Granger repeated. He paused for a long moment as though thinking. "I didn't peg our new woodworker as a man with a temper. What did you say to make him decide you needed to leave town?"

"Told him he was too new to know anything about Hope Falls." His sullen response sparked Mike's anger anew, but that was mild compared to the outraged indignation of Volker Klumpf.

"Ja!" The German stomped forward in a succession of aggravated clomps. "Only after Strode said he knew our women were ladies!"

"You were saying the women weren't ladies?" Even in the dark, Granger's expression made the object of his inquisition gulp.

"I never said that. We all know better than to say that."

"His meaning was clear." Mike negated the coward's hasty disavowal. Repeating the comment about Miss Lyman's britches would be disrespectful, but he needed to make sure everyone understood the gravity of the situation. "He also insulted Miss Higgins's character and appearance and made suggestive remarks about Miss Lyman."

"Ja, that he did," Clump avowed with much vehement nodding.

"Oh, come on." Giving up his pretense of innocence, the man launched a counterattack. "We all know that proper women don't advertise to hire husbands, and real ladies wouldn't be here."

Advertise to hire husbands? The ridiculous accusation hung in the air, waiting to be refuted. But no one corrected the man. Mike couldn't make a lick of sense out of the comment, but it dawned on him that none of the other men looked confused or even surprised.

"You're lucky Mr. Strode showed such restraint." Dunstan must have understood Mike's message. Decoy, picking up on his master's mood, bared his teeth at the object of Dunstan's displeasure.

"That settles things." Granger shared a glance with Bear Riordan, and the massive Irishman broke from the surrounding circle.

"To the privy then?" Bear waited for Granger's nod. Then he simply lowered his head, jammed his shoulder into the condemned man, shouldered him like a sack of potatoes, and strode into the night.

"Outhouse?" Mike grinned at the Hope Falls's detention cell.

With the excitement ended, dinner beckoned everyone back into the diner. His grumbling gut urged him to follow the crowd and find a seat, but his curiosity got the better of him. He waited until only Granger and Dunstan remained outside then asked what was on his mind. "Advertise to hire husbands? What was he talking about?"

"He doesn't know?" Dunstan asked Granger, sounding surprised.

"Tomorrow morning." Granger looked Mike over as though trying to discern something. "After breakfast. We have things to discuss."

"Mrs. Smythe spotted my dollhouse just before we left for Hope Falls. I had it brought down to the parlor for crating, and she caught sight of it." Lacey tilted her head. "Why do you ask?"

"She's commissioned me to make one for her." Naomi rubbed her temples. "I've never spoken with Mrs. Smythe about it. I didn't know she'd ever seen the Lyman Place miniature! But in the pile of mail today I found this. It's the 'second installment' payment because I didn't send back the first."

"Why didn't you tell me earlier this afternoon?" Lacey huffed as she scanned the missive. "And where's the first part then if this is the second?"

"I checked every piece of post—twice. It's not there. It's not as though a letter requesting a custom dollhouse would be difficult to find amid the ad responses." Naomi crumpled the remaining letter and fumed. "Draxley didn't just stop sending telegrams and distributing messages—he must have opened any that looked thick enough to have money enclosed. It's a wonder he didn't get his hands on the second letter and steal it, too!"

"Bad business all around." Evie scooted toward the head of her bed in order to make room for Lacey. With Mr. Lawson already ensconced in the study for the night, they couldn't converse freely in the adjoining parlor. Somehow Evie and Cora managed to find two small beds—practically hammocks topped with mattresses—in one of the abandoned houses of Hope Falls, so everyone crammed into their room.

"If Draxley did take Mrs. Smythe's first letter and steal the funds she enclosed, how will we be able to fill the order?" Cora eased herself beside Naomi, causing the bed to shift softly. "I mean, I know the second letter contains more money, but is it enough to even purchase the necessary supplies? What about the specialty pieces?"

"Mrs. Smythe paid well." *Very well.* Part of the reason Naomi hadn't been able to confide in Lacey that afternoon was her shock. Aside from the dawning horror of the situation, she simply hadn't been able to register such a large sum. Of course, she only received half of it, which created the current problem. "With God's help, a little ingenuity, and some hard work, I believe I could fully furnish a six-room dollhouse without overextending the amount."

"Then the timing is the only problem?" Lacey brightened. "Why don't you just have those specialty German pieces delivered directly to Mrs. Smythe since the passage to America already takes so long?"

"Because that's only part of the problem." Naomi smoothed the letter again. "I can't furnish a house that hasn't been built. With the advance funds she enclosed in the first letter, I would have beenable to commission a master craftsman to devote his entire attention to this as a special order. Even then I would have needed to be working based on its dimensions until it arrived here."

"And now you don't have the money to commission the house." Evie considered for a moment. "What if we raised the money?"

"It's too late." Naomi pushed against the floor, making the bed sway. "The project would have been incredibly ambitious to begin with, and I've already lost two months! There's no time to find a craftsman, work out the project details, and pray he gets them right and ships it to me on time! Nor can I try to find a house that's already constructed—Mrs. Smythe has some specific requests here."

"What if you took away the distance?" Cora put down her foot and stopped the swaying. "What if you could speak to the craftsman, monitor the construction, and not waste time waiting for the shipping?"

"I suppose it might be possible." Too anxious to sit still, Naomi hopped up and began pacing the narrow space between the beds. "But even so, I couldn't pay a reasonable fee! This is highly skilled labor—artistry, really. Anything I could scrape together would be laughable at best, insulting at worst."

"But the Hope Falls sawmill can. As of tonight, all of the workers are paid by the company." Lacey beamed at Cora, who beamed back as though they shared a secret. "Including our new carpenter."

Mr. Strode. Naomi sank back onto the bed, overwhelmed at the prospect. "We hired him as a carpenter and joiner to help construct the mill. What makes you think he'd want to build a dollhouse?"

"What makes you think he wouldn't?" Evie grimaced. "Especially since the alternative is going to the woods and cutting down trees."

"That's more masculine." Naomi didn't even know why she was arguing. "The men accept that because he's working for the mill."

"The men will accept the way we decide to do things." Cora set her jaw, reminding everyone of her newfound determination to put Braden in his place. "Every man does the work he's contracted for."

"What about the work I'm responsible for?" Naomi needed to be fair. "Evie needs help with the cooking, and laundry doesn't wash itself."

"Remember, we've lost a good dozen—well, a bad dozen—men. We all know we can thank Mr. Strode for the removal of the latest bad egg." Evie grinned. "That means less work. So long as Lacey bakes the bread and we get a jump on things in the morning, I'll manage."

Cora set her bed swinging again, as though the motion helped sort her thoughts. "We never decided what I'd do once Braden no longer needed a nursemaid. I'll take over the laundry for a while. I don't mind washing our clothes, so long as the men continue to see to their own. Arla's been kind enough to take on their mending."

"Unless we're pushing you to take on a task you don't want." Lacey peered at her. "You seemed so happy while you transformed my old dollhouse, I just assumed you'd enjoy a fresh challenge."

"Yours was a labor of love," Naomi tried to explain. "And I loved working on it. But it was a hobby, tiny projects spaced out over years. This is entirely different, and I'm not at all certain I can finish in time. I'm hesitant to inflict such a close-looming deadline on anyone else—especially a man who's already working."

"Mr. Strode is waiting until Hope Falls is ready for a carpenter. Meanwhile, he's been hired on prospectus, and we're paying him a retainer for the time when he's needed." Lacey shrugged, oblivious to the way everyone was staring at her after all that business jargon. "What he does until that time is negotiable."

"What if Mr. Strode doesn't want to negotiate about this?" Naomi knew she was looking a gift horse in the mouth, but somehow she sensed a cavity looming ahead, waiting to swallow her hopes.

"Ask," Evie ordered. "You might be surprised by his reaction."

"All right." Naomi accepted that she wouldn't get much sleep that night thinking about this. "What's the worst that can happen?"

EIGHTEEN

Braden kept the smile glued to his face until the doctor departed, still marveling over the "incredible progress" his patient had made. Only when he was certain he was alone did Braden turn his head into one of his plethora of pillows and give the hoarse shout he'd been choking back for the past half hour. Even that small movement screamed through his knee, intensifying the already bone-deep ache.

"Breakfast!" If the smell of food weren't enough to turn his roiling stomach, the cheery voice of his erstwhile fiancée managed.

She exhibited the uncanny ability to show up whenever Braden felt his worst. It wasn't enough for Cora to see him trussed up like a Christmas goose, trapped in a doctor's bed. No, the contrary woman flitted into his room every time Braden was least able to be civil.

"Take it away," he groaned, not bothering to lift his head.

She plunked the tray on his side table with a jangle of abused dishes and cutlery. "You don't have to tell me to leave anymore, Braden. I already agreed to find my place in the world without you."

Still not daring to look up from his pillow, Braden blindly groped the air, searching for her. He found some sort of fabric and grabbed hold of it, keeping her at his side. Clinging in spite of a sudden onslaught of slaps and scolds, Braden focused on controlling his body. He focused on taking shallow, measured breaths until his stomach retreated to its customary position beneath his ribs. *Finally.* Braden looked up. He'd caught Cora by the apron strings.

The irony wasn't lost on Braden. Leading strings, they were

called, because mothers the world over bid their children hold on tight in crowded places. A boy began the transition to manhood only after Mother had "cut the leading strings." Independence meant not being tied down. But here Braden was, a grown man of twenty-six, clutching a woman's apron strings as though they were a lifeline.

Because they were. Those strings were his final, tenuous connection to Cora. If he let her storm from his room for the second time in as many days, he deserved to lose her. If he was honest, Braden would admit he already deserved to lose her. But he'd also admit he was a greedy bounder who wanted far more than he deserved.

So he held on, not letting go until Cora stopped twisting, turning, and generally flailing about like a fish caught on a hook. Her contortions traveled along the apron strings, through his clenched fist, and reverberated to his knee. By the time she stilled, Braden felt like the landed fish—green about the gills.

From Cora's expression once she got a good look at him, he probably looked as good as he felt. Without a word, she dipped a clean handkerchief in the washbasin, wrung it out, and draped it across his forehead. Then she set herself in the seat beside him.

"I came across the doctor in the hall, mumbling about your most excellent progress this morning." She didn't bother beating about the bush. "You're pushing yourself too far, too fast, Braden."

Yes—but still not far enough. Yesterday Granger sent the telegrams to set Dunstan's plan in motion. They'd dangled the bait; now it was only a matter of time before their prey came skulking into their trap. *I have to be out of this bed before they arrive.*

But first he needed to apologize to Cora and make things right.

"I didn't want *you* to go." He gritted his teeth, repositioning a few pillows to brace his back before gesturing toward the covered breakfast tray she'd brought. "My stomach couldn't take the smell."

"Is it still bothering you?" Cora shot the tray an apprehensive look, as though it might jump up and bite one of them at any moment.

"No, it's passed." He struggled to find the words then gave up and offered a simple confession. "I don't know how to apologize."

"Well, you never did, and I won't expect you to start over a bout of queasiness." Cora subtly nudged the tray farther from him. "It was my own fault for assuming you meant to expel both of us."

He'd managed to make a hash of that to make Cora begin offering apologies. Braden took a deep breath and tried again. "No, I don't blame you for making that assumption. I've tried to evict you often enough. I've been a first-rate cad since the day you arrived here."

"Worse than a cad." Her gaze became a green-and-blue battering ram. "A demanding, order-spewing bully entirely without feeling."

Her assessment stunned him. When the sense of shock began to recede, Braden recognized the familiar tingle of pricked pride. "However irritable I may have been, I am not without feelings."

Cora began hazarding guesses. "Entitlement? Anger? Jealousy? I'm curious, Braden, just what types of feelings you believe you've shown during the past two months. The only emotion I've seen that even remotely recalled the man I loved was your fear for Lacey two days ago. Even then, your self-indulgent petulance overshadowed all else."

"A man feels far more than he shows." Braden pushed aside his mounting indignation and tried to explain what he could. Even if she hadn't called him self-indulgent, he wouldn't discuss the shame, guilt, and despair he'd been battling. "You can't deny that I've been protective of you women and determined to get back on my feet."

"When your protective instincts devolve to the point where you threaten to call law enforcement and evict us from our own property—simply because it's legally held under your name—it's no longer admirable." She crossed her arms, closing herself off. "As for your will to recover, I wonder at the source behind your motivation."

"What do you mean?" Braden would've paced the room if he could. "Right now I can't protect any of you women. I can't do my part to start the sawmill. I'm all but useless as long as I lie here." It killed him to say it out loud, but how could she fail to understand?

"So you want to force everyone to do things your way. If Hope Falls remained a failure, no more than a ghost town, would your will be so strong?" She rose from her chair, looming over him like an avenging angel. "Would you push yourself half so hard if you weren't fighting to wrest control of Lyman Estates back from Lacey?"

Unwilling to lie, unable to explain his other reason for pushing so hard, Braden condensed his protests. "That's not fair."

"Tell me about it," Cora countered as she gathered up the tray and swept from the room. "But that, Braden, was *the wrong answer*."

"I have to make it right." Miss Higgins looked at him, green eyes alive with anxious hope. "Are you willing to help me, Mr. Strode?"

Mike didn't even have to think about it. For all he knew, he *couldn't* think. Not when she made him feel like the answer to all her problems. How could a man turn down Miss Higgins? "Absolutely."

She blinked, probably taken aback by the speed of his answer, then gave a low, husky laugh that sent tingles down his spine. "I suppose this means the others were right. They said it wouldn't hurt to ask you, but I never imagined you'd make it quite so easy."

"It's work." Mike shrugged it off, but something stuck in his craw. If it was just work, why did it bother him that the women encouraged her to ask? She made it sound as if the others knew he'd be easy to convince. Did he seem so susceptible to feminine wiles?

"You're frowning." She now wore the same expression. "Why?"

"I don't just agree to anything a pretty woman asks." Mike wouldn't go forward with her thinking he could be manipulated.

Once a woman glommed on to that notion, it was practically impossible to convince her otherwise. Hadn't it taken years of refusing to play her games before Leticia tired of trying? His late wife and her mother seemed to think they'd purchased him outright when he owed—and gave—nothing more than the protection of his name and his best efforts to fulfill the sacred vows they'd made.

He wouldn't let another woman think him so gullible a mark. Not even if she stood there, lovely and lush as the forests around them. Belatedly, he realized that he'd let her know he found her pretty.

But she'd already suspected as much—or at least her friends did. Or maybe they hadn't. *If not*, Mike winced, *they certainly will now.*

"It's simply a business proposition." The sparkle in her eyes seemed to say she liked being told she was pretty—even if in such a roundabout way. Her pleasure at the backhanded compliment made Mike relax a little. "Whatever your reasons, I'm grateful you agreed."

"I do have reasons!" Opportunity stared him straight in the face, and Mike had been too busy ogling her to notice until now. Here was his chance to secure a home for Luke. "One reason, really."

"Oh?" She pulled back, looking suddenly wary. "What's that?"

"My son." Praying that she'd understand, that his instincts about Miss Higgins were correct, Mike pressed on. "Luke. He's ten, and I came here hoping to find a good town where I could raise him." Suspicion softened then sharpened. "Is he with your wife?"

"No." Mike drew a breath. "Luke's in Texas with my sister, waiting for me to fetch him. My wife passed on a few months ago."

"Oh." A kaleidoscope of emotions rippled across her face, leaving behind any trace of the wariness. "I'm sorry for your loss."

"Thank you." He couldn't tell her not to worry, that he'd lost more on the day he married Leticia than on the day he buried her. "I was hoping I could work hard enough to make it worth you letting me bring Luke home with me—whenever you all think the time's right."

She probably didn't realize she was doing it, and probably no one else would have noticed, but Mike was looking hard enough to see her nibble on the inside of her lower lip while she thought it over.

"The thing is. . ." The silence—and the nibbling—unmanned him. The thought that he'd blown his chance made him begin babbling. "Luke's already started learning carpentry. I haven't had a chance to show him much in the way of joinery, but he has the makings of a fine apprentice. I understood there wasn't a place for him while I was working with the lumbermen, but I figured it'd be easier to keep an eye on him once construction began. He'd even come in handy."

"All right." Her cool words cut across his frenzied speech.

For a second all he could do was stare at her. "All right?"

"Yes, Mr. Strode. You've agreed to help me with a very difficult and detailed project, sure to consume all of your time for weeks to come. In return for your assistance, your skill, and the heartwarming love you exhibit for your son, you may bring Luke to Hope Falls." She paused for a moment. "I'll have to discuss timing with the others, but it won't be long before you'll need to make a trip for supplies. I would hope you could pick him up then."

Mike wanted to kiss her, but all he could do was nod. "If you're willing to let him watch and try his hand at some of the more minor detailing, it would even be a good chance for him to learn."

"Not to sound desperate, but I'm happy for any help I can get." She smiled and extended one delicate hand. "Do we have a deal?"

He wrapped his entire hand around her soft one. "Deal."

NINETEEN

Y ou're not keeping up your end of our agreement," Cora chided, steering the ponderously pregnant Arla back to the bentwood chair they'd brought outside for her to use. "You need to take it easy."

"Seems as though I've done nothing in days." Arla Nash grudgingly allowed herself to be settled into the seat, legs up on a stool.

Cora scoffed. "You're working twenty-four hours a day!"

"Nonsense." Arla picked up her needle and began stabbing stitches into another of a dishearteningly long parade of holey socks. "You'd feel the same way, sitting around day in and day out. I'm not accomplishing a blessed thing, resting on my laurels!"

"Do you think setting hens don't accomplish anything?" Cora intentionally chose Arla's favorite animals in the modest Hope Falls menagerie. "Because you're doing the same thing—the human way."

"I'm incubating?" Her friend put down the sock and laughed until her shoulders shook. "That's one way of looking at it. But I must say that this isn't turning out at all the way I envisioned."

"Although we're happy to have you, you know we weren't informed of your situation when we hired your brother." Cora hadn't quite managed to forgive Mr. Lawson for packing his newly widowed, heavily pregnant sister out to the wilderness for the sake of a mere job.

"It was an unpleasant shock when my brother told me we needed to move. I did think he could have left me back in the city to mind the house, but he refused to leave me alone." Arla sighed. "I dared ask him whether he might forgo this particular opportunity and await the next, but he's anxious to secure a future for the baby. I'm afraid Mr. Nash didn't leave us much after the estate settled."

"I understand." Some of Cora's resentment toward the engineer ebbed away. "We went through the same thing when Papa died. Evie had to sell the house after the money ran out. Then she worked her fingers to the bone setting up her diner and keeping us going."

"We are blessed in our siblings." Arla stroked her stomach fondly, her voice catching slightly. "I always hoped to have at least two children, so neither one would ever have to be alone."

"You never know." Cora finished pinning the last of the freshly washed garments across the clothesline and steeled herself to start another batch. It never ceased to amaze her how much filth their skirts collected out here—and that wasn't even counting Lacey's mining getup. "There might still be another man for you."

Even as she spoke the words to Arla, Cora wondered if they'd prove true for herself. Having found the right man and lost him, was it possible to love another in the same way? Or was a second love doomed to play second fiddle to a memory, always second best?

"I hope so," Arla murmured. "Even if it seems disloyal to Mr. Nash's memory, no woman wants to be alone for a lifetime."

"No." Cora agreed, plunging her paddle into the steaming vat of wash water. Her hair frizzled instantly. "We all hope to find love."

"Since everyone needs love"—Arla started sticking her needle into the fabric again—"you'd think it would be easy to find."

"You'd think so," Cora agreed, watching her clean, soapy water turn gray, then brown, then blackish. It had been the same with Braden. They'd been so clearly, purely in love. But time changed things, tragedies muddied the waters, and it took a long time for the filth to fall away. If you were patient, things settled. If you kept agitating the water, things never cleared up, never improved.

If someone asked about Braden, Cora wouldn't be able to say whether she was letting things settle or trying to stir things up. Maybe, just maybe, it was better to let Braden decide for himself.

Decision to help Miss Higgins made, the deal to bring Luke home to Hope Falls in place, and the troublesome fool still locked away in the privy, Mike sat down feeling better than he had in months. It didn't hurt that the table all but vanished beneath a bountiful breakfast.

The fare wasn't fancy or unexpected like those Scotch eggs. Still, Mike never met a man who'd turn down hot coffee with a heaping helping of fluffy flapjacks smothered with butter and syrup. Even the cougar he'd noticed before looked less like he was snarling down at the diners and more like he might be licking his chops.

Riordan and Clump made for good company at the table. They knew that the time for talking was after a man filled his stomach. They ate in companionable silence until they'd done justice to the food. For the first time, Mike didn't pepper them with questions; he was saving those for his meeting with Granger later that morning.

Mike was also loathe to lose the newfound camaraderie of his logging team. These men moved from working at his side to backing him last night. Mike had no doubts they would've fought alongside him if needed, the sort of friendship usually forged by years. How could he explain that he wouldn't be working with them much longer?

"I'm going to borrow Mike for a bit." Granger clapped a hand on his shoulder and addressed Bear. "He'll join you at the worksite."

With that, Mike didn't need to explain anything. Bear nodded, got up, and made his way out the door. Clump followed, one of the last of the men trickling into the bright sunlight of a workday. In almost no time at all, Mike and Granger sat alone in the diner.

"There've been a few changes since I arranged this meeting. You've already spoken with Miss Higgins, so you know the bind she's in." Granger poured a cup of coffee and eyed Mike through the steam. "And since I've spoken with Miss Higgins, I know about your son."

It seemed to Mike that the room shifted. Everything around him came into sharper focus. In his conversation with Miss Higgins, he'd revealed his vulnerability because requesting her assistance in return for his own made for an even trade. Now Mike needed Granger's agreement to finalize the bargain—a different dynamic.

Alert but not allowing himself to be anxious, Mike waited. He waited while Granger took a few slugs of coffee. He waited and fought off thoughts about what the man before him might want. He waited until Granger realized he'd go right on waiting for however long it took for the other man to explain what he wanted.

"Dunstan does the same thing." Granger scratched his jaw. "Waits out a conversation so the other man spills his guts."

Mike raised a brow and drank more coffee to hide his grin. He could be compared to far worse than a man like Dunstan. The hunter didn't seem to speak much, but he commanded respect when he did.

"Most men would've told me about their boy, I expect. Tried to convince me what a good lad he is and how he wouldn't cause any trouble." Granger tilted his head. "Why aren't you convincing me?"

"I don't like it when people go on and on about their progeny, so I try not to inflict my parental pride on others." Mike saw the smile but couldn't relax yet. "Ask questions. I'll answer them."

"Why didn't you mention the boy when you first got here?"

"When would I have worked it into the conversation?" Mike shook his head. "From where I stand, Hope Falls sets a fast pace."

"From where I stand, you don't have trouble keeping up. When you aren't already a step or two behind, that is." Granger pulled a folded newspaper from his pocket and laid it on the table. "You're the only man in town who hasn't read this—one of very few who didn't find their way to Hope Falls because of it." He pushed the paper to the middle of the table, but kept it anchored beneath his hand.

"I was warned this is a strange place, but I'm not sure I follow what you mean." Mike had never held a more convoluted conversation in his life. They were no longer talking about him helping Miss Higgins or determining whether or not Luke was welcome. Mike's fingers itched to snatch the paper and make sense of things.

"This paper holds an unexpected answer to some of your

questions about the way we do things," Granger advised. "But since it didn't bring you all the way out here, I want to know what did."

In spite of the gallons of coffee Mike downed that morning, his mouth went dry. He'd told Granger to ask his questions, and now he was honor bound to answer. A couple of dry swallows bought him time.

"You read the telegram." He croaked out the most honest answer he could give. "I needed work, and I was told I'd find it here."

"A man with your skill set can, if you'll forgive the pun, make a place for himself just about anywhere." Granger flattened his palm against the paper and leaned forward. "It makes me wonder why you'd decide to raise a child near the dangers of a new sawmill."

"Boys can find danger wherever they're raised," Mike hedged. "Hope Falls seems as good a place as any—and better than most."

"I'm not saying it's not a good place to find yourself—but I'd be a fool if I didn't know it's a better place to *lose* yourself." The steely glint in his gaze belied his wordplay. "So why are you here?"

"For Luke." That gallon of coffee sloshed bitterly in Mike's stomach. He'd prepared to answer a few questions, but he hadn't reckoned on Granger's astute appraisal of his situation. He made his message clear: either trot out an explanation or ride out of town.

"Most would say I married above myself." Mike forbore to mention that he didn't agree with the general consensus about his bride. "Leticia was an only child. Now that she passed on, my in-laws demanded they be allowed to raise their only grandson."

"And you won't fork him over." It wasn't a question, though Granger looked curious. "I can understand that. What I don't understand is why your in-laws thought they could force the issue."

Again, Granger didn't ask. Mike still answered. "They can't."

"They shouldn't," he corrected. "But I've more than my fair share of experience with wealthy flea-brains who think money gets them whatever they want." Granger paused. "It usually does."

"I know." Mike sucked in a breath. "You're right about the reason I chose to come here. I'm doing my best to get us lost."

"Don't let anybody else find out." Granger took his hand away from the paper. "Go ahead and read it. You'll find it interesting, but I don't think it'll make you change your mind about staying."

"It won't." His relief was so intense, he didn't grab the paper. Mike realized his mistake when Granger picked it up again.

"Probably shouldn't say this. . ." The other man tapped the paper against his palm as though deciding whether or not to pass it over. In the end, he shoved it toward Mike. "But I'm saying it anyway. Don't let this change your mind about Miss Higgins either."

"What?" Mike turned around so fast he worked out a kink in his neck that'd been pestering him since yesterday. It was just in time to see Granger slap his hat on his head and walk through the door.

"What does this have to do with Miss Higgins?" Knowing there was no one to hear him ask, he muttered the question and started scanning the newsprint. The first page ran an article about trains, but a quick read turned up nothing out of the ordinary. On the other side, columns of classifieds paraded up and down, jostling against each other all the way across the page. Mike turned back to the first page to make sure he hadn't missed anything important. *Nope.*

A prickle of unease raised the hairs on the back of his neck. Mike carefully turned the thin paper over again, looking closer at the jumble of advertisements. A single ad took up more space than any three, demanding attention from the bottom third of the page.

> *Wanted:*
> *3 men, ages 24–35.*
> *Must be God-fearing, healthy, hardworking single men*
> *with minimum of 3 years logging experience.*
> *Object: Marriage and joint ownership of sawmill.*
> *Reply to the Hope Falls, Colorado, postmaster by May 17.*

Mike read the thing through three times before laying it back atop the table. Only then did he realize he'd been gripping the news sheet hard enough to poke his thumb clear through the page. He propped his feet against the bench across from him and leaned his head against the wall, trying to take in the irony of his situation.

Trying to outrun a past where he'd married for money, Mike stumbled upon the only town in all of history where the women were trying to hire husbands. It was his own mistake, multiplied by three and magnified by the men who came to "apply" for the position. All his questions, the unexplained oddities of Hope Falls, and the bits and pieces he'd seen firsthand joined together with what he'd read.

Now he understood why the men answered to the women. It explained why men worked for room and board to start. It even made sense that they began to offer wages when, as one man put it, there was only one more "girl up for grabs." The odds of winning a wife had changed. After all, Granger claimed Miss Thompson, and then Miss Lyman chose Dunstan, leaving only the youngest of the three without a fiancé. The poor girl was about to be deluged with would-be suitors.

The only thing the ad didn't explain was why Granger thought it would change Mike's opinion of Miss Higgins. Did he think Mike would think less of her for not joining the other three in a husband hunt?

Mike snorted. If anything, it reassured him that the woman he'd agreed to spend months working alongside wasn't a mercenary female desperate to nab a husband. It probably took great strength of character to withstand her friends' pleas and refuse to join them in this farcical scheme. How could this advertisement make him think less of Miss Naomi Higgins? *If anything*, Mike decided as he shoved the distasteful thing deep in his pocket, *I admire her more than ever.*

TWENTY

*H*e *thinks I'm pretty.* No matter how Naomi tried to push the inane thought aside, it kept bubbling to the surface of her thoughts. All day yesterday, like a tune she couldn't get out of her mind, the phrase hummed in her head. *Mr. Strode thinks I'm pretty. Me. . .pretty!*

It was distracting. It made her smile. It would have been downright mortifying if anyone suspected her of such foolishness. Of course, no one caught on. Naomi was far too sensible for such girlish foibles. At least that's what she sternly reminded herself when she woke up with the chipper refrain ringing in her ears.

Unfortunately, Naomi found her own reprimands surprisingly ineffective. It was, to say the least, disconcerting to be ignored by one's own self. Though it did explain why Lacey found it so easy to disregard Naomi's sage advice—there were things a woman's heart found far more interesting than plain, old-fashioned common sense!

And Mr. Michael Strode is one of them. Little wonder she'd found the notion of working with him so unsettling; those qualms were the last vestiges of her instinct for self-preservation. They must have been the last. They'd gone quiet since the moment Mr. Strode told her, in a roundabout way, that he found her attractive.

Naomi knew how dangerous this was. She knew she shouldn't entertain the hope, not even for the briefest moment, that Mr. Strode might be interested in a more permanent sort of partnership. Because even if he indicated interest, Naomi couldn't allow things to progress beyond mutual regard. Newly widowed, Mr. Strode was trying to build a new life for himself and his son. *Far too fine a man*, Naomi lectured herself, *to overlook my checkered past.*

By the time she'd gotten through breakfast, she'd worked very hard to talk sense into herself. It didn't take Naomi long to figure out that she'd fixated on the carpenter as an appealing alternative to her real suitors. With that sobering realization, she managed to replace the happy little "he thinks I'm pretty" hum with a "he deserves better" refrain. It sounded as sprightly as a dirge.

"Granger tells me you're ready to get started." A deep voice broke through the plodding rhythm of her new favorite dirge.

"If there's nothing to interfere." Naomi made it a point to sound brisk and businesslike, but couldn't help returning his smile.

"It's all been arranged on this end," he assured her. "I didn't bring my toolbox, but I can fetch it in a jiffy if it's needed."

Naomi gave a rueful shake of her head. "I'm afraid things aren't nearly so neatly arranged on my end. The furthest I've planned is to set up a work space. Beyond that, I'll need to do some digging to find my own materials so we can create a scale for the project."

"We get a workshop?" Mr. Strode's eyes sparkled like a child's who spied a bulging Christmas stocking with his name. "Lead on."

"First, you'll need to lower your expectations." She couldn't help but laugh, picturing his reaction to what lay ahead. With that, she took him to the short row of houses behind the diner, pausing at the threshold of the second building. "This is where we'll work."

The door swung open to reveal a modest-sized room adorned with a block table, two chairs, and a questionable-looking old pipe stove. The dirt floor had been hard packed by the miners who'd lived there and would be fairly easy to sweep clean. Three windows, covered with cloth to keep out the elements, let in plenty of light.

"Strong light," Mr. Strode approved, making a quick circuit around the space. "We'll need another two tables—work space for each of us and a display station for completed or in-progress pieces. If none are available, I can put a pair together this afternoon."

"That won't be necessary." Naomi felt her shoulders relax and realized she'd been anxious for his approval. "Tables I can provide, but we're going to have to sort through some things before we clear them off. Things have been so busy since we got here. Anything we didn't immediately need got shoved into storage."

"It doesn't take long to clear a table," he assured her in the confident voice of a man who hasn't seen the task ahead of him. After Naomi opened the house next door, he revised his opinion.

A low whistle escaped Mr. Strode. "I believe I spoke too soon."

"How could you know?" Naomi asked, torn between amusement and resignation as they stood on the threshold. Boxes and bags, crates and trunks, luggage of all sizes crowded from floor to rafters, with a few pieces of furniture thrown in to keep things interesting. "Clearing off a table is one thing, but I didn't know how to explain that we'd have to clear out a house to get to the tables first."

"I see." Mr. Strode looked up, looked down, ducked his head through the door, and swiftly pulled it back. "Not to criticize the plan, but it would be less hassle for me to build the tables."

Naomi shuffled closer to the door and glanced at the chaos within. Like the sun, it was best seen in glimpses. Otherwise its full power made a person close their eyes and turn away. Even in small doses, it was overwhelming to take in the sheer mass within.

"It's worse than I remembered," she admitted. For a fleeting moment, she wondered whether Lacey had managed to organize the colossal mess of the mercantile by ferrying merchandise here. But another quick glimpse revealed nothing from the storeroom. "When we were packing back in Charleston, everything seemed important. If you left something behind, it might take weeks to order a replacement."

"So instead you borrowed a page from Noah and brought two?"

"No." The giggle escaped before Naomi could even try to stop it, but it erased Mr. Strode's dawning chagrin at his outspokenness. "Between the four of us, we probably brought along a few spares."

"When you put it that way,"—he braved the threshold and squeezed inside—"it doesn't seem so bad, for four women."

"Er. . ." Naomi wondered if discretion wasn't the best course of action but decided in favor of full disclosure—some of her things might have been misplaced, and she didn't want to go through explanations. "All things being equal, how about two out of four?"

He eyed her incredulously. "You mean to say there's *more?*"

"The next house." Naomi gestured to the right, where an almost identical structure stood. Doors shut, it looked unprepossessing.

"The whole house? Another like this?" He sounded faintly awed, but Naomi found it encouraging that he didn't just sound faint. The prospect of going through everything made her think longingly of a nap. How must he feel, faced with the task of hauling it all out?

"We made some attempt to categorize things," she soothed. "So we won't tackle the second house. My supplies should all be here."

"So we're going in after more than just the tables." Mr. Strode squared his shoulders and eyed the Herculean challenge ahead. "I'll haul out whatever you want, so long as you don't expect me to open things up. It wouldn't be right to go through ladies' luggage."

"That's fine, since I'm not even sure what I'll find!"

Five hours and countless boxes later, Mike began to suspect this was retribution for his thoughts on how building a dollhouse would be easier on his back. At the start, he figured it looked like there were more things crammed inside than there really were because the eye couldn't focus on individual pieces. He'd been wrong.

The farther he burrowed into Miss Higgins's storage, the more he marveled at how much a one-room structure could hold. He'd practically built a fort out of the pieces she immediately rejected— and not the size fort he'd hammered together for Luke back home. The saving grace of that pile was Miss Higgins's offhand remark that she needn't look through them—they all belonged to Miss Lyman.

If Mike had to slap a ratio on it, he'd say that two-thirds of the contents of the house went to the fort. In comparison, the heaps surrounding Miss Higgins seemed downright reasonable—especially since they owed most of their bulk to two tables and a small shelf.

"Why don't I tote these over to the workshop and out of your way?" Mike gestured toward the shelf and one of the tables. The other table made itself useful as a type of sorting station.

"Yes, let's do that." She snapped shut the satchel she'd been looking through and added it to the heap nearest Miss Lyman's fort. "If you'll take the table, I'll get the shelf—it's not heavy."

"Spruce is surprisingly light," Mike agreed. In general, he wouldn't want a woman lifting any furniture, but he was learning that the women of Hope Falls were a determined and capable breed. He'd save his protests in case she tried to move something heavy.

"Is that why?" She slid her hands beneath a shelf and lifted without much effort. "It's surprisingly sturdy without being dense."

"Yep." He shouldered the door open and set down the table, unable to hold the door open for her if she went through first. "You'll find a lot of crates, ladders, and ship masts made from it."

"I never knew." She tucked the shelf into a corner and smoothed her apron. "As part owner in a prospective sawmill, I suppose I'll need to brush up on the types of wood and what they're used for."

"Start with the softwoods," he suggested. "Pine, spruce, fir, and even cedar grow hereabouts, and that's what you'll be milling."

It was a novel experience, talking business with a woman. Or rather, talking business with an *interested* woman. Mike thought of all the times he'd tried to share something of his craft with Leticia. She waved him away, refusing to hear about "trade." Wasn't it enough that she allowed Luke to come home covered in sawdust?

"They're called softwood?" Miss Higgins's astonished query amused him. "All things considered, isn't that a bit of a misnomer?"

He shrugged. "It's a classification based on the tree itself. Evergreens are generally less dense than trees that shed their leaves. They grow faster, so the layers aren't as compacted."

"How fascinating." Eyes alight with interest, *she* was fascinating. "If you don't mind, I'd like to learn more as we work."

"It would be my pleasure." Mike couldn't remember a time when he meant it more. "I'm not the sort who requires silence to work."

"But you do require sustenance." Miss Higgins squinted at the sky when they exited the building. "It looks about time for lunch."

"I'll never turn down a good meal." Mike happily followed her to the diner, where a medley of smells made his mouth water.

"Oh!" Miss Higgins held up a finger and backed toward the door. "I'll be right back. I forgot something!" With that, she was gone.

"Strode." Until Dunstan's greeting, Mike didn't notice him. Like any good hunter, he had a way of blending into the shadows.

"Dunstan." Mike joined him, taking a seat nearest the swinging kitchen doors. He avoided the man's injured side, where Decoy hunched beneath the table. "How goes it?"

"I'm trussed tighter than a turkey," he grunted. They lapsed into companionable silence for a moment before Dunstan added, "Don't remember if I thanked you for helping haul me out of the mine."

"Don't mention it." Mike watched as the other man dug around in his pocket and pulled out a new knife sheath of tooled leather. Mike accepted the gift with a nod of recognition but no words. Neither one of them wanted to talk about what happened to his old one.

Miss Higgins bustled back in, clutching a grubby lump of cloth trailing a mangled set of ribbons. She paused for a moment to look around the room, apparently satisfied to see no one but the men. Then her eyes widened—she'd caught sight of the massive wolfhound curled up under the table.

"Does Evie know he's here?" Her murmur scarcely made it across the room.

"Yep. Miss Thompson says he's earned a place—just not at mealtimes." Dunstan reached down to scratch between Decoy's ears. "And not in the kitchen. The other women are in there now."

Mike thought he heard her mumble "excellent" beneath her breath as she crossed the room and came to a halt in front of the mounted cougar. He watched as she gave the cat a considering glance, set down her bedraggled bundle, and began tugging at one of the benches. Before Mike could offer to help, she'd worked the bench closer to the wall and climbed up. She looked quite pleased with herself until she realized she couldn't reach the thing she'd set on the table.

"It's the hat." Dunstan sounded as though he was trying to hold back his laughter—probably because it made his ribs hurt.

"Yes it is." Naomi held a finger to her lips, signaling him to hush. She wanted to get things in place before Lacey decided to investigate. Unfortunately she'd hit a snag; now that she could reach the cougar, Naomi couldn't stretch far enough to get the hat!

"It's a hat?" Mr. Strode sounded as though he had doubts about that, but Naomi forgave him since he was kind enough to pass it up. He'd see that it was a hat as soon as she got the thing situated.

Only now that she had her hat in hand, so to speak, she couldn't decide quite how to place it. Too far back and it wouldn't make enough of an impact, but the ears presented another problem entirely. No matter how she tried, Naomi couldn't further squish the already-squashed accessory to fit between the cougar's ears. Nor would it balance atop the furry tufts. The more Naomi failed, the more she imagined the great cat was laughing at her paltry efforts.

Until she pulled a packet of hairpins from her apron pocket. Jabbing hairpins into place, Naomi discovered, was far easier when the subject of the primping couldn't feel anything. In almost no time at all, she'd anchored the hat at a jaunty angle, with one ear artistically uncovered. As a finishing touch, she tied a large bow beneath its hairy chin. Then she hopped down to survey the results.

"Please forgive my earlier skepticism," Mr. Strode apologized. "I failed to consider your superior knowledge of feminine frippery."

"Obviously." Naomi swallowed a snigger at the sight. Lacey's prized pink hat, now squashed and stained almost beyond recognition, listed drunkenly atop the snarling beast. Tattered ribbons dangled limply over one eye to tangle in its whiskers. It was perfect—especially since the cougar faced across from the HATS OFF TO THE CHEF sign

Evie carted clear from Charleston.

"I suspect there's a good reason Dunstan's got the giggles?"

"Sure is." Dunstan stopped chuckling. "But I don't giggle."

"Who has the giggles?" Lacey popped through the swinging kitchen doors, caught sight of the newly adorned cougar, and froze. Slowly, as if seeking something lost, she smoothed back her hair. "My hat. . ." She turned to Dunstan to demand, "You went back for it?"

"Later that night." Suddenly the hunter looked uncomfortable. "You tried so hard to retrieve it, and then you said that thing about how a gentleman would pick it up. . .so I went and picked it up."

"Why didn't you tell me?" Lacey's mushy, in-love-with-a-man-who-saved-my-hat expression changed. "Why didn't you give it back?"

"I couldn't very well waltz up to you and present the thing on a silver platter, so I shoved it in one of those rooms you had filled with stuff." Defensive and sheepish, Dunstan glowered. "You were bound and determined to run me out of Hope Falls. Remember?"

"What's all the commotion in here?" Evie and Cora joined them. Cora gasped. "What on earth have you done to that poor cougar?"

"Don't look at me." Lacey held her hands up. "I just shot it."

"I found the hat when Mr. Strode and I started sorting through luggage, trying to unearth my supplies." Naomi tried not to look too pleased with herself. "I wanted to display it in honor of your engagement and decided the cougar deserved to be part of it."

"Why?" Mr. Strode's baffled query reminded her that he didn't know the story behind the cougar or its significance to Lacey.

"I met Lacey when she decided to go for a walk in the woods. Alone." Dunstan threw his fiancée a pointed glance. "Granger warned me that the women needed looking after, but I didn't expect to find a cougar stalking her. It must've been the fluttering ribbons."

"Which is why I think the hat belongs right where I put it," Naomi finished. Then she thought better of it. "If Lacey agrees."

"Well. . ." Lacey's smile flickered, and she admitted, "I certainly won't ever be able to wear it again. But it was my favorite hat. I hate to see it looking so sad and frumpy—cougar notwithstanding."

"Try to stop thinking of it as a ruined hat," Evie suggested. "Instead, why don't you see it as a one-of-a-kind souvenir?"

"Of what?" Lacey's brow furrowed. "A souvenir of what?"

"Of one of the best days of your life." Naomi tried to keep the wistfulness from her tone. "The day you finally met your match."

 TWENTY-ONE

"Is this the one you've been looking for?" Mike asked after he'd brought Miss Higgins back into the storage area. To the very back, a three-foot-square crate crouched atop a lacquered cabinet.

"What do you mean, what I've been looking for?" She moved to his side, the better to see around him. "I've been looking for a lot of things today, and I've found very nearly all of—oh!" Whatever else she'd meant to say was lost in a soft exhalation of happiness.

Mike tried not to think about how much he liked hearing her go all breathy. "There's something you've been waiting for. All day yesterday and all day today you've looked up every time I've stepped through the door. You check what I'm carrying, sometimes shake your head, and almost always go right back to whatever you're sorting."

He didn't add that he liked the way she looked up, eyes alight with expectation, every time he passed through the door. He didn't tell her that what kept him hauling things out of this one-room house was the chance that any item might be the thing she hoped for. He wanted to see her face when he carried it to her. But since that mysterious item happened to be huge, heavy, and stamped on every side with the word FRAGILE, Mike settled for that sweet little sigh.

"It's the dollhouse!" She turned to him, eyes shining. "The replica of Lyman Place that I restored and furnished for Lacey."

"The one that impressed the lady so much she hired you to make another one?" Curiosity getting the better of him, Mike started looking around for the crowbar he'd barely used this whole time.

"One and the same," she confirmed. "I'll go get Granger so the two of you can transfer it to the workshop. We'll open it there."

With a swish of her skirts, she all but ran from the room, barely giving Mike enough time to dig up his missing crowbar before she returned with Granger in tow. And Miss Lyman, and the two Miss Thompsons, and a woman who looked ready to give birth any moment. Mike couldn't recall having ever seen her before, and he was pretty sure there could only be one woman in Hope Falls expecting a child.

Actually, until two minutes ago, he'd been fairly sure there were no women in Hope Falls who were expecting a child. So maybe, Mike decided, he needed to stop making assumptions and get to his side of the crate. Granger already stationed himself on the far end.

Once in position, Mike waited until Miss Higgins herded the rest of the women outside and out of the way. Then he and Granger lifted the crate—which wasn't as heavy as Mike first thought, but unwieldy enough to require two men—and half shuffled, half walked it over to the workshop next door. They hadn't set it down before Miss Higgins bustled in, brandishing his crowbar and directing them to set the crate atop a console table she'd tucked into the far corner.

"Thank you." Mike snagged the crowbar when she turned to speak with one of the women currently congregating near the entrance.

In a few minutes, he removed the top panel and pried off the front piece to reveal. . .cotton batting. With him supporting the house from the bottom, Granger eased what remained of the crate to the floor. Mike offered Miss Higgins his knife when she drew close, rewarded for his efforts when her fingers brushed against his.

After a few slight tugs to pull the packing away, she began slicing open the cotton, letting it fall like snow and drape around the house. When she stood back, she revealed an astonishing replica of a Georgian brick home, complete with two faux marble pillars bracing the architrave above the door. From dormer window to gable to mullioned windows, they'd executed every detail impeccably.

"Oh." Miss Lyman's hand went to her throat. "Do you know I'd forgotten how beautiful Lyman Place is? How many memories it held. . ."

"Memories can be kept forever, but you can only live in one place at a time." Miss Thompson gave her a quick hug. "Better to choose the people we love than hold on to a place we once lived."

"You're so blessed you could bring Lyman Place with you!" The younger Miss Thompson brought the focus back to the dollhouse.

"Yes." Miss Lyman straightened her shoulders and moved toward the table. She touched the side of the structure, and with a little pressure, it turned on the table. "My home away from home. I'm so glad I didn't let you talk me out of bringing this, Naomi!"

"What?" Mike tore his gaze away from the model, which he surmised revolved on a sort of broad turntable, to stare at Miss Higgins. The lovingly crafted details evident on the exterior of the house would surely pale in comparison to the loving attention she'd lavished on the rooms within. The idea that someone would willingly abandon such a masterwork, an unquestionable labor of love, boggled his mind. He had to know. . . . "Why would you ever leave this behind?"

"How quickly you forget the mountain you moved to reach this crate! With so much to oversee already, I didn't want Lacey to bring along something so large and difficult simply to spare my feelings."

Her feelings were reason enough, but Mike didn't care what motivated Miss Lyman to bring the thing. He was just glad that she had. At that point, the women clustered around the table, pulling tiny wooden boxes lined with more cotton out of every single room. Within the boxes, Mike saw, lay the furniture and frilly bits females used to cover perfectly good hardwood floors, mantels, and walls. Feminine exclamations of delight accompanied the excavation of each room's box, driving Mike back to the storage next door.

On his way he noticed that Granger was nowhere in sight. No fool, the head of the logging operation skedaddled once he finished the heavy lifting. That left Mike with nothing but time on his hands and little left to go through. Most of the room had been emptied—he'd carted Miss Lyman's possessions to a separate building and carefully kept everything Miss Higgins already went through off to one side. By now there wasn't much left, aside from the lacquered cabinet that he'd found supporting the dollhouse.

It sat on squat little cabriole legs, oddly fashioned of mahogany inlaid with blond oak—an uncommon combination, since blond oak didn't echo the rich red tone of the mahogany. Then, too, the broad oval shape of the piece was perplexing. Square, rectangular, or even circular tables and cabinets were all common enough, but doors to fit an oval piece were difficult to execute evenly.

Upon closer examination, he saw that the design worked onto the top surface was a fancifully elaborate letter *N. For Naomi*. Mike traced it with his fingertips, more intrigued than ever now that he knew it didn't belong to Miss Lyman. Custom pieces like this became costly, and he wondered whether she'd commissioned the unique design or if someone special presented it to her as a gift.

Tiny golden hinges, expertly recessed along the back, tattled that the top lid lifted. Mike stopped tracing the letter, dropping his hands to run beneath the edge. There he found a tiny button. He pressed it before he could talk sense into himself, hearing the slight click of a released clasp before the lid angled upward.

A recessed shelf occupied the middle of the piece, but the design of the doors caught his attention. They were oval because they'd been designed to loosely bracket a chest of drawers. When he opened the doors, small spikes with slight bends at the tips thrust from each side. Tightly wound spools of sturdy thread and colorful embroidery floss, neatly ordered by shade, stood at attention beside more incongruous windings of wire, fishing line, and even twine.

Having identified the piece as a sewing cabinet, Mike wasn't surprised to see a small pair of silver scissors, a magnifying glass, and a matching slender tube for needles. Nor did the various yarn hooks and such give him pause. But there, neatly laid along the side, sat something very familiar—a combination tool set.

Mike knew what he'd find if he opened the case: a small-grade chisel, gouge, screwdriver, tack puller, gimlet, scratch awl, and brad awls in four different sizes—all hand-forged steel and all interchangeable for use with the included hardwood handle. Impressed with the quality and sure that the size would suit a young boy, he'd ordered one for Luke from the Montgomery Ward catalog a year ago.

Mike quietly closed the doors and lid of Naomi's workbox. His discoveries eradicated any doubts that this dollhouse was a whim, the sort of poorly planned project sure to end in disaster. Miss Higgins knew full well the complexities ahead, and she'd undertaken the challenge with the confidence of an experienced craftsman.

Craftswoman, Mike corrected. *One I'll enjoy working alongside.*

"Do you think he'll like it?" Naomi scrutinized the parlor, reaching in to nudge one of the mantel candlesticks a smidge farther inward. "I know men don't usually think much of dolls and dollhouses, but we're going to be putting in long hours working on the next one."

While she didn't expect Mr. Strode to share her enthusiasm for all things miniscule and perfectly ordered, Naomi did hope he would find the work interesting. Nothing put a damper on her enjoyment more quickly than someone who didn't savor the process of creating the pieces or worked as though rushing through an unpleasant task.

"What's not to like?" Cora looked up from where she sat on the floor, cross-legged, the box for the ballroom half unpacked amid the cushion of her carefully smoothed skirts. "It's amazing!"

"I wish I had these full-sized!" Arla exclaimed. At some point, Granger had brought in a small rocking chair for Arla to sit comfortably amid them. She'd pulled it up to a table and was gingerly unwrapping the pieces that belonged to the nursery. Arla held up a wicker bassinet tiny enough to rock in the center of her open palm. "However did you make this, Naomi? It must have taken you days!"

Naomi laughed and admitted, "I cheated. It's a regular cradle made out of sandalwood with braided broom straws glued on top and painted. To tell the truth, it went quickly once I learned the straw bent more easily if I soaked it overnight in a bucket of water."

"Clever." Evie turned the house slightly so she could place the baking table in the center of the kitchen, offset so it didn't block the stove and scrub sink already situated against the back wall. She let out a little squeak of pleasure as she unwrapped the next bundle. Tiny rounds of cheese, braided loaves of bread, and a cone of sugar—complete with tiny wire tongs—spilled into her hand.

"You thought of everything!" From Evie, this was the highest compliment any kitchen could receive. "When you've finished your work for Mrs. Smythe, I might have to beg you to make me one of these model kitchens. I'd keep it on my shelves for inspiration!"

"I'd be honored." The thought that another project might follow this gave Naomi a surge of energy. There was something galvanizing about the idea that she could keep doing what she loved.

"We're the ones who should be honored." Lacey lifted the lid to the small hope chest she'd slipped against the end of a canopy bed. She smiled, tugging out a set of tiny washcloths for the washstand. "Isn't it awful, the way we become used to the blessings we're given and stop seeing them? Honestly, Naomi, it's as though years of familiarity blinded me to how special you made this Lyman Place."

"Working on this was a gift to myself as much as a present for you," Naomi confided. "I would have gone mad if I didn't find a way to keep myself busy!" Indeed, losing herself in a thousand tiny details kept her from losing herself in a quagmire of self-loathing and sorrow. When she felt powerless to fix the mistakes she'd made, Naomi found comfort in the tiny world she kept in perfect order.

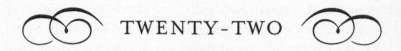

TWENTY-TWO

Today Braden would regain control of where he went and how he chose to spend his days. Just as soon as Doc stopped dilly-farting around.

"You want to run and get a protractor, Doc?" Braden asked after the doctor checked and rechecked his progress. He'd flexed his leg and brought it back one time too many, and Braden knew he couldn't conceal his discomfort for another round. *Time to move things along.*

Three months after the first mine collapse, and more than a week since the second, Braden finally reached the doctor-required forty-five-degree angle. He'd earned the right to get out of bed and into his wheeled chair—and the sooner, the better. He needed to gain proficiency in using the device. By the time the targets of his trap wandered into Hope Falls, Braden wanted to wheel like the wind.

"Congratulations, Mr. Lyman." Doc adjusted his spectacles and consulted his chart once again. "You have regained enough range of motion to progress to the wheeled chair. We'll attempt it tomorrow."

"Today." Braden couldn't wait another minute, much less a day.

"Tomorrow, Mr. Lyman." Doc eyed him with obvious disapproval.

"Listen." Braden grabbed the edge of his bed to keep from throwing the medical chart out the window. "We made a deal. You said I could get out of this bed once I bent my knee forty-five degrees."

"It would be best to be certain you can do so consistently. One more day gives me the assurance that you haven't overexerted your knee this morning in a misguided attempt to reach your goal." He tapped the chart. "Another day's rest won't do you any harm."

"Yes it will." Braden clamped his hand on the chart, trapping Doc's pencil and demanding his attention. "I've rested for more than three months. That's more than a hundred days of sitting in the same bed, staring at the same three walls, and slowly going stir-crazy. I met your criteria; I've earned the chance to leave this room. *Now.*"

Doc cleared his throat and tugged at his precious chart. When he realized Braden had no intention of letting go, he sighed. "Your determination is evident. I'll bring in the wheeled chair then."

The man staggered back when Braden released the chart then scurried from the room. Whether or not he'd return remained to be seen, but Braden's fears faded when he heard rolling wheels nearby.

Doc parked the contraption and poked his head through the door.

"Just a moment—the first attempt is always tricky. I'll need to find someone who can assist you while I hold the chair in place." He vanished almost before he finished, before Braden could protest.

He stared at the wicker chair, outfitted with wheels and a foot-rest, and groaned in frustration. So close. . .and he couldn't do a thing about it unless he wanted Doc to find him facedown on the floor. Braden considered trying anyway but decided that the foolishness of the maneuver might make Doc rescind his approval.

"Good morning." The new carpenter strolled into the room.

"Where's Granger?" Braden demanded. He would have settled for Dunstan if he hadn't been nursing his cracked ribs, but Braden recoiled at the idea of this stranger seeing him at his weakest. This was supposed to be a moment of triumph, not more humiliation!

"He just finished with the Bible reading, and now he's praying with a few of the men," the unsuitable replacement explained. "If you prefer, I'll go back and let him know you're waiting on him."

It's Sunday? Braden hadn't realized it, but that made today an even better choice. *The workers won't be going into the forest. I'll be able to spend the day with the whole town, same as any other man.*

"I can assure you,"—Doc took advantage of the short pause,

obviously still peeved over Braden's abuse of his medical chart—"that Mr. Lyman won't wish to wait a second longer than he has to."

"If it's all the same to you, Doc, I'd rather hear Mr. Lyman's decisions from Mr. Lyman himself." The carpenter crossed his arms—arms that were strong enough to get the job done. "He may not be back on his feet yet, but it's my understanding he still runs this town."

Good man, that new carpenter I hired. Doc looks like he swallowed a bullfrog. He couldn't resist rubbing salt in the wound.

"Doc's right—no sense in waiting." Braden scooted his rear as close to the edge of the bed as possible without falling off then angled slightly so he could slide into the chair. "Mr. ...."

"Strode." The carpenter crossed the room and stood beside the bed.

"Right. Mr. Strode here can help as well as anyone." Braden gave a tight smile to the carpenter and a scowl to Doc, who hadn't taken the hint. "If you'll just move the chair into position?"

Begrudging but blessedly silent, Doc decided to cooperate. He maneuvered it through the doorway without any difficulty, passing the first hurdle. If the contraption hadn't fit, Braden didn't know whether his newfound approval of the carpenter would extend that far. Having a man help brace him as Braden slid into a chair was one thing; having a man carry him to it was a beast of another color.

Doc nudged the chair right up alongside the bed and employed the locking mechanism to keep the wheels from rolling, but the next step proved more difficult. When facing him, the footrest's extended "comfort design" proved too extended for Braden to reach the seat.

With the chair sideways, he could place his legs in the vehicle, but the armrests stopped him from sliding into the chair. Braden could grasp the far armrest, but the angle was too awkward to provide any stability. In the end, Braden had no choice but to allow Mr. Strode to help lift him into the chair while Doc held it steady—locking wheels or no, the thing could still tip over.

By the time they'd finished, Braden was breathing hard. He was unaccustomed to the exertion—his upper body weak from lack of use. The pain streaking from his overworked knee didn't help matters. Inspecting his new conveyance helped mask his weakness. Braden kept his head bent, peering at the footrest, the wheels, and even the braking mechanism until he could look the other men in the face.

"It's more comfortable than I expected." Braden found he particularly liked the way the back of the chair rose so high. When he wasn't in motion, he'd be able to lean back and relax. Outside.

"Press here to unlock the brake," Doc instructed. "But before you do, put your hands on the outer rim of the wheel and tell me whether it will be awkward for you to push forward. We can always add pillows to your seat and raise you an inch or two higher."

"Let's see." Braden loosely grasped the outer rim, sliding his hands forward and deciding that freedom felt like cool metal—a sharp contrast to overly warm cotton sheets. He pulled his arms back, placed his hands, and tried again. "I'm not scrunching up to grab the wheels, and it's not a reach either, so it fits right."

"Good." Doc demonstrated again how to set the brake, had Braden release it, reengage the mechanism, and release it again before he proclaimed himself satisfied. "Now, a few things before you begin."

"A few things?" Braden all but gaped at the man in disbelief. "Maybe you haven't noticed, Doc, but I've gone through a few things to put me in that bed, then a few more to work my way back out of it. A few more and I doubt I'll ever make it through the door!"

He let his exasperation show but kept things light. No way he'd let his deepest fears spring to life in front of an audience. They did enough damage where they were, whispering in the dark. *You'll never be whole. . .never be the man you were. . .never walk again. . .*

"Your impatience fails to impress me." Doc sounded full of bravado, but he made sure to keep the chart far from Braden's reach.

"Over three months since I've been out of this room. That's plenty patient." Braden gripped the wheels and pulled back, trying to gain room enough to angle past the doctor. One good shove and—

Nothing.

While he'd been plotting, Doc nudged a wooden wedge beneath the nearest wheel, effectively ending any forward motion. Nor could Braden reverse enough to maneuver around the blockage—his back was pressed against the bed. Even if his arms reached far enough to remove the object, he'd most likely tip himself over and wind up on the ground, helpless as a turtle turned on its shell.

"In light of your earlier. . ."—Doc took a moment to choose a descriptor—"*vehemence*, I suspected the doorstop might be needed."

Wings effectively clipped, Braden gritted his teeth and waited. He noticed that the carpenter had the good sense to make himself scarce. Braden wished he could do the same thing but would have to settle for not being further humiliated in front of an audience.

"As you've already begun to discover, you will need to rebuild your strength. This is the case not only for your legs but for your core, your back, and your arms." Doc gave him the hairy eye until Braden nodded. Then he kept going. "The effort required to maintain an upright position will be greater than you anticipate. The muscle and movement needed to propel the device will further fatigue you."

"I'm overwhelmed by all this encouragement," Braden quipped.

"You will rebuild your strength, but gradually. Thus, your initial forays will be brief." Doc held up a hand, forestalling protests. "This may be extended if you allow someone to assist you."

"You mean let someone push me like a babe in a pram?" Braden couldn't hide his contempt. *First the apron strings, now this.*

"Your choice, Mr. Lyman." Doc removed the doorstop. "Mr. Strode thought of laying planks of wood over the doorsteps so you can come and go more freely. I will check on you in two hours."

Braden didn't ask any more questions. He pushed himself straight through the door and took some time in the hallway to gauge how best to move. Swift, short pushes gave more speed but took more energy. Longer, smoother motions allowed for more control with less effort. Stopping was a matter of catching the wheels and pulling back, and this, too, was more effective with longer pushes.

When Braden was satisfied he wouldn't make a fool of himself with the town watching, he rolled onto the porch. There he stopped, wanting to imprint the moment in his memory. The sun hung low enough for its rays to reach down and warm the porch. Braden tilted his head into a welcoming breeze. It brushed across his face, cool as a mountain stream, crisp as pine needles, and whispering of freedom.

TWENTY-THREE

T rapped. No two ways about it. Nor three, or four, or five. Five men surrounded her when Naomi tried to sneak off to the workshop after breakfast. Five men who all wanted the pleasure of taking her for a walk. Five very determined men, none of whom would give way to the next, and none of whom broke ranks to let her escape—er, pass by.

Honestly, the one man Naomi wanted to speak with was just about the only man who didn't insist on the pleasure of her company. It was enough to make a woman disgruntled—especially since she knew, in all fairness, that this was a mess of her own making. This wasn't the first time Naomi had cause to regret placing the infamous ad, and she harbored an unpleasant suspicion it wouldn't be the last.

"Good weather for walking." Clump had headed her off at the door. If he weren't such a sweet, earnest fellow, Naomi might have blamed him for her current predicament. After all, he'd stood in the doorway—*still* stood in the doorway—effectively ending her exit.

"I'd be pleased to act as your escort." Gent seized Clump's opening to insert himself into the conversation. Unfortunately Gent's exuberance for good manners got the best of them all. His flourishing bow caught the attention of every man in Hope Falls.

So three more had decided to swoop in, cutting off Naomi's alternate route. Until that point, she'd been steadily edging back along the wall, hoping to sidle straight back to the kitchen. None of the men would dare follow her there. Evie laid down the law as soon as they arrived: any trespassers forfeited their next meal.

"I was askin' her!" Clump's indignation was almost comical.

"Brevity is the soul of wit." Gent wasn't apologetic.

The youngest lumberman, Bobsley, tossed Naomi a grin. "Looks like you'll have your choice of company this morning, Miss Higgins."

"Some choices are better than others," interjected Craig Williams, a loudmouthed team leader who'd arrogantly tried to claim Evie from his first day in town. Evie's acceptance of Granger didn't humble the man; he merely turned his unwelcome attentions on Lacey.

"And why are you thinkin' you're one of her choices, Williams?" Bear Riordan raised one impressively furry red eyebrow, and Naomi wondered if he hadn't joined them to keep an eye on the adversarial Williams. Despite his intimidating size—or perhaps because of it—Bear's well-intentioned interference helped keep things peaceful.

"Yeah!" Bobsley, whose slight build was an asset to high climbing but didn't lend itself well to confrontation, allied himself with Bear. "You used up your chances on the other two!"

Privately, Naomi agreed. Each man chose two of the three, with the understanding that the woman he didn't name wouldn't accept his suit. Early on, when some of the men tried courting all three ladies at once, this cut down some confusion. The idea also took into account this sort of situation, so the last unengaged woman wasn't hounded by every man in town. *So why do I still feel hounded?*

"Those were the old rules." Williams smoothed his thinning hair over his bald spot with a sickly smile. "Things are different, but they specifically said we can take pay and still court the lady."

"It was understood that the courting would be done by those of us who listed Miss Higgins as a desired bride," Gent corrected.

A desired bride. Naomi felt the soft heat of a rising blush, enchanted by the description in spite of herself. Amid all the pressure of choosing a groom and praying he would accept her past indiscretion in return for the position and property she offered, Naomi never noticed that some of these men might find her desirable.

"You were clear as water that you chose Miss Thompson." Clump readily sided with Gent against this new opponent. "She didn't want you, and neither did Miss Lyman. Don't horn in on Miss Higgins!"

"Why shouldn't I? She and I got a lot in common." Smile long gone, Williams plowed ahead. "Like you said, we're both leftovers."

Naomi gasped, her brief hope for becoming a "desired bride" crushed by Williams's more accurate assessment. *He's right. Harry threw me over for Charlotte, and I'm last choice in Hope Falls.*

"Walk away, Williams," Bear growled, his face darkening. "Plenty men asked to court Miss Higgins in the beginning. She deserves to be courted by men who recognize her value—not insulted."

"It's no insult when a man offers a woman the protection of his name." Williams wouldn't back down. "My courting is a compliment!"

"A compliment that's become cliché." Naomi lifted her chin. "One you'll no doubt extend to the next unwed woman you find. I happen to prefer men who are more selective with their attentions."

Williams's eyes became beady slits. "You're making a mistake."

"No she ain't." Bobsley sounded as certain as Naomi felt, beaming as Williams, unable to salvage his pride, stomped away.

"Now that he's gone, would you like to take that walk?" Clump slid a glance toward Gent and immediately clarified, "With me?"

Naomi looked for an excuse but saw only three hopeful faces and Riordan's more impassive expression. Again she wondered whether he'd come to her defense as part of his position, or if he was one of the men who'd, as he put it "chosen" her. She'd have to ask Lacey, whose memory about which man chose whom was more reliable.

"I think the forest is large enough for all of us," she announced. Naomi owed them a chance, and she owed it to herself to learn enough to make an informed decision when the time came. At least this way she wouldn't need to go on more than one walk!

If the men looked less than enthusiastic at the prospect of a group outing, so be it. No matter what she decided, several of them would have been disappointed. Besides, this way she could rotate the conversation if things lagged or became otherwise uncomfortable.

No one said much as they left town, crossing the railroad tracks and heading into the forest. Naomi couldn't tell if they were sulking over the situation or waiting for the scenery to give them something to say. She refused to consider whether they were waiting for her to come up with a topic of conversation. They'd asked for her company— it wasn't her responsibility to keep them entertained!

The forest rose up around them, majestic pines and stately spruces pointing straight to heaven. Dappled sunlight streamed through the canopy of branches, highlighting some areas and leaving others mysteriously shadowed. Here the fresh mountain was more strongly scented with pine, with moss lending a musky note not found in town. Dry pine needles snapped underfoot with each step, a crisp counterpoint to the cheerful bird calls from high above them.

"It's lovely." Despite her decision that the men should lead the conversation, Naomi spoke first. Since arriving, she hadn't had much opportunity to leave town. If not for the pure air she breathed, she might almost convince herself that the surrounding scenery was no more real than a well-executed oil painting.

But it was real—a tangible display of God's grandeur, set down to nourish the body and inspire the soul. For the first time, she understood what lured Lacey to her solitary walks and later why her cousin insisted on accompanying Dunstan on his forest treks.

When Naomi spotted a white-and-brown-speckled feather resting atop some bushes nearby, she stopped and picked it up. Stroking her thumb upward, it felt so soft. Running downward, it resisted. *Just like Lacey—always reaching high and not stopping to look down.* The thought made her smile, and she tucked the feather into her pocket.

"You like feathers, Miss Higgins?" Bobsley squinted around, moved to the left, and gave a short hop. In a moment, he returned with a longer feather, white in the center and dove-gray at the tip.

"I was thinking of Miss Lyman," she explained as she accepted the gift. "She's sad to see her favorite old hat looking so. . ."

"Scraggly?" Riordan supplied the word Naomi couldn't find.

"Exactly," Naomi agreed. "I was thinking to spruce it up a bit, tack on a few feathers and whatnot to hide the worst spots."

From that point on, the men made a game of spying fallen feathers and fetching them for her. It nicely broke up the silence while leaving everyone free to enjoy the beauty around them.

"Will it all be destroyed?" Naomi stopped beside one of the trees, peering up at a knothole. Above a tiny black nose, reflective eyes peered back at her—most likely wondering what she wanted.

"Not here." Gent stepped forward to assure her. "I won't tell you it hasn't happened in other places, because they logged the forests right out of most New England. But it won't happen here."

"Why not?" With a twitch of its nose, her friend disappeared, and Naomi returned to the well-worn path. She hadn't given it much thought before, but wasn't this the reason Lacey's idea would work—they'd ruined most of the forestland back East? "Isn't that what logging does? Chops down all of the trees to mill the lumber?"

"Ja, this is done in some places still." Clump looked aggrieved, mirroring Naomi's newfound concern. "But, too, this depends on who owns the land and also who they hire for the working of it."

"Oh." In spite of the odd way Clump phrased things—Naomi suspected the German language put words in different order than English—she understood his meaning. "So how can Hope Falls cut enough logs for a sawmill without taking down all of the trees?"

"We're lucky to have Granger on board. Granger Mills was one of the first to head West for fresh timber sources and one of the first to stop strip-logging the sites." Bobsley's disembodied voice reached Naomi from where he traveled behind her, Gent, and Clump.

"Sometimes it's good to thin the forest." Gent gestured toward a thick stand of trees, dense branches casting shadows. "If no light comes through, the smaller trees die and nothing new can grow."

"But don't the old ones keep growing, things still the same if it's left alone?" Naomi persisted in spite of their explanations.

"Overgrown areas hide dead trees, withered brush, and dry, broken branches. Loggers avoid them or clear out the kindling before starting work." For the first time, Bobsley sounded serious. "One spark to those places and an entire mountainside goes up in flames."

"Granger's way, we clear out areas we need for construction then cull through the timber." Riordan veered around Gent and stopped a few steps ahead, patting a tree. "What do you see, lass?"

"Um. . ." *A tree?* Suddenly, Naomi wished she'd asked Michael how to identify the different kinds of wood while they were still trees. "It's not as thick or tall as some, and the branches start low?"

"Verra good." Riordan was pleased—his accent was coming out. "It's young, green, and supple. The saplings and the smaller trees make for more work with less profit. In old days, we'd take them anyway. Here and now, they stay behind to continue the forest."

Naomi broke out in a grin. "I'm so glad to hear that!"

"We are the kind you said to Williams that you wanted." Clump hooked his thumbs through his suspenders, rocking back on his heels.

She blinked, trying to understand but coming up with nothing.

"For beautiful trees and also with beautiful women," Clump explained. "We pay attention and make good choices for the future."

"Selective," Naomi murmured, fighting another blush as the men around her nodded. She'd gotten so caught up in her concern for the land, she'd forgotten the reason she'd ventured outside to enjoy it.

Lord, Naomi prayed in silence as the group headed back to town, *I know I don't deserve this embarrassment of riches, but You've put it before me anyway. They're good, kind men who've all chosen me. So why is it that I can't bring myself to choose one of them?*

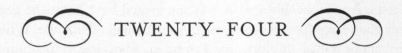

TWENTY-FOUR

W here's Miss Higgins?" By the time Mike returned, she'd vanished. To his way of thinking, he'd gotten the bad end of the deal if his brief absence meant he'd traded her company for that of Braden Lyman. The other man seemed more agreeable than Mike remembered from his first night in Hope Falls, but he was still no Naomi.

"She went for a walk with—" Granger's woman didn't finish her thought, instead shielding her eyes and squinting out toward the forest. "There she is. Looks like they'll be back in a few minutes."

"They?" Mike mimicked her motion, putting his hand against his forehead to block the morning glare. It didn't take long to spot the three, four, no. . .make that five figures walking through the trees. And only one wore skirts. *Why is Naomi walking with four men?*

For a moment he wondered whether Miss Thompson mistook her own sister for Naomi, but Mike knew which woman was picking her way down the mountainside. It wouldn't grumble his guts any to see men circling around the younger Miss Thompson like hounds after a hare.

Mike didn't want to think about why he reacted so strongly seeing Naomi surrounded by would-be swains. Nor did he want to think about why he'd been so disappointed in the first place when he'd returned and found her gone. No matter how she monopolized his thoughts lately, Mike had nothing to offer a woman like Miss Higgins. Even if she and Luke got along well—which was a big assumption, given Luke's experiences—Mike hadn't established himself in Hope Falls. He couldn't give her a home so long as he slept in the bunkhouse.

And if any woman deserved a home to make her own, it was Naomi. Any fool could see the way she longed for a house; he need only glance at what she'd done with Miss Lyman's dollhouse. When he first saw it in all its glory, rooms emptied of boxes and transformed with treasures, he'd been staggered. Naomi filled every corner and crevice, left her stamp on each nook and cranny until the model home overflowed with tangible proof of skilled hands and a giving heart.

For the first time, Mike wished that Naomi's looks didn't mirror her spirit. Her trim figure and pretty smile attracted too much attention in a town full of bachelors. If anything, he should be surprised that he hadn't seen men trying to court her before today. Of course, this was the first day the men hadn't been excavating a fallen mine or spending ten to eleven hours in the forest, so perhaps Mike had missed the subtler signs of wooing.

"I've seen soaked cats wearing less peeved expressions." Braden wheeled up beside him as smoothly as though he'd been doing it for days. "And it doesn't take a detective to see where you're looking."

"It surprised me to see the men swarming like that." Mike admitted part of the truth. "Up till now, I thought the ladies had a better handle on that sort of thing—making sure they didn't let one get outnumbered if the others could step in and even things out."

"They probably used to." Braden rubbed at a crick in his neck. "But with Evie and Lacey off the market, there are too many determined bachelors with high expectations from that consarned ad and no one else left to draw their attention away from Naomi."

Mike frowned at that interpretation. Why wasn't the youngest girl stepping in? Unless. . .the prospect of angering the town chef could easily turn a hungry man's mind from one woman to another less thorny option. "Is Miss Thompson overly protective of her sister?"

"You mean Cora or Evie? Eh, doesn't matter. You'll get the same answer either way. They're protective of each other. Cora couldn't stand the idea of coming here and leaving Evie alone, and Evie couldn't let her little sister come to the wilds of Colorado Territory without her. And all that hullabaloo when we were already engaged, if you'll believe it." Braden shook his head at the memory.

"*Engaged?*" Mike repeated dumbly, too astonished by his mistake to say more. He thought back to his first night in Hope Falls, thinking of when Granger's woman made introductions. She'd called the other Miss Thompson her sister—no one made any mention of her engagement to Braden Lyman. Nor had anyone brought it up since.

"You didn't know." It wasn't a question. Braden peered up at him, the corners of his mouth flat and tight. "You should have known Cora was taken, even if nobody told you who claimed her. Didn't you wonder why the ad only asked for three husbands?"

"The ad didn't bring me here." Mike tried not to snap at the man who was still his boss. "I caught wind of it after I got to town."

"And you made the wrong assumption about which women wrote it." Braden scowled and decided, "You look like you swallowed a slug."

Mike didn't comment, though the description wasn't far from the truth—the realization that Naomi was the last woman from the ad definitely left a lump in his throat and a bad taste in his mouth. Mere minutes before, he'd been grappling with his inability to offer this woman the stability of a home and marriage. Now he learned that if he had tried, he'd be nothing more than a hired husband. *Again.*

Lord, it looks like You've saved me from repeating my biggest mistake. Mike tried to drum up some gratitude for the intervention but came up empty. *I can't say I'm happy about the situation, but since I was reminding myself I couldn't marry her anyway, it's not as if I lost a chance I was willing to take. Help me, Lord, as I work alongside this woman. In spite of what I've learned, there's still a lot to admire about Naomi Higgins. Enough that I think I'm going to need Your help to remember the way things really stand.*

"So," Braden prodded. "What made you think it was *Cora*, anyway?"

"Think *what* was Cora?" Cora froze about four feet behind Braden. Flabbergasted to see him out and about, she'd hurried to greet him without paying any attention to the conversation going on. All she heard was his question to Mr. Strode—and though the words might be innocuous, she didn't care for his dismissive tone. Not one bit.

Even from behind she could tell she'd taken him by surprise—his shoulders stiffened that much. She could have made things easier for him by walking around his chair so they could speak face-to-face. But Cora was finished making things easy for her former fiancé.

So she waited for him to turn around, and while she waited, she became more and more irked. There he sat, in the wheeled wicker chair she'd brought all the way from Charleston. Without being asked. Without having him even bother to roll up and thank her.

Instead, like the fool she thought she wasn't, she'd rushed over to share the joy of his achievement, only to hear him speaking her name in the same tone usually reserved for creepy-crawly things. It was one thing for the man to denounce her in private, worse when he did so before their tight-laced group. But publicly? The closer Braden got to getting back on his feet, the lower the man sank.

"Cora!" Braden started to reach for her hand, but Cora crossed her arms. His smile hadn't fooled her; the man wasn't happy.

"Yes, Cora. The same Cora you were discussing?" She slid a glance toward Mr. Strode, noticing the man looked to be suffering from a stomach ailment of some sort. When neither of the men responded, she prompted, "You thought I was what?"

"One of the women who wrote the ad." With that simple statement and a glance toward the group of men bidding for Naomi's attention, Mr. Strode's sour expression made much more sense. The man wasn't ill; he was disappointed!

So our new carpenter isn't as indifferent to Naomi as he'd like to be. It took a lot of willpower for Cora to keep from smiling. She, Evie, and even optimistic Lacey all worried about their friend. It would be just like Naomi to tire of all the fuss and choose the first man she deemed marginally acceptable. Then they'd have a terrible time convincing her that an "acceptable" man was insufficient. Naomi simply didn't see herself as extraordinary.

But Mr. Strode obviously did, and that was a more important development, even, than Braden finally getting into his wheeled chair and out of that dismal room. Braden, of course, wouldn't agree with that assessment, but then Braden hadn't been agreeable in a long time. At least Cora now understood why he'd been so sour about it.

He wasn't disgusted with her. Far from it. He didn't like the idea that another man thought she was available. Even when that other man was obviously smitten with Naomi! Cora felt as happy and relieved as when they'd finally pulled Lacey from the mines.

"As it just so happens, I did help write that ad." Cora let loose the smile she'd been holding back. It felt wonderful.

"Not as one of the would-be brides, Cora. Somehow the new man in town got the idea that you were the last bride, and I wanted to know why he didn't realize it was Naomi."

"The night everyone was offered wages, the men talked about the last girl up for grabs. It seemed to me that between yourself and Miss Higgins, you were the girl. Then your sister started warning the men to keep their hands to themselves, and it seemed like she was protecting you." Mr. Strode grimaced. "I didn't know you were engaged."

"I'm not." Cora knew her comment would confuse Mr. Strode a bit, but more importantly, it would clear things up for Braden.

"Don't go mixing up the truth with trouble." Her former fiancé looked mad enough to spit. "He thought you were one of the women advertising for a husband, and I told him you were already engaged."

"True. When we posted the ad, I was engaged." She shrugged. "Hope Falls has a funny way of turning things on their heads."

"I'm getting that impression." Mr. Strode looked from Braden to her then back again, no longer confused. "It sounds like the two of you have some things to talk through, and it sounds like they're private. So I'll just leave you to it." With that, the carpenter extracted himself from their convoluted conversation. He also, Cora couldn't help but notice, headed straight for Naomi.

"What do you think you're playing at?" Braden demanded, looking positively outraged. "Telling him you're not engaged. If he repeats that around town, all the men will think you are up for grabs!"

"It's the truth." Cora sighed. "I signed Lacey's paperwork, Braden. My dowry has been returned, along with my own portion of Hope Falls. As of now, the engagement is officially dissolved."

"No it isn't!" Braden pounded his fist on the arm of his chair, making the wicker creak. "You can't end it just because things aren't going your way, Cora. We made a commitment."

Cora's jaw dropped at the vehemence of his hypocrisy. Was this the same man who'd ordered her to leave his side, leave town entirely? Was this the Braden Lyman who'd looked her in the eye and told her he didn't want her anymore? She'd had to hold his use of her dowry over his head to make him accept that he couldn't back out of their engagement. So how could this be the same Braden who'd begged her to sign Lacey's paperwork so they'd both be free?

It can't be. The man sitting before her bore more of a resemblance to the Braden she'd loved than the Braden she'd battled in Hope Falls. Staggered by the realization, Cora decided to leave him in the company of his own hypocrisy while she sorted through her conflicting emotions. She needed to decide where to go from here.

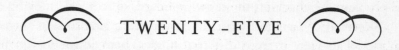# TWENTY-FIVE

The bottom floor is where the kitchen, dining room, and parlor belong." Naomi bent over the sketches scattered across the tabletop. "Since we're making this home with six rooms rather than eight, we'll need to move the study upstairs with the bedroom and nursery."

"Do you have any preference as to which room is the starting point?" Michael seemed more businesslike than Naomi remembered from the first few days. But then again, he'd been moving crates and setting up the work space. Now that the room was ready, it was understandable that he wanted to get the project fully under way.

At least that's the explanation Naomi hoped explained his sudden lack of warmth. It wasn't as though he was rude or dismissive—merely detached. As though he'd withdrawn in some way from their burgeoning partnership. Whatever the reason for his altered demeanor, Naomi hoped his enthusiasm would return. Soon.

"It needs to be one of the side rooms on the ground floor," she mused. "So either the parlor or the kitchen would be a good choice."

"What if the location of the room didn't matter?" He looked up from the prints. "Wouldn't it be easier for you to develop a room if it wasn't already locked in place? I mean to say, would it help you work if I could build the rooms first and connect them later?"

"That would make it much easier to work on the ceilings, wall coverings, and flooring." She caught herself nibbling on the corner of her lip and immediately stopped. "But I would imagine that would interfere with your work on the exterior. Doors, windows, shingles, the scalloped siding would all wait for the house to be together."

"True. . . ." He looked to be off in his own thoughts, but this was the sort of distance Naomi didn't mind. Anyone could see he was turning around options in his head, trying to find a solution to the problem. Michael left the drawing board, so to speak, moving to stand in front of Lyman Place. He moved from side to side, turned the model to view it from different angles, bent lower to run his forefinger along the edges of floors and ceilings. Then he returned, picked up a pencil, and began drawing. Quick, slashing lines across the blank page formed the now-familiar outline of their design.

Except this was shaping up to be anything but familiar. As she watched, he outlined the house, using it as a frame and running two lines across it—one beneath the eaves and another about halfway down the walls so the whole sketch looked rather like a bookshelf. When Naomi began to ask a question, he held up his left hand, forefinger extended in the age-old request that she wait a moment.

So Naomi waited. And wondered. And watched.

She watched as he added two lines, dividing the house with one-third to the right and two-thirds of the space to the left, and understood that he was leaving room for the hallway and staircase on each level. Again, she wanted to ask why he felt the need to draw again what they'd already decided, but then Michael's pencil veered to the margin of the paper, abandoning the skeletal structure. In quick succession, he drew six cubes floating around the house. He lifted his tilted head and erased the top line from each cube.

"Movable rooms." Naomi's mind raced with the possibilities of this innovation. It was an entirely new dimension for those who loved dollhouses, allowing them to arrange not only the furnishings and décor of the home but the floor plan of the house as well. "It's genius!"

"Just practical," Michael demurred but seemed pleased with her reaction. "You were right before, when you said that working on the rooms would stop progress on the exterior. This way you'll be able to work more comfortably without losing time elsewhere."

"This way I can even work on multiple rooms. I won't need to wait for paint to dry or glue to set!" Naomi was almost giddy. "It will be so much easier than hunching down, straining my neck to see what I'm doing. This makes all the difference."

He made all the difference, but Naomi couldn't tell him that. It sounded too intimate. *That's because it* is *too intimate, you ninny!* Her common sense was putting in almost as many hours on this project as Naomi, constantly delivering stern reminders and scolds. *You can't tell a man that you wake up looking forward to spending the day with him. Michael isn't one of the men who's courting you, and you already decided that you couldn't marry him even if asked. You should not enjoy his company this much. Compose yourself!*

At this rate, *Compose yourself!* was vying with *He deserves better!* as Naomi's mantra. It seemed a pity that she didn't like either one. But a more encouraging, uplifting sort of motto would be of no use in restraining her fascination with the man beside her. She hadn't known Michael Strode for long, but his strength of character set him apart from most of the men she'd spent time with.

He made no secret of his love for the Lord. In fact, her first memory of Michael was his offer to pray. Then he'd proceeded to help pull apart half a mountainside without even knowing whether he'd be allowed to stay. That spoke of a servant's heart.

Then there were the things she learned as they worked. Michael treated her like an equal, never resenting having to work with a woman. His determination to provide for his young son merited respect, as did his formidable intellect. Naomi found herself transfixed by his unique ability to puzzle through problems.

How could she compose herself when he stood so close, smelling of soap and pine, his sleeve brushing against hers? Or when his eyes lit with enthusiasm for a fresh idea? Naomi sighed and accepted her weakness. When it came to Michael, common sense went out the door.

Mike wondered if Naomi realized how long she'd been thinking without saying anything. He wanted to know what, exactly, she'd been thinking about for such a broad range of expressions to cross her face. And most of all, he wondered why on earth Naomi Higgins would need to hire a husband. With or without part ownership in a new sawmill, the woman was a prize. So how come some man hadn't swept her off her feet long before she resorted to such extreme measures?

"Is there a reason behind your decision to not enclose the rooms?" She'd apparently decided to rejoin the conversation. "I would think ceilings stabilize the unit, so won't the room be more easily damaged if it's moved around without the covering?"

"Yes." Mike tapped the drawing on the table. "But I was thinking about how much simpler it would be for you to work with the rooms open so you could reach in from above as well as from the side. Also, it makes for less work if we address the ceilings all at once, doing the painting and so forth along the undersides of the support shelves before I insert them into the frame."

"Clear advantages." She paused, clearly torn between the function of the design while they were working as opposed to the function once they'd finished.

"I also considered that the lack of a roof would make people more cautious when handling the rooms. They should always be supported from the bottom, but a closed box might encourage rougher handling." Mike wanted her to decide in favor of what made her work easier, but he wanted her to feel good about the decision.

"I agree." Until her smile returned, Mike hadn't realized he'd missed it. "The increased difficulty in this approach falls to you—there's no margin for error when each portable unit must be precisely the same dimension as the next."

"Not a problem," he assured her. "I'm known for precision."

"Oh?" Her green eyes lit with curiosity, and Mike knew he'd made a mistake. Naomi seemed to have been waiting for an opportunity to ask about his past. "How did you gain such a reputation?"

"Mark the line and measure twice; a single cut should then suffice." He smiled as he recited the rhyme. His father drilled it into his head from the time he'd been old enough to hold a hammer.

"Sound advice in a clever phrase." Naomi smiled, but she wasn't finished questioning him. "Where did you learn it?"

"My father made sure I learned that lesson long before he let me put it to use." Mike didn't mind telling her that much. Trades were often handed from father to son through generations. "I did the same with Luke when he started to show an interest in the workshop."

"You had a workshop?" She seized the word like a dog on a bone.

"Yep." How was he going to change the topic now? If he didn't derail the conversation soon, she'd keep digging for information he needed to stay buried. No matter how he racked his brain, Mike could think of only one answer a woman wouldn't question further. "I closed it down after my wife died. Luke took it pretty hard."

This, at least, was true. Although he'd manfully refused to indulge in tears when he heard of his mother's death, Luke shed a few when they visited the workshop for the final time. Mike understood— Leticia didn't involve herself in Luke's upbringing, preferring to leave the difficult task of parenting to a coterie of nursemaids, nannies, and tutors. Although not altogether indifferent, she'd been absent more often than not. Far more often.

But the workshop. . .that had been a constant in his son's life long before Luke spoke. Mike started sneaking his son into his sanctuary while the nursemaid napped and continued the visits more openly after Luke could walk. In the workshop, he'd read fables to his son, and when Luke began to write, they'd traced letters then words in layers of sawdust. While Mike worked, Luke kept himself busy, happily playing with the trains, spinning tops, and building blocks Mike gave him—toys Mike fashioned in the early days of his marriage, when he still hoped to build a real family.

Naomi seemed subdued. "You must have loved her very much. It would have been hard to stay in a place that held so many memories."

"It was hard to leave," he admitted. When he'd locked the door for the final time, Mike almost cried along with his son. Leaving behind the workshop meant leaving the place where they'd both been happiest, without knowing when or where they'd find a new sanctuary. Mike could only thank God that he'd found Hope Falls and pray for patience until he could bring Luke home to build new memories.

"It's never easy to leave what we know." A hint of hardness crept into the set of her jaw but quickly vanished as she whispered, "But sometimes it's the only choice you have left."

Mike gladly took the chance to turn the conversation around. If things went well, he might be able to answer the questions plaguing him about that ad. "It couldn't have been easy for you either."

"No, it wa—" She stopped, the unnatural pause and her widened eyes telling that she'd been about to agree with him but didn't want him to know it. Naomi cleared her throat. "It was much easier than you might think—certainly easier than staying behind."

"Why?" Mike knew better than to pry, but his inability to solve the puzzle that was Naomi Higgins goaded his conversation.

Naomi looked astonished at his brazen question but still deigned to answer him. "You might not understand, Michael. You left your home because a family member died. I left because we found out that Braden survived the cave-in. Lacey and Cora were going to find him whether Evie and I came with them or not."

The sadness behind her words tore at him, and Mike could have kicked himself for being an insensitive boor. Apologizing was the only thing to do. "I'm sorry. I didn't realize the Lymans were your only family. Did you lose your parents at a very young age?"

"My father died two days before I was born. They say I share his coloring." Absently, she reached up and traced the streak of white brightening her hair. "My mother passed away two years ago."

"My condolences for your loss." Mike was glad to know he hadn't trampled over a fresh tragedy, but he also knew that the loss of a beloved mother never lost its sting. "My mother traded this world for heaven shortly after Luke was born. At the time, I thought she'd held on so long just to see her grandson. It gave me comfort to know I'd been able to give her that final joy." More than any medicine paid for by the Bainbridge largess, Mike believed that his mother's delight in seeing her grandson gave peace to her final months.

For that, and for Luke himself, he couldn't bring himself to regret the bargain he'd struck. But he knew all to well that was an undeserved blessing. Mike ached at the thought Naomi might make the same mistake he had. Would a decade with her hired husband leave her with all the regrets and none of the satisfaction a marriage should hold? She deserved more—why could she not see it? Did she feel that her lack of family left her so alone, she had no choice but to marry the first man who'd be an asset to Hope Falls?

"A child is a joy unlike any other, and even better since no two are alike." She smiled, but her eyes swam with sorrow. "Your wife must have grieved to be unable to give Luke a brother or sister."

"Luke is enough." Mike heard his own fierceness and softened his tone. "God saw fit to bless me with one wonderful son, and I never wanted him or his mother to think he wasn't enough."

Not having any more children was one of the few things he and Leticia had actually seen eye to eye on. Despite Mike's dogged determination to honor their wedding vows, Leticia returned to her faithless ways almost as soon as she'd healed from giving birth.

Mike married her knowing it meant accepting another man's child as his son, but he'd felt no bitterness about it. The deed was done before he'd ever met the woman. Somehow he knew he wouldn't be able to accept the same situation with the same equanimity after they'd wed. Perhaps it wasn't logical or fair, but he was honest about it. For her part, Leticia refused to endure the pain again or ruin her figure.

"Of course! I didn't mean to imply that your son was in any way lacking. My thoughts were more that siblings add a new dimension to a child's life. . . ." Naomi trailed off, lost in consternation.

"I didn't take offense." He saw she didn't believe him and searched for a way to smooth things over. "Do you have a sibling?"

"A sister." If she'd seemed sorrowful at the mention of her mother's passing, now Naomi looked lost in the Bog of Despair from

Pilgrim's Progress. Blinking rapidly, she croaked out, "Married."

She seemed so distraught at the thought of her sister's marriage, Mike wondered at the cause. Perhaps she disapproved of her brother-in-law and felt concern for her sibling. Or maybe theirs was a happy marriage, and Naomi battled envy. Either way, the comparison between her sister and herself could only cause pain.

He hated to see her suffer, but more than that, Mike hated his own inability to do anything about it.

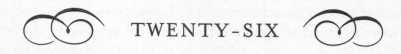

TWENTY-SIX

W hat are we supposed to do?" Cora hissed at Braden, trying to keep her voice low enough that the stranger loitering in the hallway wouldn't hear. "And who, exactly, is this Mr. Clyde Corning? You didn't discuss inviting him, and now all of a sudden *he's here!*"

This last statement smacked of the obvious, but Cora wanted to get the true urgency of the situation through Braden's thick skull. Because the man looked completely unperturbed by the fact that they had no accommodations for the "honored" guest he'd sprung on them.

"Corning's a potential investor, and I didn't know he was coming." He sounded less unconcerned than tired, and suddenly it occurred to Cora that Braden might have already worn himself out.

He'd made a habit of finding the most difficult inclines to practice rolling himself up and down several times. But this didn't satisfy Braden, who seemed bound and determined to build up his strength. The few times he'd tipped over had been due to trying to control his descent down an incline while going *backward.*

As if that weren't enough, Braden didn't even get into the chair until Doc put him through so-called physiotherapy every morning. Even the doctor himself admitted that it was a new field of medicine—pioneered by Swedish gymnasts of all things! Even though the techniques were finding widespread use for rehabilitating wounded soldiers, the process remained both inexact and exhausting.

Now that she took the time to look, she saw the telltale tightening of the corners of his mouth—the ones that said he was in pain but determined not to let her know. His color, while much improved from a week's worth of outdoor sessions, looked pale. Cora chastised herself for not noticing sooner. After all, she knew that he'd already gone through his personal gauntlet by late afternoon.

Keeping track of his schedule helped her know how to evade him. Otherwise she never would have managed to avoid him for an entire week while she floundered from one sort of feeling to another. Cornering Cora seemed to be Braden's only goal—aside from his almost maniacal determination to regain his strength. It didn't matter how many times people told him he didn't need to rush, he—

He knew better. The realization whisked away Cora's guilt over misinterpreting Braden's fatigue as disinterest. *Braden hasn't been pushing himself so hard simply to recover—he's been getting ready!*

"Oh, you knew he was coming." Cora jabbed a finger at him, stopping just shy of his nose and making his eyes cross for a second. "Mr. Corning says you invited him, and you've been working yourself into a lather readying yourself!"

"Erm." Braden uncrossed his eyes and slid his gaze over her shoulder, toward the closed door. "He didn't respond to the invitation. I didn't know if anyone was coming, much less when."

"What do you mean, 'anyone'?" Suspicious, Cora peered at him, but Braden kept his gaze firmly fixed on some spot behind her. He only refused to meet her gaze when he had something to hide. "Just how many people did you invite without consulting everyone else?"

Briefly Braden's temper flared to life, giving him the energy to push himself into a sitting position. "Now isn't the time to discuss it, Cora! Right now you need to escort Mr. Corning in here and go find Dunstan and Granger so they can join us. While the men talk, you women can bustle around and get something ready for him."

"While *the men* talk?" She gritted her teeth to keep from shrieking at the obstinate fool. "You don't run Hope Falls, Braden. *We women* do. Dunstan and Granger answer to Lacey and Evie, and we will not be treated as housekeepers while you hold court in here!"

"Stop making things so difficult!" he snapped at her.

Cora arched a brow and left the room—closing the door behind her so Braden couldn't hear what she said to Mr. Corning. As far as she was concerned, he deserved to be shut out of things for a while.

"Mr. Corning." She nudged the corners of her lips into what she hoped passed for a gracious smile. "I've informed Mr. Lyman of your arrival, and he is anxious to greet you. He'll need a few moments, so I'll escort you to the house where you can freshen up a bit."

Within five minutes she'd directed the doctor to ready Braden's chair, stopped by the mercantile with Mr. Corning to pick up Lacey and ask Dunstan to find Mr. Granger, and shooed their unexpected guest into the kitchen to wash up. As expected, Dunstan found Granger in the kitchen, which made Evie go fetch Naomi, so Cora had just long enough to apprise everyone gathered in the parlor of the situation. It didn't take long since she knew precious little. She finished before Mr. Corning emerged from the kitchen.

By the time Braden rolled in, it was good he brought his own seat. Disgruntled women monopolized the parlor—and the conversation.

Braden could hardly get a word in edgewise. He sat there fuming while the women sent him scowls and cozied up to Corning. Corning!

Of all the strategic invitations he'd sent, no one showed the good grace to respond. But Clyde Corning, who Braden only included because it might raise the saboteur's suspicions if only some of the previous investors were invited, landed right on his doorstep.

"Cautious Clyde," as he'd been nicknamed in college, made a tidy living on the stock market by selecting only the safest shares. Corning's reputation for careful investing convinced others to back Miracle Mining when geological surveys and Braden's own powers of persuasion failed. Every businessman in Charleston knew there was no better bet than a venture already backed by Cautious Clyde Corning.

A more methodical man couldn't be found. He shied away from

all but the slightest risks. So what in blue blazes brought him across the country without so much as a question asked or research piled into every nook and cranny of his meticulous, massive desk?

Dunstan kept looking from Corning to Braden, as though trying to decide what made this man a suspect. Judging by Granger's furrowed brow, his attempts to solve the same puzzle were failing. The only signal Braden could give was a short shake of his head. It wasn't as though he could outright announce that Corning didn't count as a suspect and Braden never expected him to show up.

"A pleasure to meet each of you." Corning awkwardly addressed the female population in the room and rubbed his chin. "I apologize that I didn't have the time to shave and present myself properly."

"We don't rest on formality," came Naomi's understatement.

"Do you know, Mr. Corning, that I believe a beard would look well on you?" Trust Lacey to try and hide the man's weak chin. His sister waged a constant war to help people look their best. So far Naomi was the only person who'd held out against Lacey's guidance.

Cautious Clyde went ruddy at the comment, thoughtfully fingering the sparse stubble along his jaw. "I've considered it."

Braden held back a snort. The man had probably been considering the change for years, judging it too drastic to attempt.

"What do you think, Miss Thompson?" Corning shifted slightly to better face Cora, who occupied the seat beside him on the settee.

Wait. Braden's eyes narrowed. *Why is he sitting beside her? He doesn't need to be that close. And why ask Cora's opinion, as though it matters more than Lacey's or any other woman's in the room?*

"I'd say now is a good time to test it out, while you're away from home." Cora's smile held a shade too much warmth for a new acquaintance. "If you dislike it, shave before you return. If you do like it, you can surprise everyone with it when you get back."

"Well reasoned." Corning's smile matched hers. "I'll do it!"

"I'm surprised to see you." Braden managed to break into the conversation while everyone was busy agreeing with Cora's summation. "If we'd known of your imminent arrival, we would have prepared something for you." *Like some skillfully designed questions to ascertain why you ventured so far from your well-ordered life.*

Because the more Braden thought about it, the more suspicious Corning's sudden adventure seemed. As far as he knew, the man rarely left town and never journeyed beyond state borders. *Until now.*

"Did you not see my telegram?" Corning's brows tented upward.

"We lost our telegraph operator a couple weeks ago." Dunstan stepped in to smooth things over—and closely eye Corning's reaction to this vague revelation about Draxley. Would Corning take the bait?

"Sorry to hear that." Corning looked genuinely disturbed as he looked around the room. "I never intended to inconvenience you. I should have waited until I received confirmation from you, Braden."

"It's fine," Braden lied, still digesting the fact Corning hadn't asked after Draxley. Of course, an innocent man wouldn't know the telegraph operator's name, much less inquire further. But a canny saboteur would know better than to display interest as well. Who knew whether or not Corning actually sent a telegram? *Maybe he wanted to swoop into Hope Falls and catch us completely off guard.*

If so, the tactic worked far better than Braden cared to admit. He'd pushed himself hard throughout the morning and early afternoon, and by suppertime he'd tired himself sufficiently to be grateful for the bed that had been his prison for so many months before. Right now his wits weren't nearly as sharp as he needed them to be.

"Even so," Braden prodded a bit further, "I must say I'm surprised that you took me up on the invitation. I expected a few to come, but it didn't strike me as something you'd be interested in."

"My interests might be more varied than you think." Was it Braden's imagination, or did Corning slide a glance at Cora before continuing? "A few of the men who'd asked for my input regarding the Hope Falls mine came asking me about this new sawmill you proposed."

"Oh, did they?" Lacey sounded sweet as syrup while she glared daggers at Braden. "Perhaps you should tell us who *we* invited."

"Businessmen." Braden gave an indolent shrug, as though the

telegrams weren't highly specific. "No one you'd know, really."

His sister gritted her teeth. "I didn't think Hope Falls was ready to begin inviting businessmen and seeking new investors."

"We needed to." Granger threw the weight of his experience behind Braden's decision, knowing that the women would assume he meant the sawmill needed start-up capital. As things stood, they wouldn't have been able to begin paying wages if Granger himself hadn't bought into the business. They'd all agreed that the women didn't need to know the reason behind this particular group of investors—if they knew, the girls would give the game away.

Evie gave her future husband a meaningful look and observed— in a thoroughly pleasant voice, "So you knew about this decision."

"The sawmill benefits from investors." Braden somehow summoned the energy to give a credible performance. "It seemed only right that the men who speculated in the mine should be presented with the opportunity to recoup their losses. So we contacted them first."

"Indeed." Corning gave a repugnant little snuffle, digging around in his waistcoat for a handkerchief. "Should the mill be as promising as described, the mine investors should be among the first to benefit. It's why they came for my opinion and why I came here. Given the last fiasco, I need to review things firsthand, you see."

Fiasco? The word hung in the air like a foul stench, reminding Braden that his business venture had failed so spectacularly it jeopardized even the reputation of Cautious Clyde. He tried to swallow his rage, knowing that the time would come when the safety of his mines would be vindicated and the saboteur exposed. But that day loomed long into the future, and for now Braden found it incredibly difficult to drum up the appropriate response for Clyde.

"I owe you my thanks." He almost choked on the words, the truth of them weighted like bricks. "After the failure of the mines, you would have been within your rights to denounce Hope Falls entirely."

"No, I won't denounce you." A martial glint appeared in Corning's gaze. "The mines did not fail. You promised silver, and the mine produced silver until the unfortunate, *unforeseeable* collapse."

Dunstan and Granger's eyes widened at the stress Corning placed on the word *unforeseeable,* and Braden knew they wondered the same thing he did. Was Corning consoling a friend or trying to emphasize the "accidental" nature of the collapse for another, darker reason?

Perhaps I was too hasty in writing off Corning as a suspect. Braden leaned back. Clearly the man merited a close watch.

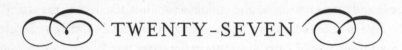# TWENTY-SEVEN

I t's time!" Arla's voice wafted downstairs on a gasp of breath.

Naomi jumped up from the armed chair she'd just claimed, thinking to settle in and get as comfortable as possible for what was sure to be another long, awkward argument with Braden Lyman. They'd scrubbed a mining cabin and scrounged up a bed for Mr. Corning while the men ate supper. Afterward, Cora caught Braden by the back of his chair, refusing to let him return to the doctor's house until the owners of Hope Falls conducted an urgent meeting.

A meeting that wasn't nearly as urgent as Arla's cry.

"Fetch the doctor," Naomi shouted over her shoulder at the men, who'd clustered together like schoolboys awaiting punishment. "Evie, you'd best get some water boiling! Lacey, bring the cloths we washed and set aside. Cora, fetch Mrs. McCreedy—Arla will want her."

And even if Arla didn't particularly want the company of the sole married woman in town, Naomi needed her calming influence. Martha McCreedy could stare down a roomful of loggers, keep up with Evie in the kitchen, and calm a heated conversation with a grace born through years of experience. Naomi could only hope the older woman would be able to help usher a babe into the world as easily.

"Oooooh," Arla panted from the bed, where she huddled on her side with her arms around her stomach. She rolled over when Naomi nudged her shoulder, staring with wide, slightly unfocused eyes.

"It's all right." Naomi reached up and pulled off the frilly nightcap

Arla favored, already damp around the rim. It wasn't warm in the room, so the layer of perspiration dotting her forehead meant Arla had been struggling for some time before she called for help.

Naomi kept her expression schooled in an encouraging smile, refusing to frown at a woman in labor. "When did the pains start?"

"What kind of pains?" Arla shifted around, obviously unable to get comfortable. "The dull, achy ones started, but I drowsed through them. My back always hurts these days, and I didn't realize that these were—" She broke off, breath stolen by another contraction.

Too close. Naomi's mind raced as she remembered everything she'd read on childbirth. She and Lacey had dug through their extensive collections of books once Arla arrived in town, determined to read up on the subject and prepare themselves for the ordeal ahead. From what she could recall, the pains shouldn't be coming this close together until the baby was practically ready to slide out!

Naomi reached for Arla's hand, trying not to wince at the force of the woman's grip. She eased back the sheet, unsurprised to find blood staining Arla's nightgown and the bed beneath her legs. *It's normal.* She reminded herself that this had been expected, but somehow the knowledge hadn't prepared her for the horror of reality.

"Don't fret." Martha McCreedy swept into the room, closely followed by Lacey with her arms full and Cora, who wedged herself between Naomi and the wall to bathe Arla's face with a damp towel.

"Her contractions are coming close," Naomi told them as they eyed the bloodied bed in horror. "Every few minutes already."

Mrs. McCreedy clucked her tongue. "Arla, my dear, you've tricked us into leaving you alone while you did all the work." She rolled up her sleeves and moved to the edge of the bed. There she softly nudged Arla's knees until her legs were tented then rolled back the nightgown and started tucking towels all over the bed.

Naomi edged to the far corner beside Lacey, trying to give Arla more room to breathe. "How can I help, Martha? What do you need?"

"To have this room cleared." Doc burst into view, looking in disapproval at the cramped quarters. "Everyone can leave, now."

"Noooo!" Arla's refusal ended in a scream as she gripped Cora's hand and shook her head. After the pain subsided, she panted out, "Cora...Martha...stay." She leaned back against the pillows, drained.

"That's it, dear." Mrs. McCreedy scooted over to give Doc his rightful place. She gestured for Lacey and Naomi to leave. "Save your strength for the next one. We'll tell you when to bear down."

Not wanting to abandon Arla, but not wanting to get in the way, Naomi skirted around the washstand and out the door. Lacey followed her, and they both stood in the hallway, not certain what to do.

"We might as well see if Evie needs help," Lacey suggested. They trooped down the stairs, spurred by another one of Arla's heart-rending shrieks. As they made their way to the kitchen, they passed a panicked Mr. Lawson. Or rather, they tried to pass him.

"My sister...is she all right?" He blinked behind his spectacles, looking like an incredibly worried owl. When Arla screamed again, he held his breath until she stopped, letting it loose in a long, shaky exhalation. "Does everything seem normal?"

"It shouldn't be long." Naomi gave him an encouraging nod, hoping he didn't notice the way she avoided answering whether things seemed normal. She didn't know much about the normal way of things, but she did know things were progressing at an unusually rapid pace.

"Come and have a seat, Lawson." The familiar bass of Michael's voice washed over her. "Let the ladies get on with their work."

"Right." Lawson scurried away as though he'd been endangering his sister by blocking their way. "Thank you for coming, Strode."

His heartfelt gratitude rang in Naomi's ears as she entered the kitchen. Wasn't it just like Michael to stand by a friend under circumstances when other men fled the scene? She noticed that Dunstan, Granger, and Braden cleared out quick as could be, not stopping to think that poor Mr. Lawson would be on pins and needles.

They all were. Naomi, Lacey, and Evie found themselves pacing the perimeter of the kitchen, loathe to let the men see their anxiety. Aside from bringing water and fresh towels and carrying soiled ones away—carefully concealed from the men, of course—the three of them didn't have much to do except wait. And worry.

So Naomi did what she always did when fear nipped at her heels. She prayed. This time she prayed while she paced, sending an unceasing flow of thoughts and requests with each and every step.

Lord, thank You for speeding this delivery. I know most women labor much longer, and in Your wisdom You spared Arla that trial. Maybe it was to spare all of our nerves because You knew what a state we'd be in. Whatever the reason, I'm grateful. Please let Cora and Martha and Doc be the comfort and assistance she needs. Please let her be all right. Please let the babe be healthy. Please, Lord. . . .

She prayed and paced until Cora burst through the room, grinning from ear to ear and announcing, "It's a girl. A teeny, tiny, perfect little shriveled raisin of a beautiful baby girl!"

Then she went back to the parlor to tell Mr. Lawson how beautifully his sister handled the delivery, that Arla was already holding her new daughter, and that Doc would be down to answer questions shortly. And then there was only one thing left to say.

The women gathered in the kitchen, clasping hands to form the prayer ring, and thanked God for the tiny miracle snoozing upstairs.

Another hour's sleep would have been nice, after turning in late last night, but Mike rolled out of his bunk at the same time as the other men. There'd been a few grumbles about his change in status when the men realized he spent all day with Naomi—practically alone. He didn't plan to give them more ammunition by sleeping in.

The others probably didn't know Lawson had dropped by the workshop to get Mike's opinion on plans for the sawmill. They didn't know that when Dunstan came rushing in with news of Arla, Lawson had asked Mike to go with him. It made sense—of the men Lawson spent any real time with, Mike was the only father in the bunch.

And while Lawson was the uncle, he'd be the man raising the babe along with his sister. Mike understood full well how nerve-racking it could be to wait out the delivery of a child. He fought against his own helplessness, knowing he couldn't soothe the pain or make sure things would turn out right. The sound of a new mother's anguished cries made any man's blood run cold.

He hadn't been thrilled to go with Lawson, but he accepted that the man needed company. Mike didn't regret going—how could he? The babe and mother were doing well, and Lawson didn't break down. What were a few missed hours of sleep compared to those blessings?

Besides, he knew full well that the women found their beds much later and awakened a solid hour earlier than he did. That thought galvanized him as he splashed frigid water on his face and rubbed the bleariness from his eyes. He left the bunkhouse, further invigorated by the chill morning air and the enticing scent of coffee. Mike breathed deep. *And bacon.* He picked up his pace.

He wasn't surprised to find the dining room almost empty, but it did prompt him to bolt down a meal that deserved more appreciation. Then again, all of Miss Thompson's meals deserved appreciation, so Mike determined to give extra attention to the next one. Or two. Or. . .

"Good morning!" Shadows smudged the delicate skin beneath her eyes, but Naomi's smile said she didn't mind the missed sleep.

"Good morning." He hid his surprise to find her already in the workshop. Mike expected her to be doing what all women did, hovering around the newborn and rushing about with tiny clothes and whatnot.

Of course, Naomi never fulfilled his expectations; she exceeded them. With plenty of other women to fuss and coddle the infant and mother, Naomi didn't shirk her responsibilities. She went to work. Her very presence in the workshop told him everything was fine.

Still, Mike knew he should ask. "How are the mother and babe?"

She positively beamed. "Quite well. Doc said Arla's labor was the easiest kind, very short, so she'll have a quick recovery. Granger is showing Mr. Corning around, which is fitting since Mr. Corning is concerned with the business side of the enterprise, so Granger is the best man to explain what we've accomplished and how we plan to proceed—they'll meet with Mr. Lawson a bit later. At any rate, it frees any of us from having to play hostess today.

"Cora and Martha are taking turns, switching between helping Evie with supper and staying with Arla. Doc will check in soon, and Lacey dragged Dunstan to her mercantile to dig up baby supplies. I expect she'll inundate Arla with piles of catalogues tonight."

"I never saw Mrs. McCreedy before last night," Mike admitted.

"The men don't see her much," Naomi assured him. "She keeps to the kitchen or watches over Arla. Martha makes a point of taking supper home so she and Mr. McCreedy can enjoy each other's company."

"That explains it." Mike began laying out the pieces he'd work on that afternoon. So far he'd spent the bulk of his time planing shingles down to extreme thinness. Now he had a stack of wood sheets, each meticulously shaved to a quarter-inch thickness. These would make the removable rooms. The stack of larger boards he'd left at a third of an inch to create the exterior and house supports.

"I think it's wonderful"—the wistful note in Naomi's voice grabbed his attention—"that they set aside time to be together."

"Spouses should make time for each other." Mike wished he could flatten the worries buzzing around her thoughts like little gnats. Of course she worried about what her own marriage might entail. The bond between a man and woman happily growing old together wasn't likely to develop with a spouse chosen without love. Mike should know—he'd failed with Leticia. Instead of stopping her worries, he should add to them—warn her away from such a disastrous decision.

But I can't tell her that I married for money. Women made this arrangement every day, but for a man to admit he'd sold himself the same way. . .it made him less of a man. Weak. *No one can ever know.*

"Did you?" She looked at him expectantly, with a trace of defiance for having dared ask such a personal, prying question.

"Did I make time for my wife?" Mike had no easy answer for that. In the beginning, he'd catered to Leticia's every demand, believing her temper would even out after Luke's birth. The physicians who knew no more of Leticia's character than Mike assured him that women were notoriously emotional when expecting.

After Luke's birth, Mike brought the babe to visit Leticia every day, even though she refused to nurse the child herself. When Leticia regained her strength, she ended the visits entirely. Dinners were eaten in silence across a long table.

His attempts to interest her in the workshop were met with open disdain. Invitations to take their son for a walk earned him a frosty glare while she informed him that nannies pushed prams—did she *look* like a servant? As time passed, Mike slowly stopped making overtures to his wife. They lived as strangers in the same house.

"I should have tried harder." The admission tasted sour. He'd been the only one trying, but Mike took Leticia as his bride. As the head of the household, the marriage rested on his decisions. There was no excuse good enough for giving up on his wife. *None.*

Sensing that she'd pushed too far, Naomi settled herself in her chair and devoted her attention to the list she'd begun yesterday.

Mike thought she'd ended the conversation until he heard her whisper, hesitant and husky, "All any of us can do is try."

TWENTY-EIGHT

It's not enough." Naomi pushed her chair back from the table an hour after the awkward end to her and Michael's conversation. Up until today, she'd been setting up the work area and poring over catalogues to place orders with German manufacturers for things she couldn't possibly make herself. Now that she'd inventoried her supplies, she realized how much she still needed to move forward.

"What isn't?" Michael stopped sawing and walked over to eye her list. A frown puckered his forehead as he read over her supplies.

"These." She circled the lower portion of her list and began reading aloud. "Tin ceiling panels, pressed cork sheets, model ship masts, wall-covering samples, linoleum, one-inch diameter wooden dowels—the manufacturers won't ship small orders. Except the wall-covering samples—I don't think those will be shipped at all."

"The ceiling panels, linoleum, and wall coverings make sense." Michael paused before asking. "Cork? Model ship masts? Dowels?"

"Cork is wonderful!" She got up and rooted around Lacey's dollhouse, bringing back a handful of items. "It's thin enough to cut, more pliable than wood, inexpensive, and it takes paint well."

She set down one of the beds and tugged off its coverlet to expose the cork nestled within the bed frame. "It's perfect for mattresses or padding-covered furniture. If you slice a bottle stopper, with a little paint it makes an excellent rind for cheese."

Naomi smiled at his thunderstruck expression as her "cheese" spilled onto the table—some already with wedges cut out. She added her pièce de résistance—a "copper" bathtub. "The flexibility allows me to cut the pieces, glue them together, and paint it easily."

"Cork it is." He picked up the tub and turned it around. "I'd only ever seen it used as insulation for walls or even flooring."

Naomi set down one of the flights of stairs and pointed to the railing. "Here are the ship masts. They're already the right size, shaped nicely, and take almost no effort to trim. I also use them for furniture." She indicted the posts on the disassembled bed.

"That'll save a lot of time carving." Michael seemed impressed.

"Oh, you wouldn't believe how much I rely on toothpicks and pieces made for ships in a bottle." Naomi laughed. "And fan blades."

Admiration shown in his gaze. "Clever—very clever. I wouldn't have any idea where to find a supplier for fan blades though."

"I found a fan maker who was closing her shop, and I bought all of the pieces she had on hand. Strips of sandalwood and balsa mostly. I use them for everything from fireplace grates to furniture. But thank heavens there are still plenty of those—I doubt we'd find an accommodating fan maker out here in the territories!"

"I can't wait to hear how you plan to use the wooden dowels."

Naomi didn't keep him in suspense. "Scalloped siding. If you cut the dowel into thin, angled rounds then layer them so the thicker bottom part overlaps the thinner upper portion, it looks like siding. If Lyman Place hadn't been brick, I would've tried it."

Michael rubbed his jaw, as he frequently did while thinking. "That's going to save me a considerable amount of time, and the results will be much more uniform than hand carving each shingle."

"Oh, I'm sure your shingles would have been wonderful." Naomi couldn't remember when she'd enjoyed a conversation more. Here she stood, discussing her techniques with a man who appreciated her method and made her feel almost as innovative as he was himself.

"There are dowels at the mercantile. I remember seeing some the first day I arrived." He looked uncomfortable, and for the first time Naomi wondered why Michael, of all people, had followed her back into the storeroom that day. Why not stay in the main area of the mercantile, grabbing spades and pickaxes with the others?

She slowly put a line through the dowels, crossing it off her list if not her thoughts. "That helps. The other thing we'll need is glass cut to fit the windows, but I don't know the measurements."

Michael grabbed a piece of paper and a pencil to start making notes of his own. "I'll write them out and take them to a glassmaker when I go to fetch the other supplies. The ship masts will be the most difficult to come by, but maybe we can place a large order since we'll use a lot on things like staircases and porch rails?"

"True." Naomi put a careful little question mark beside the item, trying to hide her smile at the way Michael listened to and was already finding ways to tailor the materials for new purposes.

"When do you need these things?" He tapped his pencil on the top of her list. "How long before the lack starts to slow you down?"

"Soon. The linoleum and wall coverings are the foundation for most of the rooms. So you should go next week." Naomi nibbled the inside of her lip, not wanting him to see her distress at the idea of him leaving. She couldn't show how much she'd miss their daily conversations and the simple pleasure of working with a partner.

"It's fortunate," she began brightly. Too brightly—Naomi realized she'd overdone and modulated her tone before continuing. "Lacey and Braden were determined that Hope Falls be a place where workers could bring their families. The little houses are so useful—if one doesn't think about the people who left them behind."

"And why." He sat with her in a moment of silence, acknowledging the losses incurred by the mine collapse. Families torn apart. "But they came in handy when Corning showed up."

"And for storage," she teased, knowing it would make him smile. "But I was thinking more along the lines of setting up a house so when you go for supplies, you can bring Luke home with you."

"You mean. . ." His face lit up as though all his Christmases came at once. "I can bring him back with me next week? To a house?"

"Well, we aren't going to put him in the bunkhouse." Naomi tried to look stern but couldn't manage in the face of his joy. "A one-room cabin is the least we can do. Aside from Arla's little Dorothy, he'll be the only child in Hope Falls. Our first family." She tried not to think about how it wasn't actually hers at all.

She's not mine, Mike reminded himself, watching Naomi return from another nature walk, surrounded by lovesick swain. *Don't interfere.*

Not that she asked him to. Actually, by the looks of it, she didn't seem to mind being swarmed every time she stepped foot outside their workshop. But try as he might to convince himself otherwise, Mike minded. He wanted to swat the suitors away from her.

It was maddening, seeing her smile at all of them and no one in particular. He'd come to loathe seeing what new addition perched atop the cougar's hat in the dining room—one of the men actually added a small bird's nest, ostensibly to go with the abundance of feathers fluffing up all over the raggedy thing. Each one of those multihued plumes reminded Mike that other men gave her gifts.

Gifts she accepted, doling out smiles in reward for shameless scavenging. Mike wouldn't be surprised to find out the men were trapping birds, just to pluck a few feathers and bring them to her. And there was nothing he could do to stop it. Nothing he could say to make her see reason. No way to reclaim her attention when they moved beyond the cozy confines of their work space and half a dozen men clamored to speak with her, sit beside her, gape at her. . . .

No. Naomi chose to put herself through this. Even worse, Naomi was going to have to choose one of the men, all now tripping over themselves to snag her smiles. Had they no pride? If Mike could join them, would he? Didn't she know she deserved better than this travesty of a courtship, where half their enjoyment came from the competition?

In two days Mike wouldn't be around to keep an eye on her and make sure none of those men stepped over the line. He wouldn't know how she handled things or how the lumbermen stepped up their attentions. The longer this went on, the more intense it became. And with Mike not present in the workshop, she'd be alone. *Unprotected.*

By the time she emerged from the diner, having shed her coat of companions, Mike worked himself into a thoroughly foul mood. When Naomi settled herself beside him to watch Braden engaging in a cutthroat game of horseshoes, he couldn't keep it all bottled up.

"How did you ditch them?" He slid the diner a sideways glance.

"Don't let anyone else hear you say that." She hushed him, but her grin went a ways toward soothing his pique. "Evie made a batch of shortbread, and she was kind enough to bring out a full plate."

"Good timing." Some of the tension eased from his shoulders. "Good to know someone's keeping an eye on how things are going."

"Oh?" Her green eyes snapped with suspicion. "How's that?"

"You shouldn't be dangled in front of the men like a piece of meat before wolves." Mike jabbed a finger toward the diner. "At least someone's keeping tabs on where you are and with whom."

"And if that 'someone' is supposed to be Evie,"—she pinned him with her gaze—"why did you decide to take on the task yourself?" *Oops.* Mike swallowed, unable to refute the accusation but not willing to own up to it—or open the door for more questions. So he borrowed Luke's method of evading the question. He snorted. Loudly.

"Don't be so dismissive." She folded her arms over her chest. "It's clear that you've been keeping tabs on me, so why deny it?"

Technically he hadn't denied it, but Mike deduced she wouldn't take kindly to the observation. It would help him think better if she didn't look so pretty, with anger making her cheeks all pink. He realized he'd waited too long to talk when she started squinting.

"It doesn't matter." He waved it away and looked fixedly at the game of horseshoes, where Braden was gleefully trouncing Corning.

"Then why did you bother bringing it up in the first place?" Exasperated, she wouldn't stop pestering him. "If it didn't matter?"

"I don't understand why you did it." He shrugged as though her answer wouldn't make much difference. "That's all there is to it."

"We go for walks because the forest is beautiful, and I can spend time with all of them at once, without obviously favoring anyone."

She sounded calmer now. "It keeps from causing trouble."

"No." Mike turned to face her again, wanting to see her face, needing to know what she might refuse to tell him. "I meant I don't understand what possessed you to put out that advertisement."

For the first time, he understood what people meant by the expression "her face fell." It was as though everything happy and bright about Naomi just crumpled until she wouldn't look at him. She looked like she might cry, and that was enough to make him want to pull her into his arms and start apologizing until he fixed it.

Only he couldn't. Mike couldn't hold her. He couldn't fix it.

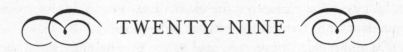

TWENTY-NINE

What a mess. Naomi stared down at her hands, neatly folded in her lap, and wished she could go back to the day Lacey talked them all into that awful ad so she could talk sense into everybody.

"It was a mistake." She hated how pathetic she sounded. She hated how pathetic she *felt*. And, truth be told, Naomi wasn't too fond of the tell-me-something-I-didn't-know look Michael gave her.

"When the mine went bust, we lost all of the money we invested in Hope Falls. Not just Braden and Lacey, but Cora and Evie and me, too. We'd all gone in together to buy shares. Lacey and Evie invested in the mercantile and café—so they stood to lose the most."

"That explains why you decided to start a sawmill." Michael didn't say it, but Naomi heard the unspoken part of the statement: *but it doesn't explain why you put out an ad to hire your husbands!*

"It's like dominoes." She knew it was cliché, but she couldn't really think of another way to explain how everything came crashing down, piece by piece. "The mine failed. The town went bust. We lost our investment, but Lacey saw a way to turn things around. Problem was, none of us knew the first thing about sawmilling, aside from what Lacey researched. And it wasn't as though we thought we could traipse into the forest, swing an ax, and fell trees ourselves."

"Right." He looked aghast at the suggestion, but beneath that she saw a glimmer of recognition. "The four of you needed help."

Naomi tried to speed things up. "But even if we had the funds to hire men, we wouldn't know who to trust. When Lacey first suggested it, we thought Braden was dead. We had no other brothers or fathers or cousins to come with us. We'd have to go alone."

"Too dangerous." If she'd thought he looked horrified by the idea of them chopping trees, it was nothing compared to the expression on his face as he considered the alternative. "You couldn't surround yourselves with strange men without protection."

Naomi nodded vigorously, glad to see that he understood their reasoning. "Exactly. But when Lacey suggested that husbands could solve our problems, we balked. Every one of us refused to listen. We decided we'd rather take the financial loss than strike out with such a far-fetched scheme. Saving Hope Falls wasn't a good enough reason to endanger ourselves and do something so outrageous."

"And then you learned Braden hadn't died." Michael demonstrated that spectacular ability to piece things together. "You said Miss Lyman and the younger Miss Thompson were coming with or without you. So they came for Braden, and you and the older Miss Thompson came to make sure they didn't get themselves killed along the way."

"That's a rather blunt way of putting it." Naomi considered it for a moment before confessing, "Very blunt—but dead right." A smile played about the corners of her mouth at the pun.

"Which brought you right back to where you started—heading for an isolated place where none of you had the strength or know-how to save the town." Understanding was dawning, but Michael didn't look happy about it. Which was just fine with Naomi, since she wasn't very happy about the situation either. "Without male protection."

"Precisely." Naomi sighed. "At this point, we were also concerned that Braden's injuries might clear the way for unscrupulous men to encroach on the property. We couldn't defend the land, we couldn't protect each other indefinitely, and we couldn't trust any men who'd be willing to follow us to an isolated area."

By now Michael was raking his fingers through his hair in obvious agitation. "Did it occur to you to just wait until Braden recovered? Until either he came home or he could look after you?"

"It occurred to us. But we'd been mourning for my cousin for weeks already. It was only natural that his sister and fiancée would rush to his side when we heard he'd been pulled from the mine." She sniffed at the memory of those intense days. "At the time, there was still some question as to whether or not he'd survive. You know about his knee, but the more dangerous injury was a severe concussion that left him unconscious for two days after he was rescued."

She fell silent, having explained all she could. Michael stayed quiet, too, and Naomi knew he was turning the problem around in his mind, trying to puzzle out a solution that was already too late. Anything more she could add ventured into very personal territory, and Naomi wasn't about to reveal the other salient points Lacey made while convincing all of them to take such drastic action.

How could a woman explain the impact of Lacey's argument that hiring a husband wasn't merely a mercenary flouting of convention, it was a chance for them to decide what they really wanted from a spouse? A unique opportunity to select a life partner who could fill those needs. Instead of waiting for a man to offer a ring entwined with a lifetime of *his* expectations, they would choose for themselves. And instead of feeling privileged to have been chosen, they would feel valued by the men who'd proven themselves worthy.

The idea awakened a dormant hope Naomi had long since left for dead. A man responding to the ad wouldn't expect an overly traditional bride. A man willing to view marriage as a partnership might value her for the prospects she brought to the table. In short, she might find a man willing to overlook her lack of virtue and even—here's where the temptation became overwhelming—feel as though he wasn't making an unspeakable compromise in wedding her.

How could she explain any of that to the man sitting beside her? She couldn't even explain it to her closest friends. And the way things turned out, Naomi couldn't justify it to herself. She'd done an excellent job of backing herself into a corner, and her only possible escape would be on the arm of a man she didn't really want.

Wrong man. No matter how kind and attentive Mr. Corning was, Cora found herself thinking the same thing every time she saw the admiration in his gaze. *Why isn't Braden looking at me like that?*

This made it difficult to keep up her end of the conversation. At a certain point, Cora realized that it didn't make much difference to Mr. Corning. So long as she contributed the occasional smile, a few nods, and the odd "mm-hmm" or "oh?", Mr. Corning kept things going. Either the man loved the sound of his own voice or else he didn't get much opportunity to speak without interruption.

Her only consolation was the dark looks Braden kept casting poor Mr. Corning whenever he looked the other direction. Of course, Cora couldn't be sure that Braden wasn't just taking exception to having another man take his place pontificating. But somehow she thought his irritation had more to do with the attention Mr. Corning was giving her. That thought alone kept her smiling and nodding.

She'd enjoyed a brief respite during supper, but when everyone bundled in their coats and gathered around a large fire, he glommed on to her again, and Cora couldn't help thinking that after all his practice, she thought Braden could wheel to her side a bit faster!

Gradually she realized that Mr. Corning wasn't yammering on any longer. He was, in fact, looking at her with that very specific combination of expectation of a response and concern that she wasn't giving him that response. But no matter how hard she racked her brain, Cora realized she'd lost the gist of the conversation entirely. She didn't know whether to agree or disagree, and the time clearly passed for a politely vague murmur to suffice. *Oopsie.*

"I'm afraid I just realized I forgot something," she hedged, casting about for an appropriate excuse. She caught sight of Evie bustling back from the kitchen storeroom with a bag of what looked like. . . "Marshmallows! I'm supposed to help Evie pass them out so everyone can toast a few over this lovely fire. You might want to find a long twig or a thin branch or something of the sort."

With that, she hopped up and hurried to meet her sister. As usual, she didn't need to fill Evie in on why she'd rushed over.

"Quite chatty, that Mr. Corning." Evie shook half of the marshmallows into Cora's waiting apron. "You'd think Braden would be so kind as to absorb some of his guest's fondness for conversation."

"You'd think so, wouldn't you? But apparently we'd both be wrong. Thank you for the distraction." Cora tilted her apron so the fluffy little treats lumped together more or less in the middle.

Evie looked from her half-empty bag to the fire, where the men were already holding out stripped branches in obvious readiness. "Well, these won't hold him off for long, I'm afraid. They don't take long to chew. . .but fires are good for more than roasting marshmallows. What if I get everyone to ask you to tell a story?"

"All right." Cora began thinking of stories, weighing options and discarding several that wouldn't hold the attention of a bunch of lumberjacks. She smiled at her sister. "My voice is well rested."

They laughed together as they rejoined the group and enjoyed their marshmallow-influenced popularity. In a few moments, the treats were passed out, and the men were briefly silent as each tried to toast their treat the perfect golden brown. The odd failure, blackened like a lump of coal, induced much teasing. One fellow seemed to get it just right, only to have the gooey morsel slide down the branch and plop, hissing, atop the licking flames.

As promised, Evie took advantage of the quiet. "I always think that a good fire with good friends needs only a good story to make it perfect. Cora, why don't you see if you can tell us a tale?"

A chorus of agreement went up around the circle, including Mr. Corning. Now that she was the focus of so much avid attention, Cora found herself grateful that Naomi hadn't allowed her to announce her newfound availability. She couldn't imagine how Naomi dealt with this type of attention so often—it was absolutely unnerving. Cora looked around the circle, her gaze snagging on Braden. He nodded, and suddenly she knew exactly which story she wanted to tell. It was a legend he needed to hear—and a lesson she needed him to heed.

"All right," she announced to the waiting group. "In honor of the fine men seeking to woo my good friend, Miss Higgins, I will tell the "Legend of the Loathly Lady." Listen well, because the moral of the tale reveals the answer to an almost unanswerable question."

"She's anything but loathly," Mr. Strode objected, giving Cora a look that told her Naomi might have one more suitor than she knew.

"Listen to the story before you judge it." Naomi, who'd taught it to Cora in the first place, smiled in anticipation. "Go on now."

THIRTY

It's one of my favorites," Naomi whispered as the story began.

So Michael listened and found himself caught up in the story woven around the campfire. He noticed that the other men, some of whom politely feigned interest at first, perked up when they realized this "lady" story revolved around Arthurian legend.

Swiftly, Miss Thompson set the scene. King Arthur, separated from his loyal knights during a hunt, is drawn deep into the forest. The king slays his deer but finds himself at the mercy of an enraged dark knight. Unarmed and alone, Arthur faces certain death by the hand of this opponent, but the dark knight offers him a deal: Return in a year, unarmed and alone, and if Arthur can answer the knight's question he may go unharmed. If he does not give the right answer, he will lose his head and Camelot will be undone. Arthur, of course, agrees to find the answer to the question.

"And what do you suppose was the knight's question?" she asked the crowd. "Something so difficult that the king's failure was certain?" After a moment, the men began to bandy suggestions around the fire.

"Why bad things happen to good people?" Clump guessed, only to be outvoted on the grounds that a *dark* knight wanted to leave the ways of evil a mystery so people could stay weak and afraid.

"Oh, I know!" Bobsley slapped his knee. "If a tree falls in—" He didn't even finish the old saw before groans drowned him out.

Naomi quirked a brow, daring Mike to make his own guess.

But Mike couldn't. Not when the only unanswerable questions

bumping around in his brain concerned the woman sitting beside him. He gave a prayer of thanks when Miss Thompson took up the story again.

"The knight's challenge to King Arthur was to discover. . ." She paused, making everyone lean forward. "What do women want the most?"

Groans and guffaws went up, the men shaking their heads.

"An impossible question indeed." Mike kept a straight face.

"I bet you could find the answer, the way you puzzle things through." Naomi gave him a small smile. "Think about it awhile."

"It's not so obvious for us men," he told her, biting back the first answer: *love.* A part of him still believed everyone wanted to be loved, but hadn't Leticia proven him wrong? What about Naomi, whose plans for the future centered around a business arrangement? No, Mike knew better than to say love was most important to her.

"Security!" Gent announced from across the way. "Women want to be looked after and to know that they and their children are safe."

"Nah, she's right. There is no good answer. Women can't pick one thing when they want so many," grumbled someone in the shadows.

"Don't be sore because you aren't one of them, Williams!" For a moment, it looked as though a scuffle might break out, but Miss Thompson picked up the story and averted the blossoming problem.

"Disheartened but bound by his word, Arthur returned to Camelot. There, his nephew, Sir Gawain, notices the king's melancholy and pries the reason from him. For the next year, both Arthur and Sir Gawain ask thousands of women for the solution to the riddle. But every woman gave a different answer from the last." At this statement, the men starting laughing, and Mike joined them.

Mike shared his answer with Naomi. "Maybe the answer is that every woman wants something different because no two women are the same. Maybe they want their uniqueness appreciated."

She tilted her head and gave him a searching look. "Clever, but I think it depends on how the man shows her his appreciation."

"Something special, just for her." Mike decided to ask his own impossible question. "How would *you* want to be appreciated?"

"Say!" a man shouted. Braden recognized the high climber but couldn't remember the name of the man talking through Cora's story. "There's a better question. What does Miss Higgins want? That's what we need to know!"

If it wasn't for the fact Braden had just been wondering the same thing about Cora, he wouldn't have any patience for the interruption. As things stood, he wondered if this question might open an opportunity to wrangle an answer to his own version. As it stood, he wasn't doing a good job figuring out what Cora wanted, much less how to convince her to let him be the man offering it!

Naomi froze, eyes wide as a startled deer, and Braden felt a little sorry for his cousin. She hated being the center of attention and usually exhibited a distinct talent for fading into the woodwork. If Braden hadn't seen it for himself, he wouldn't believe any woman could render herself almost invisible while staying in plain sight. But Naomi could go quiet, tuck herself in a corner, and watch as most of the people in the room forgot she was still there.

But that wasn't possible anymore. She—along with the rest of the women—thrust herself into the limelight when they posted that ad. *Wait.* The ad! Why were the men asking what Naomi wanted when she'd been kind enough to spell it out for them in the clearest possible terms? Even better, Cora swore she'd helped write the thing. So didn't that mean she wanted the same things on the list?

What had they required, aside from logging or sawmill experience to help get the business off the ground? He racked his brain, trying to remember the exact words. *God-fearing* was the first one. *Hardworking* was another. They'd wisely added *single* because, even though that should be obvious, some unscrupulous fellows might try to trick them. With that in mind, Braden made a split-second decision to surreptitiously have the men looked into. Just to make sure none of them had a surprise bride tucked away in another state. But hadn't the ladies listed something else? One last criteria?

"Right now,"—Naomi all but shouted to catch everyone's attention—"I most want for everyone to let Cora finish the story." The announcement left the men no choice but to quiet back down.

Then Cora was talking, and Braden forgot everything except how her hair glowed in the light of the fire and her eyes shone with mirth while she spoke and her words flowed around him with reassurance and familiarity, weaving a spell through the story. Of course, magic didn't exist anywhere other than legend. No. Such wishful thinking was just a way to spring life lessons on unwary listeners.

"Despairing, with only a day remaining,"—she looked directly at him, and Braden knew King Arthur wasn't the only one whose time ran short—"the king returned to the depths of the forest, hoping to reason with the dark knight. Instead he came upon a hideous hag tucked atop a snow-white mare. Oddly formed of sparse hair, shriveled skin, and yellowed nails, the Loathly Lady looked down upon the good king and bared her blackened teeth in a sad smile.

"She told Arthur she was the sister of the dark knight, and she would tell him what women wanted if he granted her one small request: that she be allowed to wed Sir Gawain. Horrified by the idea of handing over one of his bravest, most handsome knights to this foul creature, Arthur refused her request and left the forest."

"Ah, big mistake," someone hooted. "Rather die than let a friend get shackled to a hag? People marry for worse reasons." Eventually he realized the silence around him turned ominous and probably recalled that most of the men around him were trying to marry a woman who'd advertised for a business partner as a husband. He tried again. "Erm. That is to say, I didn't mean, you know. . ."

"Quit yer jawin' and let her finish the story," someone yelled, making the fool gratefully shut his mouth and stop his retractions.

"And again, Sir Gawain recognized his uncle's sadness and wrangled the truth from Arthur. When he heard of the Loathly Lady's request, Gawain agreed immediately. They wed the very next day, the court full of whispers and regret for the fate of this good knight."

"Well?" Bear Riordan prompted when Cora's pause lasted long enough to show that she wanted someone to ask. "Did she keep her promise? Did she tell Arthur what women want most and save him?"

"Yes. After the ceremony, she revealed to Arthur and Gawain that the thing women most want is sovereignty." Cora stared pointedly at Braden. "The ability to make their own decisions."

Dimly, Braden knew that the men were full of comments. Some agreeing, some contesting an answer obviously supported by the women around them. It might be a story, but Braden reeled at the truth. *Independence? The thing women most want is the same thing I do?*

Even more surprising was the fact that it surprised him. It made perfect sense! Hadn't his sister, his fiancée, his fiancée's sister, and even his mild-mannered cousin been arguing with him for months about their ability to make their own decisions? And he'd ignored them, making demands and handing down orders as though he had the right to personally control every one of their lives.

But it was for their own good! They put themselves in danger with terrible decisions! He protested against the guilt rising in him, but it did no good because, as Cora doubtless intended to show him, *those decisions were* theirs *to make after* my *choices blew up.*

There was an unfamiliar sensation prickling in his stomach and clogging his chest, and Braden suspected it had something to do with the sudden realization that he was a first-class idiot. *I never was before. How did everything change so much? How did I change so much?*

The cave-in. It only took one catastrophe in his well-ordered life to destroy his equilibrium—and not just because it knocked him off his feet either. One crisis took away his choices, and instead of accepting it and moving on, he tried to steal everybody else's.

No wonder Cora avoids me. He swallowed, mouth dry and tasting like the ashes of the fire. *How can I win back my lovely lady now?*

"The story isn't over, gentlemen." Naomi tried to hush them.

"What about Gawain?" By the looks of it, Strode hit on the

right answer again, naming the one element of the legend that didn't resolve happily. He received approving nods from the women, but, more importantly, his reminder that a knight remained in peril made the men quiet down in respect for the fate of the brave Sir Gawain.

"Very good, Mr. Strode." Cora made a point of acknowledging the carpenter, but Braden didn't feel any stab of envy—it was far too obvious that Strode had his eye on Naomi. "That night when Sir Gawain went to his bride, he could not find the Loathly Lady."

"Lucky man." The mutterer got a quick elbow in the ribs.

"Instead a beautiful maiden waited in her place. As it happened, her brother cursed her with hideous looks when she refused to marry as he demanded. The spell could only be broken if she married a handsome knight. Their marriage lifted part of the curse."

"Did you say 'part' of the curse?" Dunstan looked up from scratching behind Decoy's ears until the massive dog nosed his arm.

"Yes, only part." Cora's eyes gleamed, and Braden knew the last part of the story would be the most interesting. "The lady regained her beauty for half of the day but would remain loathly for an equal share. She explained that Sir Gawain could have a beautiful wife at night, in private, or he could have a beautiful wife by day, in public. But his decision could not be undone or changed later."

Corning shook his head. "There's a catch to every contract."

"What a catch." Gent twirled his beloved top hat on the tip of his finger. "To trade the respect of your peers for the bride of your dreams or maintain one's stature and live with a monster."

"It takes a strong man to choose his bride for her own sake and not for what other people will think." Naomi's cheeks glowed, and she'd half risen from her seat in a rare display of irritation.

"So tell us," Braden intervened. "What did Gawain choose?"

"He chose to listen." Cora spread her arms and looked around the circle. "Gawain remembered the answer to the impossible question and honored his bride with the thing women want most. He told the lovely maiden he couldn't make the decision for her."

The answer was so obvious it could have smacked him in the

head, and Braden still hadn't recognized it until Cora finished. His only consolation lay in the fact that the other men hadn't realized it either. Maybe that's why only a legendary knight figured it out.

"The Lovely Lady smiled and told him that, in return for listening to her answer and giving her a choice, the spell was entirely broken. Lovely she would remain for all the hours of the day and night, and none would ever see the Loathly Lady again."

THIRTY-ONE

It can't be her. Naomi staggered, guilt pressing her lungs toward her spine and shame making her want to hide. She watched in disbelief as a very elegant lady daintily disembarked down the train's folding steps. Naomi watched a very familiar face turn toward her, and suddenly it was too late to pretend this wasn't happening. Too late to seek sanctuary in the workshop and pray that the visitors were just passing through and might miss her entirely.

An enigmatic smile tilted the corners of her lips as Charlotte spotted her sister for the first time in five years. That smile pounded in Naomi's heart with the force of a battering ram. *She hates me. I know she does. But she's smiling. Maybe there's a small chance we can rebuild a relationship, that blood is thicker than betrayal and the years have softened Charlotte toward forgiveness.*

She needed to move, but that terrible mix of fear and hope kept her rooted in place in the shadow of the diner. Because her sister hadn't come alone. No. There, smoothly taking Charlotte's arm and oblivious to Naomi, stood the man who'd torn them apart. *Harry.*

Oh no. Her chest pinched, making it difficult to breathe. Five years had passed, but her first glimpse of them brought her right back to the most horrifying moment of her life. The terrible truth Naomi privately mourned and desperately kept hidden from everyone. *Lord . . . Oh Lord. . .why have You brought this upon me?* Naomi desperately sought reassurance. *Why now, when I'm so close to choosing a husband? I know things aren't going as well as I'd hoped, and I spend far too much time thinking about Michael, but still—* A sudden thought grabbed hold of her with iron claws. *Is this why You brought them? Not to restore the last member of my family but only to remind me of the heartache of choosing a man who isn't meant for me?*

She thought she might be sick, right there in front of her estranged sister and the man who'd ruined her life. *How uncivilized.* Then there was no time left to be sick because now Harry caught sight of her and began steering Charlotte over. Naomi could only watch as the Blinmans descended on her like some dark dream.

Perhaps they're going to denounce me. What am I going to do?

Smile. Or at least, Naomi tried to smile. She nudged her mouth into some semblance of a welcome. Then she took a step forward as though on her way to give the congenial greeting propriety demanded. A single step toward doom. It was all her wobbly knees could manage.

"Mimi!" Charlotte launched herself into a crushing embrace.

What on earth is going on? Naomi's mind whirled. Why was the sister who'd shunned her for half a decade now enacting this overblown reunion? Why did this embrace not feel forced and grasping, when Naomi longed for the day Charlotte would accept her?

Mimi. Naomi's nose wrinkled. She'd forgotten the way Charlotte always insisted on using the pet name Naomi disliked most but still threw herself into a tizzy if anyone dared to call her Lottie. *Funny, the things you forget,* she mused. *Almost as strange as the way one's brain stops working properly just when one needs it most.*

"How *have* you been?" Charlotte disentangled herself at last, still smiling. "It's been positively *ages* since I've seen you."

Wait. What? Why did that make it sound as though Naomi abandoned her? Her precarious smile slipped, and Naomi tried to tack it back on, too saddened by the realization that her hopes were for naught. Not that she blamed Charlotte for forbidding so much as letters—her sister had every right to cut Naomi from her life after what happened—but why enact such a grand performance here and now?

Unless. . .unless she kept her promise and never told Harry what happened. The fine hairs on the nape of her neck prickled. *Unless she somehow hid the fact that we haven't so much as written each other, and Charlotte is trying to make sure he never knows about it.*

"Since the wedding." How had she failed to notice how nasally Harry's voice sounded? "Yes, that's it. Such a long time since you left to help your cousins, and now we find you all the way out here!" Astonishment underscored this last, bringing the dawning realization that Harry—and perhaps Charlotte, too—hadn't known Naomi was here.

What a muddle. But at least she could take comfort in the knowledge that they hadn't tracked her down intending to ruin her. Charlotte's affection might be staged, but that was preferable to hostility. Her presence threatened more than Naomi now. If Charlotte started stripping away Naomi's veneer of respectability, Lacey, Cora, and Evie's reputations became vulnerable by association.

"What brings you to Hope Falls?" she blurted out once she could finally speak. It sounded too harsh. Unwelcoming. Accusing, even. Naomi dredged up some enthusiasm. "Such a surprise to see you both!"

"Naomi?" Lacey detached from Evie's side, where they'd both been gawking at the spectacle, and fluttered over to join them. She looked from Charlotte to Naomi, recognition flaring in her blue eyes. "I didn't realize we were expecting guests this afternoon."

"We weren't." Naomi knew she sounded less than gracious, but she refused to be blamed for another unannounced arrival. "I mean, I wasn't. And I don't think they expected to find me here either."

"Oh no." Harry patted Charlotte's hand. "We knew. It's the reason my wife insisted on coming along, wanting to see Naomi."

"You knew?" Naomi's heart, which only just resumed regular beats, plummeted. The sensation was so physically uncomfortable, she rather suspected that her next step would end with a sickly *squish*.

"How intriguing." Lacey tilted her head as though puzzled. "Surely you're Cousin Charlotte? The resemblance to Naomi is absolutely uncanny. But didn't you send notice of your arrival?"

"Wanted it to be a surprise," Harry chortled. "Charlotte ran across your brother's invitation, and when I told her I wanted to see this sawmill venture for myself, she refused to stay behind."

"I wouldn't hear of it." Charlotte tittered like a parakeet.

"Oh, I'll just bet you wouldn't." Lacey's sickly sweet tone didn't fool Naomi, who remembered her cousin's outrage when she'd learned that Harry had originally courted Naomi then switched.

No, Lacey. Naomi gave her cousin a pleading look and a swift shake of her head. *Don't antagonize Charlotte or rile her temper!*

"So many adventures to be had in such a wild place as this!" Charlotte tightened her grip on Harry's arm and gave Naomi a pointed look. "Why should I let my husband and my sister have all the fun?"

She might as well have kicked Naomi in the stomach. The air whooshed from her lungs, and she had to take a step back to keep from keeling over. And Charlotte knew it, too. Her sister's grin became positively feline, and Naomi suddenly knew, without a doubt, that her sister was toying with her. Even worse, she *enjoyed* it.

As the danger grew clearer, Naomi's guilt faded beneath panic. She'd probably been waiting for this chance since Naomi ruined her wedding. With Mama gone, Charlotte could finally take her revenge.

"Vengeance belongs to the Lord, but He encourages us to seek justice," Granger reminded Braden when he spotted the new arrivals.

Since Granger came back from his trip to Baltimore, having seen his brother's murderer tried, found guilty, and slated for execution, Granger had mellowed. Or maybe that was Evie's influence. Either way, Braden didn't appreciate his friend's well-meaning reminder that *finding* the saboteur didn't end things, because Braden couldn't mete out the murderer's punishment.

For some unfathomable reason, letting the court decide to hang the criminal counted as justice. To Braden's way of thinking, justice should be more along the lines of breaking a few bones before leaving him enclosed in a cold, pitch-black cave to die slowly—the same sentence his greed handed down to Braden's miners.

Luckily, Braden could shove that aside for further contemplation *after* he caught the criminal. More urgent matters demanded his immediate attention—for instance, the newly arrived suspect who'd just strolled past Braden's window. "Harry Blinman?"

"Say again?" Dunstan craned his neck to look around the paper he'd been perusing. Half curled beneath his master's chair, Decoy raised his head from his paws and cocked his ears. "Harry who?"

"Forget Harry Whoever-he-is." Granger crossed over to the window for a better look at a mysterious woman in violet. "Who's *that*?" From his tone of voice, Granger was more wary than impressed.

Braden let out an exasperated snort. "If you stop blocking the window so I can get a better look, I might be able to tell you."

By now Dunstan took the opposite side, bracketing the window and making it even more difficult to see anything. If Granger sounded wary, Dunstan sounded downright suspicious. "Fancy dame."

"Dame?" Braden snickered. "Never thought I'd hear that word coming from you to describe a lady. She must be Blinman's wife, though why any man would bring his wife here, I can't even imagine."

"I don't use it to describe ladies." Dunstan abandoned the window and returned to his paper. "And the one all decked out in purple might look like Miss Higgins, but she's a rotten egg."

"Looks like Naomi?" Braden took another look. Without Dunstan blocking part of the window, he caught the resemblance he'd missed. He fell back with a groan. "Lacey's going to have my head. How could I forget that Blinman married Naomi's sister? That's Cousin Charlotte—and I've never met her, but Dunstan just might be right."

"How did you know?" Granger squinted over to where the purple lady stood, watching porters remove her luggage from the train. "That she's a rotten egg, I mean. You can hardly see her face."

"Way she carries herself." Dunstan strolled back to his spot, careful not to block the view this time. "See how it's not just good posture?

Her chin's forward, nose up, eyes narrowed. She holds her arms stiff and straight when she directs the porters—keeping as much distance as possible. Very hoity-toity. Thinks too much of herself, too little of others, with just enough charm to hide it from the 'important' people." He nodded as Harry Blinman reached his wife's side. The woman visibly softened. "See? She rounds her shoulders toward him, making him feel bigger and stronger—building him up. For him, she's all big eyes and pretty smiles. Pure manipulation. That woman's a cobra disguised as a kitten, coiled and ready to strike."

"I don't know how you do that." Braden stared, seeing everything Dunstan described and agreeing with his assessment. "If someone asked, I'd say she was just directing the workers and then welcoming her husband to her side. Never would have noticed."

"The shift is too big." Granger rubbed the back of his neck. "She's the kind to ruffle feathers, and Evie's too much a mother hen to let it happen. If I were you, Braden, I'd make the most of my time with Blinman because, like as not, it's going to be cut short."

"I would say Harold Blinman is the last man I would've expected to have drop in, but Corning takes that honor. Remind me to thank Lawson for fielding all his questions about the mill design—and for taking him off our hands for a few hours." Braden rubbed his temple. "An entire week, and I've found nothing to indicate his involvement in the mine collapse. The most suspicious thing about the man is the sheer fact that he toddled out from behind his desk and came here."

"I've got nothing to add to that." Granger cracked his jaw. "For as many questions as he asks, they're all about the sawmill plans, logging, or supply routes. Thing is, he might be avoiding the topic of the mines because he thinks I won't know anything. We made it pretty clear I came on board to run the sawmill, not before."

"We also made it clear that I helped survey the property, recommended the geologists, and helped start the mines." Dunstan put down the paper. "But he hasn't said a word to me either. He's either very optimistic about the new venture and reluctant to bring up past failures, or Corning is trying hard to seem disinterested."

"We can't condemn a man for his lack of conversation." Braden swung his feet over the side of the bed, ready to get into his chair and greet his guests. "Maybe we can do better with Blinman. Even if he plays close to the vest, maybe his wife will let something slip."

Dunstan grinned. "Either way, I won't worry about Evie's ruffled feathers. Lacey's more than a match for any snooty miss."

"I'm not worried about either of them," Braden admitted. "It's Naomi. I can't remember hearing her mention her sister—not one single time in the five years she's lived with us. Naomi isn't a part of her sister's life, and there's got to be a good reason."

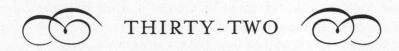 THIRTY-TWO

Y ou stole my wedding night." Charlotte turned on Naomi a moment after Harry closed the door. Just long enough so he wouldn't hear.

At least Naomi hoped he hadn't heard. She hoped no one heard, that no one would *ever* hear. Because if she couldn't make it untrue, at the very least she needed to keep it her and Charlotte's secret. The thing of it was, Charlotte didn't seem very inclined to keep it a secret anymore. That fear, more than the old guilt and shame, is what kept Naomi silent beneath her sister's scathing scrutiny.

"You slept with my *husband*," Charlotte hissed, almost exactly the same way she had on that awful morning five years before. She seemed to think the word *husband* held particular pain for Naomi, and once upon a time she'd been right. Today she probably noticed that it lacked the same impact, so she tried again. "*My* husband."

And even though Naomi knew this was all her fault, knew the shame of her sin and the aching regret for the destruction it caused... she surprised herself. How often had she dreamed of a reunion with her sister? So many times imagining that she'd be overcome with guilt again, offering profuse apologies that just might be accepted this time...but anger steadily overpowered regret.

Lord, what right have I to be angry? After what I've done, I don't deserve to grieve the loss of my innocence or still ache over the reminder that Harry betrayed me with my own sister. Not when I betrayed us all ten times worse. I know I'm in the wrong. I know it.

But still a tiny, stubborn kernel of her heart raged at Charlotte's callous egotism. That she'd intentionally stolen the man Naomi once loved, just to get pretty dresses and a more respected name in society. She hated the way Charlotte saw Harry as nothing more than a belonging to dangle in front of Naomi's nose, the trophy that forever proclaimed her ability to upstage her older sister.

Because in Charlotte's mind, Naomi hadn't betrayed a sacred moral vow or even their bond as sisters. No. For Charlotte, the cardinal trespass had been Naomi's assumption of her position—for daring to touch what *belonged* to her. Harry was just a possession.

"Is that why you came?" Naomi folded her hands in front of her then decided that made her look too much like a penitent child. She wouldn't grovel for a forgiveness her sister would never offer. Not anymore at least. Charlotte didn't know it—and Naomi knew her sister well enough to accept that it wouldn't make a difference even if she did—but ruining Naomi meant ruining Lacey, Cora, and Evie. Their connection to a fallen woman, coupled with their unconventional choices, made all three sitting targets for slander.

Naomi could no longer wallow in a bog of despair, refusing to defend herself against a crime she'd never intended to commit. Now was the time to challenge Charlotte—let her know Naomi had grown too strong to be destroyed by catty comments, snide reminders, or even outright threats. Now wasn't the time for self-flagellation—now was the time to protect Hope Falls and throw her sister off-balance.

"You tagged along to keep an eye on Harry?" She used his nickname to goad Charlotte. Sure enough, her sister's eyes narrowed, but Naomi continued. "To keep an eye on me? Make sure I didn't catch your husband's eye and tempt him into an illicit affair?"

"Don't make me laugh." Charlotte jerked at a knot in her hat ribbons, freed herself, then flung the overblown creation atop the bed. "You possess the charm and grace of a moldering turnip. Do you think I don't know the measures you've resorted to, trying to snare a husband? Everyone knows you couldn't catch a man of your own."

Naomi sucked in a breath. Charlotte wouldn't *inadvertently* destroy the other women of the town by destroying Naomi. No. Her sister *knew* about the infamous advertisement. She knew the depth of the destruction she'd cause if she alienated the only men who might overlook Naomi's past in favor of the future they could create. As much as Naomi hated to admit it, her sister was right. *I can't catch a man.* But lagging behind the bitter reminder came indignation. *Who's Charlotte to say anything, after she stole Harry from me?*

"I might not have caught a husband," Naomi's fingernails dug into her palms, "but at least I can say I didn't steal one either."

"No, you didn't." Charlotte skimmed her hand along the footboard, examined her fingertips, and rubbed them together as though trying to remove nonexistent dust. "But not for lack of trying. How very lowering it must be, to have failed like that. Tell me. What is it like, trying so hard for so little recognition?"

Naomi bit her lip, the taunt jabbing a tiny, tender spot of what used to be her pride. The fact that Harry never realized he'd bedded the wrong sister still hurt. Naomi might not remember that night, but she'd been a novice when it came to hard liquor. Naomi hadn't known better than to follow two fingers of aged whiskey with a few glasses of wine and several champagne toasts. Naomi hadn't known she'd become such an embarrassment that her sister had to drag her from the ballroom and back to the family wing. Most of all, she never would have imagined that she'd wake up in the wrong bed. If Naomi had known any of that, she would've taken the tumbler from her mother's hand and smashed it against the wall!

"Speechless, are you?" Charlotte sank down onto the mattress. "Well, I can't blame you for feeling mortified. If you can't be successful in stealing a man, you should at *least* be memorable."

And that was the crux of the matter. If Harry knew what he'd done, Naomi wouldn't have been able to leave quietly. But a small part of her hadn't forgiven him for not remembering the night he took what only belonged to her husband. Harry had no excuse. He drank with his friends. Often. He knew better than to overindulge and should have abstained on the eve of his wedding, if for no other reason than to respect his new bride. Instead he'd gotten caught up in revelry, taken too many celebratory sips, and lost his head.

Charlotte flapped her hand. "Now go away. You've made me tired, and I need rest because, unlike you, *I* always make an impression!"

Naomi left without another word, too needled to trust herself to speak, too confused by the sudden storm of emotions. She'd tried so hard not to think about Harry, and now the maelstrom hit. She found herself thinking she could almost—*almost*—have understood if he'd only realized his mistake when it was too late to undo the damage. After all, hadn't Jacob done the same with Leah and Rachel? But Harry didn't realize he'd made any mistake. He'd stumbled back to his own chambers, never noticing he'd bedded the wrong sister.

And while his ignorance saved her reputation from certain destruction…it rankled. An insult upon injury. The man who'd taken her virginity *didn't even recognize her*. Harry took her pride when he chose Charlotte, then he stole Naomi's innocence. How could it not hurt? Despite their history, Harry never bothered to notice the real Naomi. Not the woman she was, and not the woman she wasn't.

Was she the woman for him? The question flitted around Mike's mind, swooping in and mixing with his excitement over fetching Luke. *Is Naomi Higgins the woman I should marry? The right mother for Luke?*

Decency dictated that he mourn his wife for at least a year, but widowers with children were often given greater latitude—especially out West, where a man worked sunup to sundown and nannies were all but a foreign phrase. Even if some sticklers balked at a short mourning, no one here knew how long he'd been a widower.

Nor did they know Mike hadn't really lost a wife—how could he lose what he never really had? A wife was supposed to be a helpmeet, a mother to their children, faithful to her husband. Leticia, God rest her soul, fulfilled none of these, and although Mike regretted the way she lived her life and mourned his inability to reach her, he didn't grieve for her as a husband for his mate.

Still, he never imagined he'd be contemplating marriage to another woman so soon. If things were different, he'd have time to court Naomi properly. Time to introduce her to Luke and cultivate the respect and affection sure to blossom between them. Mike didn't doubt Naomi would love Luke—but his son would be more reticent. A new town, a new home, and a new workshop were a lot of big changes to take in all at once. It might already be too much, too soon.

But if he waited to woo Naomi, he would be too late. Even now, during the few days he'd spend away from Hope Falls, the loggers were closing in. *By the time I get back*, he couldn't help the bitter thought, *they'll have constructed an entire tree around that cougar.*

For now he could only keep doing what he'd been doing— praying. Mike prayed for wisdom, he prayed for guidance, and most of all he prayed that the woman he wanted just might happen to want him back and that it was God's plan to bring them together in time to swipe her from the lumberjacks. If not, surely He would have brought Mike to Hope Falls after she was safely married? Or at least not let Mike's thoughts continually drift toward her change-able green eyes.

Mike rubbed his hand along his jaw, resisting the urge to scratch the itchy growth. He'd intentionally gone without shaving for two days before leaving Hope Falls, and after four days his full-fledged beard provided something of a disguise. He prayed it wouldn't be necessary, that the threat of the Bainbridges' selfishness no longer chased his son, but Mike came prepared.

He rested in the assurance that his sister never sent their coded warning. Given the telegram situation in Hope Falls, he might have missed such a message. But Paula knew to send a written letter—addressed to the fictitious Miss Nouveau—as an additional precaution. If they'd been tracked down, there was every chance that her messages might be monitored. Mike had been surreptitiously riffling through the post ever since Granger and the women had cleaned out Draxley's office. No telegram, no letter, no trouble.

And no taking chances with his son's future at stake. As the train eased into the station, all steam and straining steel, Mike tugged his hat brim a shade lower. He grabbed the burlap sack he was using in lieu of a satchel—the better to look like a random deliveryman, if necessary—and moved in an ambling shuffle completely at odds with the urgent need to reach his son. *I was gone too long.*

He felt it with a bone-deep conviction, even though Mike never expected to be back so soon. He'd even warned Luke that it might take the rest of the summer to find a new home for the two of them. Mike realized he'd started to speed up, spurred by the thought of surprising his son. He slowed by degrees, no sudden stops or any abrupt shift in stride. Nothing to draw the attention of passersby.

The nonchalant pace took an agonizingly long time to traverse the few short blocks to his sister's house. As Mike turned the corner, he very obviously checked the street sign and squinted at the structures as though not entirely sure where he was headed. By the time he shuffled up the steps and knocked on the door, Mike felt he'd given a credible performance. It was all he could do to keep his head down so he could hide his grin. *Luke will be so happy.*

The door cracked open. Paula looked out, pale and suspicious, before she ushered him inside. She sagged against the closed door as though to brace against intruders. Her eyes, wide and troubled, made Mike's heart pound long before she confessed, "Luke's not here."

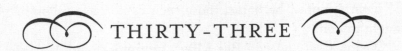# THIRTY-THREE

The sack slipped from his fingers, meeting the rough planks of the raised wood floor with an audible thunk. "What? Where is he?"

"Safe." Paula pushed away from the door. "For now at least."

"Where?" Mike repeated, tensing to bolt out the door and take off running as soon as his sister told him where to find his son.

She laid a restraining hand on his arm. "Mrs. Roberts has him, but you can't go haring after him. If you do, you might as well carry a banner proclaiming, 'Follow me, he's right this way!'"

"Yeah." Mike closed his eyes, forcing his fists to unclench, his shoulders to relax, his breathing to slow. When he had himself under better control, he followed Paula to the table and drained a glass of water. "When did they come for him? How did you know?"

"God watches over His own." Paula refilled his glass and slid it across the table. "I kept in mind what you said about not leaving Luke alone but not taking him around more than necessary—that he might be recognized. So when I needed to go to market last week, I took him over to my friend's place. It does him good to romp around with the other boys a bit. Then he's just one more child in a group—easy to overlook by someone snooping around, peering past fences."

"Are they?" Mike scraped his chair back from the table and flattened himself along the wall, peering through a crack in the curtains. "Looking over fences? Skulking around, asking questions?"

"I'm afraid so. There were two of them waiting for me when

I came back with my groceries, wanting to know if you'd been in contact, if I'd seen my nephew, if I planned to see him soon." Paula smoothed back a strand of hair. "Thank the Lord I thought to put the pot roast in the icebox before I fetched Luke from Mrs. Roberts. If I hadn't stopped by home, those men could have followed me straight to him!"

"Thank God, indeed." But Mike's gratitude couldn't mask his own lack of foresight. No matter his intent, he'd left Luke behind, left him vulnerable to the hired men sniffing around Paula's place. As the picture became clearer, he turned to face his sister again.

"A week, you said?" He waited for her nod. "Why didn't you send the letter and the telegram? I would've boarded the next train!"

"We've been under surveillance since the day they came." Paula started wringing her hands but stopped when she realized it. "Two of them I know by sight. One short, stocky, all in gray with a squashed-in nose. Sits on the bench on the far side of the street for hours. Doesn't move, doesn't blink. He's more rock than man."

"I didn't see him." Mike headed for the other window to check.

"You wouldn't. We can't see the bench from here. Besides, it might be the other one. Tall and gangly, wears all brown, likes to stand in the grouping of trees on the other end. Sometimes they're both out there at once, so we couldn't get by on either side without them seeing. They follow me to market. They follow my husband to work. Our telegraph operator told me they threatened him if he didn't write down a copy of anything I sent or received, and I just know they'd steal the mail from the drop. As long as I didn't send word, they had no reason to stay. I kept hoping they'd leave."

"Well, now we'll be hoping they stay." Mike put his arms around his sister, trying to absorb the tension he'd put her through. "How do you check on him? How does Mrs. Roberts know what's going on?"

Paula's shoulders squared and she stepped back, smiling for the first time since he'd walked through the door. "Our neighbor—she's gotten on in years and her son's away on business, so I do the shopping for her as well. She uses the oldest Roberts boy to do other errands and send messages. So that's how I warned them, and that's how I hear about Luke and know he's still safe."

"That's brilliant." Mike knew she needed to hear how well she'd done, needed to know that her worry and caution had been worth it. "There's no other person in the world I would have trusted to take care of him, and no one could have protected him better. Thank you."

"Don't be silly." She dabbed her eyes and blotted her nose with a hanky and stuffed it back into her apron. "After all the ways you've helped me? I'd do anything for Luke. Ask and it's done."

In spite of himself and the situation, Mike felt the beginnings of a grin. "I can't tell you how glad I am to hear you say that. Now tell me, have you ever gotten a book of wall-covering samples?"

"What are you talking about?" Cora tucked an errant strand of hair behind her ear and tried to concentrate on Martha McCreedy's explanation. She wasn't managing very well, unable to make out most of the words beneath her own panicked chorus of, *No, it can't be.*

Because if Martha was right, there was nothing they could do. And after they worked so hard to see Arla and baby Dorothy through the birth, Cora's mind refused to accept that. Arla would be fine simply because she had to be fine. Or because too many people had died on—or in—this mountain during the past year. Or because Mr. Lawson certainly wasn't up to the challenge of raising his niece. But whatever the reason God chose as the most compelling, Cora couldn't see beyond her blind need for things to be all right.

"No," she interrupted Martha, only to realize that the older woman hadn't been speaking for a while. "You're wrong. When I checked on her this morning, Arla was fine. A little tired, but that's to be expected. She's very excited about our plans to make a nursery, and when she's not with Dorothy or napping, she's knitting. The most dangerous thing in Arla's life is those knitting needles."

Martha's eyes brimmed with compassion and resignation. "I'm

sorry, dear. But you're going to have to face the truth and send away for a nursemaid. There won't be much time to find a good one."

"I'm getting Doc." Cora abandoned the half-finished ironing but found her exit cut short when Martha grabbed hold of her elbow.

"He's already with her." Martha didn't let go immediately. "And you can't go storming in there, demanding to hear pretty lies. Soon enough Arla will know deep down that it's too late, and if you don't start making preparations, she'll be fretting over Dorothy's future instead of enjoying what time she has left. Don't make it worse by pretending things are all right; make it better by promising a mother you'll make sure her daughter is cared for."

Cora jerked her arm away and glared. "Hope is not a pretense. Giving up doesn't give God room to work and show us His will."

"*His* will, Cora. Not yours. Not mine." Martha took a deep breath. "Hope as hard as you can and pray harder still, but prepare yourself for the worst. Send for a nursemaid. If Dorothy needs her, she'll be ready. If she doesn't, I'll happily send the woman home."

"She seemed fine this morning." Cora sniffed, trying to ease the prickles of fear and sorrow. "She's seemed fine since Dorothy was born. How did I miss this? Could we have done something sooner?"

"Childbed fever comes on like this." Martha patted her hand.

"I thought it presented by the third day. We're past that."

"It can come on as late as ten days after the birth," Doc's rough voice interjected. He hunched his way forward, burdened by bad news. "If it were just the stiffness in her joints and the headache, I would be suspicious. But she's cold and clammy to the touch, didn't want me to move any of the blankets she's heaped atop herself to try and keep warm. The cold fit confirms puerperal fever, I'm afraid."

"Some women pull through, don't they?" Cora heard the shrill of her own demand and tried to soften it. "Arla might not die?"

"Few women live once they've contracted it. It's an infection of the blood itself, not something to be isolated for treatment." He set down his bag and rummaged through, pulling out various bottles. "Next will come the fever—the heat is terrible, so put her in a cool bath until it subsides. She'll have a powerful thirst, so let her drink her fill until her stomach starts to pain her. Then she won't want to eat, and she must if she's to continue feeding the babe."

He pointed to a small brown bottle, giving directions on dosage and timing to lessen nausea. Then he gave other instructions for a green-bottled syrup to help her sleep. "For now, make her as comfortable as possible. I'm sure Mrs. McCreedy's already spoken with you about seeking out a nursemaid. I'll come back later."

Cora made it to the nearest chair and plunked herself down. *Not Arla,* she began to importune. *I know I've used up more than my fair share of prayers lately, begging for Braden's recovery and asking for good men for Evie and my friends, but Arla. . . Oh Lord, why would You take Arla so soon after giving her the joy of a daughter? When Dorothy will already never know her father, why imperil her mother? I don't understand. How could it be Your will to orphan an infant?* Cora swallowed against the tears. *Everyone needs to be loved.*

"I don't like her." Lacey plopped onto the settee, not bothering to modulate her tones. "Charlotte may be your sister, Naomi, but I refuse to claim such a condescending cow as any relative of mine!"

"You will *not* antagonize my sister." Naomi fixed her cousin with an icy glare. Lacey may be adept at social sparring, but there was nothing Charlotte loved so well as sharpening her claws on another woman. And this time she'd dipped the points in venom.

"Listen." Lacey leaned forward, dropping her voice so Cora and Mrs. McCreedy wouldn't hear her all the way up the stairs. "I'll admit, I held a bias against Charlotte even before I met her. You've never complained or spoken ill of her, but I've not forgotten Mr. Blinman courted you first, and she intentionally cozened him into marrying her instead. I can't imagine you've forgotten either."

"No." Naomi tried for a wry smile and felt it fall flat. "Some things a woman never forgets." *Even if she can't remember it all.*

"She wears your face but hasn't your heart. I can't understand how two sisters so close in age can be so far apart in character."

"Different fathers, different upbringings. I went to boarding school here in the States, but Charlotte's father insisted she be educated at an exclusive finishing school in France. Mother fought against it, but in the end familial tradition held sway." Naomi shrugged as though she could nudge away the painful memories.

She didn't tell Lacey that she and Charlotte had been close when they were little or how badly she missed her sister when she went to school. She and Charlotte begged and pleaded when they'd learned they were to be separated so often, but their tears changed nothing. Two decades and one debacle later, Naomi knew tears still changed nothing. Whatever connection she and Charlotte once shared had been severed long ago. A quick, clean end might not have done so much damage. But it had taken years of distance and difference to unravel their bond, leaving Naomi with frayed feelings worn raw with regret.

Lacey harrumphed her back to the present. "Well, the French ruined her, I say. I could just throttle Braden for bringing her here." Her face screwed up as she recited in a low voice, " 'No one you would know.' Ugh. Trust a man to forget the important things."

"Braden might not consider it important when so much time has passed and Hope Falls is in need of investors. He meant no harm."

"I suppose." Lacey fell silent as Cora bustled down the stairs, waiting to drag her into the conversation. "Cora! You'll never guess what's happened. Braden's invitations brought two more arrivals!"

Cora joined them, eyes downcast and nose reddened as though from sobbing. Or perhaps from trying not to sob. Sometimes it was difficult to tell. "There'll be one more new person soon enough."

"What's wrong?" Naomi guided Cora to a chair when it looked as though she might simply sink to the floor. "Who else is coming?"

"A nursemaid." Red-rimmed eyes rose to meet their scrutiny. Her voice lowered to an almost inaudible mutter. "Arla's taken ill."

"I'll get Doc!" Lacey practically leaped from the settee.

"He knows." Cora's pronouncement had them all sit back down.

Tears slipped down her cheeks as she told them, "Childbed fever."

"No." Naomi's jaw dropped, and she struggled to compose herself. Childbed fever took almost every mother it chose. So few women survived, the diagnosis might as well be a death sentence.

"But..." Lacey's protest sounded feeble. "The birth went so well."

"There's still hope we might contain the fever and bring it down." Despite the words, Cora looked as worn as their hopes.

You work miracles where You wish, Lord. I pray You see fit to bestow one on Arla and let her live to be a mother to Dorothy. She adores that baby girl, and I know she'd never make her daughter feel unwanted or flawed just because Dorothy's father has passed away. Naomi's heart clenched at the thought and the memories behind it.

Lacey rallied before any of them. "What can we do to help?"

"Keep her cool and comfortable, lots of water. I've contacted an agency, and they're sending a nursemaid for Dorothy. She'll arrive tomorrow. Doc put in an order for ice. Arla gets agitated when he comes in—when anyone but Martha or I go into the room actually." Cora frowned. "Mr. Lawson isn't handling things well. As soon as he heard, he rushed up to see her. Then he left—and hasn't come back."

"Perhaps it's best that he grieves now so he can be strong if he needs to handle the worst," Naomi ventured, although privately she couldn't imagine leaving her sister's side if Charlotte were the one suffering. Time took away precious things, leaving family with nothing to hold on to. How could anyone let go a moment early?

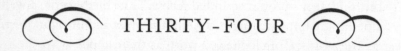

THIRTY-FOUR

Mike struggled to hold on to his patience, anxious to hold Luke and see that he was fine. Unfortunately, patience was one of those virtues he found easier to cultivate than to exercise. Generally he felt patience was a good thing. He worked to have stores of it so he could wait through difficult days, months, years. . .an entire marriage. But longsuffering was a completely different sort of patience than the kind that kept a man from stomping around, being short with shopkeepers, and generally buzzing around like a demented bee.

He wrestled with his agitation with each step, each word, each stop he made to gather Naomi's dollhouse supplies. Mike and Paula hatched the plan together. She'd go about her daily business, stop for the wallpaper samples, and drop them off at her elderly friend's house with instructions for Mrs. Roberts. When the Bainbridges' henchmen had gone for the night, she would place one of the white patterned squares in the front window to signal the all clear. If the wallpaper remained in the morning, Mike would grab Luke and hop on the first train out of Dallas. It didn't matter which direction the train headed—he could always double back after they were safe.

Meanwhile, Mike would gather everything on Naomi's list. He forced himself to move slowly, unhurriedly, like a man going about his normal daily business. If anyone followed him—and he caught sight of The Stone several times during the course of the afternoon— they'd find nothing suspicious in his activities. Thankfully, it kept him busy. If he'd had nothing to do, Mike would've gone mad.

Actually, that part remained in question. He'd taken a bed at a lodging house, careful to make sure that the room he shared with four other men had a back window. While they slept, he'd slip out and return to Paula's street under cover of darkness. Mike would conceal himself well, wait for daylight to dawn, and watch for the wallpaper. If one of the lackeys appeared, he'd wait them out.

He lay awake the entire night, going over possible scenarios and praying that Luke was fine and they'd escape without leaving any trail behind. Other than Paula, Mike had no family. He'd left his friends behind when he skipped town. After this, the Bainbridges would have no leads left to track. They'd have to accept defeat.

The thick, almost smothering darkness of night began to thin. Mike sat up, his legs on the side of the bed, his hand fisted around the burlap sack. He waited, watching black soften to charcoal, charcoal seep to gray. Mike edged to the window, thankful that none of his roommates protested leaving it open on a warm summer night.

He lowered the bag, swung his leg over the sill, and slid down. Staying in shadows marginally darker than the rest of the world, he pulled his hat from the sack and tugged it low over his brow then moved into the night. Mike hid himself in a cluster of trees as morning dawned, illuminating the streets with watery light. He smiled to see the white square in the window, glowing with promise.

Somewhere inside that house, Luke slept. He'd always been a sound sleeper—his head hit the pillow and he slept like a log. That was good—he needed Luke well rested and in good spirits for the journey home. *Home.* Strange how quickly home became a workshop in Hope Falls and the woman who ran it. Mike hoped his son would see the town—and Naomi—as he did.

They'd specifically instructed Mrs. Roberts not to tell him about the plan ahead of time. Exceptional as Luke was, ten-year-old boys weren't known for their prowess at intrigue. They couldn't hide all their excitement, and if one of the Bainbridges' men caught a glimpse of Luke peering through the window in anxious anticipation, things would get very ugly, very fast. To make sure that didn't happen, Mike planned to wait it out, take things nice and slow.

Or agonizingly slow, as the case may be. Mike couldn't remember the last time dawn's soft light spilled forth so gradually. The sun decided on a leisurely morning, but Mike couldn't afford that luxury. He shifted his weight from one foot to the other and back again, peering around the tree trunks in every direction to make sure no one arrived. To make sure no one was watching him in return.

Finally, the day began. Women bustled about, lighting cook fires and sending spools of smoke into the crisp morning air. The piping voices of young children joined the background. Smells of bacon, coffee, and biscuits ventured from open windows to scent the air and tempt slugabeds to the breakfast table. And still no sign of the men who'd been lurking in the lane for more than a week. Even better, Mike didn't see anyone else set up watch on the street.

As casually as he could, Mike swung his now-heavy sack over his shoulder and ambled across the way and down toward the Roberts' house. After a nonchalant glance around to make sure no one looked interested in his destination, he nipped behind the house itself. A tap on the frame of an open window. A few endless moments while his heart slammed against his ribs. And then a small boy was shoved through the opening, hair ruffling as he descended, a book of wallpaper samples clutched against his chest. Mike caught him and slapped a hand over Luke's spreading grin before he could shout a greeting.

The last traces of bleariness vanished. Luke's eyes widened as Mike raised a single finger to his lips, warning to keep quiet. He pulled back his hand and caught Luke again, this time when his son flung himself into his arms. This time Mike picked Luke up and didn't let go until they were tucked away on a departing train.

"Where are we going, Dad?" Luke burst out as soon as Mike told him it was safe to speak. "This time we stay together, right?"

"We're sticking together, and we're going home." Mike wrapped an arm around Luke's shoulders. "There's someone I want you to meet."

THIRTY-FIVE

N aomi!" Her sister's trill pierced through the workshop window, which Naomi left uncovered even in the drizzling rain. Overcast though the day might be, some natural light still shone through.

For a brief, cowardly moment, Naomi considered ducking beneath said window in hopes that Charlotte would peek in, see an empty room, and keep walking. But Arla's rapid decline had strengthened Naomi's resolve to make the most of her time with Charlotte. Perhaps they'd never be reconciled—Naomi knew she didn't deserve forgiveness even if her sister were the sort to extend it—but perhaps they could blanket the past in a newfound peace. *I have to at least try!*

So she stood up, brushed her hands against each other to dislodge some sawdust, and waved through the window. "In here!"

Astonished by a deluge of icy drops, Naomi hastily pulled her arm back inside. She'd been focusing so intently, she'd not registered that the morning drizzle became a downpour. Now that she noticed, Naomi realized the biting chill seeped into the workshop, too. As her sister flung the door open, Naomi headed for the modest cookstove. She added logs until the fire blazed hot and bright.

"So this is where you escaped to!" Charlotte swept over to warm her hands by the fire, gaze raking the room in abject disapproval.

"The workshop isn't an escape." Naomi recognized the lie as it dropped from her lips. Even without Michael's conversation and smiles, the workshop remained her refuge. Primarily, it was a place to work—but in her work, Naomi found an escape. Focusing on minute details distracted her from the many hurts haunting Hope Falls.

At the house, Arla moaned in pain and baby Dorothy wailed for her mother. In the diner, well-meaning lumberjacks vied for her attention and reminded her just how limited her choices for the future had become. Everywhere else, Charlotte sniffed her out like a hound chasing a hare. And the daily train stops heightened hopes she shouldn't have but never brought Michael home with Luke.

None of that followed her into the workshop. . .until today.

"Well, it's not *my* idea of an escape," Charlotte conceded in a tone that implied she held higher standards than her sister. "But it is out of the rain and away from the diner where that Evie woman acts like she owns everything and won't answer questions. Would you believe she told me to make myself useful or make myself scarce?"

Naomi smothered a chuckle by pretending to clear her throat. "Yes, well, Evie does own the diner and doesn't answer to anyone over how she runs it. I know it seems strange the way we do things, but in Evie's kitchen, if you're not helping you're in the way—and, yes, she'll tell you so. The men aren't allowed inside at all." She tacked on this last in an attempt to soothe Charlotte's indignation.

"She did seem to have her hands full." Charlotte unbent a little. "I vow, Naomi, you could *hear* the men sniffing on the other side of those batwing doors! They all tromped in once the rain started coming down in sheets. Something about dangerous conditions—sticky summer sap and slippery rain making things too difficult."

"Oh, I didn't realize." Naomi closed her eyes, knowing she needed to go join Evie in the kitchen or at least help Lacey come up with a way to occupy the displaced workers. As she knew from previous experience, rainy days made the men ornery, and the last thing they needed was for a fight to break out in the diner. Again.

But she had so much to do. *I'm already short on time, and somehow everything takes longer when Michael isn't here with me.*

"I assumed not." Charlotte gave another sniff as she looked around again. "So this is where you spend your time, cobbling together tiny knickknacks? When Mother shipped you off to Charleston, I never imagined you'd resort to taking up a *trade*." She managed to make honest work sound like the lowest sort of crime.

"How fortunate," Naomi murmured, giving her sister a faint smile, "that my choices are not limited by your imagination."

Charlotte tittered as though amused, but her eyes narrowed. "Yes. Your unconventional choices have brought you unexpected options. However will you decide among your throng of suitors?"

Her shoulders slumped forward, but Naomi recognized the sign of defeat and pulled them back before her sister could comment. Now was not the time to indulge in morose feelings and show weakness. Now was the time to show her sister that she'd moved on. That she'd rather be sitting in a sawdust-strewn workshop in the middle of a mountain storm than pouring tea as Mrs. Harold Blinman.

"I don't know how I'll choose." She screwed the silver-plated cap and brush onto the cut-crystal paste pot Lacey gave her instead of admitting that the only man Naomi might consider didn't see her as anything more than a fellow worker and friend. *How can a woman choose a husband when the man she wants doesn't offer for her?*

Not that she could have chosen Michael. Choosing him would mean telling him about her past, and then he wouldn't want her anyway. When he remarried, Michael would choose an upstanding woman to be the mother of his children. Naomi picked up the tiny crib she'd been gluing, inspecting the rails while she thought. *Michael is too good a father to give Luke anything less than a good mother—a shining example of what a wife and woman should be. Not me.*

With a sharp crack, four of the crib rails splintered away from their frame, broken by Naomi's clenched fist. She carefully set the piece down, knowing better than to further reveal her inner tumult. She shrugged at Charlotte and announced, "Not sturdy enough. I'll drill deeper impressions with my awl before gluing the rails. Everything that goes into the dollhouse has to be strong enough to withstand being grabbed by children and shoved about the room."

"If only there were so easy a test to eliminate unsuitable husbands." Speculation lit Charlotte's avid gaze. "Although, I must say, you've done an admirable job of making sure they're all impressively strong. Perhaps you need to see how they temper all that raw physical power before you make your final choice?"

"Perhaps." Naomi didn't see any harm in agreeing with her sister when Charlotte accepted the crushed crib as Naomi's barometer of her own work. Besides, anything that bought her more time before she was trapped into accepting one of the men couldn't be so bad.

"Worse, much worse." Doc shook his head as he whispered his assessment of Arla's condition. "Her pulse is over one hundred thirty beats per minute, and the white coating of the tongue is darkening. You'd best say your good-byes while she's awake."

Cora gave a mute nod, unable to muster any further response. She drew a bolstering breath as the doctor took his leave. For two days she and Martha had watched over Arla, bathing her with cool cloths, giving her water, coaxing broth down her throat. Almost insensible with the fever, Arla no longer protested when Lacey and Naomi took turns through the night so Cora could close her eyes.

"We failed." She looked at Martha now, stricken afresh by their inability to avert the tragedy. "What can we do for her now?"

"The same as we have been. Pray, keep her as clean and comfortable as possible. But for now, I need to find Mr. Lawson and tell him he won't get another chance to say good-bye to his sister." Martha's lips tightened in disapproval, adding a few more lines to those already creasing her cheeks. "Doc will have given Arla something, so bring her Dorothy. Let her hold her daughter one last time so the happy memory can ease her heart on the way to heaven."

Blinking back the tears she'd seen mirrored in Martha's eyes, Cora grasped the banister and pulled herself onto the first stair. Every step seemed so much harder than before, weighted with sorrow unalloyed by hope. They'd fought for Arla's life and lost. Cora might have been better able to accept the failure if it didn't wear the face of her friend and shape the fate of her beloved baby girl.

She pushed open the door to see her friend propped up against a multitude of pillows, draining yet another glass of water. Arla's hand shook as she replaced the empty cup, knocking it against the side of the table and then the top before managing to set it down. After being insensible with fever throughout the night, an ice bath that morning had revived her to an almost miraculous degree. For a moment, Cora thought perhaps Doc read things wrong, that they'd lessened the fever boiling Arla's blood enough to give her a chance.

"Will you bring me my Dorothy?" Face flushed and eyes bright, she looked like a happy young mother as she asked for her daughter. But the flush warned of fever regaining its stronghold, and Arla's bright gaze looked wide and glassy rather than joyous and alert. One hand pressed against her swollen abdomen as though holding back pain, and her breaths sounded sharp and shallow between each of her words.

"Of course." Cora crossed the room, lifted Dorothy from the bassinet Lacey ordered weeks in advance, and straightened the tiny white cap frilling across her forehead. She cuddled the tiny bundle close, drawing comfort from her sweet warmth as she returned to the bedside. A few rearranged pillows helped provide the support Arla couldn't manage so Cora could tuck the baby into her mother's arms.

"Precious." Arla snuggled close to her daughter, rewarded with a gummy little yawn as Dorothy snuggled back. "Such a blessing."

"Yes she is." Looking at the baby, Cora couldn't help but share her mother's smile. There, in Arla's arms, lay a blessing to believe in. The miracle of life lessened the disappointment of death, if only just enough to help a grieving heart hold faith.

Arla's shoulders sagged, and Cora hastily slid another pillow beneath her friend's forearm to keep the baby supported. She wouldn't take Dorothy away unless Arla asked her to. That tiny daughter wouldn't know many moments in her mother's arms, so each second became something to cherish, blanketing a soon-to-be-orphaned child in the knowledge and depth of her mother's love. When Dorothy grew, she'd hear the words, be told by friends and family how Arla adored her—but this moment, this half-formed memory, could be hidden in her heart forever, an underlying certainty every child needed.

"Thank you." Arla's whisper drew Cora's gaze from Dorothy. Her friend's flush had deepened even in that short a time. "For helping me. For helping bring my daughter into this world so I could hold her even a few times." Tears rendered them both silent for a while.

"I wish I'd been able to help more," Cora finally burst out.

"Will you?" More than tears and fever brightened Arla's gaze. The hand not supporting Dorothy reached out, fingers curling in Cora's sleeve. "Will you help my daughter? See that she's fed?"

"I already took care of it." She patted her friend's hand then enclosed it with her own. "The nursemaid came this morning, Arla."

She blinked, her gaze unfocused for a moment. "Good." Arla blinked a few more times, obviously fighting against the medicine. She grimaced, knees drawing toward her stomach as if to ward off a sudden wave of pain. Arla curled herself around Dorothy until the spasm stopped. Then she cupped her daughter's cheek, pressed a final kiss to her forehead, and lifted Dorothy. "Will you take her, Cora?"

"Of course!" Cora gently accepted the fidgeting baby and unwound the top blanket. Even such a short time with her mother made Dorothy overly warm, and fussing gave her a moment to collect herself. She shifted in her seat so Arla could look at her daughter as she drifted off into peaceful rest. "See? She'll be just fine."

"Thank you. My brother can't take her. " Arla's hand clutched hers again as she fought to finish before sleep claimed her. "But I can rest, knowing you have Dorothy. I trust you, Cora. Like. . .a sister."

Cora suddenly realized what her friend meant. "Wait, Arla!"

But her friend's grip already went slack, Arla's eyes drifting shut as she whispered, "Trust you. . .with Dorothy. Take care of her. . . ."

# THIRTY-SIX

I've taken care of everything!" Charlotte sashayed into Naomi's workshop the next afternoon, eyes alight with triumph and mischief.

Too tired after helping look after Arla through the night and distracted by the knowledge that their efforts weren't succeeding, Naomi didn't understand what her sister meant. At least not until Charlotte moved aside and began ushering lumbermen into the room.

Rory Riordan edged in first, instantly making the room feel half its size. Gent trundled after him, unwrapping a sodden scarf and flinging water droplets on everyone nearby. Bobsley bounded in next and rabbited over to the stove, looking very pleased with himself. And, though she couldn't spot him at first, Naomi heard Clump's distinctive, heavy tread bringing up the rear. He shouldered himself between Gent and Riordan, beaming with open enthusiasm.

"Never enjoyed the rain so much as today," he announced loudly.

"We should have asked about your work before." Riordan sounded partly apologetic, partly interested, and entirely uncomfortable—as any very large man would feel if surrounded by delicate miniatures.

"You did ask!" Naomi found her voice, if not her wits. "We've spoken of it during several of our walks together, remember?"

"Yeah." Bobsley sauntered over to the table displaying the replica of Lyman Place. "But picturing things ain't half so good as seeing them. That's why we hopped on your sister's invitation to pay you a visit and maybe lend a hand so long as this rain keeps up."

"Lend a hand?" Naomi repeated faintly, shooting her sister a look she couldn't even name. Part glower, part disbelief, part plea to fix this awful mess. Needless to say, Charlotte disregarded it.

"Absolutely!" Her sister glided to a stool in the far corner and waved one leather-gloved hand to indicate the worktables. "Just yesterday we discussed how you already know they're strong but wanted to see how they balanced that considerable strength with the other, finer qualities a woman might hope to find in a husband."

"Such wisdom alongside such beauty." Gent swept his ever-present top hat from his head, dousing everyone anew with dislodged rainwater. Incidentally, the gesture also revealed sooty black smudges and streams where the water passed through his dyed hair.

Riordan moved away, found himself too close to Charlotte, and shifted back as though he'd been poked with a knitting needle. Clump shot Gent an unacknowledged glare and made a fuss over brushing water from his beloved suspenders. Bobsley missed the entire thing, his nose mere millimeters from the mullioned windows of the Lyman Place model as he squinted, trying to view the rooms beyond them.

"This is no wisdom of mine," Naomi refuted, hard pressed not to giggle at her gaggle of suitors. Really, it wasn't funny. Lack of sleep and a myriad of emotions were just converging and making her somewhat silly. Though in all honesty, the men's antics didn't help.

She suddenly wondered what Michael would say if he saw their workshop invaded by her earnest, bumbling beaus—and her smile faded. Michael wasn't here, and she didn't know when he'd make it back. And even if Michael were here, he wouldn't be actively seeking her company; he merely accepted her presence as a business necessity.

Then, too, if Michael were here, there would be no interruption. After all, the men respected another man's work—they just didn't consider extending the same courtesy to a woman's work. Naomi remembered how these men tried to take away her tools and bodily lift her from working through the landslide to free Lacey. Their strength lay in their muscles, perhaps, too, in their protectiveness and obvious willingness to help in any little way.

But they were weak when it came to understanding how to approach her, how to respect the woman they strove to win as their life's partner. The thought was downright depressing. One man worked alongside her but didn't seek her hand. Four other men vied for her hand, but her only options would never want to work alongside her. *Charlotte is right. . . . I need to learn more about them and let them learn more about me. Maybe something can come of this after all!*

"Wisdom, whim, or what-have-you, I'm glad." Clump crossed the room, barely needing to stoop beside Bobsley for the same view.

"Well." Charlotte regained everyone's attention, gave a dainty sneeze, and said, "I do believe it's an excellent idea for your beaus to prove that they have the patience, creativity, and gentle touch needed to bring my sister's dreams to life. First, in building your dollhouse and later, so you can build your lives together."

If Naomi saw her sister smirk at that last, maudlin sentiment, none of the men caught on. Whatever game Charlotte played to amuse herself, it seemed to their advantage to follow along. Trouble was, Naomi didn't understand where Charlotte's enmity had gone. Why was Charlotte working so hard to help orchestrate Naomi's wedding? The only explanation she could think of made Naomi cringe. *Does she think I'm still in love with Harry and might try to win him back? After all that happened, he's the last man in the world I'd want . . . But maybe Charlotte's trying to protect us all from my past mistake.*

She tried to give her sister a reassuring smile as Charlotte slipped from the workroom, lamenting that sawdust made her sneeze. Whatever her reasons, Naomi appreciated that her sister was trying to make her choice easier. Amid so many disappointments, this unexpected alliance—however oddly motivated—warmed Naomi's heart.

Perhaps God did bring her sister to Hope Falls to remind her not to lose her head over the wrong man—but maybe He'd also brought the chance to heal old wounds. His blessings changed things.

Naomi didn't have to force her smile as she approached Bobsley and Clump, still trying to peer through tiny windows. She gestured for Riordan and Gent to join them then placed her hand on the house.

"Let's see what happens when we turn things around."

No going back. Braden watched as everyone piled small stones atop Mrs. Nash's grave. Prayers had been lifted, hymns sung, memories shared, and tears spilled over the now-covered ground. Funny how he'd never noticed that people buried these things alongside their loved ones, as though cold earth could actually absorb hot grief.

Her passing had been unexpected, swift, and awful for those who'd grown to know the woman and helped care for her through the birth of her daughter and later the futile fight against her fever. Lawson refused to speak, as though his mouth were a Pandora's box of pain that he couldn't allow to be unleashed in public.

Cora cuddled the baby close, tears slipping down her cheeks in a nonstop stream that told of a deep friendship Braden's fiancée had established with the now-dead mother. She looked in sore need of comforting, and Braden promised himself he'd go to her. *After.*

For now he waited as everyone filed away from the grave site, waving Granger away when it looked as though his friend might try to wheel him off. People probably thought the long, difficult rise up the uneven path wore him out, but he was staying because he chose to. Because the weight of his own guilt, shame, and grief pressed hard against his chest, demanding release before he could leave.

I should have come sooner. When he was finally alone, Braden pulled out a bandana and quietly—because sound carried through these mountains, even if no one could see him—shed his own tears. He wept for each wooden cross marking the ridge, for each man who'd died in the mines he'd cut deep into the neighboring mountain. His chest heaved with sorrow at the knowledge that several of the plots held nothing more than names, their owners never found. *Lost forever.*

Why, God? Why let this happen? Why let them die? Braden's heart cried its own lament. *Why didn't You let me die with them and save another in my place? They didn't deserve their fates, and I didn't deserve Your grace, even if I didn't cause the collapse.*

When the tears slowed, Braden looked over the ridge. Below, a sparkling stream wound through the lush forest. In a land of such abundance, the loss of life seemed senseless and wasteful. He rolled over the uneven dirt, brushing his fingers over every wooden cross and praying for the souls they represented. He knew each name, could envision each face, and for the first time since the tragedy, this didn't haunt him. Finally, Braden saw the blessing in his knowledge.

If I hadn't insisted on personally hiring every worker, meeting every man, who would mourn them this way? Braden came to the end of the row, his tears slowing to a stop as resolve replaced sorrow. *More important, who would hold their murderer accountable?*

"Her?" Nose flat against the window, Luke jabbed his stubby little finger against the glass each time he caught sight of a woman. "No, she's too blond, and you said Miss Higgins has black hair, so maybe . . . Her? Or maybe that one—no, that one's got to be too old. How 'bout her—no, she has a baby already so she must be a Missus not a Miss."

So far he'd pointed at Miss Lyman, the elusive Mrs. McCreedy, and the younger Miss Thompson who happened to be holding Mrs. Nash's newborn. Mike didn't spot Mrs. Nash herself and assumed she must still be recuperating—or maybe just taking a little afternoon rest.

"No, none of those." He pried his son away from the window and smoothed down the bangs tufting up at all angles. "Now calm down. You'll see the workshop and meet Miss Higgins in just a little bit, and it's nothing to get overexcited about in the meantime. Got it?"

"Why not?" Luke blinked, tilted his head to the side, and stated, "You are, and I know why. It's 'cuz you like Miss Higgins."

"Well," Mike hedged, wondering how on earth his ten-year-old boy figured that one out so quickly. "I know you'll like her, too."

Luke's grin grew wider. "Just not in the same way you do, Dad."

This needed to be nipped in the bud before his son mentioned this to someone else—especially if that someone else turned out to be Naomi. He had enough obstacles without his son adding to them. Mike crossed his arms. "What makes you think something like that?"

"Aw, come on! I'm not some little kid anymore." His son raked a hand through his hair, sending shocks springing up at random intervals across his head. "You catch yourself, but you almost say her first name—right? It starts with an *N*. And when you talk about her, you smile with your eyes the way you used to. It's *obvious!*"

Mike held up his hand to stop his son's litany. Luke's voice had risen with every reason, and the now-stopped train couldn't mask it. Besides, the obvious thing was that Luke was right—he wasn't a little kid. After dealing with the death of his mother, losing his home to grasping grandparents, and evading dangerous thugs, Luke started the transition from boy to young man. *And an observant one.*

"What's obvious to you might not be so easily seen by others." *I hope.* Mike smoothed Luke's hair again. "So keep it down."

"Then you admit it?" He clamped a hand atop his head as though trying to plaster his hair in place. "That I'm right this time?"

"I'll tell you this." Mike leaned down as he whispered, waiting for Luke to shuffle a step closer. Then he added, "I admit nothing!"

"Aw, Dad. It's not something to be embarrassed about." Luke gave him a good-natured cuff on the arm. "You found a woman *with her own workshop.* I'd be more worried if you *didn't* like her!"

And with that bit of irrefutable logic, his ten-year-old son turned Mike's difficult decision into a forgone conclusion. Luke, who'd never met Naomi, held no doubts about how special she was. So why should he, who'd spent so many hours enjoying her company, waste another minute trying to argue away his deepening attraction?

"Got your rucksack?" Mike asked, shouldering his bulging bag.

"Yep." Luke narrowly missed slugging him in the head as he

swung the sack over his shoulder and darted out into the aisle. He didn't slow his pace until he'd gotten through the car, down the steps, and off the train altogether. Then he stopped to gawk at the town around them, effectively boxing his father on the steel steps.

"Scoot over, son." Mike resisted the urge to nudge the back of his son's knees with the tip of his boot. The gesture might lessen Luke's newfound dignity as he greeted Hope Falls for the first time. Mike scanned the group, his gaze hitching on Naomi's smile and staying there. In that moment, it felt like he'd come home again.

"What"—Luke's tone mixed trepidation and wonder—"is *that*?"

So much for dignity. Mike grinned as his son inched to the side and gaped at the group of people now crowding around the engine. Or, more specifically, at the massive, brindled wolfhound circling them.

"Dunstan!" He called the hunter over, knowing Decoy would follow his master. Meanwhile, Mike clapped a hand on Luke's shoulder so he'd know not to be frightened of the approaching beast. "I need to make introductions, but your dog's stealing my son's attention."

"Decoy, right?" Far from being frightened, Luke moved forward. He glanced at Dunstan. "Dad said a big dog helped save some people trapped in a mine, but I didn't realize he meant one *this* big!"

"He comes in handy." Dunstan's reply might have sounded cool, but the corners of his mouth quirked as though holding back a smile. He snapped his fingers, made a motion, and the wolfhound promptly lowered his hindquarters and sat. The movement didn't make him any smaller, but the show of obedience reassured Luke—and Mike, if the truth be told. Somehow he'd forgotten just how large Decoy was.

"Can I pet him?" Luke's hand twitched, belying the effort it took to ask permission instead of reach for the gray-black fur.

"Let him sniff the back of your hand first," Dunstan instructed. "Dogs are like horses that way—like to get a sense of you before they let you touch them. It's kind of like a handshake."

"Yeah?" Luke beamed as Decoy gave his hand a thorough snuffle.

"Now you can pet him. See how his ears went back? That means he's relaxed. Just remember, if they went flat against his skull, that means to get back." Dunstan kept up a steady stream of instruction, though it was easy to see Decoy loved being scratched behind the ears. No one could see the way his tongue lolled out as anything but bliss.

"Well, now that Decoy's approved of you, you're officially welcome in Hope Falls." Miss Lyman stood on Dunstan's other side. "I'm Miss Lyman—the other person stuck in the mines until Decoy led my friends and your dad to come dig us out of there. It seems your father has a knack for showing up in the middle of difficult days."

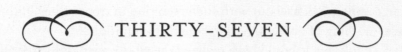 THIRTY-SEVEN

*M*ichael *has a knack for showing up when he's needed.* Naomi drank in the sight of him, from the unruly hair she wanted to run her fingers through to the smile lines drawing attention to his deep brown eyes and the broad shoulders she'd cried on the first day they met. Had it really been just under a month since he came to Hope Falls? It felt as if she'd known him a lifetime and missed him for half that.

"And who, pray tell, is *that?*" Charlotte twirled her parasol, gaze fixed on Michael as though committing his features to memory.

"Mr. Strode." Naomi's hackles went up at her sister's appreciative murmur and discreet ogling. Discreet ogling still counted as ogling. Charlotte had no business going goggly-eyed over the way Michael stood there, silhouetted by the late afternoon sun.

"Your carpenter?" Charlotte practically purred. "Now I begin to see the appeal of staying shut up in that sawdust-strewn room."

"The Hope Falls carpenter," Naomi corrected, unwilling to let Charlotte see that she hated making the distinction. *Not mine.*

"My, my. How very precise you're being." Her sister gave her a knowing glance. "It looks as though Lacey is finished explaining about Mrs. Nash, and the boy's wandering off to walk with that massive mutt. Isn't it the perfect time for you to introduce us?"

"Of course—why don't you get Harold while I fetch Mr. Strode?" Naomi knew full well that Charlotte hadn't included her husband in that "us," but she seized the opportunity to give her sister a subtle reminder. The fact that it also allowed her to approach Michael alone, if only for a scant moment, added another reward.

"Welcome back." She swept toward him, moving as quickly as possible to greet him before her sister intruded. Naomi wanted to give him a hug or at least clasp hands, but couldn't. She knew better than to single Michael out with such attention in front of her suitors, to say nothing of giving Charlotte such ammunition.

"Thank you. I should have realized the whole town didn't turn up to greet us." He kept the words light, but his gaze held hers, strong and steady. "It's never easy saying good-bye to a friend, and I know you'd become fond of Mrs. Nash. I'm sorry for your loss."

"Loss is never easy." Charlotte swept into the conversation, positioning herself as close to Michael as possible. "Of course, the arrival of an old friend and the promise of new acquaintances means life continues. The reminder makes any loss somewhat more bearable."

Michael looked poleaxed, but Naomi couldn't tell whether he was overwhelmed by her sister's charms or caught off guard by her boldness in inserting herself into their private conversation. Additionally, it looked as though Charlotte's ambiguous statement had perplexed even Michael's ability to puzzle things together.

At best, Charlotte was saying that Michael and Luke would ease the grief Hope Falls felt at losing Arla. Possibly she meant that she herself along with Michael might provide the distraction and entertainment needed to lighten the dreary day. But the worst interpretation of all seemed most likely: Charlotte had insinuated that she—who'd never exchanged so much as a word with the deceased—needed comfort and expected to find it in Michael, her new friend.

Not that Naomi could call attention to the inappropriateness of Charlotte's conversation. Her sister would claim the best of intentions, casting Naomi as petty and petulant. *Am I being petty? Is it really Charlotte's words that I find objectionable, or am I looking for offense because she barged in to Michael's homecoming?*

"I didn't realize your sister planned to visit." Michael's comment was part question, part answer. At least it explained why he'd looked vaguely confused and definitely at a loss. Michael hadn't been trying to puzzle through Charlotte's meaning at all—he'd been busy looking for her connection to Naomi. And he'd found it.

"Nor did I, but she and her husband arrived the day after you left. Apparently Mr. Blinman was one of the previous investors Braden decided to invite." Naomi noticed Charlotte hadn't bothered to fetch Harold for introductions. "Mrs. Charlotte Blinman decided to join him on the journey. As you guessed, she is my sister."

"*Younger* sister, though I'm certain you would have guessed that, too." She peeped from beneath her fanned lashes, pretending shyness but obviously expecting his swift and admiring agreement.

Naomi fought a sudden urge to step on her sister's toes. Wasn't it enough that Harry chose Charlotte for her youth and supposedly better ability to bear little Blinmans? Did Charlotte have to trot out their age difference to make her seem spinsterish to Michael?

"No, ma'am." Michael either didn't notice or pretended not to notice the astonishment then fury flashing across Charlotte's face before she composed herself—most likely to avoid getting wrinkles. "I can't say I would've guessed that, seeing as how a smart man doesn't go around speculating on the age of ladies he's just met."

But a smart man does *soften the blow of calling an obviously vain woman "ma'am."* Naomi struggled against giving in to giggles—not because of Charlotte's indignation, but because Michael hadn't played her sister's game. He'd deliberately refused to flatter Charlotte at Naomi's expense and almost complimented her instead!

Charlotte's simper held a slight edge. "An excellent policy."

"We do look very much alike." Naomi intentionally sounded apologetic. Hopefully it would appease her sister while letting Michael know she regretted putting him in such a difficult spot.

"Could almost be twins." Michael must have caught another flicker of Charlotte's irritation because his jaw set and his eyes sparked with mischief. "Same height, similar features and coloring. When you're wearing bonnets or hats, a man would be hard pressed to tell you apart at first glance."

"In time you'll notice how our disparities outweigh the similarities." Her sister scraped up a smile and twirled her parasol. "Until then we'll take care you don't confuse us."

Naomi sucked in a sharp breath, sickened by the veiled allusion to their past. Her sister kept her claws sharp and tinged with more than malice. The attack seeped into Naomi's soul, stealing her joy at seeing Michael again. He didn't know the history behind Charlotte's seemingly innocuous comment, but he saw its impact.

The warm brown of Michael's gaze sharpened. "You're distinctly different, and I could never mistake one sister for the other."

"Never say never," Mrs. Blinman cautioned, casting her sister a meaningful glance. "As Naomi can attest, you wouldn't be the first."

Mike looked from Naomi to her sister and back again, reaffirming his conviction that no man with an ounce of sense could confuse these two women after a moment spent in their company. From afar, the resemblance might mislead, but certainly not up close.

He hadn't lied when he said he wouldn't have guessed Naomi to be older. Mrs. Blinman fancied herself a coquette, but those fancy frills and simulated smiles couldn't sweeten the bite beneath her comments. Her sham sophistication, as with any poorly laid veneer, aged her. In fact, the woman reminded him of his mother-in-law.

By contrast, Naomi's simple dress and fresh face didn't detract from her beauty. Like finely grained oak, she needed no adornment save what God granted already. If affectation aged her sister, Naomi's unadulterated loveliness seemed almost untouched by the time. *Forty years from now, she'll be every bit as beautiful.*

"Just as we dislike being thought of as interchangeable,"—Naomi spoke stiffly and with an underlying fierceness, unsettled by her sister—"you can't judge Mr. Strode by the mistakes of other men."

Her sister's smile grew more feline. "How silly of me, when it's so clear Mr. Strode has. . .distinguished himself with you."

She took the words and twisted them with her tone, implying

impropriety where there was none. Mike didn't like the way Naomi had gone pale early in the conversation and not yet regained her color. When she'd mentioned her sister, he'd gotten the idea the two weren't close. Now that he met Mrs. Blinman, he understood why.

"Mr. Strode distinguishes himself with everyone he meets." The green in Naomi's eyes sparkled with an emerald brilliance her sister could never match. "Aside from his work, he's unusually observant."

It didn't take heightened powers of observation to see that Mrs. Blinman wasn't pleased with the way the conversation was going. "Perhaps he is. Then again, you make things easier by refusing to style your hair to conceal that bizarre white streak of yours."

"Why would she ever want to conceal it?" Mike challenged.

"Most ladies do not flaunt their oddities." She sniffed in disdain. "You must admit, Naomi's coloring marks her as outlandish."

"Unique." He barked the word. "Refusing to hide who she is doesn't mean Miss Higgins flaunts herself. It means she's genuine."

"What I am," Naomi intervened while her sister spluttered, "is genuinely excited to meet your son. I see he's returning from his walk with Decoy and Dunstan. Looks like he's enjoying himself."

Mike nodded, taking a moment to switch gears. In a few moments he'd gone from happy homecoming to the sad news of Mrs. Nash and had been unable to relish his reunion with Naomi thanks to her catty sibling. Now he had to push all that aside and make sure Naomi took to Luke and Luke liked Naomi back. He swallowed against a stomach spasm, and Mike belatedly recognized the sensation as nerves.

Lord, You know the desire of my heart. You know I've sought Your guidance about Naomi, and now I seek Your assistance. The timing feels rushed, more now than when I left Hope Falls. But if it's right, if You've planned this path, please pave the way.

"Luke!" He called his son over, wishing Mrs. Blinman would flit away to offer the three of them a little privacy. No such luck.

"Yeah, Dad?" Luke came running up, stopping suddenly enough to raise a small puff of dust and make Mrs. Blinman take a step back.

"Son,"—Mike brought his son to stand in front of him and clapped his hands on the boy's shoulders—"I want you to meet—"

"Miss Higgins?" Luke burst out, eyeing the women in blissful ignorance that he'd revealed how much Mike talked about Naomi. Luke couldn't tell that Mrs. Blinman realized the significance of his ignorance any more than he could tell which sister was Miss Higgins. His brows knit. "I mean, one of you is Miss Higgins?"

"That's right." Mrs. Blinman swept in front of Naomi, who'd already started to come forward with her hand extended. She reached out one perfectly manicured hand and pinched Luke's cheek as if he were still a toddler. "Aren't you the most adorable little boy?"

"No." Mike heard his thought echoed by both Luke and Naomi.

"I am not little. Or adorable." Luke rubbed his reddened cheek, pulled his shoulders back to look taller, and gave Mrs. Blinman a well-deserved glower. "And I don't think you're Miss Higgins."

Mrs. Blinman looked indignant at the reaction. "Well, I never—"

"My sister never said she was Miss Higgins." Naomi nudged her sister out of the way with a touch more force than was absolutely necessary, and Mike had to hide his grin. She stooped down a smidge and held out her hand for Luke to shake. "And your dad never said what a strong grip you have! Nice to finally meet you, Mr. Strode."

Luke, visibly puffed up by the way Naomi addressed him, pumped her arm another time to prove his strength. "You can call me Luke."

"Thank you. Please call me Naomi." She returned his grin, and Mike started to relax. "Now, you have a very important decision to make, Luke. I know what your dad would choose, but this time it's up to you. Would you like to go to the diner for some of my friend Evie's cooking, or do you want to stop and see the workshop first?"

"Workshop!" Luke burst out without even thinking it over then laughed when Mike groaned and rubbed his stomach in a sad way.

"Tell you what." Naomi straightened up and held out her hand in invitation. "We'll go to the workshop while your dad saves seats."

"Deal!" Luke plunked his hand in Naomi's without reservation.

As the two of them left, Mike's heart swelled with pride and hope. "She's good with children." Mrs. Blinman watched her sister go then turned with a sorrowful expression. "Such a pity she's barren."

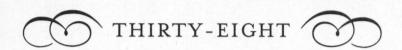# THIRTY-EIGHT

W hat?" Mike couldn't muster up the more polite, "Excuse me?"

"Unable to have children." Mrs. Blinman shook her head in a regretful sort of way but finished with a shrug. "Barren."

"Why are you telling me this?" Mike's astonishment swiftly turned to ire. "How could anyone know that when she's unmarried?"

"How do doctors discover any condition?" Another dainty shrug made her ridiculous parasol bob. "There are symptoms when women lack the ability to bear children, though I won't detail those signs."

No children. Mike suddenly understood this was the missing piece—the final detail as to why Naomi never married. A woman like that didn't resort to hiring a husband without several reasons, and she'd only revealed the least personal ones to him. That, more than the condition itself, gave him pause. *But why would she confide that to me when I'm one of the few men who haven't tried to court her? She'd have no reason to give me such intimate information, and it's not something she'd want to discuss under the best of circumstances.*

Again, he couldn't help but see the irony. Not only had he found the only two women who might "hire" him for a husband, but they happened to be the same two who wouldn't give him a child of his own blood. Leticia because she carried another man's baby. Naomi because she couldn't carry any at all. *But does it matter? Luke is the son of my heart, and while I wanted to give him siblings, he's fine.*

In the midst of muddling through his thoughts, he realized Mrs. Blinman had started talking again. In his opinion, she talked too much.

"It's the reason why Harry chose to marry me instead." She tilted her head toward a well-dressed man in conversation with Mr. Corning. "He originally courted Naomi, but when I finished school and came home from France, Harry decided I would be the wife he needed."

What kind of man would choose her over Naomi? The fact that she would consider taking her sister's suitor makes her a poor choice. Mike did his best to hide his incredulity, struck by the memory of Naomi's wistful expression when she told him she had no family left because her sister had gotten married. "Your husband originally courted Miss Higgins? Is that why the two of you aren't close?"

"Jealousy ruins relationships." She gave a dramatic sigh. "I came to Hope Falls hoping to mend fences, but I can see that it will not work. How can I blame Naomi for being heartsick over Harry?"

Her words packed a punch that left him reeling. Mike struggled to make his lungs work. "Are you saying that she still loves him?"

She blinked at him, eyes widened with surprise. "Of course, Mr. Strode! Her first love is something a woman can never forget."

I couldn't have heard that right. Naomi paused one step away from passing the workshop window. She rubbed behind her ears and waited.

"Say it again!" Clump urged. "I want to try to remember how."

"Oh, it's nothing special," Charlotte demurred. "You can say the same thing in English or German, since you're multilingual."

"Stuff sounds so much better in French," Bobsley proclaimed.

"All right. To say 'I have a noble bearing,' it's: *Saviez-vous que vouz avez le nez d'un cochon?*" Charlotte repeated the phrase that had stopped Naomi in her tracks.

It had been a long time since Naomi had used her girlhood French lessons, and Charlotte learned the language in its mother country, but she knew without a doubt her sister hadn't complimented Clump's noble bearing. She'd asked him if he knew he had the nose of a pig! Clump begged her to repeat it, but Gent said it was his turn. "Now, what was that thing you said before about my fine manners?"

"One moment." Charlotte issued a string of sneezes, and Naomi was glad to remember that her sister couldn't stay around sawdust for long. *"Vous êtes plus dense que les arbres que vous hacher."*

Naomi swallowed a surge of anger as kind Gent—whose manners trumped her sister's—carefully repeated that he was denser than the trees he chopped. Charlotte was systematically insulting her suitors and compounding the crime by teaching them to go around insulting themselves! If any of them remembered the words and repeated them to someone fluent in French, they'd be laughingstocks.

"Charlotte!" She thundered into the room, unable to hold herself back until her temper cooled. "A word with you, please."

"Naomi! I was just entertaining your beaus while we waited for you to get back from showing Mr. Strode and his son to their house." Slyly suggestive and innocent all at once, Charlotte made it sound as though she'd done nothing wrong—and that Naomi was inappropriate to want to see Luke's reaction to the house she'd helped ready for him.

"Outside, please." She gritted her teeth, turned on her heel, and listened as Charlotte sneezed her way out of the room behind her. Naomi didn't trust herself to speak—or the men not to overhear—until they'd passed the buildings used for temporary storage.

"What do you think you're doing?" she demanded once stopped.

"Filling in." Charlotte inspected her nail beds. "Providing amusement so they wouldn't stop to wonder at your interest in Mr. Strode. You really shouldn't abandon your suitors like that, Mimi."

"I didn't abandon anyone." Naomi narrowly kept from mentioning the way Charlotte and their mother abandoned her after one night's mistake. Even in her anger, she knew there was no comparison—her mistake made her unworthy of understanding. But her failures hadn't ruined her ability to understand the feelings of other people.

Charlote rolled her eyes. "Let's not quibble over word choice."

"No, let's." Naomi refused to let her sister off the hook. "Your

266

words, to be exact. You will not insult any of my friends, my suitors, or any Hope Falls workers again—not in English or French."

"Don't get overexcited. It's not as if they knew what I said."

"*I* know." Naomi struggled to put her outrage into words. "Why do you think it's all right to mock people, whether they understand it or not? Maybe it's even worse if they don't know what you're saying because you're taking advantage of their trusting natures."

"You've been in the country for far too long, sister." Charlotte's eyes held a predatory gleam. "Don't mistake foolishness for trust. Trust should be reserved for after someone earns it."

"Why? Why should everyone have to go around assuming other people are unworthy when only a small percentage ruin things?"

"That percentage can create a lot of trouble, and you know as well as anyone that even the so-called good people misstep. The fact that your suitors extend such confidence to either one of us attests to their lack of wisdom. They've barely met me, and they certainly don't know you any better." Charlotte's taunts sliced into Naomi. Her sister possessed a talent for vicious truths. "Stop acting so high and mighty, Naomi. Don't pretend you're better than you are, and don't pretend your suitors are more than clodpolls."

Naomi slapped the wall with the flat of her palm, welcoming the distraction of its sting. "They're far more than you'll ever know."

"How can they be, when they know so little?" Charlotte countered. "Tell me, were you planning on being honest with the man you'll marry? Warn him beforehand he's taking on damaged goods?"

A few sentences, and Naomi needed to defend herself. Unfortunately, she didn't have much to say. "I've been praying about it, but I won't know until I choose the man. Obviously I'll need to tell him that I'm not innocent, but I would hope to find a husband who would want to know the entire truth and be able to forgive it."

Her voice grew fainter with every word because aloud they sounded every bit as ridiculous as she'd feared but had tried to convince herself otherwise. Charlotte laughed at her admission.

"Now who's the fool?" she spat. "No man wants to know the

entire truth about anything, much less hear how another man beat him to his bride. Besides, what makes you think you could tell him, even if you found so spectacular an idiot as to offer forgiveness?"

"I'd find the strength. He deserves to know. If I'm going to promise to honor a man for a lifetime, I would need to from the start." Naomi stiffened. "And forgiveness isn't idiocy. It takes an incredible amount of strength to forgive a wrong and keep loving."

"It's not your secret to tell." Charlotte's hands curved into claws. "Listen, you self-important chit. Why do you think I didn't denounce you the morning after we dragged you from my marital bed? Because news of your betrayal would taint Harry's reputation, too. Neither one of us should suffer slander and ridicule so you can seek absolution from whatever man you convince to take you as his bride."

With that, Charlotte huffed off, layers of skirts billowing like a ship with sails unfurled. There was no way of stopping her, so Naomi's future depended on Charlotte's ability to stop herself. Because as much as she hated to think of it—she now realized she'd been avoiding thinking of it—Charlotte made sense. Only their continued silence could protect the Blinman name and Naomi's reputation.

I can never be honest with my husband. Naomi sagged against the splintering wood wall. *He can never know the worst of me.*

 THIRTY-NINE

The best part about coming back was waking up, knowing Luke was safe with him and they could spend the day with Naomi. He and Luke spent yesterday afternoon exploring first the town then some of the outlying forest to help his son settle in. Mike resisted his impulse to ask Naomi along—it was clear she and the other women needed some time to recover from Arla's death.

In spite of Luke's enthusiastic approval of the woman Mike "liked" so much, Mike needed the two people he cared about the most to get to know each other. And Mike needed to start waging his campaign to win Naomi's heart. He'd known he lagged behind the loggers, but her sister's revelation yesterday meant Mike wasn't just competing with the lumbermen; he was up against the memory of the man who'd hurt her.

It didn't help that the memory—and the man who'd made it— happened to be wandering around town. If Mike didn't have so much lost time to make up for, he might be tempted to run the fool to ground, ask him what he'd been thinking, and hold him accountable for making Naomi think she didn't deserve more than a hired husband. Lucky for Blinman, Mike would keep busy convincing her otherwise.

Besides, the man shackled himself to Naomi's sister. That should suffice as punishment until Mike got things squared away. He couldn't wait to get started. For the first time, he ate one of Miss Thompson's delectable breakfasts without noticing what she served.

Instead, he kept an eye on Naomi as she wove around the tables, bringing out platters of food and rounds of fresh coffee. He barely managed to keep track of the conversation but paid closer attention when Dunstan invited Luke to go fishing with him and Decoy that morning.

"Good time for trout," the hunter was saying. "And until my ribs are better healed, there's not much hunting I can get done."

Luke wriggled on the bench, unable to hide his excitement. "Can we go, Dad?"

"I don't know." Torn between his obligation to Naomi's workshop and wanting to make Luke happy, he hesitated. "I've been away from the workshop for days now. There's a lot to do."

"Please, can't we go together? You were gone a long time." His son hadn't blinked since Dunstan issued the invitation. His eagerness, and the reminder that Mike hadn't been able to spend time with him for a while, broke down Mike's protest.

"Lacey'll be keen to come along," Dunstan mentioned. "Might be easier to ask Miss Higgins to join us and make a trip of it."

"I'll ask her," he promised. When the diner emptied out, Mike edged off the side of the bench, told Luke he'd be right back, and snuck into the kitchen.

"No loggers allowed," came a curt order from the stove where Miss Thompson hovered.

"It's Mr. Strode," her sister corrected and offered him a welcoming smile.

"Is there anything you need?" Naomi bustled over with a steaming pot of coffee, worry in her gaze.

"You," he blurted out then quickly added, "if the workshop can wait another day. And Miss Lyman, too. Dunstan's invited us for a morning of fishing, and Luke's raring to go."

"You're hooked into it then." Naomi gave a gentle laugh as the other women rolled their eyes.

"Obvious pun." Miss Thompson shook her head. "You can do better than that, Naomi!"

"Well…" She pursed her lips for a moment as though considering. "I suppose I could have said that with Luke invited, he couldn't worm out of it—but on the balance I thought that one was worse."

"It is," Mike assured her. "Who wants to be likened to a worm?"

"Ah." Her smile widened as she teased. "So you'd rather be hooked?"

He couldn't find a suitable answer for that, and the sudden pause brought a blush to her cheeks.

"Oh, cut line!" Miss Thompson stepped into the breach and brought on a new round of groans.

"I think you should all go. With Dunstan out of commission, we don't get meat like we used to. The kitchen could use a bountiful catch of fresh fish."

"I didn't want to neglect our work either." *Our.* He liked saying it when it meant him and Naomi. Especially when he could still see the vestiges of her blush over talking about hooking him.

"Luke can help us make it up later," she said firmly. "Every boy should go fishing with his father—and it'd be criminal not to give him a special outing on his first full day in Hope Falls."

"I'm game." Miss Lyman pulled down a large wicker hamper and plunked it atop a table. "Braden plans to take his investors around a bit, so the Blinmans and Mr. Corning will be occupied."

This was sounding better and better—Mike hadn't even considered the idea that Naomi's sister and old love might intrude on the fishing trip, but he was heartened to hear they couldn't.

"I wanted to join in the first time you told me about this place." Corning gestured around. "It sounded like a perfect business proposition."

"It should have been." Braden knew he needed to say more, to get the conversation rolling and pry information from his suspects, but the sight of the collapsed mine before him stole his speech.

Blinman's chortle made his hands fist. "Nothing's perfect."

"Oh, phoo! I'm standing right next to you!" The man's wife pouted prettily. Why the woman insisted on joining them on this trek escaped Braden's understanding, unless she was trying to avoid the morose tone in town. If that was her reason, she'd failed miserably. The mines were as much a grave site as the place they'd buried Arla.

"I said no*thing*, darling, not *no one*." Blinman backpedaled and swiftly changed the subject. "Though the mines seem an awful waste."

"Yes." *Of life.* Braden's eyes narrowed at Blinman's renewed interest. "It was a devastating loss of irreplaceable resources."

Blinman furrowed his brow. "Irreplaceable, you say? I wasn't aware that cave-ins could actually destroy a mine's ore."

"They don't." Corning took a few steps closer to the blocked entrance, squinting at the small opening they'd made to free Lacey and Dunstan. "Reaching silver is a dangerous and difficult business to begin with, and the collapse destroyed the access points."

Braden noticed that Corning mentioned only silver. If only someone mentioned the gold—that secret only he and Owens had known about—Braden could catch his killer. But no one whispered a word about gold or Draxley or Owens, and his time trickled away.

"Then it's not irreplaceable." Mrs. Blinman brightened. "It's just buried treasure! Would it really be so hard to go after it?"

"Yes." Braden kept from snorting in disbelief. Buried treasure? Did the flea-brained woman think a shovel could salvage things?

"Why?" Blinman's eyes narrowed. "They went in after the collapse and pulled you out. Didn't they shore up the cleared tunnels? Couldn't we get a team in there and work around the collapsed areas, go even deeper if that's what it would take?"

"You would send men into an unstable mine, directing them to dig into shifting rock and knowing they could die at any minute?" Braden eyed Blinman in disbelief then speculation. He hadn't considered that the killer might openly suggest reopening the mine, but he should have. The saboteur's greed couldn't be denied.

"Mr. Lyman!" Mrs. Blinman sounded shocked and affronted. "My husband asked about the supports and specifically mentioned working around the dangerous areas. How could you make such an accusation?"

"It was a question, not an accusation," Corning observed as he started up the uneven incline and gestured to the small opening. "And not a foolish one either. Like Harry mentioned, men have already gone back into the mines since the collapse. He most likely didn't realize they barely managed to unblock enough to get in."

Why is Corning defending Blinman? Granted, the man always had a peacemaker streak, but were they working together to reopen the mine?

"Surely that could be widened." Mrs. Blinman waved a dismissive hand. "That passage looks far too small for a grown man. I simply can't imagine why they didn't make it bigger in the first place."

Braden circled around until he had a clear view of both Blinman's and Corning's faces. He wanted to see their reactions as he said, "True. They made a much bigger opening after the first collapse."

Instant impact. Corning's brows jammed together in consternation. Blinman's practically disappeared into his hairline. Mrs. Blinman, who hadn't been facing them, whipped around fast enough to dislodge her silly little bonnet. Each one evinced surprise and hesitation but not a single shred of shame or guilt.

"Did you say 'first collapse'?" Corning scrambled down the rocks, away from the opening he'd been examining with such interest.

"Do you mean that the mines shifted again shortly after the first collapse because things were so unstable?" Blinman clarified.

"No." Braden didn't hide his anger. "A month ago the mines caved in again, this time trapping my sister and her new fiancé."

"But that's three months after the initial event!" Corning jumped down the final boulder and wiped his palms on his waistcoat. "Why would your sister go into the mines?"

Avid speculation lit Mrs. Blinman's gaze, conflicting with the practiced innocence of her tone. The woman probably hoped Lacey had been meeting Dunstan for a tryst and was looking for juicy gossip to spread around back East.

"Obviously they'd already considered reopening the mines." Blinman moved closer to his wife. "Perhaps the second cave-in will have made things more settled, and they can try again in the future."

"No." Braden said. "Those mines won't open again." And he was starting to worry that he wouldn't be able to unlock their secret.

FORTY

T he secret to catching fish is—" Naomi didn't get to finish her advice before Luke broke in.

"I know. Patience." He looked like it took a mighty effort not to roll his eyes. Luke didn't recognize the irony of his own statement.

"If you know the importance of patience," his father spoke sternly, "then you'd know that you're not demonstrating your mastery of the skill by interrupting Miss Higgins."

Luke's face fell. "Oh. Right. Sorry, Miss Naomi." They'd agreed yesterday afternoon when she showed him the workshop that "Miss Higgins" sounded too stuffy to keep using. The boy didn't know that Naomi made the decision partly because this way Michael wouldn't have to stop using her first name. It would seem a natural progression that wouldn't raise so many eyebrows if he slipped.

"No matter. You'll get plenty of practice today," she assured him. "That's always the second part of learning something. First you know it. Then you practice it. Then you master it. At least you're already over the first hurdle."

"Yeah!" Luke brightened and looked at his father. "Dad taught me. He says that patience is the secret to everything."

"Almost everything," Michael corrected with a grin. He shifted his gaze to meet Naomi's then added, "Every once in a while you find something special, and you don't want to lose it by waiting too long."

Her breath hitched at his intensity. A warm, swoopy feeling in her stomach made her almost giddy. Michael looked at her as if *she* was something special—and he didn't want to wait before letting her know it.

Perhaps he'd missed her company during his trip—the same way she'd missed him? The swoopy feeling intensified, and it took real effort for Naomi to pay attention to Luke's comments as they reached the bank of the stream where Lacey and Dunstan already laid out an old blanket.

"I asked Cora to join us," she told Lacey. "She said she might bring Dorothy along in a bit."

"Did you tell her Braden wasn't coming?" Lacey looked up from where she'd been tying a hook to her line. "She might be more keen to join us if she knew he wouldn't be."

"She knows." Naomi gave an absentminded wave and went to join Luke and Michael.

"Squishy." Luke palmed a handful of mud, closed his fist, and watched it ooze from between his fingers.

"A mite too squishy," Michael warned. "Worms like their dirt more solid. Let's move back a bit and try again."

Naomi grabbed the empty pail and shuffled up the bank a few steps then lowered herself into a precarious squat alongside the men. This time she picked up a clump of moist earth, rolled it between her fingers, and watched it crumble back to the ground as Michael proclaimed it a good spot.

Decoy bounded over to shove his muzzle into the small hole Luke started. The massive dog nosed around before pulling his head back, shaking back and forth, and sneezing all over the boy.

Luke's laughter held the high, joyful pitch of childhood as he reached out and hugged the wolfhound. "I think he's saying it's a good spot, Miss Naomi. Let's prove him right."

She decided to forgo rootling around in the dirt, preferring to keep them company while the boys tugged long, slippery worms from their snug mud homes. Naomi made sure to enthusiastically praise each and every find, with particular attention paid to size, color, and width of the various specimens Luke presented before dropping them into the bucket.

"Oh, a wriggler," she improvised, running out of comments on worm appearance. "If I were a fish, I'd definitely notice the way that one twists around."

"You know? I think you're right." Luke's hand veered away from the pail where he'd been about to drop the critter. "Better keep this and make sure he's the first one I use. I want to be sure and get a good start."

Naomi tried not to wince as he stuffed the wriggler into his back pocket but couldn't refrain from issuing a warning. "Whatever you do, do not sit down until you've put the bait on the hook."

"Right." Luke gave a solemn nod. "He won't wriggle if I squash him, and then he's no better than the rest."

Michael gave a snort of laughter, his gaze dancing with their shared merriment. "All right. That should be enough to get things going." He rose to his feet with an easy movement and held out a hand to help Naomi straighten up.

"All ready there?" Dunstan thrust poles at Luke and Mike. "Bait 'em up then. I sprinkled the area with crushed beetles already, so there should be plenty of prospects swimming around. Just keep calm and quiet, drop in the line, and wait for the tug."

"I've got my wriggler!" Luke's exaggerated whisper didn't pass for quiet, but no one reprimanded him. In no time at all, he'd plunked himself on the bank, leaned up against Decoy's furry bulk, and strung his line into the water.

"You look mighty pleased with yourself." Lacey sounded amused.

"Yep!" Luke squinted over at her, beaming. "I'm sitting in the shade with my dad, the world's biggest dog, and my new friend Miss Naomi. What more can a man want?"

"Not much." Michael settled himself next to Naomi, so close that the brush of his shoulder made her shiver. He looked at her with the same intensity as before, folding his hand over hers to adjust her grip on her own fishing pole. "This is just about perfect."

Thank You, Lord. Mike woke up the next morning with a smile on his face and praise in his heart. For a few moments he stretched out in his bunk and offered up his appreciation for Naomi, for Hope Falls, for the way Luke had taken a shine to both.

He grinned all through breakfast, even when some of the loggers attempted to engage Naomi in conversation. *Let them try*, Mike decided, feeling smug. *I get to spend the entire day with her while they're all out chopping down trees.*

In fact Mike was focusing so hard on how he'd arrange the day once they got to the workshop he almost didn't notice the rain pelting them when they stepped outside the diner. The cold, stinging drops made him prompt Luke to button up his coat, but Mike remained preoccupied with how he planned to spend the day. Just him, Naomi, and Luke—

And four merry woodsmen. Mike opened the workshop door to find the room filled to the rafters with the last people—aside from the Bainbridges and their lackeys—he wanted to see. The surprise stopped him cold in the doorway until Luke shoved his way into the room.

"Good morning, Naomi!" He dripped his way across the floor to join her near the stove. "What are you making? Can I make one, too?"

"Well, here's another one that sounds just like us." Bear Riordan raised a bushy red brow and grinned. "Lucky for you, Miss Higgins has a big heart and a bigger project for us to help with."

"Is that what's going on?" Mike moved to hang his hat on the peg by the door but found it—as well as those beside it—already occupied. "Have we fallen so far behind since I left Hope Falls?"

"We were behind before we began." Her easy smile made him wish twice as hard that their workshop hadn't been invaded by loggers.

"Since there's been a lot of summer showers, Mrs. Blinman wrangled us a way to keep busy and spend more time with Miss Higgins." The edge of Bobsley's tongue hung out the corner of his mouth as he focused on fine-sanding a miniscule wooden square.

"And it's fun." Clump looked up from where he crouched on the floor, an old cloth draped over an older crate and covered in tiny gray lumps of who-knew-what. "Salt clay is good, but I didn't know of it until Miss Higgins helped me make a batch a couple days ago."

"Clay?" Luke zoomed to look over Clump's shoulder. "Do you squish it into shapes and stuff? What are you trying to make?"

"Salt and water on the stove, cornstarch and cold water in a bowl, then mix it all together and knead it like bread." Naomi creaked open the steamer trunk at her side, tugged loose one of the drawers, and pulled out what Mike recognized as a vanity jar.

He watched in a combination of irritation and pleasure as Naomi handed it to Luke. Pleasure because she did such a wonderful job of including his son and making the boy feel important. Annoyance because apparently she'd done the same thing for a bunch of men.

"I keep mine in this powder pot because the lid screws on tight and keeps the clay from drying out. Why don't you look at the things in the Lyman Place house and choose something to make?"

"Sure!" Luke grabbed the crystal jar and hurried away. Instead of grabbing something as soon as he got there, he began taking inventory of everything in the dollhouse. He looked so serious trying to choose something to mold for Naomi that Mike smiled.

"Not the rocking horse," Clump cautioned. "That's what I'm making now, with the clay and snips from my bristly brush for mane and tail. I already finished the cat for the kitchen last time." Sure enough, he pulled out the tiny figure of a crouching cat, painted in black and gray stripes with little white-tipped feet.

"Nice work." Mike didn't have to like the way Clump cozied up to Naomi, but he believed in giving credit where credit was due. Then the idea struck him. If he found out what the others were working on, he might be able to help them finish. So they could leave.

"Hello, Strode." Gent perched on a three-legged stool, hunched over like an overgrown crow as he painstakingly chiseled at a small white block. The scent of lye stung the air when Mike drew near.

"Soap carving?" Mike tried to sound interested rather than disappointed. This was a task he could do nothing to hurry along.

"For marble busts." Gent straightened up and stretched before extending his work. "This is William Shakespeare. For the study."

Sure enough, Mike could make out the beginnings of a nose over The Bard's trademark goatee. In spite of himself, he was impressed by Gent's ambition and solid start. "Very creative, using soap."

"The shavings help discourage ants and other creeping things." Naomi carefully replaced the silver brush of her paste pot, her graceful motions making Mike wish lye frightened off larger pests.

He gave Luke an encouraging nod as his son settled down cross-legged by Clump's clay-working crate. Then he wandered over to where Bobsley sat, so closely sawing and sanding flattened blocks.

"I dunno if we're going to paint these or paste paper over the sides," the high climber commented. "Painting would be quicker, but Miss Higgins says that fabric makes them look more like real books."

"Books. Also for the study, I take it." Mike's heart sank. If Naomi wanted the shelves filled with books, he could expect Bobsley popping into the workshop every time a cloud crossed the sky.

"Well, first I made this here fur rug to go in front of the fireplace." Bobsley dug around in his pocket and produced a patch of fur half the size of Mike's palm, roughly cut to look like a bear hide. "I seen the one in the fancy house over there, so I caught a squirrel and set to making one for Miss Naomi. But she says there's really only room for one fur rug in a house, so I'm on to books."

"That'll keep you busy for a good while." He tried to sound hearty, but Mike heard the bitter note beneath his cheery words. It was glaringly obvious this wasn't the first time the loggers invaded the workshop, and he didn't like knowing they'd stormed the castle in his absence.

How much time had they spent with Naomi? And how much progress had they made while he'd been gone? The smile he'd hitched on his face slid off as questions mounted.

"Not as busy as Bear." Bobsley gestured to where Riordan sat, bent nearly double over a table littered with headless matchsticks.

"What are you making?" Mike's curiosity got the better of him, since he couldn't usher the intruders out the door anytime soon.

"Shutters." With a single blunt fingertip, Bear nudged one completed set across the rough surface of the worktable. The squared matchsticks, divested of their sulfur-dipped ends, had been fitted and glued at slight angles within a larger frame. The tilted edges looked remarkably like raised shutters, perfect for a dollhouse.

"That's impressive." He didn't try to pick one up—they might not yet be dry. "These will look even better after we paint the trim."

"They're all so creative and patient, working on these things." Naomi favored the entire room with a brilliant smile. "If you ask me, this dollhouse is shaping up to be something very special."

To a man, they agreed. Mike could tell that the men were all thinking along the same lines; a project with Naomi at the helm couldn't be anything less than extraordinary. A woman like her demanded the best a man could give, and they would work their fingers to the bone before admitting defeat. None of them were just working on dollhouse pieces. They were working to win the woman.

"I'm sorry to say that you'll be losing us, but we really must go home." Charlotte clasped her hands over her bosom as though sincerely wrenched at the prospect of leaving Hope Falls. Or as though she thought the town would feel bereft after her defection.

Sadly, Naomi didn't feel that way at all. She wouldn't have believed it, after the extremes they'd come through in the past, but the longer her sister stayed, the more strained things became. She'd breathe easier after Charlotte left. And as for Harry. . .well, Naomi long ago saw his betrayal in choosing her sister as a blessing. In spite of everything—or perhaps because of it—she didn't want him.

After a too-long pause, the men figured out that Charlotte expected protests and requests that she prolong her stay in town. Muttering and grumbling, they made a suitably incoherent response.

"Yes. I, too, need to be getting back to the office." Corning stood, but he didn't seem much taller than when he was sitting. "Rest assured that I will tell anyone who asks that the Hope Falls sawmill is a sound proposition and an absolutely worthy investment."

"Our stay here has been marked with sorrow." Charlotte regained the proverbial floor. She probably interpreted the men's restless shifting for regret at her imminent departure rather than a disgruntled signal that she should stop holding up everyone's dinner. At any rate, she didn't sit down so they could start eating.

"The passing of Mrs. Cash gave you reason to mourn, and I simply can't ignore the fact that now Hope Falls needs a reason to rejoice." She utterly ignored mutters over her mispronunciation of Arla's last name, instead flinging her arms wide as though to embrace everyone in the room. "So before we take our leave, I intend to put together a party. A sort of backwoods ball, you could say. I'll arrange for music and dancing and refreshments so we can all enjoy one final evening together. A very...special evening."

A chill of foreboding raised gooseflesh on Naomi's arms. The way Charlotte paused before saying "special" was cause for concern.

"Any dance will be special, since we ain't never had one before." One of the men lessened the room's expectant tension.

"Ah, but this one will be very special indeed." Charlotte's gaze sought Naomi's, and her smile held more than a hint of triumph. "You see, in but a few nights' time, my sister will reveal the secret she's been keeping from all of you. Or I'll do it for her."

Naomi's heart skidded to a stop. It didn't simply skip a beat; it jumped, sputtered, and ceased working altogether. *She can't mean it. What about her protests that the past would harm her and Harry?*

"See how shy she is?" Charlotte made sure every eye in the room took in the heated flush creeping up her neck like a mottled rash. "That's why she needs her sister to give her this nudge. If I don't do something before I leave, Naomi might never reveal which of you men she wants to marry. She's too afraid of insulting the others!"

Relief brought air back into her lungs and even more blood

rushing to redden her face. *She didn't mean* that *secret. Charlotte's just being dramatic. This won't ruin me, it just. . .* Naomi's thoughts hitched as Charlotte gave her deadline.

"In two nights, my big sister will choose her groom!"

FORTY-ONE

W ho is he?" Lacey wasted no time demanding an answer. As soon as they shut the door to the house and sent baby Dorothy upstairs with her nursemaid, the women rounded on Naomi in curious indignation.

"I don't know." Naomi sank into a wingback chair and moaned.

"Why is your sister forcing your hand?" Evie couldn't sit, too agitated to do anything but pace the parlor. "We all agreed you'd have as much time as you needed to choose a husband. No rushing, and at least two of us need to approve your selection beforehand. Did Charlotte know this before she waltzed in and dropped her decree?"

"Even if she didn't know the particulars, she knew better than to do this." Cora sat on the settee, spine ramrod straight. "I say we don't go along with it. Why should any of us dance to her tune and let her play puppeteer with Naomi's future? It's idiocy."

Naomi cleared her throat, if not her mind. "It's already done." If she didn't go through with Charlotte's well-publicized plan, her sister might very well decide to reveal a more interesting secret. After all, Charlotte probably didn't trust Naomi to keep quiet, and Colorado Territory was such a long, long way from back home.

"She's right." Lacey retraced Evie's circuit. "Charlotte's whipped Naomi's fellows into an awful lather. If Evie or I hadn't yet selected our fiancés, we could circumvent this. As it stands, we won't be able to buy more time for Naomi to decide. The men will be insulted and up in arms if she balks now. And Charlotte knows it."

"She's very astute," Naomi admitted. "She played this well."

"I have a few other descriptions I'd use before 'astute' occurred to me," Evie harrumphed. "But why is she playing at all?"

"Isn't it obvious?" Lacey's nonchalance made Naomi worry anew.

"Is it obvious?" She winced at the quaver weakening her voice.

"Charlotte's jealous. She knows Harry chose the wrong wife, and by now Harry's had half a decade to realize his mistake. Braden's invitation threatened her—she came to make sure her husband didn't harbor feelings for Naomi." Lacey stopped pacing in favor of shredding the ribbons dotting her skirts. "Now she's making sure Naomi's solidly married, just in case Harry invests in Hope Falls and takes it into his head to come down for another visit!"

"Well, we all knew I'd have to choose one of them eventually." Naomi decided to lay out the facts and try to hide the doubts and protests thrumming through her thoughts. "And since I'm holding up your and Evie's weddings and drawing out the loggers' expectations, it couldn't go on much longer. At this point, I'll have to choose."

"It's all my fault." Lacey plopped down onto the settee with enough force to make Cora pop up before sinking back down. "If I hadn't convinced you all to run that accursed advertisement, Naomi wouldn't be trapped in this predicament. At the very least, I should have waited to announce my engagement with Dunstan until you'd had more time to get to know the men and make an informed decision!"

"Poppycock." Naomi snorted. "It's not your fault I joined the ad, and after your private adventure in the mines became so public—with the men seeing you in those pants!—you had to announce your engagement. Stop taking credit for my mistakes, and help me choose."

"I've always had a soft spot for Clump," Evie confessed. "If not for Jake, I would've chosen him. You know he'd work hard to be a good provider, cherish his family, and not take you for granted."

"Clump has a good heart." Naomi's own estimation of the sincere

German echoed Evie's sentiments almost exactly. But Clump didn't make Naomi's pulse pick up pace when he walked up, smiled, or spoke.

"So does Riordan. He's breaking up a fight or helping Granger every time we turn around. And you know a man that size can care for his own. You could do worse than a gentle giant," Cora advised.

"That's true, too. Riordan looks like a Goliath, but he acts more like a David." Naomi couldn't say that, for all his gentleness, Riordan's sheer size made her skittish. She couldn't marry him.

"Bobsley's too young." Lacey flatly refused to consider the flighty high climber with the good-natured grin. "Gent's too old."

"I wouldn't say that." *I might think it, but I wouldn't say it!* "He's extremely conscientious, always thoughtful and well-mannered."

"Excellent. Do keep him in mind if you ever decide to hire a butler." Lacey's wry tone made it clear that Naomi hadn't convinced anyone she considered Gent and his top hat to be a viable option.

"What about Mr. Strode?" Cora ran a palm over her face as though trying to wipe away the day's difficulties. "He's fairly new, but I think you've spent more time with him than any of the others."

"I like him." *I want him. I'd choose him in a heartbeat!*

Naomi ruthlessly reigned in her thoughts. Michael deserved a wife he could trust, and after her discussion with Charlotte, she owed her sister her silence. She couldn't tell him what she'd done, what kind of woman she was—even if she thought he'd overlook it.

The next words pained her before they were born. "But he's not one of the men who's courting me, so I can't consider him anyway."

"You don't have much time," Evie mused. "But if he's the one who suits you best, consider giving him something to think about."

"That's not a bad idea. Try persuading him. He might be more interested than you suppose." Lacey brightened. "Dunstan was."

"Thanks for the advice." Naomi forced a chuckle. "But I'll never be as persuasive as you. We're very different women, cousin."

You have no idea just how different, and I hope it stays that way.

"You have to change it." Cora circled the fingers of her left hand around her right wrist and hung on tight to keep them from fluttering around while she spoke. "Since you didn't make it to dinner last night and you're the supposed head of Hope Falls, you can stop Mrs. Blinman's attempt to bully Naomi. Say you'll help!"

"So that's why they didn't leave this morning?" Braden sat still for a moment, mulling over this new information. "When I left Blinman and Corning yesterday, they sounded bound and determined to be on their way. If the doctor hadn't slipped me some morphine yesterday afternoon, I would've been there last night to intervene."

"You can be there now," Cora urged. "While it's mainly about refusing to let Naomi be pressured into a loveless marriage, there's another reason why Hope Falls shouldn't be holding this dance."

She waited for him to mention Arla so she wouldn't have to speak around the lump that clogged her throat whenever she thought of her friend. But Braden sat there waiting for her to continue.

"Arla! She hasn't been gone for even a week," Cora burst out.

"I know." But Braden didn't look at all like he really understood how inappropriate this dance would be. He stared out the window into a distance only he could see. "So many deaths."

She waited for him to acknowledge Arla specifically, to snap to his senses and declare he'd look after his cousin instead of letting Naomi be sacrificed for the sake of some stupid advertisement. And when he finally did speak, his thoughts surprised her.

"There's a lot that's not fair, Cora. Mrs. Nash's death, leaving her child orphaned, Naomi needing to pick one of her suitors so fast... None of this is fair." He pointed out the window. "But it pales in comparison to the men who died in the belly of that mountain, buried alive by the greed of a man I've yet to catch."

"Draxley's dead." Cora didn't follow his reasoning and wondered whether Doc had snuck Braden another dose. Normally she'd say it served him right for pushing himself too hard, but right now she needed Braden to be able to think clearly and act strongly.

"I know." His arm fell to his side, fist clenched. "So's Owens. But what about the man who convinced Owens and Draxley to sabotage the mines? We don't know his name, so he escapes any justice."

"That's not something I can solve. I'm busy trying to figure out how to keep Charlotte from ruining Naomi's life—and you don't seem to care!" Cora pinched the skin between thumb and forefinger, refusing to start wringing her hands or pacing. She'd promised herself she'd stay strong any and every time she talked to Braden.

Braden swallowed and faced her. "I care, Cora. But Naomi's a grown woman who can choose her own husband. The men on that ridge beside Mrs. Nash can't hunt down their own killer, can they?"

Cora was about to tell him she'd come back after his medication wore off when something clicked into place. "The investors."

He nodded miserably, confirming her blossoming suspicion.

"You invited the previous investors because you hoped the saboteur would be greedy enough to show up and say something so stupid and so obvious we'd all know what he'd done?" Cora gaped at her fiancé in disbelief. "That's beyond far-fetched, Braden!"

"It was all I could do." He rubbed the back of his neck. "I thought I'd lost my last chance, but this dance gives me another opportunity to question Blinman and Corning. I can't cancel it."

Cora felt her pulse thud at the base of her throat and raised a hand to cover it. "What about Naomi? What about little Dorothy, who'll someday hear that Hope Falls threw a party days after her mother's death? What about what you owe the people who still live?"

"Like the Loathly Lady in your story, Naomi can make her own choice." Braden gave a weary sigh. "And what makes you think little Dorothy will stay in Hope Falls? Lawson might move on, you know."

"Not if I marry him, like he asked, so I can be a mother to Dorothy." For the first time, Cora spoke of the promise she hadn't meant to give Arla. "I assured Arla that I'd take care of her daughter, and Mr. Lawson can't do it alone. Dorothy will stay."

"You're adopting this child?" Braden sat up, exuding anxious energy. "And you didn't think to discuss it with me before now?"

"No. You're busy pursuing your own vendettas. Our engagement is dissolved, and you don't see fit to honor my friends. Why would I discuss any of my decisions with someone like that?" She couldn't keep the scorn from her voice. "If it came down to you or Dorothy, there wouldn't be any question. I choose the child, and I choose to keep my promise to a friend who deserved more from this town."

She left before Braden could summon a response. No argument he concocted now could change her mind. He wouldn't help Naomi, and Cora couldn't help Braden. He'd failed her for the final time.

"You need more time." Mike didn't waste words when he finally got a moment alone with Naomi. He'd been trying to pull her aside since her sister's announcement, but she hadn't so much as stepped foot in the workshop since. The lumbermen abandoned all attempts at logging, keeping Naomi hopping with their final, desperate attempts to woo her. Mike pushed away his bitterness over failing to do the same. Now he had this one chance, mere moments before the dance began, to make her listen.

"We'll catch up on the dollhouse." Naomi's eyes, made even greener than usual by her verdant dance dress, looked tired. "With all the things the men have made, we can make up the time."

"That's not what I meant." He curled his fingers around her elbow, feeling the warmth of her skin through the thin fabric. "I meant you need more time to make the biggest decision of your life."

"Why?" She blinked at him, more remote than he'd ever seen her. "It isn't as though my options are going to improve or expand. I put out the advertisement; I've gotten to know the men who responded. The men are waiting. Lacey and Evie's weddings are waiting on me."

"Hasn't anyone told you you're worth waiting for?" He rubbed his thumb along the soft fabric, wishing he could touch her without any barriers between them. "I don't think there's a man in that clearing or a single one of your friends who'd disagree with me."

"Well, there's one." She gave a sad smile, and suddenly Mike knew, without a doubt, Naomi was thinking of Harold Blinman.

"Any man who'd let you go didn't deserve you to start with," Mike whispered fiercely. "If you can't see that, then I'm right. You need more time to come to terms with your past before you can promise any man your future."

Now Naomi's eyes sparkled, but they were wet with unshed tears. "What do you know about coming to terms with the past, Michael? Some mistakes, once made, color everything that follows."

"Only if you let them." He wasn't whispering anymore. "But if there's any part of you that still belongs to Blinman, you shouldn't accept another man. You know I'm right. Don't do this."

"What do you know about Harry?" She looked as surprised and wounded as if he'd slapped her across the face. "Why do you care?"

"I want better for you." He stepped closer and abandoned his attempt to talk sense into her without pressuring her further. Mike cupped her cheek in his palm. "I would wait for you, Naomi."

Longing flashed through her gaze, and her gloved hand rested atop his for a moment. She closed her eyes, and when she opened them, he saw only grim determination. She dropped her hand. "You shouldn't."

She rushed off into the night, leaving behind a half-heard addition. "You'd only find out that I didn't deserve it."

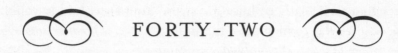

FORTY-TWO

Shaken by Michael's unexpected offer, hardly able to breathe while regret pinched her ribs like a remorseless iron cage, Naomi ached to tell him the truth. To see if he still thought she was worth waiting for or if he'd denounce her as the worst sort of woman.

She didn't think she'd like his answer, even if she could ask the question. Ringed with lanterns and pressed by the promises she'd made her sister and her friends, the dance floor held all the charm of a gallows. Each step felt leaden, her stomach swimming in her shoes. Naomi knew full well she didn't dredge up a smile for anyone.

Lord, if I'm not to be with Michael, why did You let him return my regard? I know my sins; I've confessed and repented. So why this torment? If he didn't want me, I could move forward with my plan to accept Clump. But how can I do that now, knowing Michael might feel the same way I do? Knowing that I can never find out because I'm bound by my promise to Charlotte and my own unimaginable past?

She managed to nod and murmur her way through a dance with Corning before her suitors queued up. The phonograph Charlotte dragged from the house sounded as scratchy and sore as Naomi's throat felt from swallowing back her tears. But the music played on, and so did the farce her life had become. Gent took her for the first dance.

Admittedly, she didn't pay close attention to what he was saying until she caught a smattering of French. The words acted like a cold dousing, dragging her forward to face the moment.

"I'm sorry." She concentrated on not tripping over his boots. For some reason, her movement seemed disjointed and surreal. "You know, my French is rusty. Would you mind repeating that for me?"

"Ah, that caught your attention." Gent beamed down at her through a particularly enthusiastic swirl. "Your sister said it would. I practiced all day to memorize the inflection. *Votre premier amour n'a pas que vous voulez, et pas plus que ces hommes.*"

Your first love didn't want you, and neither do these men. Naomi stumbled as the words hammered into her. Stunned, she barely held on and finished the dance. Luckily, Gent seemed pleased by her dumbfounded reaction until Bobsley cut in.

"Good evening, Miss Higgins." Stiff formality made the young man seem awkward—though, then again, that might be due to his jerky movements and abysmal dancing. For a while, it took all of their concentration to remain upright. But soon enough, he spoke in stilted French. *"Vous n'êtes rien, mais une salope skunk-cheveux."*

You are nothing but a skunk-haired slut. Naomi went stock-still at the denouncement, causing the well-meaning Bobsley to tromp on her foot. The mishap bought her a few moments off the makeshift dance floor, but even so the world seemed to be spinning around her.

"Pardon?" Riordan hunkered down into the seat beside her when Bobsley left to get her something to drink. "That's a wonderful color on you, Miss Higgins. And I wanted to tell you—"

"Wait. Did my sister teach you something special in French?" At his nod, Naomi closed her eyes and braced herself for his words.

"L'homme que vous mariez vous haïra autant que notre mère."
The man you marry will hate you as much as our mother.

"Well." She sucked in a sharp breath and tried to hold back the bile burning the back of her throat. "I hardly know what to say."

"Here's your milk, Miss Higgins." Bobsley pushed a cool glass into her hand, and Naomi gulped it down gratefully. The burning sensation receded, and she didn't feel in danger of being sick.

Until Clump joined them. Well-meaning Volker Clump led her back onto the dance floor, tromping her feet with his too-heavy tread and battering her heart with his "compliment." His German accent clotted the French pronunciation, but Naomi heard each damning word. *"Votre nuit de noces sera encore pire que celui que vous avez volé."*

At that, Naomi mumbled an incoherent apology and excuse then rushed from the dance floor. Alone in the darkness of the night, she broke into a run. Each step pounded out her sister's final curse.

Your wedding night will be even worse than the one you stole.

"You don't mean that." Cora stared at him as though he'd sprung from his wheeled chair and begun a series of handstands and cartwheels.

"I do." He wanted to reach for her hand but knew he didn't have the right. Instead he forced out the words lodging in his throat. "If you want to go and dance, I'll hold baby Dorothy for you."

She squinted at him and laid a cool palm against his forehead. "Are you feeling all right Braden? You're not acting like yourself."

"Good." He decided to be blunt since he wasn't much good with words anyway. "I've been acting like a horse's rear end for months."

"Well." She pulled her hand away, and Braden fought the urge to snatch it back. "That's new. Since when do you admit you're wrong?"

"Since every time I try to control something, it goes wrong." He looked at the white bundle she cradled in the crook of one arm. "She seems healthy and happy, and so do you. Motherhood agrees with you."

"Do you think so?" A hesitant smile lifted the corners of her generous lips—the first smile she'd given him since she told the Loathly Lady legend. "I constantly worry I'm not doing it right."

"That's my fault, Cora." His smile faded so she could see his seriousness. "I should have told you what a wonderful job you do, taking care of people. You have a comforting touch, encouraging smile, and just enough starch to keep things interesting."

"Oh." She blinked then ducked her head and fussed with the baby's wrappings. "That's. . .well, that's the nicest thing you've said to me since I came to Hope Falls. Which isn't saying much, Braden."

He bowed his head. "I know. I have a lot to make up for."

"Well, it would have been a very nice thing to say anywhere," she relented, still focused on the baby. "But why would you try to make up for your behavior? You were grieving the loss of your men, dealing with a lot of pain, and trying to protect all of us."

"And failing to treat you like a grown woman fully able to make her own decisions." Braden stated it outright. "If I have any chance of convincing you to reestablish our engagement, I'll need to prove that I realize what a treasure you are. No matter my struggles, I shouldn't have stopped cherishing the amazing woman God brought into my life. Cora, I'm sorry for the way I acted. I just hope you'll let me make it up to you someday."

Confusion flitted across her features. "Then why did you offer to hold Dorothy so I could dance with someone else?"

"Because I'm giving you the one thing every woman wants." He reached up and clasped her hand in his, unable to keep from touching her. "I'm respecting your choice—whatever it may be."

After all, respecting was a far cry from accepting, should she make the wrong decision.

She stayed quiet for a long time but didn't pull her hand away. Braden clung to it and the hope that she'd see the change God had been working in him since the day of the cave-in. He had a long way to go still, but he figured Cora already knew that. He'd taken a bad turn and gone a long way down it. Getting back to the place where they'd been before meant a return journey.

"You listened." She squeezed his hand, but Braden didn't think she realized she'd done it until he squeezed back. "Why now? What changed?"

"I'm done chasing things I can't change at the expense of the people I'm supposed to cherish." His voice sounded croaky, but at least he forced the words through. "You were right. I should have called this thing off. Naomi looks like she's about to burst into tears, the men are circling her like jackals, and I haven't gotten a single clue from Corning or Blinman about the mine collapse."

Her brows slammed together. "Don't blame yourself for not finding the saboteur." Her whisper sounded a bit hissy. "Just like you need to stop blaming yourself for the accident."

"I have." Something like peace swelled in his chest. Cora still cared—he could build on that. "But I do blame myself for losing you. I want to win you back, Cora-mine."

A ghost of the gamine grin she used to wear flashed across her face. "I won't stop you from trying."

"Good because someday not too far off I intend to get out of this wheelchair." Braden grinned. "It's the only way I can get back down on one knee."

A fleeting smile, the shimmer of tears, and Cora's expression grew shuttered. "Before you start thinking you'll reestablish our engagement someday, you need to know that I've discussed Dorothy's situation with Mr. Lawson. At length."

No! Braden couldn't speak, could only scream a silent denial. After all they'd been through, he couldn't have lost her to Lawson!

"I turned down his generous proposal, but he agreed it would be in Dorothy's best interests if we honored Arla's last request. As of today, Dorothy is mine. I plan to raise her as my daughter, Braden."

He reached out and tucked back the blanket obscuring the newborn's face. Dorothy wrinkled her nose and let out an agitated gurgle, flailing one tiny fist before settling back into sleep. "She's beautiful. Any man would be blessed by the pair of you."

Cora smiled again. "Did you have anyone particular in mind?"

Not thinking, Naomi's steps carried her along the familiar path to the workshop. She flung open the door, strode inside, and grabbed her apron as she always did. Then she realized what she was doing. Her legs shaky, she barely made it to the chair before the sobs slammed together in the back of her throat, cutting off her air.

Charlotte found her bent over, clutching the apron like a lifeline and gasping for breath. The tears streaming down her face made her sister look hazy, as if rubbed by a zealous eraser. "What do you want?" Naomi choked on tears and bone-deep pain.

Charlotte sneezed. "To apologize." Another sneeze. "What I did was awful, petty, and cruel, and I can't tell you how sorry I am, Mimi."

"I hate that nickname," she protested thickly. Somehow it symbolized the way Charlotte always disregarded her feelings. That made it something important. "Don't call me Mimi, and don't give me your apologies when you don't mean them. I understand that you hate me, and I understand why. Leave it at that and leave me be, Charlotte."

"No! You don't understand. How could you? I've been jealous of you my whole life. You got to stay home while they shipped me to another continent," Charlotte burst out. "Then when France became the home of my heart, they dragged me back to the States so I could see my big sister marry some well-to-do man from a distinguished family. I stole Harry because I wanted to prove that I could make Mama proud, too—that I was just as good as you are. But look how that worked."

"I'm not apologizing again," Naomi snapped, trying to hold on to her anger. She couldn't handle or help her sister's old hurts, but they seeped toward her heart. Didn't Naomi know how it felt to be sent far away? To feel second best to her sister? She'd never realized Charlotte experienced some of those same feelings.

Another sneeze and Charlotte squeezed her hand. "I'm not asking you to. I'm talking about how I failed. Harry married me so I could bear him an heir—and I haven't. One miscarriage, and no more."

Naomi's wall crumpled at the forlorn grief in her sister's voice. She reached out to stroke Charlotte's black hair, an awkward attempt to comfort the sister who'd become such a stranger to her. "That's not your fault. You're not a failure—Harry seems happy."

Charlotte said something but lost it to another round of sneezes. When she caught her breath, she said, "Can we go outside? It's a warm night—we can go for a little walk in the woods where no one will interrupt us. I'm not ready to rejoin the dance."

"Neither am I." Naomi stood, still clutching her apron. It gave her hands something to do, a simple comfort she desperately needed. They walked side by side, slowly at first, both of them loathe to draw attention to themselves. When they reached the woods and Charlotte stopped sneezing, she started to walk more quickly.

"What's the hurry?" Naomi hurried after her sister, pulling up short when Charlotte stepped up a series of small rocks to look over the edge of a steep drop. Darkness blanketed the area, and the recent rains probably meant slippery moss scattered around those boulders. She hung back.

"Aren't you coming?" Charlotte turned around and beckoned.

"No. Why don't you come back down here?" Naomi suggested. "As I recall, it's a very long drop from up there. One of us might slip."

"Well that's fine." Her sister gave a sharp laugh and pulled something out of her pocket. Moonlight glinted off the barrel of the pistol she pointed toward Naomi. "Since one of us is supposed to."

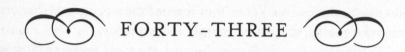

FORTY-THREE

It wasn't supposed to be like this. Mike glared at each man who spoke to Naomi, reserving a special intensity for the ones who danced with her. The lucky ones who could put their hand on her waist and smile into her eyes while they swayed to the music.

Although, in all fairness, Naomi didn't seem as graceful as usual. Her movements seemed abrupt, jerky, and downright clumsy at times as she tripped over her partners' feet. Mike felt something akin to satisfaction at the idea she was as unsettled as he was.

"Shouldn't you be asking Naomi to dance, Dad?" Luke's anxious query made him look down. "Because you know lots of other guys are, and you don't have much time left to convince her to choose us."

Us. Mike's jaw clenched at his son's innocent comment. Luke already saw the three of them becoming a family. Mike wanted the same. But none of that did any good if Naomi didn't choose them.

"She looks kinda upset." Concern crinkled Luke's brow as they watched Naomi jump back from Clump and rush away from the dance area. He pushed up his sleeves. "All right, Dad. Now's your chance. You go follow her, and I'll take care of the guy who made her cry."

Mike caught his son by the back of the collar before the boy could go do something foolish. "You don't know what happened. Promise me you'll leave Clump alone. Trust me, he's a good guy." When he wasn't trying to steal Naomi for himself at least.

"Okay. So long as you go get her." Luke pointed toward the

workshop. "She went that-a-way, so you better get a move on!"

His son's eagerness made Mike want to cry and punch something all at once. It was his fault. He'd raised Luke's hopes along with his own. And, unless God intervened sometime tonight, both of them would suffer major disappointment before the sun rose again.

Mike approached the workshop in time to see a set of skirts disappearing around the corner. For a moment he hesitated. Naomi obviously wanted to be left alone—but it looked like she might be headed for the woods. The memory of the stuffed cougar she persisted in decorating stuck out in his mind. The forest was too dangerous to let her go wandering around unprotected. Especially at night.

Quietly, Mike crept around the side of the shop and headed for the woods. In the distance he could make out two figures. While relieved Naomi wasn't alone, the idea of leaving two women to wander the woods by themselves made him uneasy. He decided he wouldn't intrude—just shadow them close enough to keep Naomi in sight, far enough to give her privacy. She probably needed to talk through her choice.

The farther the women went into the woods, the closer Mike followed. Otherwise too much cover separated him. He'd be of no use if he had to scramble through thickets and bound over boulders. When the women reached a clearing—the edge of a cliff face really, Mike stayed behind in the shadow of the woods. The wind carried their conversation to him, and Mike realized Naomi's companion was her sister. He'd just started to wonder if he shouldn't leave them to talk things out when Mrs. Blinman pulled the pistol from her pocket.

Mike started forward but realized his presence might startle the woman into shooting. Even if he didn't startle her, the knowledge that there was a witness might provoke her to violence. Desperately he scanned the area for closer cover and found none. The trees where he stood provided the nearest foliage, and the closest rocks were situated on the cliff edge behind the women. For now he had no choice but to stay concealed and wait things out.

"What are you doing?" Naomi stared at the weapon, eyes glued to the one threat Mike never suspected—a danger he couldn't reach her in time to prevent. "When did you start carrying a gun, Charlotte?"

"Since the day I boarded the train for Hope Falls. The mountains are a dangerous place for anyone," Mrs. Blinman singsonged and cocked the pistol. "But they're particularly threatening to me. Harry never suspected why our cousin invited him and the other investors 'to inspect the sawmill,' but I suspected. Braden found out the collapse wasn't an accident, didn't he?"

Still hidden, Mike bit back a groan. He'd been so focused on getting Luke home, he hadn't bothered to question Braden's blasé explanation about those special invitations of his. Now that Mrs. Blinman said something, it made perfect sense. Had Braden Lyman been sitting beside him, Mike would have been tempted to do violence.

"It was you who sabotaged the mines?" Naomi sounded flabbergasted. "Why would you bother arranging a cave-in?"

"Money, you flea-brain." She gave a bone-chilling laugh.

"But you don't need it. You have Harry and a house and fine clothes—anything you want." Naomi twisted some fabric in her hands.

"Not anything," her sister snapped. "Harry won't take me home. After all I went through to marry him and get that honeymoon in France, I couldn't convince him to stay there. He forced me to come back to America, no matter how much I begged to go back home."

"I don't see how the mine collapse would change that." Naomi slid forward, the shift so slight Mike might have imagined it.

"Of course you don't see. You never did see what was right in front of your face." Another cackle. "I took Owens as my lover. When the mine struck gold, I convinced him to manufacture a false cave-in so we could buy the other investors out for next to nothing. Then he'd go back in with a new crew, reap the riches, and we'd be off!"

"But you didn't tell him you planned to kill Braden." Naomi

seemed to understand something Mike could only guess at.

"No. I arranged that with Draxley. Why split the profits and dodge suspicion if we didn't have to? But Owens, sentimental fool that he was, got himself killed by racing back to save our cousin. Not that it mattered. Sure enough, Braden lived." She grimaced in disgust.

"Most of us were glad about that." Naomi shifted again. "Now, do you want to tell me why you're pointing a gun at my head?"

"Because you, dear sister, are going to climb those rocks and fling yourself over the edge. I'll make sure everyone knows you couldn't stand the thought of marrying anyone other than Harry. Your mad, unrequited love has built for half a decade, and you snapped." The crazy woman snapped her fingers to further illustrate the point.

Slowly, Mike pulled off his boots and started edging out of the woods, making as little noise as he could manage. If Naomi planned to jump her sister, he wanted her to know he was there for her. He wanted to get as close as possible to the crazy woman with the gun. He saw Naomi's eyes widen when she caught sight of him, but otherwise she kept her calm. Better, she kept her sister talking.

"Why kill me?" Naomi scooted again, making Mike's breath catch. Could she be trying to grab her sister's pistol? "What's the point?"

"I'm your closest relative. Your shares in Hope Falls—and the mine—will come to the sister you so recently reunited with." Mrs. Blinman waved the pistol and adopted a sorrowful tone. "Imagine my devastation, after I worked so hard to help you find a husband of your very own, that you decided to end your life over my Harry."

It seemed like ages passed since Mike started creeping up the cliff side, cautiously balancing amid small, sharp rocks. He sent up a prayer of thanks that he'd thought to remove his boots—the rocks against boot heels would have given him away in a heartbeat. Finally, he'd gotten close enough to risk lunging at the lunatic.

But Naomi beat him to it. With a deft motion, she untwisted the fabric she'd been bunching and unbunching in her hands. She pulled it taught and flung the thing upward, diving to the side in a cloud of sawdust. Her sister started sneezing immediately, finger tightening on the trigger and sending a bullet ricocheting off the nearest boulder and back into the woods behind all of them.

When Naomi dove to the side, Mike lunged. He caught Mrs. Blinman around the waist, hand closing over the wrist holding the pistol. For such a tiny woman, she had a surprisingly strong grip. He had to slam her arm against the ground before she released it.

For a moment all three of them lay there, gasping for breath. Mrs. Blinman punctuated the silence with a few more sneezes before Naomi got to her feet. Without speaking, she refolded what Mike now recognized as her work apron—and the source of the sawdust cloud. He couldn't help but grin at her brilliant makeshift weapon.

"Sawdust sneezes," her sister wheezed. "Crude, but effective. I should have remembered how hopelessly provincial you can be."

"As opposed to being a scheming, lying murderer?" Naomi glared down at her sister. "If that's what passes for sophistication these days, then I'm well rid of it. Just as I'll be well rid of you."

"Not so fast." Charlotte's sneer made Naomi's blood boil. "You can't prove anything—and you know you have to let me go. Otherwise I'll tell the world my big sister's sordid little secret, won't I?"

"No." Naomi froze, fighting the now-familiar clench of fear. "No one will believe an adulterer, saboteur, and murderer."

"People believe the best story," her sister spat out. "If you turn me in, I'll turn out your dirty laundry. Imagine how the gossips would love it—they'll gleefully pick apart a whole family!"

"What is she talking about, Naomi?" Michael's deep, steady voice made her nerves flutter more than ever.

"Nothing." She rubbed the bridge of her nose, searching for a solution to this impossible situation. She couldn't let Charlotte go— Braden deserved to find justice for the mine sabotage. And even if he didn't, she couldn't live with herself if her sister went on to hurt some other person, family, or even an entire town.

But she couldn't stand to have Charlotte tell Michael what a despicable, lowly woman she really was. The look on his face when he saw her unmasked would hurt more than a thousand Harold Blinmans. *Why are you leaving it up to Charlotte?* A small, brave voice surfaced from deep inside her. *You can't set her free, and she'll hurt you if she can. Don't let old guilt give her new power.*

"On Charlotte and Harry's wedding night, Mama gave me hard liquor to steady my nerves. Everyone was talking about me, staring to see if I'd fall apart. Then there were the toasts. And the punch." She remembered the sensation of floating and tried to capture that same detachment. "I don't remember anything, but I awoke in Charlotte's bed the next morning—in place of the bride."

"I don't believe it. You would never, not in a million years. . ." Michael rubbed his forehead as though trying to push away the thought. "All that about a man mistaking one sister for the other. . . Do you mean your sister's groom never realized his mistake?"

"No. It can't be true. I would've known. . . ." Harry emerged from the forest, visibly shaken and staring at her as if he'd never seen her before. "Why would you say something like that, Naomi? Did you hear me coming and think I was eavesdropping? Because I wasn't. I came to find you and your sister since you'd been gone so long."

"She said it because it's true, and I'm going to tell everyone," Charlotte crowed. "You went to bed so drunk you didn't recognize that the woman wasn't your wife. It's a wonder you did anything to be ashamed of, in that condition." She gave a crude snicker.

"Why didn't I remember? Why didn't anyone tell me?" Harry went pale and looked as though he was going to lose his dinner.

"Would you have wanted to know?" Naomi steeled herself for the answer. "Would it have made any difference, or would you have helped them ship me off and get rid of any difficult questions?"

Michael kept his gaze locked on the ground, unwilling to even look at her. That hurt more than Harry's refusal to answer her.

"Michael." She whispered his name, pleading for understanding. "I didn't mean to do it. I didn't plan on it or want to. I don't even remember anything except becoming ill when Mama told me."

"Your hair," Harry burst out. "I would've noticed your hair."

"Mama and Charlotte took pains to hide the white streak that night." Naomi closed her eyes at the memory. "So I'd look young enough to maybe catch the interest of some other gentleman. Not that I was at the party for long—I got so confused Charlotte took me back to the family wing so I could go to bed and sleep away the fog."

"Wait." Michael's head jerked up from where he was pinning Charlotte's arms behind her and tying them together with the apron Naomi had passed him. "Your sister is the one who took you to bed? After she tried so hard to hide your hair?"

Naomi understood what he was suggesting, but her mind couldn't make the connection stick. Not until Charlotte rose to her knees and hissed at Michael. That's when she knew. Michael saw what she never had.

She bent down to stare her sister in the eye. "You did my hair so I'd look more like you. You kept giving me champagne and making toasts to get me tipsy. You took me upstairs and put me in your own bed. . . . I should have realized someone undressed me. The maids would have taken me back to my room if they found me there. Even a drunken groom would notice his bride wore a red dress instead of white!"

"Yes. Your shame and guilt kept you from asking too many questions or examining your memory too closely." Charlotte cackled. "How else was I going to fool Harry into thinking he'd married the young innocent I pretended to be? A little sleeping powder for you and lots of bourbon for Harry, some creative juggling, and voilà. Stained sheets the next morning to make my husband happy."

"I never stole your wedding night." Naomi sat on the nearest boulder, her knees unable to support her. Relief and rage at this revelation robbed her of any strength. "You stole mine."

"For all the good it did me." Charlotte snorted. "Harry turned out to be as useless as you, but the secrets do me no good now. I'll tell them to anyone and everyone if you turn me in for the mines and trying to make you walk over the cliff," Charlotte promised. "You and Harry won't be able to hold your heads up."

"The mines?" Harry looked confused, and Naomi knew he really had just joined the conversation. Quickly, Michael filled him in.

"No one will believe you." He echoed Naomi's earlier hope.

"Gossips love a good story." Charlotte jerked against the binding Michael made from Naomi's apron strings, unable to get free.

"I'll give them a better one." Harry's face filled with wrath. "A selfish, grasping adulteress who seduced a good man, sabotaged a mine, and tried to kill her own sister. When she failed, she went mad and her poor husband had to place her in an asylum, where she screams obscene stories from the mess of her mind."

"You wouldn't put your wife in an asylum—it'd be the sort of scandal you want to avoid." Her sister's bravado couldn't hide her fear.

"Better than the sort you'd create if everyone didn't dismiss your ramblings for insanity." Michael's face hardened. "And considering the things you've done, I don't question that you're insane. The asylum will stop you from hurting anyone else."

But there was nothing he could do to heal Naomi's hurts. He didn't know how to banish the haunted look in her eye as Harry took her sister away, condemned by her own evil madness to a life of misery.

"Do you think I could've stopped her?" The choked question brought him to her side. "If I'd fought harder with my parents so they never sent her away? Maybe I could've helped her. . . ."

"No." Mike decided they'd bypassed propriety by this point and folded her into his arms. Her hands crept up his chest and locked onto his shoulders, hanging on as sobs wracked her small frame.

When they slowed, he slipped a finger under her chin and forced her to meet his gaze. "It's not your fault. Not Harry, not the wedding night, and not the mines. You've shouldered her blame for the past five years—lay that burden down, Naomi."

"She used me." Naomi winced. "But my mistakes paved the way.

No matter how guilty Charlotte is, I'm still a fallen woman."

"No you aren't!" His hands closed around her upper arms, making her stand straight and tall. "If Blinman didn't look so sickened by the whole thing and I didn't know your sister orchestrated the situation so skillfully, I'd be tempted to beat him to a pulp for taking advantage of an unconscious woman. No man has that right, and no woman should bear the responsibility for what was done to her."

"But I'm still responsible for letting Charlotte trick me, for being so morose I drank enough liquor not to notice her machinations. If I hadn't been so wrapped up in my anger over her and Harry's betrayal, I wouldn't have been vulnerable to her plans."

"Have you confessed those mistakes? Repented of them?" He almost missed the nearly imperceptible bob of her head. "Doesn't the Word say that if you've done that, He's faithful and just to forgive you and purify you from unrighteousness?" Another stronger nod.

"Then why, Naomi, do you continue to doubt your own worth?" He slid one hand up her arm, over her shoulder, and into her loosened hair. Mike let the silken strands slip through his fingers. He knew what he had to do next, and he dreaded it. But he couldn't expect her to be brave if he hid things from her. "You're not the only one who's needed that sort of grace. I know I did—and still do."

She tilted her head back and looked at him through half-lowered lids, apparently enjoying having him play with her hair. "I'm sure it wasn't anything so horrible."

"I didn't marry my first wife for love." Reluctantly he stopped toying with the texture of her silky locks. "I married for money."

Her eyes snapped open in shock. "Why did you do that?"

"I just said." Her surprise was almost comical. "For money."

"No. I meant why did you need the money?" she pressed him. "I know you. There had to be some very important reason to make such a sacrifice."

"You believe in me that much?" He had a hard time getting the words out.

"No less than you believed in me." Naomi reached up to thread her own fingers through his hair. "You saw in a second what I never considered because you were looking for an explanation while I was busy wallowing in blame."

"My mother had consumption, and she was dying a slow, painful death. Dad passed on not long before and didn't leave much of anything behind. I'd just sunk my money into my workshop with nothing left to pay for the doctors, medicine, and help to keep her comfortable until God called her home." He resisted the urge to lean back like a cat, pressing against those soothing fingers.

"See? I knew you had a reason. And even if you entered into it for the wrong reasons and struggled afterward, you got Luke." Seeing her smile, Mike reached up and pulled her hand down, clasping it against his chest. What was the old saying? In for a penny, in for a pound. . .

"Luke's the reason Leticia needed to marry in a hurry." Mike brought her other hand up so that he held both. "He doesn't know. I don't want him to ever know, but I won't hide things from you."

"I won't tell him." She looked down at their entwined hands then back up. "Now I understand why you were so horrified by my ad. It touched on a sore spot, didn't it?"

He tightened his grip. "That, and I couldn't figure out why such an incredible woman had such a hard time finding a husband."

"Now we know each other's secrets." She brushed her thumb back and forth across his knuckles, sending chills up his spine. "Do you still mean what you said before the dance?"

"Which part?" Mike found it hard to think at the moment.

"The part about how I'm worth waiting for?" She tried to duck her head, but he released one of her hands so he could tilt her chin back up.

"Absolutely." He looked into her eyes for a long moment then lowered his head for an overdue kiss. After several more, he pulled away and drew a ragged breath. "Just don't make me wait too much longer!"

EPILOGUE

Hope Falls, August 30, 1887

Luke grasped Decoy firmly by the collar, both hovering a respectful—or perhaps apprehensive—distance from the fidgety bunch of brides. The cheery notes of Gent's fiddle grew fainter. Soon they would fade altogether in the late summer sunshine—it was time.

"Ready?" Cora twitched her nose, trying to stop the telltale tingle of tears to come. *You can't fall apart before the ceremony starts!*

"One last time then?" Naomi reached out and snagged one of Cora's hands and one of Lacey's. Evie swiftly joined in and closed their circle. "Since we'll no longer be 'The Lovelorn Logging Ladies'!"

"I forgot one of the responses was labeled that way!" Lacey's giggle was punctuated with a suspicious sniff, and Cora knew she wasn't the only one struggling against swelling emotion. That in itself was telling. Lacey almost *never* cried.

"It's a good reminder of just how blessed we are." Evie's smile lit her whole face. "The music's ending—we'd best offer up some of our thanks."

"Dear Lord," Naomi began, and all four of the women bowed their heads.

Cora didn't close her eyes, unwilling to unleash the tears yet. She prayed along with the others all the same, cherishing the sisterhood they'd forged through sheer determination and difficult decisions.

"Thank You for the men we're about to marry. Thank You for the burgeoning success of our humble sawmill. We know we went about things wrong and struggled through those mistakes, but today we're reminded of how You can shape all things to Your will and for our good." Naomi paused for a moment, and her voice cracked when she continued. "But most of all, thank You for the sisters surrounding me. They are the family of my heart, even as we branch off into our own marriages. I pray we maintain that bond, and I pray that You use it to strengthen Hope Falls for generations to come."

"Amen." Cora joined the whispered chorus and groped for a handkerchief. Keeping her eyes open hadn't helped in the face of Naomi's prayer. The words echoed the hopes of her own heart too closely.

"You're gorgeous," she told her sister for the dozenth time that day after they'd all wiped their eyes and the final note of "Great Is Thy Faithfulness" faded away. "Let's make Granger goggle all the way down the aisle."

"Oh, Cora!" Evie gave a watery smile, took Cora's proffered arm, and they started forward.

Every man stood, and when the women reached the first row, Cora heard Volker Klumpf's order ring out.

"Hat's off to the chef!" At the words, every man swept his hat from his head and held it over his heart.

Evie's laughter rang out, joining Granger's deeper notes in a harmony that boded well for the marriage and set the tone for the wedding. The lighthearted gesture helped Cora gather herself, and she managed a heartfelt smile at Braden.

Because every step that brought her sister closer to her groom brought Cora closer to Braden. A bittersweet longing lodged in the back of her throat, and Cora barely managed to answer when the preacher asked who gave Evie away to be married.

Soon enough Evie would walk her down the aisle. Braden wanted to wait until he could stand through the ceremony, so today they stood as best man and maid of honor for all three couples.

As soon as the whoops died down for the new Mr. and Mrs.

Granger, Lacey started down the aisle. With her full skirts and long—at least for the Territories—train, she looked a vision. Normally Braden would walk her down the aisle, but there wasn't room enough for her splendor and his wheeled chair. Besides, he was standing as best man for each of the three grooms. So Dunstan and Lacey dredged up another escort.

Dignified and handsome, with touches of gray threading through his hair, Lacey's escort was undeniably dapper in his jaunty bow tie. Luckily, Decoy was also tall enough to cut an impressive figure as he led the bride down the aisle. When the preacher asked who gave Lacey away, everyone laughed at the wolfhound's single authoritative bark. His part finished, Decoy politely edged out of the limelight and sat at attention beside Braden's chair while his master pledged his troth.

But as wonderful as the wolfhound was, Cora believed Naomi's escort topped them all. Dressed to the nines in a top hat and tails, brandishing a silver-topped cane Lacey slipped him that very morning, Luke Strode looked every bit as proud and happy as his father. Arm stretched high to support the bride, he visibly counted the steps so he could, as he'd put it, "get it right for Mama Naomi."

When they reached the end of the aisle, he rose on tiptoe to kiss her cheek. Amid many female tears and good-natured male whoops, he took his place beside Decoy and beamed through the rest of the ceremony.

By the time the last couple said "I do," Cora had gone through all six of the handkerchiefs she'd tucked up her sleeves and her cheeks hurt from smiling so much. She gave each of the brides a hug for good luck while the loggers scrambled to form what they called "the kissin' queue," lining up to buss each bride on the cheek.

Cora threaded through the crowd, retrieving baby Dorothy from Mrs. McCreedy and feeling grateful for something to snuggle. The weddings were wonderful, and Cora knew Braden would be back on his feet soon, but the entire thing did leave an unmarried woman feeling a bit wistful.

Apparently she wasn't the only one to have that reaction.

"Well," Bobsley sighed to Riordan after they'd filtered through the kissing queue, "that's it. Last one's spoken for by the mill owner, so I reckon we'll be bachelors for a good long while yet."

Cora's heart twisted for them. She had Braden—the real Braden—to look forward to. These poor loggers had come up here looking for love and were sticking around empty-handed.

"Or maybe not." Clump joined the other two and pulled something from his pocket. As always, excitement increased his accent. His darting glance missed Cora as he rustled a battered sheet of newsprint from his pocket and showed his friends. "Haf you ever heard of mail-order brides?"

Kelly Eileen Hake
Mistakes, Love & Grace!

Kelly received her first writing contract at the tender age of seventeen and arranged to wait three months until she was able to legally sign it. Since that first contract a decade ago, she's fulfilled twenty contracts ranging from short stories to novels. In her spare time, she's attained her BA in English Literature and Composition, earned her credential to teach English in secondary schools, and went on to complete her MA in Writing Popular Fiction.

Writing for Barbour combines two of Kelly's great loves—history and reading. A CBA bestselling author and member of American Christian Fiction Writers, she's been privileged to earn numerous Heartsong Presents Reader's Choice Awards and is known for her witty, heartwarming historical romances.

A newlywed, she and her gourmet-chef husband live in Southern California with their golden lab mix, Midas!

Discussion Questions

1. Sometimes it's healthy to find a fresh start, and sometimes we try to run away from our past. Between Naomi and Mike, who would you say was running and who was beginning again? Why? What's the difference?

2. The issue of forgiveness winds through the story in more than one way. What about you? If you were in Naomi's shoes, would you find it harder to forgive Charlotte for what she'd done, or would you have struggled much more to forgive yourself? Why is that?

3. A lot of the characters in this series have high expectations for themselves. How does this transform into self-doubt, making them overly willing to believe the worst about themselves? For the characters in the story, this issue leads to more mistakes. Does that happen to you? How does it tie into forgiving ourselves for shortcomings?

4. Throughout the series, the four heroines—Evie, Lacey, Naomi, and Cora—are more than friends and business partners. Facing the loss of their parents, their homes, and more, they banded together to form their own family. Do you have friend-family members? Is there more of a danger of letting yourself be talked into something (like, say, advertising for husbands!) than there would be otherwise? Why could this be an issue, and how can you guard against it?

5. In the beginning of this novel, and throughout the series, Braden maintains that he loves Cora enough to let her go—or, in this case, push her away. What is his rationale? Is he right? What is the difference between protecting someone you love and betraying the love you share, and how did he go wrong?

6. In light of Braden's trauma (both mental and physical), do you think Cora would be right to forgive him and trust him with her heart again? How does this fit into the "in sickness and in health" vows of marriage?

7. When Cora relates the myth of the Loathly Lady, she says that the thing women most want is sovereignty—or to be able to make their own decisions. How is it an expression of love, trust, and respect when someone more powerful allows us to make our own choices? Who first gave us this incredible gift, and what does it mean for our relationship with Him?

Other books by
Kelly Eileen Hake

HUSBANDS FOR HIRE

Rugged & Relentless

Tall, Dark, and Determined

PRAIRIE PROMISES

Bring the entire Prairie Promises series home in one volume—and experience the humor and romance of three bridal situations gone awry in Buttonwood, Nebraska.